It's Always Us

STACY WILLIAMS

ISBN: 979-8-9890449-5-5 (ebook)
979-8-9890449-6-2 (paperback)

Cover Design by Erika Plum

To those who don't believe in love. Those who've never felt it or know what it's like to be cared for—loved so deeply that someone would give it all up for you. It exists. But first, you have to have hope. Only then will you recognize when it appears.

Prologue

MARK

Eight Years Ago

I scan right and then left. "Roscoe thirty-five! Roscoe thirty-five! Hut! Hut!"

The ball hits my hands, and I jog back. One, two, three steps. My eyes roam. *Wait for it. Wait for it.*

I dodge a defensive end diving for me, slipping to the right. My heart pounds its steady beat, bumping against my ribs, my adrenaline soaring to the highest level.

Thump-thump. Thump-thump. It's all I hear.

Wait for it.

I sprint forward and scan. *There it is.*

I pull my arm back and thrust it forward, releasing the ball into the air. I watch it fly.

My hands round into fists, tracking its path. The ball spirals toward its target and . . . drops right in. The crowd roars, and it kicks my lungs back into rhythm.

I flex my arms, squeezing them together. *I did it!* My team charges me in crazed elation, their hands smacking my helmet and hitting my pads.

I jog off the field, letting our kicker take his place as more teammates and coaches reward me with praise. Only thirty-four seconds between me and winning the first game of my college career.

I pull my helmet off and stand with my team, watching the ball fly through the goalposts. Fans erupt again, but their loud chorus doesn't quiet this time.

I take a seat on the bench, resting my forearms on my knees. I did it. I made it . . . just like she said I could.

I push up, turning my back to the field. My eyes drift over the stands, section by section, searching. A burning ache erupts in my chest, wanting to believe she's here somewhere.

"Let's go, Sandberg!" I'm tugged from behind back toward the field and the reminder that this is the only thing I have left, but my eyes won't leave the crowd, needing her to be here—proof that I wasn't wrong.

I join my team and the chaos in the middle of the field, trying again to force myself to let go of what was and focus on what is. All there is left for me. This. This game, these guys, and to continue to prove I'm worthy of being here.

"Nothing but 'W's' this season!" someone hollers, gripping my pads.

I shake hands with the other team, talk to reporters, and then join my team in the locker room. Everything moves fast, but my mind is stuck somewhere far away.

I've worked so hard, and it paid off, but the one I need is gone. Vanished. She just disappeared.

I tug on a shirt, and a hand lands on my shoulder.

"Come on, man. We're hittin' the pub for some grub," Higgins says.

"I'm not—"

His arm slides around my shoulders, steering me in the direction of the after-party. "Nah, you're coming. This is just the beginning, Sandberg. You better remember me when you're at the top."

It's dark and late when I fall onto the edge of my bed in my tiny dorm room. Two hours of constant noise, replays, and plans for the season ahead, but I heard none of it. My mind was lost in what used to be and the place I want to be again.

I rest my arms on my knees and run a hand over my face. *How could I have been so wrong?*

I pull my phone from my pocket and stare at the screen. Her name calls to me, but my gut pinches tight, warning me of what will happen if

I tap her name. The same thing that's happened since I said goodbye. But what if . . .

I close my eyes, still able to feel her lips on mine as she told me she'd see me soon. Her eyes and mouth delivering the promise.

I need to hear her voice one more time. To know she was real. That what we had wasn't only my imagination.

I tap her name.

The phone number you are trying to reach is no longer in service.

I grip my phone, wanting it and the hope it holds to crumble into a million pieces. I check the time. 12:42 a.m.

My finger taps the second number. It rings and rings and rings. Over and over again.

I end the call, giving up. I want to banish her from my mind and what I thought we had. What I knew we had. The only thing I thought was mine and always would be. The only love I've ever known. But it wasn't real.

I reach for the mini-fridge and pull a can from the door. The tab cracks and hisses, and I take a long, slow drink. The cold liquid soothes my thick throat, but I need it to numb my heart and mind.

I guzzle the last of it and pull another, seeking quick relief. I tap her name again. The same automated message plays again and again. I pop another tab and lie back, staring at the ceiling as everything starts to dull into a tolerable haze. I float. Anger and frustration lift as hope settles in to take its place.

I wasn't wrong. It wasn't a lie. It couldn't have been.

I see her face. Her blue eyes. Her gentle smile. Her faith in me.

I squeeze my eyes shut tight as my world spins. Her words surround me.

"I'll see you soon."

Chapter 1

LEX

The thick liquid swirls around the rim of my wide-mouth glass. I watch the translucent streaks recede into the blood-red pool. The pungent smell stirs the waves of nausea rising in my stomach as I try to keep my miserable heel-clad feet from running out the doors.

This is what I want. This is what I want. This . . . I push out a long, slow breath. *This . . . is what I want.*

You know that feeling you get in the very depths of your gut when something isn't quite right? The one that sets off warning bells or sirens that are supposed to kick you into high gear and generate action.

Some people call it instincts, others the gift of fear. I'm not exactly sure what it is or where it comes from, but over the past few months, I've gotten really good at ignoring it. Tonight, every form of internal alarm system is going off, and it's so loud I can't hear anything else.

I tip my glass to the side, wondering what would happen if my unsteady hand slipped and this detestable, fermented sludge ran down the front of my stiff ivory dress.

"Alexandra."

The startle of a familiar mousey voice prevents the first drop, and I turn to see Gail Chambers making a beeline for me with a group in tow.

"Alex, these ladies are my best friends. They've known Seth since he was a toddler and have been dying to meet you."

The tiny, prim, and proper woman loops her arm through mine as if we're best buds. It's not that Gail isn't friendly. She's just never been that fond of me, or really, I'm not the princess she imagined for her son.

The women gather around, and I squeeze back, unsure I want to be included in their little plastic circle. I realize there's a frightening similarity between my dress, which I hate, and the style and appearance of my future mother-in-law and her posse. My stomach rolls again, and I clench my teeth, forcing a polite smile as she introduces me to each of her friends.

I offer my hand, receiving each meticulously pampered and manicured one in return. The last desperate housewife offers one of those prissy handshakes that involves only a few awkward fingers, clearly appalled by my rough, grease-stained hands despite my light pink polish.

A nervous laugh escapes Gail as her friend studies her hand, ensuring I didn't leave any residue behind. "Oh, yes, I told you all how Alex volunteers at her grandfather's garage from time to time." *Volunteers?* "Young women these days and their need to master the skills meant for the opposite sex." Her condescending laughter makes my stomach punch itself.

This is what I want. This is what I want. This is . . .

I inhale, scanning the overly decorated room for Seth, needing rescue. When I don't spot him, my alarm system activates the panic mode. The only cheese and cracker I choked down rises in my throat, a cold sweat creeps up the back of my neck, and my feet tingle with the urge to sprint to the nearest exit.

While the former county fair beauty queen and her band of BFFs babble on about necessary skill sets and changing times, I stare into the glass in my shaky hand, contemplating a spill as my escape plan.

"So, you work on automobiles, then?" one of the women, whose name I can't remember now, asks with a little too much 'Eww' in her tone for me to care to answer. But because I'm mostly polite, I respond.

"Cars, trucks, SUVs, things with engines." I force my lips upward as they all half laugh—the nose tipped-slightly-in-the-air, snooty kind.

The laughter halts as they study me like I'm some kind of new trend that challenges their highly strict values. It's my cue to find somewhere else to be in this twinkle-light-flower-infested room.

"Alex is taking some classes and assists Seth at the firm, but once they're married, you know how it is. Wifely duties take over."

Her ability to make excuses for my line of work never ceases to amaze me. Helping Seth move his office furniture doesn't even remotely qualify as working for his firm. As far as schooling, I'm enrolled in a single program working toward an ASE certification, as in Automotive Service Excellence.

School was never my deal, but working with my hands, specifically on cars, is where I belong. I grew up in my grandpa's garage, filled with foul-mouthed men and the scent of oil and brake fluid. Those men are my family, and that garage is my life.

I want to get married, have a family, and work on cars. That's my dream. It's simple. It's not flashy or grand, but it's mine. But here I stand in a room full of people who will never understand me or the thrill of diagnosing a broken vehicle, repairing it, and returning it to its grateful owner.

The pool of women I've encountered in my life that seem to understand my career choice could be counted on one hand. There are even fewer men who appreciate it for more than assuming I'm some chick who cluelessly tinkers under a hood because it's 'cute.' *Gag.*

Women in the garage are rarely accepted, but someday, Grandpa's garage will be mine, so I'm doing what I can to give myself the best leg up when that day comes.

Wanting no part of the load of crap being shoveled out here, I excuse myself. "It was nice meeting you all, but I need to find Seth."

They all nod in unison.

"I'll catch up with you later about dress shopping," Gail chimes in an overly eager tone that causes my feet to move even faster.

I weave my way through people, most of whom I've only briefly met over the past two years, searching for the man who's supposed to be helping me through this. The one who's supposed to be standing by my side yet never seems to be present when I need him most.

These are his people, his family, and his friends. If I had it my way, I'd forgo all this pomp and circumstance. Unfortunately, my ideas were vetoed immediately once Gail got wind of our engagement. But maybe this extravagance is giving me the time and observance I need to put things in perspective.

I stop at the bar to set down the glass of wine I didn't order and would never drink. Chugging it is an appealing idea if I didn't think it would come right back up. Then again, maybe that's not such a bad plan.

"Hey, Pal."

I turn to the man who's taught me everything I know, his slightly wrinkled gray button-down shirt only mildly fitting over his short, broad frame. He leans an elbow on the bar, surveying the room.

"Hey, Grandpa."

"Your mom messaged me. She got caught up at work."

I nod, wishing I could get back to working on the truck that came in this afternoon with a valve cover leak.

"This is quite the setup. You doing all right?"

My eyes roam over the room filled with people and things representing nothing of the world I belong to or my preferences. The white linen covered high-top tables with elaborate pale pastel floral centerpieces and hundreds of twinkle lights strung from one end of the room to the other. It's all elegantly stifling and stiff, just like my dress.

I tug at the scratchy material around my neck. "Yeah, it's all a bit . . . bright." I spend my days in coveralls or jeans covered in grease and grime; T-shirts and flannels are my go-to. All this flowery vibrance is nauseating.

Grandpa chuckles. The low, gravelly sound so familiar eases the waves of panic, cresting higher and higher with each passing minute. "That it is. How are your nerves? Time is ticking."

I can't meet his gray-blue eyes because this man will see right through my shaky conviction. "They're holding on." I try to joke, but it comes out flat.

In my periphery, I see one of his bushy gray brows arch as he studies me. I pretend to search the room again, attempting to ignore his prying eyes.

"No one is forcing you to do this."

My head snaps in his direction. I'm used to Grandpa being blunt, but this comment came out of nowhere.

"What?"

He rests his back against the bar, turning his attention to the room full of men and women dressed for the Kentucky Derby. This was supposed to be an informal engagement party for family and friends—a.k.a. Gail's family and friends.

"All this," he gestures around the room with his head. "I want to be sure that this is what you envisioned when you think about the rest of your life. Seth is a good guy, but he's not . . . "

Don't say it. Don't even say it.

Every muscle throughout my body constricts, and I turn to face him, stopping him before he says it. "Grandpa, this is happening. This is what I want." A sour taste fills my mouth with those five words, my stomach in full revolt.

He doesn't look at me, likely knowing I'm full of crap. He releases a long exhale through his nose, and there's that slight whistle that's always there.

"Sometimes, the comfort and reliability of a Buick seem like a safe bet, but a Mustang . . . it's where real fun and living happens."

I stare at him as he pushes away from the bar. The man who's raised me, at least where it's counted most. The one who knows me better than anyone. He just had to do it.

But this is what I can't handle right now. I can't have him putting thoughts in my head that don't belong there. Thoughts that haven't belonged there for a very long time. I've never been able to rid myself of them no matter how hard I try. Thoughts I don't have space in my head for, especially tonight.

The rotten old fart drops a bomb of wisdom and leaves me standing here as he heads back to the fresh trays of cream puffs and crab cakes.

He just had to say it. He had to put it out there.

I glare at his back as my dress suddenly shrinks around my chest, and my need to flee escalates. *Where in the hell is Seth?!*

I move toward the doors leading to a small deck needing fresh air.

I push into the cool night air that's filled with the overwhelming stench of cigar smoke.

"Alex." Seth's voice catches me off guard. He stands off to the side, surrounded by his college buddies and their ladies. "Come here and hang out with us."

My feet stay put as I glance over my shoulder at the party inside that's for us, yet we've spent the whole evening apart. *What's new?*

My positive attitude hits rock bottom, and my desire to be here evaporates like the billowing smoke around me. Tired of me not listening, that little voice of my innermost being screams. *This is NOT what I want!*

Seth takes another puff of his cigar and closes the distance between us. He leans down to kiss my cheek, and the smell is repulsive. I wrap my arms around myself as my skin breaks out with goosebumps at the recognition of what's happening—of what's been happening that I've chosen to ignore.

"We've been catching up." He shrugs off his jacket and places it around my shoulders. One of his arms comes around me and pulls me toward his friends.

I join their little smoke-filled group, trying not to breathe while an unspoken war rages within me.

Buick. Mustang. Buick. Mustang. Buick. Mustang.

As the Buick talks next to me, I can only think that the Mustang is long gone. My heart sinks yet again to the toes of my overly-priced and horrendously uncomfortable shoes.

"So, Alex, does this mean we all get free oil changes when we're in town?" One of the guys asks, pulling me from battle. When I realize who said it, it's accompanied by a smug smirk, like it's some kind of joke. *Pompous dick.*

"It's buy ten, get one free." My voice is quiet as my mind spins with sudden awareness.

The women in the group giggle like I said something funny, and Seth's arm slides around me. "Alex runs the shop. She's got guys to handle the dirty work."

I've got guys to handle the dirty work? I might actually vomit. I'd change oil every day for the rest of my life as long as I don't have to sit behind some computer or work in an office.

This isn't new. These comments, the condescending little jokes, and this weird type of protectiveness as if I need help to explain the work I do because it can't possibly be serious. I guess I'm finally hearing it all loud and clear.

What the hell have I been doing?

A chill runs up my spine as heat consumes me. I try to breathe through the smoke and the vice cranking tighter around my ribs.

It's not my problem these people are too close-minded to think a woman might genuinely enjoy fixing things—like cars.

It's time for me to go before I melt down and make a fool of myself in front of people who really don't care to know me other than I'm becoming Seth's wife. *Seth's wife.* I'm not even sure who that's supposed to be because I'm afraid it's not me.

I've been a flight risk for the past two hours, but my timer just went off.

"I have a valve cover leak waiting on me," I announce to no one in particular, pushing Seth's jacket off my shoulders and handing it back to him.

He frowns. "What? You're leaving?"

"Yes." My heart begins to race with the need to run. *Mustang.*

"Are you all right?" He follows me to the doors.

I stop, peering up at his freshly shaven face and golden-brown eyes while my heart hammers away at the thought of what I'm about to do.

"What do you think of this dress?"

"What?" His brows tip in so far they almost meet.

"This dress," I whisper, running a hand over the stiff, ugly, plain material covering my body. *Punch. Punch. Punch.* My heart bangs against my ribs as if it, too, is searching for the one who isn't here. The one who hasn't been here in so long but it has never been able to forget. "What do you think of it?"

He studies me like he's noticing I'm wearing a dress for the first time. "I think you look beautiful. It's stunning."

My heart sinks into a pit of disappointed despair. *Buick. Mustang. Buick. Mustang . . . Mustang. It's always been the Mustang.*

"I have to go."

I swing open the doors, and all the bright whiteness of the room shocks my senses into flight mode. I make a run for it, not taking even a second to think about what happens next.

Chapter 2

LEX

I roll over and smack my vibrating phone. I have no idea what time it was when I crawled into bed, but when sleep never comes, you can't blame it all on a bad dream. It's all real, and with daylight, I have to deal with it.

I want to hide in bed and bypass the day, especially talking with Seth. It's going to suck, and that's a vast understatement.

I prefer to reserve confrontation and difficult conversations for someone else. I'm an avoider, which is precisely what got me into this giant shame-ridden mess. But now, I have to strap on my big girl boots and deal with the consequences.

I push myself up, my body springing to life with anxiety.

"How in the hell did I let this happen?" I whisper, shoving my hands into my messy, tangled hair. I pull my knees to my chest, needing the morning air to cool me.

Two years. I've dated Seth for two years, and it's taken me all that time to wake up. I told myself I could marry Seth and let him believe I wanted to. Grandpa said no one was forcing me to do this, but I was forcing myself.

For two years, I've been going through the motions, allowing myself to get wrapped up in an idea of what my life should look like. I dated a stable guy and molded myself into his life, but all I've been doing is running from the past by planning a future that shouldn't be mine. I told Seth I would marry him because that would mean I'd finally moved on like it was some kind of proof that I'd actually been able to let go.

I rest my forehead on my knees as my empty stomach twists into a giant knot, heaving bile into my throat. I fill my cheeks with air and blow it out slowly.

I've lied to myself, my family, my friends . . . Seth. I've pretended to be someone I'm not. To love a man simply because I've never been able to stop loving another.

I pretend. It's what I'm good at. I pretended and made it through school. To be ok when life is hard, disappointing, and full of hurt.

I can't keep lying to everyone. To myself. I can't keep trying to convince myself that I'll somehow be able to move on because I won't. All this time, all these years, and I haven't been able to. Maybe I haven't tried hard enough, or maybe sometimes, when someone steals your heart, you just don't ever get it back.

I'm tired, and my heart aches with years of grief I've tried so damn hard to ignore. It's time to face it and accept I will never rid myself of him. The one person who will forever linger within me but can never be mine.

I inhale, filling my lungs as I run my fingers over the bags underneath my eyes. I have to drag myself from this bed and get to it. Seth should be relieved, but he may not see it that way.

Still curled into a ball, I let myself roll to the side, hitting the bed. My phone vibrates on my nightstand. Reluctantly, I grab it to see who it is. Seth.

I ignore it. I can't talk to him right now. The longer I wait, the worse it'll be, and I should have done this long ago.

I force myself right side up again, pulling my hair back into a loose ponytail and straightening my T-shirt. It's tattered and holey, but the most comforting possession I own.

I tug the neck up over my mouth. *I wish everything was different.*

My phone buzzes again, but only once this time, followed by a quick second. I grab it from my nightstand, focusing on the words.

SLADE: U ok?
SLADE: Krissy's on her way.

I haul myself the four feet to my dresser, needing to get downstairs and make coffee before the house fills with questions about why I left the party. I know my mom will be here any minute, but Krissy will be a good buffer.

I tug the shirt over my head, tossing it aside, and pull on a sweatshirt. I force myself down the stairs, not even bothering to stop in the bathroom, even though I know I look like I'm in need of a rehab facility—one that specializes in compulsive lying. I wonder if it would be an in-patient facility. Maybe then I'd be excused from having to tell Seth our engagement was off.

"Well, you look like you've been dragged behind a truckload of shit. Are you hungover?"

Grandpa sits at the table with his coffee and newspaper, as he has every morning since I can remember.

I shove a single-serve coffee pod into the machine and hit the button. "No."

I've not been hungover often, but I'd trade a good case of too much liquor for the emotionally sick feelings swirling in my belly. I shove a mug under the spout, and it clangs.

"Something crawl up your ass, then?"

I rest my back against the counter, turning to face the man who stirred the pot and left me to deal with the boilover. I slump in surrender, knowing he'll understand. He might be the only one, so I need to spill it before my mom and Krissy get here.

"Grandpa, I need to tell you something."

His gray eyes move to mine over the rim of his reading glasses. I slide my hands in the front pocket of my oversized sweatshirt. I know this man will support me, but it doesn't make my admission any easier, so he's the best person to test it out on.

He folds and closes his newspaper, waiting patiently.

"I'm not marrying Seth."

I might be wrong, but I've known this man my whole life. Unless I'm losing touch with reality, I think I see the slightest hint of a smile.

"Ok." He clasps his rough and worn hands, resting them on his paper. "Is that it? Anything else you want to tell me?"

I focus on my neatly painted pink toes, wishing I'd picked purple. "I'm not sure." I don't need to look at him to know that one of those overgrown eyebrows creeps upward again.

"Does Seth know?"

"No. I'm telling him this morning."

The coffee maker spurts and sputters beside me as it finishes its task.

"Well, shit. That'll be fun. I guess you'll need the morning off?"

I can't help my soft smile. "Yes, that would be appreciated. Thank you."

"My pleasure. I never thought you should marry him."

My head pops up. "You didn't? Why didn't you say something? You waited until last night to fill my head with all that Buick-Mustang talk, but didn't think to say something before."

"Would you have listened?"

My head falls to the side. "Maybe."

He laughs his boisterous, low chuckle. "Pal, we both know *you* needed to see this. I'm just glad you opened your eyes."

He sips his coffee while I stir enough caramel creamer in mine to double the quantity.

"Anything else? Hurry up before you have to break your mother's heart with this news."

I dread telling her about as much as I dread talking to Seth.

"Isn't this enough?"

His eyes peek at me from the corner as he picks up his paper and pushes out of his chair. *Oh, man. Here it comes.*

He sets his mug in the sink, standing beside me. "Pal, you get yourself out of this little mess, and then it might be time to shit or finally get off the pot."

"What's that supposed to mean?"

His fingers run over his scruffy jaw. "It's been long enough." His voice is softer now. "I know you might need a little time, but you've got to stop this . . . just checking off the days. One way or another, you've got to start living, and there's only one way you're going to be able to do that."

I stare at the floor, not needing this today. "Too much time has passed. He's long gone, and after what I did . . . "

He pats me on the shoulder, stepping away. "Maybe, but you're never gonna know what time can do if you keep this up."

He opens the back door, leaving me with his profound words of wisdom.

My lips tip upward, barely. They quickly fall when I hear him holler over the rumble of his truck. My mom walks in the back door in her daily black scrubs with her light brown hair twisted up in a clip.

"Hey, honey. I'm so sorry I didn't catch you last night. One of the residents was having a bad night, and I got caught up. By the time I got there, Gail was making rounds and telling everyone goodbye. Seth said you left." She frowns as she deposits my used-up coffee pod in the garbage and reloads it with a fresh one.

My mother is beautiful and vivacious. She has an addicting personality, and people gravitate toward her. She's youthful, vibrant, and has a knack for attracting the wrong men.

She works at a long-term care facility, caring for those who can't care for themselves. She's amazing at her job. How she looks after the people assigned to her is inspiring. She's just never been that attentive to me.

"It's ok. I needed to get out of there. It was all . . . too much."

She crunches the pod in the coffee maker and pushes start. "You feeling ok? You're looking a little . . . "

I sit at the table, preparing to destroy another one of my mother's dreams. Before I can, Krissy steps through the door.

Slade has worked at the garage for as long as I can remember and is the big brother I never had. His sister, Krissy, is sweet and perceptive, and I need her to be on her game this morning. I'm sure he sent her to check on me, wanting to avoid any 'girly shit.' I'm thankful knowing how my mom will take this news, and I need backup.

"Morning, ladies." She glances at me, raising one meticulously groomed dark eyebrow before setting her travel mug on the table and sliding onto a chair. "How are you?"

I pull my mug close again, needing the warm comfort and wishing I'd left my security shirt on underneath my sweatshirt.

"Oh, nerves are just getting the best of her. It's only a few months, and you'll be off relaxing in the sand." My mom busies herself straightening the kitchen as if she's speaking from personal experience.

"Actually—" I start, but Krissy jumps in.

"Slade and I looked for you last night." She eyes me like she's hunting for a hidden clue.

"I had to leave." I peek at her carefully while she continues to study me. "I didn't want to be there."

My mom's entire body turns to face me. "Did something happen? Was Gail overwhelming you with details? I'll talk with her and tell her that you're nervous and—"

"I'm not nervous." I blurt. "I'm just . . . not marrying him." As the words leave my mouth, both women gasp, and it's as if I can feel the oxygen being sucked out of the room. I force my gaze up. Krissy's glossy lips hang open, and my mom stands frozen at the sink, disbelief written all over her face.

"What?" My mom's question is clipped, and I close my eyes. "You're just nervous, honey." She sits next to me, placing her hands over mine. "It's completely normal. It's a big change, and lots of decisions are being thrown at you." She pushes a strand of hair out of my face. "You need to get some sleep and—"

I cut her off. "No. This isn't nerves. I can't marry him. I should've never even been dating him." The truth punches me in my stupid face. I rub my forehead.

My mom grips my hand tighter. "What are you talking about? Seth is perfect. How can you possibly think you don't want to marry him?"

He's not Mark. My hand slides over my mouth like I admitted it out loud. I slip my other hand from hers, resting it in my lap. Not making eye contact is easier, while everything Grandpa said consumes my mind.

"Well, ok," Krissy says calmly, but I roll my head to the side to see her perfectly lined eyes as wide as saucers. "I didn't see this coming." Her eyebrows fall. "Or maybe I did."

My mom ignores her, running a hand over my hair. "Honey, you to need rest and—"

I stop her, unwilling to listen to all the reasons why I'm not thinking clearly. "I know you think Seth is perfect, and he might be, but I can't marry him. I don't feel for him the way I should, and if I'd been myself with him instead of pretending to be someone else, I'm pretty sure he wouldn't want to marry me either." I hold my mom's hand, comforting her now. "I should've realized this all sooner, but . . . "

I stop myself because she won't get it. My mom's idea of success in life is finding a man and setting yourself up with money and security. Love is optional. This belief led her to the other side of the country while I was in high school, and it wasn't until it all fell apart that she came home.

"Have you talked to him?" Krissy jumps in with a sympathetic tone.

"No, I'm going to see him this morning."

My mom stands, moving back to the sink, frantically scrubbing Grandpa's mug. "It's too late for this. Things are being booked and arranged. What are people going to say? You'll wake up tomorrow and realize it's just the pressure getting to you."

I can't think about what everyone will think and say. Most of them don't know me anyway, but still. My eyes meet Krissy's understanding gaze, and I'm so grateful she's here.

"Better now than after." She pats my hand in comfort. "Anything Gail has arranged can be canceled. There's still plenty of time."

Gail is going to blow a gasket. I take a deep breath.

I push out my chair and stand. "I have to shower and talk to Seth. I've already let this go on far too long, and he needs to know."

My mom reaches for my arm. "You don't know what you're doing. Seth is everything you could ever want. This is a huge mistake, and you'll wake up a week from now and realize everything you could have had." She grabs my hands, pleading. "This is your chance to have a life and future. With your issues, an opportunity like this doesn't just come along every day."

There it is. A quick jab in the gut. I inhale, pulling myself up despite feeling an inch tall. "That may be true, but I can't marry him."

"Alex, this is your chance. He's perfect."

But not for me. He's not the one I want. He never has been.

"I know you don't understand this, but he's not . . . at least not for me."

I leave her disappointed stare and carry myself upstairs to shower, hoping I'll find the courage to face Seth and then figure out how to keep going when pretending isn't an option anymore.

The glass door reads *Chambers, Macavoy, Dunn & Associates*, and I tug it open, entering the elegantly styled waiting room of the law firm. Thankfully, the receptionist, Marcy, isn't at her desk, so I head down the hall to Seth's office to make this as quick as possible.

Seeing his door open, I approach only to find Marcy resting her butt and thigh on the desk next to him as she leans toward his computer. It should irritate me, but it doesn't. I don't even care, which is exactly why I'm here.

My shaky hand knocks and Marcy quickly removes herself from his desk, redness tinting her face.

"Hey," Seth says. "I tried to call you."

"I'll go check on that." Marcy scurries out, and I step aside, letting her pass.

I shove my hands in my pockets. "I wanted to talk to you in person."

He frowns and rolls his chair back. "Everything all right? You left so early last night."

And you didn't even call or come by to make sure I was okay. The thing is, I knew he wouldn't, and I didn't want him to. *How did I let this happen?*

My mouth feels dry as guilt creeps up my throat. "I can't marry you," I blurt out in a rush, scrounging for the courage I desperately need.

He laughs, leaning forward and resting his elbows on his desk. "What?"

My eyes meet the gray carpet squares. "I'm sorry. When you asked me to marry you, I shouldn't have said yes."

His chair creeks, and I peek up to see him leaning back, arms crossed now. "You just realized this?" He looks slightly amused, as if this is some kind of joke.

"Yes."

His phone beeps and Marcy informs him that his buddy, Jeremy, is on the phone. He reaches forward and picks it up. I wrap my arms around myself, seeking security while I wait for him to finish his conversation about their tee time.

When he hangs up, his eyes meet mine again as he rests back in his chair, getting comfortable. "Sorry, I'm meeting the guys at the golf course this afternoon."

I stare at him, wondering if he remembers what I just said. I inch closer, dropping my arms and giving my sweaty hands some air. "Seth, I'm not marrying you," I say, feeling more confident.

His light brown eyebrows pull together. "And that's it? We're . . . not getting married." His voice is calm but firm.

I cross my arms over myself again. "I can't marry you, and I don't think you want to marry me . . . at least the real me."

When he doesn't say anything, I risk another glance at him, and he's staring.

"What does that mean, Alex?"

I don't even know how to explain it, but I try. "I hated school. Did you know that?" I ask, knowing the answer. "It was really difficult for me, but cars make sense. I like working with my hands, getting dirty, and making broken things new. You think because I'm a woman, it's silly or a hobby. Sometimes, I think you're embarrassed by it. You try to explain it away as if there's something wrong with me working in a garage."

I tuck my hair behind my ear. My fingers land on my stud earring to twist. "It's what I want to do for the rest of my life. I won't ever hold an office job or something you find more . . . suitable. I won't ever be a wife who sits at home, prepares meals, shops, or plans parties. I won't be golfing."

"I know you love working on cars, but our life will change once we get married. You won't have to do that anymore or work at all."

I inhale, frustration rolling through me that he's not hearing what I'm saying. "I don't like fancy dinners or clothes." I peer down at my stained jeans and boots. "I'm terrible at socializing. You know this. Especially with strangers, but that's part of your life and what you want. You love it. I hate it, and when I go out, I want to sit in a quiet bar and watch a ball game where talking is optional."

He stares at me, unmoving.

"Those are all the things I should have told you on our first date and so many more. If I had, I'm pretty sure you would've never asked me out again." When he still doesn't say anything, I channel Grandpa. "Seth, why do you want to marry me?"

He sets his chair in motion, rocking slightly, and I assume it means he's thinking. It shouldn't be this hard.

"You're beautiful and . . . different. You never expect anything from me. You've always been there, supporting me and encouraging me. You understand my long hours and when things come up. You let me hang out with my friends and never complain when I don't make it over to see you or I have to cancel. You . . . "

He stalls, and I give him a second to hear what he doesn't say. "Don't you think it's weird we don't spend that much time together? Last night was a party to celebrate our engagement, and we weren't even together. When I left, did you even wonder why?"

He comes to his defense. "I was with my friends."

My heart picks up pace as a heat wave washes over me. I speak softly. "I know, and that's ok, but that's probably not how two people who love each other would behave."

"So, this is it, then? We're just done," he snaps, straightening in his chair.

"Seth, it's been two years, and you don't love me. You love the person you want me to be or who I let you think I am. You love that I'm around. Isn't there a part of you that picked me because you knew it would drive your mom crazy, and I'm as low maintenance as they come? You like not having to be around me if you don't want to." He pushes his chin out but doesn't say anything. "I should have seen this before now. I'm sorry."

His eyes narrow, and the long moment of silence makes me itchy. I shove my hands back in my pockets, knowing I don't have anything more to say.

Eventually, he leans forward, sitting tall and resting his arms on his desk. He clears his throat, his jaw set and jetting out. "I guess you're right. I should be a whole lot more hurt than I am."

I can't tell if he's being a jerk or having a revelation, but it doesn't matter. I pull his ring out of my pocket and set it on the edge of his desk.

"I'm very sorry that I let things get this far."

He scoffs, averting his eyes. "Me, too."

I turn but stop in the doorway. "It's my fault. I've spent years trying to be a lot of things. I didn't mean to mislead you. You deserve a wife who is exactly who you think she is and doesn't want to be anywhere else."

I leave his office and walk straight out of the building, shame creeping up my throat and into my eyes. I climb into my truck and start the engine, but I sit, taking deep breaths to calm my shaking body. *How did I get here?*

I know how. I was trying to fool myself into believing I was over Mark and forcing myself not to love him. I couldn't do it.

I said goodbye once, but I've never let him go. Grandpa is right. Somehow, I have to.

Chapter 3

MARK

Three Months Later

"It's an emergency. I'm doing it, and don't even try to talk me out of it!"

I push through the crowd, keeping my head low to avoid being stopped for pictures and autographs.

I glance at the signs above, searching for the arrow that will point me in the direction of the rental lot. I need this to be quick. I've waited long enough, letting fear get in the way, and time is running out. This is my last chance, and I don't have a second to think twice.

I hear a long exhale on the other end of the line as I scan the board for my name. I have no doubt my older brother is running a hand over his face. I turn to see a phone raised in my direction and step away quickly, hoping I dodged it.

I walk quickly through the lot, scanning the cars.

"This is a terrible idea," Shane grumbles, but I don't have time for his grouchy, sour attitude. This is my life.

I find my car with the keys in the ignition and toss my duffle bag in the back, wasting no time climbing in. I switch my phone to the speaker.

"You told the GM and your coach this is an emergency? Have you really thought this through? You're walking in there blind. You have no idea what you'll face."

Sean, my younger, more sensible brother's calm questioning goes in one ear and out the other. I know exactly what I'm doing. I don't know if I'm walking in completely blind, but I can't say I know what to expect either.

These guys care. They're looking out for me, just like they always have. Even though we aren't brothers in the traditional sense, they have my back and always will.

The three of us were tossed together in a group home when I was eight, and we've been each other's family ever since. Some bonds are thicker than blood ever could be.

I have no idea what the outcome of this will be. I know what I need it to be, but I'm very well versed in things not turning out how I want them to. This is my last shot at getting the one thing I've always needed.

"This is a life emergency!" The urgency in my bones needs to calm the hell down. I can't walk in there acting like a lunatic, but my panicking ass needs this to work. "I know where I'm going, and I know what I need. Other than that, I'll be calling plays on the fly."

See calm. I can be calm. I do it every day on the field. *Shit! This has to work.*

There's silence on the other end of the line until Shane, the big, negative one, adds his two cents, which I know I'll likely ignore.

"This might be the dumbest idea you've ever had. What happens when this blows up in your face?"

Idea? Ha. I wish this were my idea. My play. I'm taking advantage of the last opportunity I might ever have, and there isn't a thing that will stop me.

"I appreciate your vote of confidence, Shane." I bite back.

"Hey, I'm watching out for you. You're supposed to be heading to Vegas. That is what you need to be doing, not chasing a fantasy."

My grip tightens on the steering wheel as the heat of irritation rushes through my body. I know when I need to be in Vegas. I'm supposed to be in a team meeting first thing in the morning, preparing for the game and then practice. I'm supposed to be on the plane with the rest of my guys in two days, aiming to get us one step closer to the playoffs.

I crack the window. "This isn't a fantasy. This is my life, and I've been given a chance."

I proceed through the security gate, hoping for Sean's gentle confidence before I lose my last ounce of patience that's dangling off a cliff by one finger.

"Just take a second to think about what you're doing and what happens . . . afterward," his calm voice advises. "You need to be prepared for this not to go the way you want. Don't forget, she's the one who left you high and dry. It's been a long time, Mark, and a lot has changed."

He might as well have socked me right between the pecs. Right where it hurts all the damn time. Never changing. Pain that I've just gotten used to. But it's always there, lingering. Wondering. Hoping. Living and breathing, begging for another chance.

Underneath, way deep inside, there's this need to know that I wasn't wrong. That somehow, this was all some big misunderstanding.

The memory of her just . . . disappearing still burns like hell, but I'll never believe it was because she didn't love me. I can't. I just can't.

Sean's right. Everything has changed, but I haven't, and I know exactly what I want and need. I've always known, but there's a real possibility I've never been what she's needed. Maybe even then.

I swallow the uncomfortable tightness in my throat.

What I don't need is any more of their negativity infiltrating my desperate, spontaneous, maybe totally and completely insane plans. But it's all I've got, and I've never been one to play it safe.

"Mark," Shane's put on his coaching pants now, and that tone makes me want to hang up on his ass.

I don't need a coach. I need my brother, who understands we might only get one chance at true, undying love if we're lucky. I had mine all those years ago, and now, unexpectedly, I've been given an opening, and I'm sure as hell taking it.

"We all know if she's seen social media, your confession, and long-withstanding pining will seem a bit hard to believe," Shane says.

I laugh. If he were sitting next to me, I'd cackle in his big, grumpy mug. "Thanks for keeping tabs, but we all know that's complete bullshit."

"You think she'll see it that way?" Sean asks carefully.

It's a good thing I love these guys as if they were my flesh and blood because if they were anyone else, I might literally reach through the phone, and fists would be flying.

The thought that she might not believe me has me rolling down the window, needing the cool air to prevent me from thrusting the door open and upchucking my dinner. I know what the world thinks I am, but it couldn't be further from the truth. I like people. I like women, but there's only ever been one woman who's ever had my heart. The rest have been my best attempts at distraction that never worked.

I take a calming breath, knowing I'll likely have to explain it all at some point, but first, I have to know if she even gives a shit. From what I understand, there's at least a shred of hope she does.

"Yes, I made some really stupid decisions. We all have, but it's been years. Nothing has happened outside of those posed photos. She'll see that."

At least, I hope she will. I'm not perfect, and I've made mistakes like everyone does, but there's a huge difference between being seen as a playboy and actually being one.

I hear Sean exhale this time, and I know it's him because it's not filled with exaggerated condescension. "Good luck, bro. I'm rooting for you."

Shane grunts, something I can't make out.

I need a few minutes to myself. "I've got to go. I'll call you guys later."

"Whatever happens, make sure you're on you're A-game in Vegas. I want to beat your ass in the playoffs," Sean jokes, lightening the doom they seem to think I'm walking into, but my mind is only on the task at hand. I play to win, and I'm playing for everything.

"Mark," Shane barks in his overly protective, coach tone. "She's getting married. If you walk in there, you have to be good walking out alone." That isn't even a possibility I can consider at the moment. "I want a phone call when this is done. No going into hiding while you have one of your monstrous diva meltdowns. You call us."

My head falls back, and I push air out between my lips, waiting for the damn light to turn green. "Fine. Don't worry. I've got a good feeling about this."

My brothers groan in unison, and I have no doubt both are rubbing their temples. I can't help but grin, and it feels good. They know I'm not one to sit on the sidelines. I've always played like I might never again. It's risky sometimes, but it's gotten me to the top. Even if I was a play-it-safe kind of guy, this is not the time to do it.

"If I had a dollar for every time I heard that," Sean mumbles.

"This is different, boys. I'm finally doing what I should have done a long time ago. No matter how it turns out, I have to know. I just hate it's taken me this long, and it's under these circumstances, but this is it. My last shot. You bet your asses I'm taking it."

The old, red brick A-frame building stands just as it did eight years ago. The garage doors still list the same services in the same old white paint. The doors are shut and locked up tight, but the lights blaze from within.

For eight years, there hasn't been a single day I haven't thought about this place or the woman I have no doubt is inside working late into the night to rid herself of . . . something. I'm here, and I want to know what that something is. I have a ridiculous desire for that something to be me.

I've loved this woman more than half my life, and that love is more alive today than it was eight years ago when she kissed me goodbye and told me she'd see me soon. Week after week came and went, but she never did. She changed her number, dropped out of my life, and went on as if we never happened at all.

All this time, I've been watching like a full-time, non-threatening stalker. I've monitored her extremely minimal social media activity, wanting her to be happy. I know better than anyone you can't believe everything you see on a screen, but my Lex is missing. I know the woman I love still has to be inside the made-up version I saw in the few posts over recent years. No one can tell me my Lex isn't still in there.

Until she walks down the aisle and promises the rest of her life to that schmuck, I won't accept we aren't meant to be together. Not until she looks me in the eye and tells me she doesn't love me anymore.

Maybe I've completely lost it, and coming here is the most preposterous thing I've ever done, which would be saying a lot since I've done some really stupid shit. But it's been years, and I haven't been able to let her go. I'm not about to now. At least not without her telling me she wants me to and actually believing her.

I climb out of my rental car, taking a slow, deep breath to calm my racing heart. This is it, the defining moment for the rest of my life. I'm either going to walk away, finally having to face the devastation and utter heartbreak I've drowned out with hope, or convince her that what we were is everything we can still be.

Outside the door, I hear metal clang to the floor and a string of gentle curses that causes one side of my mouth to tip up. My nerves still stand at attention, but they stop shouting upon hearing the voice of the one that used to lay in the grass and tell me all I could be.

I inhale deeply, my stomach crawling into my throat as I prepare to put it all on the line. I'm not sure I've ever been more nervous in my life than I am at this very moment.

I need to shore myself up and walk in with my game face on. I need her to hear and believe every word that comes out of my mouth. If the Lex I knew is on the other side of this door, I have no doubt she won't be doing much of the talking.

My pulse pounds in my ears as I man up and slowly pull the door open. I quietly step inside to the smell of grease and car fluids. Fortunately, the door is unlocked, but I hate that I can walk in without any hindrance. If nothing else comes from this, I'll make sure she locks the door.

Country music plays in the background, and Lex stands across the space on a stool, bent over the hood of an old Chevy Silverado. She's in worn jeans, a white T-shirt, and steel-toed boots, all resembling the girl I used to know. Her long blonde hair falls around her, held back by a bandana as she tugs on a wrench, trying to force a bolt loose.

The roar of my heart softens at the sight of her. I swallow and shove my hands in my pockets, steadying myself for a battle I have no choice but to win.

"Somehow, I knew you'd be here."

As if in slow-motion, I watch her body startle, her hand slipping on the wrench, and then she quickly settles as if she recognizes my voice. She doesn't turn around, but her grip loosens on the tool as she straightens.

"It's been eight years and 134 days, and there hasn't been a single one that I haven't thought about you."

She stands perfectly still, her head hanging. After what feels like an eternity, she slowly turns, her boots hitting the floor as she steps down from her stool to face me. Her pale blue eyes hit mine with the force of a freight train, and it stuns my cardiovascular system, stalling it. All my instincts flare with the need to go to her, but I stay put. I can't. Not yet.

My gut squeezes tight again as she takes me in. Her eyes trace over me, and I'd give my entire fortune to know what she's thinking. I stare back, the ache in my chest as raw and real as ever.

This version of her, in old clothes and covered in grease and oil, is still the most beautiful woman I've ever seen. I want to smile, but my nerves prevent it. It takes everything in me not to wrap her up and beg her to come back to me. To tell me that I'm not completely insane.

Her head falls forward as if to inspect her tired and worn boots. One of her hands runs down her shirt.

It's only a moment before those empty blue eyes drag back up to meet mine.

"Why are you here?" Her voice is so gentle, it's painful.

I have to be very careful. My next words need to be articulate and precise. "Because I couldn't go one more day without seeing you and risking the chance of losing you forever."

Her brows twitch but quickly relax as her eyes roam over my face.

Her eyes draw closed, and she presses them together tight. I watch her chest rise and fall. My body tenses with the realization that I can't read her like I used to. A pit slowly forms in the bottom of my stomach, and I need to slide a cover over it before I fall in.

I take one step closer, and she stiffens, so I stop. I want to beg to know what happened. To understand. To know if I really had it all wrong. If I was a complete fool.

But I can't. The pain would pull me so far under I might not find my way out.

"I know you're getting married in a couple of days. Are you happy?"

The lonely sound of a sad country song fills the silence, and I break out in a cold sweat, waiting for her answer.

Please say no. I want to know what we can be again.

She turns and walks to the workbench, pulling a shop rag to wipe off her hands.

"How do you know that?" Her question is soft but curious. When I don't respond, she shakes her head. "I can't do this."

Shit. I knew this wouldn't be easy. Panic starts to kick in, and I need to calm the hell down. It's like I'm in the fourth quarter with fifty seconds left, and I'm down by eight. I need a touchdown and a two-point conversion, and I only have seconds. I have to hit my mark, and it has to count.

Screw it. I'm here for a reason. This is my chance.

I stride across the room, not hesitating, and reach for her. I gently grab her elbow and turn her toward me. I force myself to release it even though everything in me wants to pull her close, hold on tight, and never let go.

Her eyes stay on the floor as if she's afraid to look at me. I focus.

"I'm not leaving here until you tell me you're happy. You convince me of that, and I'll wish you well and never bother you again." She doesn't move. "Lex . . . "

Her head snaps up, her eyes wild. "Don't call me that."

Part of me wants to grin at hitting a nerve, but I resist. I search her eyes. Having her this close but yet so far away is pure torture. My fingertips tingle with the need to touch her again.

I've longed for this moment, but the short distance between us feels like a canyon, and I loathe every millimeter of it.

"Please tell me," I beg. "I have to know. I can't spend the rest of my life wondering."

Her eyes remain on the floor. Her hand pushes the loose hair out of her face, but it falls right back. "There's nothing left for you here."

It comes out smooth and cool, a sledgehammer, straight to my gut. I suck in air.

Shit. No. No. No. This can't be happening. He said this wouldn't be easy.

I force myself taller, remembering how to fight. "If I believed that, I wouldn't be here. I think exactly everything I need is right here."

I take a huge risk and wrap my hands gently around her arms, easing her closer. I use one finger to tip her chin up, forcing her to look at me.

Her eyes finally meet mine. "I've missed you every single day."

She pushes me away, taking a step back, her chin returning to her chest. "We didn't fit then, and we don't fit now. We're different people, and we don't belong together."

"Liar," I say, grabbing her attention. Her wide eyes flick between mine. "There have never been two people who belong together more than you and me. I don't know who or what made you believe differently, but it's bullshit. No one knows you better than I do. I don't care how many years have passed. I still know exactly who you are."

I take a desperate step closer, needing to close a bit of the space between us. "I knew you'd be here tonight. I knew it. I know those boots on your feet are the same brand, maybe even the exact same pair you had on when I kissed you the very last time, and I know they're a size seven and a half. I know you listen to this horrible, depressing country music because it drives your hard-ass grandfather crazy, and somewhere along the way, you learned to like it."

I take another step closer, her body so close to mine, and she watches my every move. I take one of her hands, holding it. At first, it's stiff, but it quickly goes limp as I surround hers in mine. I want to take it and pull her away with me, but I can't.

I breathe her in. Her scent, one I could never forget, is exactly the same. I push a strand of loose hair behind her ear, and she watches every move. "I know anything besides having your hair down and loose gives you a headache."

I lift her hand. My thumb traces a path across her palm. "One of my favorite things was seeing the grease and dirt left behind from all your hard work because it makes you so damn happy."

"I'm not that girl anymore. She's gone." There's a slight quiver in her voice I don't miss.

I wrap my arms around her waist, pulling her body flush with mine. Her quiet, stubborn ass only releases the tiniest gasp, but everything in me tells me she feels it, too.

I stare into her eyes, trying to ignore the fear filling every pore throughout my entire body. "I don't believe that. I will never believe that."

She relaxes against me, her arms between us, and I know. I know somewhere in there she's here with me.

I lean just a little, my mouth close to her ear. "I don't care what's happened or how long it's been, but I beg you not to go through with this wedding unless it's really and truly everything you've ever wanted."

Her hands slide down my biceps and rest on my forearms. I've never hated a shirt to this extreme in my life.

"I've missed you so much," I whisper.

Her hands drop to her sides. "It's time for you to go now."

My heart hits the stained concrete floor. I don't release her. I can't. "Don't do this, please. I don't know what happened, but I know I wasn't wrong about what we had. It's once in a lifetime, Lex."

I don't even care how pathetic I sound. I can't have been wrong.

"Stop." She shoves me away this time and retreats, putting space between us. "You need to go." Her chest moves in and out quickly.

Her dim eyes find mine, and pain spears through my chest, wanting to know where the girl I love has gone, but I know pushing her won't do any good.

I swallow, trying to pull forth my last shred of dignity and ounce of hope—the very last bit.

I take a step toward the workbench. Each inch of distance is like peeling a Band-Aid off a festering wound. "I'll go, but I'm never giving up. You and me, it's the only thing that makes sense." Even as I say it, the doom of this being the end begins to steamroll my fear.

I pull an invoice sheet from the counter and a pen. "Here is my phone number. After tonight, I have to be in Vegas for a game." I set the pen on the paper, turning back to her. "I will do anything you ask me to, but I won't give up. Not until you tell me straight up that you never loved me."

I give her a chance, searching her eyes long and hard. I suck my stomach in tight and wait for those words to kill what might be the only good left in me.

She only wraps her arms around herself, with what I think might be tears gathering in the corners of her eyes. I want to punch something.

"Please go."

Two simple words that strike like a thousand-pound gavel.

I take her in a few moments longer, trying to understand everything I don't. Her sad eyes cause my throat to constrict, and the pain is so great I can't bear it.

I walk to the door, gathering myself and clearing my throat. "Don't walk down that aisle unless you're certain it's the rest of your life because I will never believe it's not supposed to be us. You and me. Forever."

I pull the door open, and a rush of cold air hits me. I stand in the doorway, needing to look at her one more time. My hand finds the spot on my ribs that's been permanently branded and will burn for eternity.

"You can deny it, but it's always been us, Lex." She hasn't moved an inch, and I try to memorize every detail of her. "Lock this door. If you work here at night, it needs to be locked."

One hand moves up to tug at one of her earrings. It's a nervous habit, and it's just enough to know I've gotten under her tough-as-nails skin.

"I've missed you, and I have this strange feeling you've missed me, too." I drop my gaze to the floor, knowing I've given it my all. "This life is hard enough. We both need you to use that number."

I step out the door, letting it clang shut. I wait, making sure she locks it before I carry myself back to my rental car, praying she'll call. It's been eight years, but she's getting married in two days. She has to use that number.

Chapter 4

LEX

I rub my swollen, crusted-shut eyes. There's a tearing sensation as I pry them open, and they burn. I lie perfectly still, letting my chest rise and fall while trying to ease out the arrow shot straight through my heart. It's painfully suffocating, as if my lungs are filling with fluid.

My entire body aches with the torment of reliving every single moment of last night over and over again. Every single second hurts like hell, but that doesn't even begin to describe the pain I saw in Mark's eyes as he stood at the door, telling me he'd missed me.

Mark. I let out a long, slow breath, swallowing the lump that reemerges in my throat. I squeeze my eyes shut tight, unable to believe that he was really here. *Mark was here.*

Hearing his voice, feeling his touch, and having him tell me he's thought of me all this time is definitely not what I need, but I can't say it's not everything I've ever wanted. I didn't need to lay here all night thinking about every word he said and wondering if it was all true, but I did.

If it's possible it's true, then why now? Why would he wait all these years and come back now? Two days before I was supposed to get married. How did he even know?

If social media can be trusted, which is about as reliable as an old Dodge Neon, then Mark has dated nearly half of the female celebrity population. Coming back, telling me he loves me, seems . . . ridiculous, and I have to wonder if I'm just the thing that simply got away. I'm nostalgic, a dream, a memory.

But if the guy that walked into the garage last night is the Mark I knew—the one I fell in love with at sixteen and have never stopped—then coming here and telling me all of that was putting his entire heart on the line.

Mark is a bleeding heart on his sleeve guy, hiding behind a fun-loving exterior. He's tough as steel, but even pipes crack when too much pressure strikes those hidden weak spots. But he'd never let anyone see. Only those he completely trusts, and at one time, that person was me. It's hard for me to believe that after what I did, he'd still allow me that kind of vulnerability.

I want to see and talk to him, to know if what he said is real and true. I want to run away with him, run so far the pain and the past disappear. But there are reasons why I didn't follow Mark when he left, and not one part of those reasons has changed.

I roll to my side, pulling a pillow over my head. Trying to ignore my feelings for him when he was far away was hard enough. Trying to ignore them after last night is impossible.

He appeared before me, tall and strong, looking so much the same but completely different. Those chocolate brown eyes stabbed me clear through.

I squeeze my eyes shut, knowing it would be easier if I could just forget. But, no. He was so self-assured and confident, as if he knew exactly what he was doing. It was almost more than I could withstand. Everything he said, all the things I've dreamed of hearing him say, each word piercing the facade I've spent years molding into place.

I bury my face further, the burn consuming sore eyes and throat all over again. I might have believed he was a figment of my imagination. But then, he touched me.

The trace of his fingers still lingers on my skin. Gentle but commanding. Soft but sure. But those hands, the moment they held me close, my body tucked into his, that was it. One second longer, and I wouldn't have been able to let him go. I would have welded myself to him and stayed there forever.

Those freaking hands. The hands of the one and only man I have no choice but to accept my heart will ever belong to.

But that's exactly the problem. When you love someone, not only with your whole heart but your body and soul, too, you'll do whatever it takes to protect them. To let them be free. To save them. To let them live the life they were always meant to have.

A fist rams into my stomach again with the vision of his beautiful, handsome face staring back at me. My skin warms with a sticky sweat, and I toss the pillow to the side. A groan mixed with a whimper, full of self-loathing, escapes for not telling him the truth—that I could never marry a man unless it were him. But telling him wouldn't change a thing.

I drag myself out of bed, doing the same thing I do every day—keep on going.

I throw on old jeans, a T-shirt, and a flannel, then brush my teeth. I fill my cheeks with air and let it out, seeing my face in the mirror. My eyes look like two puffy, red squishies. *Crap.* I slather the swollen, red circles under my eyes with cream, hoping it contains sympathy and works magic this morning.

I avoid eye contact in the kitchen, but Grandpa's way too observant eyes follow me as I pop a pod in the machine. He's like an old coon dog, but instead of tracking rodents, he catches a scent in the wind and sniffs out a dip in my emotional state.

I reach into the fridge for creamer as he folds his paper, waiting. I peek at him out of the corner of my swollen eye. He folds his glasses and drops them in his shirt pocket, eyes dead set on me.

"What the hell happened?" His voice is set, ready to beat the crap out of someone.

I turn and face him, resting my butt against the counter. Having no fight left, I surrender. If there's anyone I can tell about my late-night visitor, it's this man. He took care of me after Mark left and has helped every day since.

I wrap my hands around my mug and hold it close to my chest for comfort. "Mark showed up at the shop last night. He thought I was getting married."

"Sandberg?" He stares at me, waiting for confirmation. I nod. "Ha! It's about damn time!" He claps his hands, a smile replacing the former severe concern. "What in the hell took him so long?"

"This isn't good news," I whisper as if someone will hear us.

"Like hell, it's not! He's the one you should've been marrying. He's finally wised up and realized it, too. Did you tell him you called it off?"

My brows pull together, where a headache is gathering. "Grandpa, nothing has changed, except he made it. He's living his dream. My life is here, and I still can't . . . I'm only good at one thing, and that thing is here."

"Bullshit. Cars that need fixing are everywhere, and your struggles never mattered to him." His irritation is evident, but I ignore it.

"The shop is here, you're here, and this is my life. You know as well as I do, I can't just work somewhere else."

"You also can't live the rest of your life afraid of the world. I know it's difficult, and people have a hard time understanding, but, Pal, I won't be here forever." He sets his empty mug on top of his paper. "The shop shouldn't be your entire life. At some point, you have to let people in. Not everyone will disappoint you. You're missing out on a whole world out there and a man who'd give up his throwing arm for you."

I stare at the floor, unable to handle his words today. A mixture of rage and unbearable heartache erupts in my chest, and it's all I can do to keep breathing steadily.

He comes to stand beside me, his shoulder rubbing against mine. I'd really like to shove his old ass, but I don't because he loves me.

"I don't care what anyone else says or thinks. You're the smartest and bravest person I know. And . . . you're one hell of a mechanic. You work circles around every one of the guys at the shop, and they know it. I didn't teach you everything I know to hold you back. Quit limiting yourself. It's ok to go see what's out there."

I swallow the massive growth in my throat. "Yeah, just like that. It's not that easy."

"Pal, life isn't easy. You know that better than anyone, but it's not as scary when you let people in who care about you. People who want to help and love you." He reaches to put his mug in the sink. "Mark is one of those people. He's giving you another chance. If you're smart, you'll take it. All that nonsense about nothing changing is a load of horse shit. Things have changed. You've changed, but that boy didn't show up last night for anyone other than you."

"After eight years? I'm not enough. I never have been," I choke out.

He turns toward me. "Apparently, he disagrees. You've never been able to not love him, and I've watched how hard you've tried. Shit, you almost married the wrong guy. Maybe you should let yourself love the right one." He points at me. "He came back for you."

I grip the counter, hoping it will hold me together. "It's not just about me. I won't let—"

"More horse shit." He raises his hand, stopping me. "I understand why you did what you did. Back then, I might have even agreed with you. But now, he's a grown man. He's strong and capable, and I don't think you're giving him enough credit." He leans against the counter beside me. "You need to ask yourself if this is still about protecting him . . . or you." The creases around his mouth deepen as he eyes me long and hard.

I can't look at him. My shoulders sag, and I slump under the weight of his pointed question and stare.

He steps toward the back door but stops. "Did he sign the posters in my office?"

I suck back the tears that want to fall, my eyes burning with a fresh wave. "Seriously, that's what you're worried about?"

"Hell yes! Unless you get your head out of your ass, he's not likely to come back." He shakes his head, reaching for the door. "I'll see you at the shop unless you decide to quit being a jackass."

"Oh, thank you," I sniff. "That's helpful."

"Best advice you're likely to hear all day," he winks, stepping out the back door and closing it behind him.

I sink into a chair at the table, pulling the invoice from my pocket. I unfold it, running my finger over the numbers.

Why now? Why, after all this time? Because he thought I was getting married?

I cradle my head in my arms, thinking about everything Grandpa said and letting people in. Mark laid his heart bare last night, and I have a good idea of how much that cost him. Despite space and time, I know him, and that kind of honesty and vulnerability was painful. The question is, what do I do about it?

I step into the shop, and the metal door bangs closed behind me. The compressor drill zips as Trig sets another tire.

"Hey, I need a brake light check." Carson's southern drawl comes from his spot inside the driver's seat of a white Jeep Compass, one long leg hanging out.

A horn honks, and I reach over to press the button to open one of the doors so Wind can pull a car over the pit.

"Yo," Slade yells, signaling he's far enough, and I press the button to send the door back down.

The noise suddenly dies down, and I find all eyes on me. Even Trig's hands still. The baby-faced, wanna-be race car driver earned the nickname Trigger because he has a trigger finger when it comes to tools, and we rarely find him without one in his hand.

Ugh. Seriously?

"What the hell happened to your face?" Carson asks, leaning out of the car.

These are my friends, my family, and they don't treat me differently. To them, I'm just one of the guys. But when my eyes are puffy and red, and I look like I haven't slept in days, these men turn into soldiers ready for battle. Their furrowed brows and somber faces make my empty stomach roll into a ball and bounce around as if it, too, is searching for a place to hide.

"Stop." I let my head fall to the side in exhausted annoyance, trying to lessen the tension in my shoulders and neck. "Everything is fine. I'm tired, and I have a terrible headache. Now, get back to work."

Carson's eyes squint just a little.

"You sure? Because I have no problem kicking someone's ass this morning." James, who we call Wind because he drops bombs like it's his full-time job, asks. With broad shoulders and a slight belly to match, the man places his hands on his hips.

"I'm sure." I shove my hands in my pockets, uncomfortable with all of their serious attention.

"Is this that time of the month again?" Carson asks with a hint of a smirk, and my heart squeezes at him, lightening the mood. "I'll buy beer, and we can watch a game tonight."

"I'll throw in on that," Wind says, one dimple peeking through his beard.

"How about you keep your bad gas away from me for a few days?" The guys laugh, and I can't help but smile.

"Get to work, boys! Wind, you can take that shit outside, or I'll fire you for workplace indecency," I hear Grandpa holler, saving me.

Slade, yet to ask questions or speak, only watches me as the guys razz Wind and get back to work. Except Trig, who walks over, side-hugs me, and then returns to the impact gun to tighten up lug nuts.

All morning, it's like working in a field of prairie dogs. Eyes stare until I meet them, and then they duck away. Each pair pop a peek in my direction and then dart away again. Even Trig's hands slow for the briefest moments to watch me.

These guys, each of them, covertly inspecting me as if I might fall to pieces right before their eyes. It's annoying as hell, and they suck at it. The funny thing is, if I broke down in front of them, they'd be running for the hills. Except for Trig, he'd at least hand me a shop rag to fall apart in.

I wipe my hands on a rag and toss it on the workbench. The headache forming in the back of my skull over the past couple of hours is pounding in full force, and I know it's time to quit.

The rusted, heavy metal door to the garage bangs closed, sending shooting pain through the top of my head and into my ears. Grandpa greets a customer, but his eyes drift to me as if he's conducting a thorough evaluation of my mental state.

Our morning has been swamped with oil changes and flat tires, but the guys will have to finish up this round. I'm tapping out.

I put my hands over my ears as the compressor drill squeals and pick up my pace down the short hallway to Grandpa's office. I step in and close the door behind me, needing insulation from the noise.

I fall into his old, worn chair, laying my head on the desk. It screams from stress and lack of sleep. I roll my head to the side, my eyes catching on the cheaply framed posters of Mark in uniform, arm cocked, and poised to throw the ball. The man with the boyish personality and the most handsome face in the entire world. It's as if his dark brown eyes are staring directly at me. Those eyes that I've dreamed would someday stare across the space at me one more time, and last night they did.

I want to tell him I'm sorry for not keeping my promise and how much I've missed him all these years, but it wouldn't change anything.

I rub my temples, staring at the posters, when Slade pushes through the door and slowly lowers his large frame into the chair across from me.

The tall, bearded, and tattooed man slumps down, twisting the cap off a bottle of water.

I close my eyes, still rubbing my head. "Did he send you in here?"

He only grunts.

I should have known that Grandpa wouldn't keep his mouth shut. Now, I have to deal with worried puppy dog faces because these guys care, and even though I know they want to be sure I'm all right, I could handle some privacy.

"He said you're having a rough day."

My eyes roll to peek at him from under my eyelashes, and I know at least he got the full Mark scoop. My body crumples a little further, and I close my eyes.

"He's worried he was a little hard on you this morning." Slade's voice is low and soft.

I pry one eye open, squinting at him. "Seriously?"

He scratches his beard, clearly uncomfortable with this little heart-to-heart. This man, solid and hard to the core, doesn't do feelings. It's why we get along so well. We keep things locked down tight and in the dark where they belong. With him, I know I won't ever have to talk about or confess things I don't want to.

"Want to talk about it?" he asks, his leg bouncing.

Slade is asking me if I want to talk. *What the hell is happening to my life?*

"No."

Slade's head rolls to the side, stretching his neck like this is painful. It is. So painful.

"He's been brooding around here all morning. He's in a shit mood, and we're all suffering."

I let my head fall to the desk again. "He's such a drama queen sometimes."

"Only when it has to do with you." I lift my head just enough to meet his green eyes. "He thinks it's all his fault. He's worried he's holding you back. Preventing you from seeing what the world has to offer. Afraid he didn't do enough to get you the help you needed or do more to show you that you can do anything. Yada, yada, yada." He guzzles half his water. "Is he right?"

"What?" I grumble, the side of my face pressed to the desk. The cool surface feels good against my cheek.

"Is he right? Are you sticking it out here because you're afraid?"

Despite the sledgehammer slamming into my brain, I pull my head up to face the man who, besides Grandpa, understands what my life is like and watched me try to stitch myself back together when Mark left. I know he cares, but I don't need one more person on my ass about this.

"What are you talking about? You know Grandpa and this shop are everything to me. This is what I want. You know how much I love it."

"What about him?" he points a long, grease-covered finger at the poster.

His growly, bluntness is pissing me off today. What happened to being best friends who are happy never to discuss the sucky, painful parts of life?

He rearranges his body to sit taller in the metal chair that is three sizes too small for him. "I heard he came here last night. Shit, Alex. Don't think we won't be talking about you being here late at night by yourself or that fact you didn't have the damn door locked."

I roll my eyes and then regret it as the pain radiates through my head. I decide against biting back with the news that I do it all the time and have for years. There was a time when I'd come here with Mark. Obviously, he hasn't forgotten.

I force air in and out through the intense ache, both the physical and emotional. "I knew he told you. Man, you all are worse than women in a salon. Seriously. I don't need the rest of the crew in that part of my business." I stab him with a glare and then rest my head in my hands.

We sit with the dull sounds from the garage filtering in while he waits for me to answer the question.

"I have no clue what to think about him," I say quietly.

"I think you do, but I also think Cal is right. You've spent the last how many years trying to get over him because you're scared. Going after him means having to step outside your comfort zone."

I stare across the small space, my irritation quickly revving into anger. "It's more than a comfort zone."

"Is it?" He twists the cap back on his bottle and rests it on his leg. "You don't need to be afraid. If he loves you, it'll be ok. And even if he doesn't, it'll be ok. I think you need to prove that to yourself. Otherwise, you'll never know and be stuck right here, in the middle, continuing to torture yourself."

I'm dumbstruck at his possible insightfulness and can only watch as he stands.

Having had enough for today, or maybe a lifetime, I snap back. "It's not that simple. It's not just about me. You both know it's so much more than that."

He runs a hand over his beard, exhaling. "Alex, how long is long enough? When does the cost of trying to protect someone become too much?" He stares at me, his eyes telling me he might know a little something about this. His gaze drops to the floor. "At what point does protecting them begin to do more damage than the risk of them learning the truth?"

He reaches into his pocket and tosses a small bottle of Ibuprofen on the desk.

"Maybe it's time for you to let yourself be happy and quit taking on a burden that was never yours to bear."

He leaves the office, and I can only stare at his back as I swipe the bottle from the desk, wanting to throw it against the wall. Instead, I grip it tightly as my stomach churns, wondering if I can even keep two pills down.

When in the hell did he become so . . . logical? It's that simple. Ha. Right.

I groan, pulling a bottle of water from the pack in the corner, pop the pills, and chase them with the room-temperature liquid.

I rest back in the chair, those dark eyes boring into me again. I've never been weak. I haven't had the luxury, but Slade's right. I am scared. I'm scared out of my mind. Everything has changed, but going on like this isn't an option.

Going after what I want means becoming vulnerable to a world that doesn't understand me or my struggles, no matter how good I am at hiding them. What I'm certain of, though, is that I've never been afraid of Mark.

Maybe it's finally time I do something about it, or as Slade said, I'll spend my life wondering, waiting, and so far, that's been miserable. I push back from the desk, terrified out of my mind, but Mark suffered through it for me.

Now, I guess it's my turn to put my heart on the line and find out if he really meant it—everything he said.

I wasn't enough before. I'm not sure I'm enough now or that there's anything left of us beyond what was. Maybe too much time has passed, and all the things that stood in the way before remain, but if nothing else, he deserves to know that there hasn't been a single day I haven't thought about him, too.

Chapter 5

MARK

I toss my duffle bag on the bed, checking my phone. Again. I gave her every minute I could until I had to catch my chartered flight to Vegas. There are approximately twenty-four hours left, and this time tomorrow, I'll be on the field, and she'll be married . . . to someone else.

I stare at the small, stocked refrigerator against the wall. The tiny bottles inside call to me, promising to help me forget. There was only a short time in my life when I indulged before Shane and Sean showed up and literally kicked my ass sober.

The feelings that led me to the bottle back then are far too familiar all over again.

I force my feet to the window, smart enough to know one binge would never be enough. My vow to never turn into them is stronger than my desire to numb the pain momentarily.

My eyes trace over the city below. All the glittering signs offer relief. A million things at my fingertips that, with one phone call and some cash, I could bury the pain in . . . at least for a while. I contemplate it, sorting through a list of options, wanting something, anything, to make it better. But reality voices its strict-ass opinion, and I know when it's over, that feeling of my heart being gutted from my body with a dull blade will still be there.

I pull the blackout shades closed to hide the sun and strip below. I fall on the bed, unable to bear the stabbing pain in my chest that comes with knowing it's over. What was I thinking? I know what I thought. I thought

I would walk back in there, and she'd remember, but Shane and Sean are right. It's been too long, and everything has changed.

I place a hand on my chest, needing the pain and tightness to ease. Somehow, I have to play the game tomorrow, and not only that, I have to win.

I roll on my side, hoping it will help, but all I see is her light blue eyes. They were empty—all the soft, quiet joy and determination was gone. I don't know what caused it, but I likely just made it worse.

My phone buzzes, and I snatch it up, my small sliver of hope instantly going up in smoke.

SEAN: You all right, bro?

I already told Shane and Sean what happened, so I'm not responding. I called them late last night after I drove around for an hour, seeking some kind of resolve that never came. The last thing I need to hear is their 'I told you so' disguised as sympathy.

I close my eyes, wanting sleep to envelop me and ease the excruciating reality that Lex will never again be mine.

Shit. Maybe she was never mine at all.

I try to calm my body and mind, but my phone buzzes again. My team management ensuring I'm here and set for tomorrow's game. Another reason I need sleep. I have to be one hundred percent focused, and after not sleeping last night, I need it now.

I tap on an app, and the soft sound of rain fills the dark space around me. I close my eyes, swallowing the blaze creeping up my throat, and try to shut down the slow-burning ache of wanting something that never was.

Another fist hits me square in the chest as I force myself to face reality. Everything I've held on to, the hope of what might be again, is gone. What I thought Lex and I had was just some figment of my imagination. It was all me. One-sided. I clung to her when I had nothing and no one else. The one person who I thought truly loved me.

I don't know how long I lay there, lost in the fake rainstorm when my phone vibrates next to me.

Every part of me needs to close it in a drawer and forget about it until the morning, but the destructive part requires proof that it's not Lex.

SHANE: You're going to be ok. Focus on the game tomorrow. It's what gets us through.

I want to throw my phone against the wall and watch it break into a million pieces. Hope. That's what got me through. Hope that, somehow, I'd have Lex, but she told me there was nothing left.

Done with it all, I power off my phone and toss it somewhere on the bed. I curl into a ball and try to find sleep so I can at least be great at the only thing I have left.

I open my eyes to a pitch-black room, trying to remember where I am. It only takes a second for it all to return like a nightmare I still need to wake from. I stretch my stiff body and pat around on the bed, hunting for my phone to check the time.

When my fingers locate the slick metal device, I power it back on and wait for the incoming load of messages I've missed, except for the only one I still want.

It's ten 'til six, and I should eat dinner. I quickly scroll, making sure I don't miss anything important. *Ha. Important. That word has a whole new meaning.* Alerts about recent emails and reminders pop up. Then, social media notifications fill my screen. I have messages from a couple of the guys about the game tomorrow. And then Maggie, the sister I've always wanted.

Shane married Maggie under unusual circumstances and then fell madly in love with her. Now, Sean is building a family with Andie and her son. The two of them have everything I want, and it's a fist to my windpipe.

MAGGIE: Let us know you're ok. Please, for me.

Another knife to the gut.

ME: I'm good. Sleeping. Preparing for tomorrow.

I toss my phone to the side and rub my eyes, needing calories and to hydrate, but food is the last thing I want. I have tape I should be watching and plays I should be visualizing, but all I can do is lie here, dreading everything that comes next.

Closing my eyes and letting the darkness settle around me again, I hear my phone buzz. I ignore it. It buzzes again.

Dammit! Why won't everyone leave me alone?

I search for my phone and tap the screen, lighting it up.

UNKNOWN: Where r u?
UNKNOWN: Exactly

I sit up so fast warm blood rushes through my head, and I see stars. The messages were sent an hour ago. *It can't possibly be, can it?* I stare at my phone in shock, my heart racing with disbelief. My fingers shake as I try to figure out how to reply. I keep it simple, praying it's her.

ME: Who is this?

I wait for the three dots, but nothing, and then after ten minutes, they still don't appear. A hundred hours later, a relief so great washes over me that it brings tears to my eyes.

UNKNOWN: Alex
UNKNOWN: Here.

My head spins around my pitch-black room as if, somehow, she's actually here. *Shit.* My phone buzzes in my hand.

UNKNOWN: Vegas

I push off the bed and onto my feet, trying not to fall over while I get a clue as to what to do.

She's here. Lex is here. How? Why? Shit!

I don't care. She's here and not there. She's not there with that suit-wearing . . .

I quickly text her where I'm staying and my room number. Luckily, team security is still with the team in New York, or this would be a whole lot more complicated. I turn on a light and survey my room, realizing all I can do is wait.

So that's what I do. I wait and watch my phone for every minute of the thirty minutes until I hear the light knock. I sprint to the door and don't even bother to look in the peephole before throwing it open.

Her long blonde waves fall over her black zip-up hoodie, her blue eyes hitting mine with the force of being sacked and knocking the wind out of me.

I don't hesitate to grab her and pull her to me as the weight of a lifetime of longing lifts. There can only be one reason she's here, and it has to be because this isn't over. *We* aren't over.

She comes to me, wrapping her arms around me and sliding them up my back, just like she used to. My body fills with panicked astonishment that this can't possibly be real. I slide my fingers into the back of her silky hair, holding her to me. This is everything I've needed and the only thing I'll ever want.

I don't even breathe for fear she'll disappear or I'll wake up and find out this is all a dream. I try to take in every inch of her warm body pressed against mine.

She's here. Thank God. Tears prick my eyes, and I can't let her go.

After a few long minutes, I risk pulling away, desperate to understand. I bring my hands to her face, keeping her close. "What are you doing here?"

Her tired eyes search mine. "I had to see you."

I can't prevent the quick little dip my stomach takes, wondering if this visit isn't what I want it to be. I search her face in return, searching for clues.

I release her, tugging her inside and noticing she only has the bag on her back. I watch her, still stunned and waiting for her to tell me . . . something.

"I can't believe you're here." My heart is still beating a thousand times a minute. "I thought . . . " I can't even finish it.

I think I see one side of her beautiful mouth almost tug upward. "I couldn't. I called it off months ago."

It's all she says. *Months ago?* I can't help the foolish smile that creeps across my face. She couldn't marry him, and my girl still uses as few words as possible.

"Thank God. You have no idea how happy I am to hear that."

She bites her bottom lip, this time preventing her smile, but it quickly falls away. "Everything you said, was it true?"

"Yes. Every single word."

Her eyes drop to the floor, and her shoulders sag. "I'm sorry." Her voice is painfully soft. "I'm so sorry. I have so many—"

I step closer, taking her face in my hands again. "Shhh. It's ok. You're here, now."

My heart pounds to a new rhythm of hope and joy and disbelief. She still feels the same under my fingertips. I breathe in her familiar scent—sunscreen with a hint of car oil.

"Tell me I wasn't wrong," I beg, needing to hear her say it. "Tell me what we had was real, that I didn't make it all up."

She studies me, her eyes, the lightest blue, trace over my face. "You weren't wrong." Her throat bobs as a large knot lodges itself in mine. "It was so real." Her soft voice quivers as her eyes flick between mine.

I slowly close the distance between us and press my lips to hers. Once. Twice, quick and soft, even though nothing about what is running through me is soft and gentle.

My lips linger on hers, relishing the feel of her mouth on mine and finally being able to accept that this is really happening. It's like finally coming home.

I slide my fingers into her long strands, and it only takes a second for her to reciprocate my need. She angles her head and parts her lips, and I'm gone. Her hands move over my chest to my neck, holding me close. Heat and desperation collide. As our tongues twine, my hands find her hips seeking more as if years haven't been more than a day.

I kiss her like I've dreamed every night, over and over again, neither of us breaking for air. This is everything I've missed and longed for. Her nearness and familiarity. The feel of her body against mine. The taste of her mouth. The way she knows me and cares for me. The kind I've never known before or since.

I walk her backward to the edge of the bed, slowing our frantic and hungry kisses. "I love you," I whisper, bringing my forehead to hers. "I've always loved you. I never stopped. Not for a second. I couldn't."

Her hands fist my shirt like she's afraid I'll disappear.

I never want this to end. I can never go back to life without her. The thought of having to say goodbye to her again is unimaginable. I won't do it.

I stare into her eyes. "Marry me."

She blinks. Then, blinks again. "What?"

"Marry me. I want you. All of you. Forever. There isn't a chance I can go back to life without you. Marry me."

Her light eyebrows scrunch together. "What?" she asks again, making me smile. "Mark, there's so much—"

"I don't care. Marry me. Tonight. Here."

"Marry you?"

"Tell me you don't love me, that you haven't loved me all these years, and I won't ask you again."

Her eyes fall closed, and I see her admittance. "Mark . . . "

The way she says my name is like no other, and a flash of heat climbs from the depths of my core, spreading to the surface.

"Lex, it's always been us. It will always be us. Nothing will change that. Marry me."

She lifts her chin, her eyes opening as she searches my face, weighing . . . something.

I tug her closer, resting my forehead on hers, waiting.

She pulls her bottom lip between her teeth. "Ok."

Chapter 6

LEX

Mark's large hand surrounds mine, and I stare at our linked fingers. The warm, safe, secure feeling is exactly the same, despite the roughness and callouses from years of perfecting his skill.

He charms the smitten white-haired old lady behind the desk of the small white chapel, ordering our drive-thru ceremony and insisting that our expedited nuptials remain private.

He squeezes my hand, glancing at me like he's making sure I'm still here, followed by a grin that shows off his perfect white teeth. That confident, cocky grin that's always done funny things to my insides. The feeling I've missed every day.

This is absolutely insane, but it's the best kind of insane I've ever felt. This man is a drug. He's completely intoxicating, and just being near him makes everything and anything seem possible.

He hands over a credit card, and the woman takes her time explaining how our ceremony will proceed. All I can do is memorize all the new details of the man I never thought I'd see again, let alone get to call mine, but this time forever.

A smile tugs at my lips as Mark releases my hand to slide his arm around me, pulling me close and kissing my forehead.

"This is the best day of my life," he whispers.

Driving Miss Daisy finally finishes her instructions and directs us to sign the paperwork. Next up, we'll become husband and wife. *I can't believe we're doing this.*

Mark tugs me to a corner as we wait for our turn in the chapel, holding me close and keeping his back to the reception area. "You ok?"

I tip my chin up to meet his eyes. His dark brown irises are littered with flecks of gold. His olive-toned skin is smooth underneath a subtle layer of scruff. His black hair, trimmed close to the sides and long on top, is different from the close-cropped style he wore in high school. He's even more beautiful than I remember.

I reach up to push a couple of longer strands off his forehead. "I forgot what this feels like."

He smiles, wrapping me up so tight. His once tall, lanky body is now the strong, lean frame of a man.

We stay like that until our number is up and we're called back. Mark takes my hand, and we walk down the short aisle. It's exactly perfect, only the two of us. There's no extravagance or grand formality. It's simply us promising our lives to one another, legally, this time.

When we reach the end, the officiant waits dressed in a suit and a horrifying toupee. Mark's eyes widen, and he gestures toward the rug that could be made of goat hair and slightly cocked to the side. I bite my cheek and pinch his hand to keep from losing it.

The man shuffles through the paperwork as if he's performed marriages for the last century, and even that feels entirely right. Mark maintains a solid grasp on my hand, linking my fingers with his as our expedited ceremony begins.

I steal a glance at him out of the corner of my eye, wanting to cement this moment in my memory forever. The strong, confident man standing next to me, the young man I fell in love with so long ago.

I let out a long, slow, and steady breath, allowing myself not to think just this once. To be in this moment with him.

I turn my head, lifting my chin to peek at him. His shoulders are pulled back, and his filled-out muscular body makes him seem taller. Mark was always a little high-strung, but secure. There's a new self-assurance about him that only comes with experiences and living, something I've not had or done. I've been afraid, but with Mark, it all doesn't seem quite so scary.

He turns toward me, taking both my hands, as he jumps right into reciting his vows, promising to love me until the end. I offer them in return, knowing I never had a choice. He wrote his name on my heart all those years ago.

Mark scoops me up and carries me over the threshold of the hotel room, drops me on the bed, then falls onto it next to me.

"How does it feel to be Mrs. Sandberg?"

I scoot closer to him, unable to get enough. "Eh, it's ok."

He rolls, the entire weight of his body pressing down on mine. "Take that back," he glares, that playful stare sending rockets off inside my belly.

I try not to smile. "Fine." I study him, noting the thin lines around his eyes. "Like it's too good to be true," I whisper, afraid if I say it any louder, it'll all come to an end.

It's as if this is all some crazy dream that I'm going to wake from and have to go back to living without him. He rolls to the side, and I bury my face in the chest of the man who's molded his body to help him become the best quarterback in the NFL.

His arm slides around me, pulling me closer. Our legs tangle, and my body is flush with his. I want to stay like this, hidden and safe, savoring that he loves me and we're joined together forever. I halt the questions about tomorrow from forming. I've waited my entire life for this night with him and spent years trying to accept I'd never have it.

Mark kisses the top of my head and runs his hand down the length of my loose hair. "Tell me what you're thinking."

I inhale, filling my lungs with his spicy, clean scent. It used to be the distinct smell of the cheap bar soap the group home supplied. "I can't believe I'm here with you," I whisper. "I wish . . . I wish I could go back and do things differently. I'm sorry I didn't . . . I was . . . " All the emotions of the past few days overwhelm me, and a tear slips down my cheek.

His long fingers spread over the small of my back. "I've had a lot of time to think about what I was asking and what it would've been like for you. I didn't realize how selfish I was being, but for a long time, I just thought—"

"You would've never made it if I hadn't let you go." I run a finger over the long scar above his right eye, still wanting to erase all the pain that put it there.

The warmth of his body dissipates as he pulls away slightly. His finger lifts my chin upward, forcing my eyes to his.

"I don't believe that. I carried you with me every day, hoping I could be what you wanted again."

More tears spill over as guilt punches me in the stomach for ever letting him think I didn't want him.

"Mark, I'm sorry. I'm so sorry. I couldn't go with you, and I couldn't live with myself if I was the thing that prevented you from achieving your dream. You needed to be free . . . from everything." I pull in air, willing myself to hold it together. "I couldn't let anything get in your way. You needed to get out of there and have a chance at everything you worked so hard for. Everything you deserved."

"Shhh." He wipes my tears away with his thumbs. "It doesn't matter anymore. It's us now. We don't ever have to go back to that."

I sniff, unable to stop my next question from forming and slipping out. "What happens tomorrow?" I peek up at him, his dark eyes intense and set on me.

"I don't know." His honesty is both reassuring and awakens a new wave of anxiety about what we just did and what's to come. "I want this night with you. Just the two of us, where nothing else matters."

He pushes a strand of hair out of my face, and I lift up to press my lips to his. His fingers slide further into my hair, holding me there. His mouth takes over mine, and my hands find the hem of his shirt and tug.

He releases me to pull his shirt over his head in one swift motion, his fingers instantly moving to the zipper on my sweatshirt and then easing me up to remove my tank top underneath.

His hands cup my face, his eyes holding mine. "I was tested during my preseason physical, and it's been a very long time. I've always used protection."

My eyes roam his face, seeing the truth of his statement. "I'm on the pill."

Left in nothing but my black bralette, his eyes rake over me as a small smile tugs at his lips. "You are even more beautiful than I remember."

I can only stare at the man before me. His smooth chest is chiseled with muscle, but his ribs are marked with . . . I narrow my eyes, trying to read the black script lettering. I sit up, carefully lifting my hand to run my finger over the words.

Perhaps your love will make me forget all I wish not to remember.

My eyes jump to his as he watches me, remembering the words he read. Alexandre Dumas. *The Count of Monte Cristo.* Those words. The nights we lay in the grass dreaming about what might be. The very words I've held onto all this time, needing to make them true for him. Loving him enough to allow him to live without ever having to remember.

"It's only ever been you that could make me forget." His voice is low and ragged.

My eyes flick between his, and I see the honesty of his words. The need for him overwhelms me. The same need since I kissed him goodbye all those years ago. It's never wavered. Never faded. Not even a little bit.

I climb to my knees, my hands gliding over his chest to his neck, pulling his mouth to mine. His tongue swipes against mine, stealing my breath.

Warm, sure hands slide up my spine as he lowers me to the bed, the weight of his body pressing down on me. My fingers dig into his back, keeping him close.

His thumb runs underneath the lace wrapped around my ribs as he trails kisses along my collarbone.

"I love you. I've never been able to stop," I whisper, needing to say it. "I tried so hard, but I couldn't."

His kisses halt, and he presses up on one elbow, finding my eyes. "I love you, too. So much it hurts." He presses his forehead to mine, a devilish grin that's insanely familiar creeping across his face. "Baby, this is just the beginning. From now on, it's you and me, always."

Chapter 7

MARK

My buzzing phone pulls me from bliss, but the small, warm, soft body tucked beside mine reminds me that I finally have everything I need. She's it, and she's my wife.

My hand finds her bare hip as I push her hair away with my chin, placing a soft kiss on her neck. There's no way I slept enough last night, but I will survive on stupid, happy adrenaline.

My phone vibrates again. I snatch it from the nightstand, seeing Rob, my agent's name, which is strange for it to be so early and on a game day.

I carry it to the bathroom and accept the call, speaking softly so I don't wake Lex. *My wife.*

I grin, peeking back at her blonde hair fanned over the pillow.

"Hey, Rob. What's up?" I close the door as his voice fills my ear.

"Please tell me the rumors aren't true."

I rub a hand over my face, trying to sort through getting Lex to meet me back in New York. "I'm not sure what you're talking about."

"Seriously. The buzz on social sites is that you got married last night. There are no pics but unnamed sources. The supposed Vegas chapel is listed, and details of the quick nuptials are making the rounds."

I sit on the side of the tub, thinking through my response.

"I don't like that you're taking a minute to think about it." He sighs, and I have no doubt my longtime agent is running a hand over his face. "What the hell is going on? You know how I feel about surprises, and part of our agreement is that you don't do stupid things that end up making me look bad. Where are you?"

"Vegas." That's an easy answer.

"Shit. Are you with the team?"

"No."

"Why the hell not?" His usual calm demeanor quickly turns to full-on irritation.

"I had an emergency."

"The kind of emergency that involves a Vegas wedding chapel the night before a big game? Do I need to remind you that keeping your standing is critical for next season?"

"There's nothing to worry about. I'll be on my A-game."

"Shit, Mark. You know there's more to this than that. If you lose—"

"We won't lose. I'm ready. I'm more ready than I've ever been."

"Is that because you did something last night that I need to know about?"

I let out a breath, rubbing my temples while I think about what this all means. This is the part that I didn't think about. The part where I don't get to call all the shots on how things go in my life. The part where I have commitments and contracts and an overloaded schedule, and Lex . . . All I know is I need her with me.

"If I tell you, it stays between us."

He mutters a few words I choose to ignore. "You know our deal, but that doesn't mean I won't kill you or move on when our contract ends."

"You won't leave me. You like me too much." I try for charm, knowing it won't work this time.

"Spill it, Mark, before I dump your ass to fend for yourself."

"I got married last night." He lets out a string of colorful words, and I try to remain calm.

"That's great. Congratulations. Don't you think you could have given me a heads-up or an invitation or taken a second to think this through? When this leaks, and it's already started, your ass will be grass. Not to mention when your latest spontaneous flare-up comes crashing down in your face with divorce papers and—"

I stop him right there, my easygoing, blissful state quickly morphing into furious defense. "Divorce?" I hold back the laugh that would be smothered in irritated sarcasm. "Yeah, never happening, so you can let that worry go."

"Mark." He says my name like a parent trying to hold their tongue to keep from saying what they really want to say. "Everything you've worked for is riding on the outcome of this season and your shoulder holding up. We don't have room for tabloids and major headlines and . . . scandalous outbursts."

Scandalous outbursts? I want to yell, but I bite my tongue so hard it might bleed. I want to punch something. Maybe myself, square in the face.

Lex asked me straight up last night what happens today, and this . . . this is what happens. I have to jog onto the field in a matter of hours and not cause a media ruckus.

The problem is, I won't be letting her out of my sight, but I don't know how to do that and keep my job and prospects running smoothly.

I run a hand through my hair. My fingers grip the long strands tightly, causing pain to spread throughout the top of my scalp. "Let me get through the game today. We win, and this won't matter. I paid the chapel to ensure it would remain private. They may be spilling tidbits, but there were no pictures. These places rely on keeping things private. They'd be morons to talk."

"Shit, Sandberg, we deal with the biggest idiots of them all every day." He's almost crossed over into yelling, but he pauses, toning it back. "What does your organization think you've been doing?"

"I told them I had an emergency."

"This just keeps getting worse. Did you spend any amount of time thinking any of this through?"

My temper reawakens. Last night was the most important night of my life, and I won't feel bad about one second of it.

"I didn't think it through. I don't know what to do now besides get my ass to the stadium and win this game. Then I'll figure all this out later."

"I bet your wife will love to hear that."

His ridicule is the last thing I need at the moment, but he's right. I have no idea what to say to the woman lying in bed right now—the one I need to sleep in my bed every night. We've been apart for so long, and she's not been a witness to this side of my life.

"If this makes the rounds and you don't win the game, I have no idea how to fix this. I hope she's everything you think she is." *She's more.* I clench my jaw so hard my molars grind. "Keep her on the DL for now. Win this game, and let's hope this settles quickly, at least to get you through the rest of the season. After that and your shoulder surgery, we need teams to still be interested in what you have to offer."

The blunt reminder of all that's ahead of me feels like a two-ton weight bar being set on my shoulders, and one of them needs repair.

After this season, I'm a free agent and want out of the city, now more than ever. I need a team and organization that's willing to take a chance on me post-shoulder repair. Rob's right. Giving them any additional negative impressions or the idea that I don't take my status seriously might kill my chances.

"I hear you."

"Be smart from here on out. Don't make this worse than it already is, and make sure you win today."

"Yeah, no pressure, right?"

"Hey, it's the name of the game. I hope you don't regret this."

Suddenly, the entire world rests on my ability to win, keep news of my marriage off screens, and somehow explain all this to Lex.

"I have a lot of regrets, but don't worry, I'll do what I have to do."

I hang up, not caring for any of the thoughts running through my head about what that really means, but I don't have time to think. I have to talk to Lex and get ready to win a game.

I turn on the shower, letting steam fill the room while I figure out exactly what to say to Lex. All I want is for her to go to the game and then meet me back in New York so we can be together. What I know is she'd hate the city, and her life is back in Ohio.

After showering and drying off, I open the door to find her sitting on the edge of the bed, fully clothed, with her backpack zipped on the floor beside her. When she doesn't look at me, a cold sweat envelops my still-damp body with the realization of what she might have heard. *Shit!*

The last thing I want to do is try to make this better and then leave her, but it appears she might beat me to it.

My stomach hits the carpeted floor.

Her eyes finally drag up to meet mine. "I didn't want to just leave this time."

"What?" My cold sweat turns into full-on panic, and my heart starts sprinting while my legs remain still.

"I guess we should've thought this through."

My words are tossed back at me, and I know she heard. *Fuck. Fuck! FUCK!* I close my eyes, wholly inadequate to handle this when my ass needs to be in a car on the way to the stadium in thirty minutes.

"Lex, what you heard—"

She stands, shaking her head, her eyes trained on the floor again. "I have to go, and you have a game to win."

I quickly step in front of her, blocking her exit. "So, you're just going to go, disappear like you did last time?" I see the slap of my words on her downcast face.

I step toward her, wanting to take it back, but my anxiety shoots through the roof and is freefalling. "I don't want you to go. I want you to go to the game. I want to know you're in the stands."

Her tired, bright blue eyes meet mine, but I can't read the look on her face, and I hate it. I used to be able to tell everything she was thinking.

I push through the blood pooling in my ears and the sweat collecting in all the places I just washed. "Then I want you to meet me back in New York. I want to be with you." I don't even try to hide the desperation in my voice, knowing my time is ticking down.

"But none of that is going to happen." The surety of her soft words strikes me right in the throat. "I'm going home, and you . . . have a game to win. I don't want to be a problem or a distraction or whatever else might cause you to have more regrets."

I jam my hands into my hair, unable to handle the pressure of needing to get this right with everything else that's crashing down on me. My chest constricts, and my hands shake.

"There's *no* part of me that regrets this. That's not what I meant." Her head drops again, and I move my unsteady hand to bring it back up. "Lex, that's not what I meant. There's a lot that's going on. I have to make it into the playoffs, and then . . . " *I don't know!*

Her eyes flick between mine. "I think maybe we got ahead of ourselves. We got caught up in the past, not thinking about all that's changed. We've changed, and our lives are . . . separate."

My lungs quit working, and I suck in air, but it's painful. "Shit! No! Don't do this!" I pace with the need to fix this, but I don't have time, and the reality is neither of us can stay. "I love you."

Her quiet voice has me frozen. "Maybe it's not enough. Maybe it never has been. Maybe that's why it took eight years for us to get here, realizing that too much time has passed and everything has changed. We've changed, and our lives are so far apart."

The defeat and sadness in her voice are like a hand being shoved straight through my chest.

"I just need time to figure this out. I need to get through this season and then—"

She reaches for her backpack and throws it over her shoulder. "It sounds like you just need to get through today."

I grab her face in my hands, desperate for her to hear me. "This isn't over. This wasn't a mistake. I don't have a single regret except for not coming back for you sooner. I need you." Maybe if I keep saying it, she'll hear me.

She doesn't move, her eyes holding mine. Then she pushes up on her toes, kissing me. Gently, softly, and then she swings her arms around my neck, pulling me close. She hugs me tightly. So damn tight and doesn't let go. "Go win this game."

I wrap her up, wanting every moment of this to seep into my body.

All I can do is release her as she pulls away, her eyes holding mine. One side of her mouth tips upward, but only barely. Then, just like that, she opens the door and is gone.

I want to run after her and carry her with me wherever I go, but I can't. I have a team and an organization depending on me to carry us through to the playoffs.

But this isn't done. I don't know what happens now, but Lex and I will be together.

SHANE: Shit, Mark. What's this about you getting married?
MAGGIE: Did you get married? Were you drunk? Shane's about to blow a gasket. *Laughing face emoji*
SEAN: LOL. Did you get married? Are you lashing out?
SEAN: Bro, what's happening? You better answer.
ANDIE: You little shit. Are you trying to one-up us?
SEAN: Babe, I'm down for creating a new scandal with you.
MAGGIE: STOOPPPPP!
MAGGIE: No more scandals. I don't have time to kick anyone's ass.
SHANE: Good luck getting out of this one.

Chapter 8

LEX

Stepping into the house, I'm grateful Grandpa isn't home and will probably be gone all evening playing pool and watching football with friends at the bar. I drag myself up the stairs and into my little room, my tiny place of peace and solitude. It's been my home since I was fourteen when my mom left Ohio to move to Florida with the momentary man of her dreams. Since then, it's been Grandpa and me, but tonight, I'm glad he had somewhere to be. I need a minute before his subtle interrogation begins.

After a long, hot shower and using every ounce of water in the tank, I crawl into bed, needing to sleep for the next week. I grab my phone and power it back to life to check the score.

I want to watch the game, like I've secretly watched every other game of his career, sometimes over and over again, just to see him. But seeing Mark's face on the screen will only force me to dissect all the emotions I packed up and carried back home with me.

From his side of the conversation this morning, I heard how important this game is, but by the distraught tone of his voice, I know it's more than that.

It wasn't just his words, but that tone told me there's so much going on in his life that I don't know about. It all made me realize we don't know or understand each other like we used to. We've lived worlds apart. How could we?

I said vows to the man I used to know, the one I said goodbye to at eighteen so he could chase his dreams. At one time, we knew everything about each other, but this morning made it clear that not only has time passed, but we now live in separate worlds.

I'm afraid we got caught up in who we used to be, and I'm not sure how we make up for lost time . . . apart.

I can't bring myself to think we made a mistake or to regret marrying Mark. I can't. It's all I've ever dreamed of and still everything I want.

My phone buzzes to life with notifications. I have two voicemails. The first is from my mom, which I can't listen to. I have no doubt her words are filled with concern for my future, disguised as her checking on me.

The next is from Linda, which I'll ignore for now. I'm sure it's about scheduling dinner, but it's a conversation I can't handle tonight and just another reminder of all that's happened in the last eight years.

KRISSY: Come over. The game is on.
KRISSY: These guys smell.
KRISSY: Save me.

There's only one person I want to talk to, but he's currently a little busy. I click on the app, find his team, and see that the New York Liberties are leading in the third quarter. Relief washes over me even greater than I imagined.

It's always been my fear that I'd get in Mark's way or hold him back, and I have no intention of doing either now.

I pull the covers over me, settling for whatever tomorrow brings. One thing is for sure. Life will go on. It always does.

Only this time, as I fall asleep, it's with the hope that my future will include Mark.

I blink. My eyes take in the early darkness as my pillow vibrates. The buzzing stops, and I roll over, pulling the covers tighter around me.

Just before I reach the land of suspended consciousness, my stupid phone starts buzzing again. It's too early to talk to anyone. I hold the pillow tighter around my head until I realize I can't breathe and surrender. I search for my phone, hitting the button to silence it, but before I drop it, the name on the screen is the one I thought I'd never see there.

I swipe to answer as my heart stutters and sends my stomach swirling with nervous anticipation.

"Hey," my sleepy morning voice croaks out.

"If you didn't answer your phone, I seriously think you would've seen my head explode and all the little brain particles drift into the atmosphere." I bite my lip, trying not to smile at Mark's dramatics. "Where are you?"

"That'd be tragic."

"Ha. I see you're still hell-bent on using as few words as possible."

"I just save them up for when they really matter."

He laughs, and it's that laugh that stretches my mouth to limits it hasn't ventured into since I last heard it.

"Lex, where are you?" he barks, forcing us back on track. It's demanding, and I like it *way* too much.

My hidden grin turns into a yawn as I rub my puffy eyes. "Home."

"Good. You left so quickly that I didn't get to tell you to text me. I got home late and didn't want to wake you up to be sure you made it."

"Did you win?"

"My own wife didn't watch my game?"

The word rolling off his tongue sends my stomach soaring into a backflip, and I want him to say it again.

"I couldn't watch," I tell him honestly because there's no use in pretending anything anymore.

"Why?"

Such a simple question, yet so difficult to answer, especially when I want to respond with truth. I take a second to gather my thoughts, and he waits as he always did.

"I didn't want to see your face."

He laughs again, and it sends warmth from my head to my toes. "Baby, some women only watch the game to see this face."

"Shut up." He's not wrong. I see what women post and talk about. But now, he's married . . . to me. A smile tries to break free, but I quickly yank it back, with the reminder that he's . . . wherever and I'm here. "I didn't want to see you there . . . far away again."

"We're just starting, Lex. You and me." His tone is instantly serious and intense. Manly and direct. It's new, and I don't hate it. "I don't care what we have to do. I can't live without you, so whatever has to happen, we're going to do it." He says it matter-of-factly, and I almost believe how simple he makes it sound.

I roll to my side, holding the phone tight against my ear. I need to be brave and unpack all the thoughts I shoved into my backpack and left zipped up tight. "But we don't know each other anymore. You have your life, and I have mine. So much time has passed, and everything around us has changed."

"I know you, Lex, in all the ways that matter, and you know me."

"I don't know if that's true," I say, biting my lip, recalling his tone and words to whoever he was speaking with on the phone in the bathroom.

I hear him push out a breath, and I don't know if it's frustration or angst. "What do you want? Please, just tell me. If this was a mistake to you, then say it."

His direct question catches me off guard. All I hear is anguish now, and I hate it.

I'm careful with my words. "*You* are all I've ever wanted, but . . . I'm not sure I understand what that means. We aren't the same people. I don't know anything about your life beyond what I see on the screen, and most of that has been you with other women."

That last part slips out, but at least it's honest.

"Lex, I was a fucking idiot. None of that was what it looked like." His tone is forceful, and I want to believe him.

"I think maybe we got caught up in the moment and the past the other night, and I . . . I don't know where we go from here. I've never wanted to get in your way, and I won't now."

"Lex, seriously, how do you not get it?" His soft, gentle voice has a lump forming in my throat. "You are my dream. *You* are all I want."

"How can you be sure? I'm not the same girl I used to be." I try to tease, but the reality is that I'm not the same person I was, and neither is he.

"I see that," he says plainly. "Lex, I don't want to be here. I want to be wherever you are." I hear his frustration and imagine him running a hand through his hair. "I know we can't make up for all the time we've been apart, but I just need to know that you still want to be with me now."

"What does that mean 'be' with you?" I ask the question I'm pretty sure neither of us has an answer to.

"I don't know." It sounds like defeat, with reality settling in.

The silence between us lingers for a few moments. All I want is to be back tucked inside his arms where the rest of the world and this distance between us doesn't exist. It was so easy there. Here it sucks more than ever.

"I need to tell you something that might sound really bad." His voice cuts into my longing.

Just when I thought it couldn't get worse. My stomach takes a dip, and I give it a second to pull itself together. "Ok." I say it, but I'm not sure I want to know.

"Rumors are floating around about us getting married."

"What? How?" He was careful and paid triple to keep things private.

"I don't know, but I know better than to think anything stays off the feed for long. Since we won, one of the reporters asked about it after the game like it was a joke. I spun it, but—"

"You won?" I smile despite my confusion.

"Damn straight, I did. I just married the woman of my dreams and had the best night of my life. There wasn't a chance in hell I'd lose that game."

A wave of heat rolls through me, remembering our night together. "I don't understand."

His pause pulls me right back to the here and now.

"I need to keep us quiet for a while."

Us. It sounds nice, but also like a problem. My empty stomach folds in on itself, hiding this time. I bring my knees closer to my chest, tucking myself into a ball.

When I don't say anything, Mark continues. "I know that sounds bad. If I had it my way, I'd be shouting from the rooftops that we got married, but . . . this is part of my life now. I can't do that. A lot is up in the air, and if my organization found out my emergency was getting married and spending the night doing things other than focusing on the game, they'd fry my ass. The media will run with it and spin it and . . . I can't have that."

I don't even know what to think about what he just said. There are so many questions wrapped up in all of it, but the thing that rises to the top is that he doesn't want people to know about me. I'm not sure how I feel about that.

"So . . . I'm a secret?" I ask carefully, wanting to make sure I understand while my insecurities come strolling out to play.

"Shit. No. I mean—"

"Mark, just tell me what you mean." It's my turn to get frustrated and demand answers.

"I don't know if I can explain this in the next five minutes before I have to leave for an appointment. Lex, this is part of my life. The part I didn't think about and pulled you into when I made promises to you. I'm sorry. So many things could go wrong if we become a headline at the wrong time."

"Like?" I need more than that.

"Reporters hunting you down to be the first to show your name and face. If they're going to do that, you have to be with me where I know you're safe."

I can definitely do without that. "What else?"

"I'm a free agent after this season." He pauses. "Where I play next year is anyone's guess. I need to stay in good standing and not cause a stir that will give other organizations reason to question my commitment or dedication. I want out of the city. You'd hate it here, and I intend for us to be together."

My stomach that's stuffed itself inside my ribs peeks out, but only a little.

"So . . . we wait until the season is over, and then we try to figure out if this will ever work?" I'm not trying to make this more difficult. I just want to understand . . . something.

"Lex," he says my name like he's begging me to understand, but that's just it. I don't. I don't understand anything about where we are or what in the hell we are supposed to do. And for now, I guess that's how it has to be.

"Look, I know you have to go."

"Lex, just stay with me. Ok?"

"Yeah. Sure."

I hear him push out a long breath. "Please don't be upset. I can't handle this right now. This isn't how I want it to be."

"Me neither."

"I'll call you later." He's back to being adamant. "I love you."

I can't help but wonder if love is enough. "Yeah," I say softly. "Bye."

Mark and I are married, but we still can't be together or even tell anyone. Not that I want to tell anyone anyway. I don't care if it stays between us for now. I just can't help but feel like it's more me that's the secret and less us.

It's another thing that's changed over the years. I trusted Mark with everything all those years ago, but now, I'm questioning things, and it's the absolute worst feeling in the world.

I groan at the realization that it's Monday, and I can't stay in bed all day and hide from my life. Knowing there's no way I'm going back to sleep, I dress and carry myself downstairs. I need coffee and the shop to get my hands busy working on something.

I find Grandpa in his usual spot at the table.

"Nice to see you're home. Want to talk about where you disappeared to?"

I pull a mug from the cabinet, careful not to make eye contact for fear of what his overly aware eyes might see. "No."

"Do I need to worry?"

"No." If he knew what I'd been up to, he'd probably be skipping down the street.

"Linda and Bree stopped by yesterday morning, hoping to catch you. Bree brought you flowers." He points to the small bouquet on the counter. "That girl bounced in here like joy on steroids."

Bree. My heart squeezes with thoughts of the little girl and her big, innocent eyes. I reach for the small bright bouquet and lift it to my nose as my gut jumps up and smacks my heart, dampening its joy. I've helped take care of Bree when Linda has needed it. She's a special little girl, but even as young as she is, her life hasn't always been easy.

"What's waiting at the shop?" I need a car to fix and fast.

He folds his paper while I put fresh water in the vase.

"Dodge Ram was towed in yesterday. Won't start. But your mom has called me twice. Stop avoiding her so she'll quit calling me." He stands, brings his mug to the sink, and then swings his arm around my shoulders. "Pal, I'm not exactly sure what's going on, but I'm here when you're ready."

I set the flowers down, letting my head rest on his shoulder, knowing I've never questioned where he stands. "I know, old man."

We stand in silence for a second before the emotions get too high for the both of us, and he drops his arm, stepping away.

"I'm meeting the guys at the diner and then stopping by the store. Let me know if you want something."

I finish arranging the flowers in the jar before placing it in the center of the table. The bright colors bring a touch of cheer to the worn, dull space. I run a finger over a delicate, bright, yellow petal of a sunflower. I had twelve hours of happiness to fill my sad, lonely insides. I want more than twelve hours. I want a lifetime.

Chapter 9

MARK

I wince as my physical therapist rotates my arm, checking my function and mobility, that's becoming more and more limited. The day after a game, the pain is incredible, and my stomach rolls as my torture agent finally eases up.

"Sit tight while I grab a few things."

"How about a saw? You might as well completely sever it from the rest of me."

Tyler steps away, pulling something from the table beside me. "I'd think about it, but you'll need it next week, and I'm in the business of helping you make it there."

I take a couple of deep breaths, knowing I'm living on borrowed time. I've been Band-Aiding this injury for the last two seasons, and I'm paying for it in more ways than one.

As soon as the season is over, I'm walking straight into surgery that will hopefully repair the separation so I can start physical therapy and get back into training. I need time to show I can still throw the ball, maybe even better.

What's not factored in is my wife, and my current projection has me unable to be anywhere near her in the coming months. I might have to convince her to come to me, but after what I told her, I wouldn't blame her if she told me to go screw myself.

Telling her our relationship needs to remain quiet was unfair, and I know it hurt her. I feel like the biggest asshole in the world. She's the absolute last person I'd ever want to hurt, but my words and request did. I knew it the instant she bit back.

I have to show her that she's not something I want to hide. I know why she might think that, but she's dead wrong.

She was right when she said that we've changed and don't know each other like we used to. Lex has changed. The tentative, quiet girl is a strong-ass woman, and even though her words are still few and she's difficult to read, she knows how to stand her ground. I freaking love her even more for it.

"All right, let's get you hooked up and see if we can get the pain to come down." Tyler sticks little patches to my skin. "You doing ok? You're awfully quiet."

My mouth might be quiet, but the voices in my head are loud as hell. "I have a lot on my mind." And my right shoulder feels like it might actually be detached and hanging on by the ligaments.

"You should be flying high after that win yesterday."

"Yeah, well, this isn't helping." I gesture with my head to my shoulder, pain shooting through me at the simple movement, and I suck in air. "Did you watch the game?"

"Yeah. I was on a date, but I would've rather watched it alone."

"That bad, huh?"

He finishes with the patches and hooks up the cords. "I hate dating. I asked if she was fine watching the game, and she said yes. Then, she whined about how long the game was. Why can't women be honest about what they want? If she didn't want to watch the game, why didn't she say so?"

"Maybe you're dating the wrong women." I try not to sound annoyed, but part of me doesn't give a shit today.

He chuckles. "Sandberg, I'm sure with all the women you've dated, most have only told you everything you've wanted to hear."

There's been one who hasn't. "I haven't dated that many women." I want to smack down his assumption, but then I want to punch myself, knowing it's not just *his* assumption. It's what everyone thinks, and I have no one to blame but myself.

He laughs. "Right."

"Don't believe everything you read, Ty," I spit out, my irritation with every single thing creeping higher.

Buttons beep as he presses them. "You're saying I shouldn't put stock in the rumors that you got married the other night."

He laughs like it's the most ridiculous thing in the world and pisses me off. I should be happy that people think it's fake news, but I want the entire world to know I married the only woman I've ever loved.

When I don't respond, he continues. "Well, maybe I'll take a cue from you and keep things light. Dating is too much work."

I rest back and try to clear my mind, waiting for the pain to lessen. I've let the world think I'm a playboy. I'm a flirt, and I like to have a good time. But it's easy to put on a show when you know that once the lights turn down and everyone goes home, you're still left with a giant hole that nothing can fill.

I'm no saint, and I've done some really stupid shit that I regret, but I was young and dumb. I never met someone who could get me to forget Lex. So, I quit trying.

She's the only one I've ever wanted to date, to be committed to, and now she's my wife.

Shit. I need to date my wife.

Lex said we don't know or understand each other, but we haven't changed that much. That was clear as ever to me the other night. She and I belong together. I just need a little time to remind her of all the reasons why.

I toss my keys on the counter, grab a water bottle from the refrigerator, and then pull my ice pack from the freezer. My apartment is finished with the finest things someone can buy, and tonight, it's emptier than ever.

On my way to my bedroom, I stop at the floor-to-ceiling windows and stare down at the city. It looks like thousands of fireflies zooming around below. For years, I've stood here, reminding myself I made it. I'd survived and overcome. I'm living the dream.

There was a time when I wasn't sure I'd make it to my next birthday. I was removed from the hell I lived in and thought my life was over. I didn't know where I was going or where I'd end up. Never in my wildest dreams did I imagine I'd be here. I have it all, but like all the other times I've stood staring out at the world, there's one thing missing.

I take a sip of water, allowing a soft smile to creep across my face as I dial her. As it did this morning, my heart skips, anticipating her voice. My excitement begins to slump on the fourth ring, but then—

"Hold on." I hear a clang and a bang, and I know exactly where she is. The fact that I can call her and talk to her is everything. It's not the same as kissing her or having her body tangled with mine, but I'll take it. For now.

After a few seconds, she's back. "Hey."

"Is the door locked?" It's after hours, so I assume she's alone. Well, I hope she's alone. The thought of her being there late with a guy causes every muscle in my body to tighten.

"What?" The music dies, and then there's silence.

"Did you lock the door? If you're there by yourself, the door needs to be locked so no crazies can get in."

"That's only happened once." I know by the way she says it one side of her mouth is creeping upward.

I long to see her perfect lips. "Are you alone?"

"Yes."

Thank God. "Is the door locked?"

"Yes. Slade gave me a talking-to the other day as well."

The hairs on my neck prick to life while a roar awakens in my belly. "Slade?" I don't care for the name or the fact that it's likely attached to a man who gets to be around her every day.

"He's a friend. He's worked here almost . . . "

She doesn't have to finish. I know the end of that sentence is something like, almost as long as you've been gone. I hit the video button, wanting to see her face when I ask my next question.

It takes a second and her face appears. "Hi."

A black bandana holds her blonde hair back, the long strands falling around her shoulders. She has a smudge of grease on her forehead, where she scratched and left a mark. A lot has changed, but some things are exactly the same. She's in her element, and it's still the sexiest thing I've ever seen.

"I wanted to see your face." That earns me a slight smile. "This guy, Slade, do I need to hate him as much as I want to right now?"

Her head falls to the side slightly, and I'm not sure how to interpret that, but I don't like it.

She shakes her head. "No. He's just a friend." Her eyes drop away. "He's my best friend."

It's a punch to the stomach. "That used to be me. You should know I have every intention of shoving him to the side."

She bites the corner of her bottom lip, and I want to kiss her. "You've never been good at coming second."

"Damn straight, I haven't. Never when it comes to you."

Her fingers find her stud earring and twist it as she studies me through the screen.

I head to my bedroom, confident with my plan.

"I know I was an asshole this morning, and what I told you hurt you." Her fingers continue to twist around and around. "My schedule is chaotic and full, at least until the season is over. You have no idea how much I wish it were different, but this is my life. I have contracts and agreements, and I don't always have a say in how things go. This is one of those times if I want a chance of signing with a team that's going somewhere next season."

I sit on the edge of my bed, readying myself to ask a question I'm a little terrified to get the answer to. I've never been one to shy away, and I need to know where we stand.

"Lex, I need you to be completely honest with me."

Her blue eyes, the color of the shallow waters of the Caribbean Sea, stare back at me. "Ok."

"I know things aren't perfect or even remotely close to how I'd like them to be, but do you think you'd consider dating me and getting to know one another again?"

Her brows raise and then quickly move inward. "What?"

"I know we can't date like normal couples, at least not yet. I can't be there with you the way I want to be, but I want to date you in whatever way we can."

"Date?" Her frown hasn't eased, and I can't tell if she hates the idea.

"I want to eat dinner with you, even if it has to be over the phone. I want to talk to you before you go to bed like we used to. I want to be the one who knows everything about you again. I want to know your tones and your breaths and your faces, and I want you to know mine. *I* want to be your best friend."

Her light eyebrows tip in further. "You want to date me. Like long-distance phone dating?"

"Yeah, or however you'll date me, given our current unaccommodating and unique situation. I'll call, video, text, write long love letters, whatever you want. I just have to get through the end of this season, and then . . . "

Her eyes drop away and I realize what I said. *Shit.* I detest the distance between us.

"Lex, look at me." She doesn't. "Please." It takes a second, but her eyes finally make their way to mine. "No letters. I want to talk to you. I want to see your face all the time."

Her lips press together slightly, which used to mean she was thinking. "I guess I'll date you." A playful smile appears, and dammit, she's going to kill me.

"You guess?"

"I mean . . . I already married you, so I'll give dating you a go."

I fall back on my bed and hear her laugh. It's the first time I've heard that sound, and it's so powerful it creates a burning sensation in my throat. I give myself a second and then bring the phone to my face again. "Thank you for giving me a chance."

"You're lucky I married you. I'm not sure your form of dating will work out for us. I'm not much of a talker."

"Baby, I'll just listen to you breathe on the other end of the line." She has no idea how much I mean that.

"You're still a flirt." Her cheeks turn a bit pink, and this not being able to touch her thing is for shit. "Where are you?"

"I'm home. In my room." I move the phone to show her my space.

"How is it living in the city?"

"I've gotten used to it. At first, I loved it. The constant busyness and hustle, but I miss the quiet and calm. I'm ready for a change."

"What's on your shoulder?"

I press on the ice pack that's beginning to thaw. "Ice pack. My shoulder is shot. I have to have surgery as soon as the season's over. I'm afraid I've waited too long."

She sits on a stool, propping her phone on the workbench.

"Will you have that there . . . in New York?"

I remove the ice pack and prop my sore body against my headboard, not wanting to talk about this part but knowing we have to. "Actually, in Phoenix. I have the best surgeon, and Sean's there. He and I will train together in the offseason once I'm ready." I hesitate to share the next part, but I want to be open with her. "Rumors are the Kingsnakes might be interested. Their quarterback is done after this season, and it'd be a nice change. Playing with Sean would only sweeten the deal."

She nods but doesn't say anything.

"This surgery has to work, and I'll have intensive physical therapy. I have to prove that I can still throw, or any interest will die. New York could be history, too, if they want to change things up."

One cheek scrunches, creating a small crease to the side of her mouth that's new. "Is this all why you and I would be a big deal? I'd make it appear like you weren't taking things seriously."

I weigh my head from side to side. "Lex, it's all business. Each organization wants to have the best team, and the best teams have loyal and focused players. Getting married the night before a big game shows where my focus was. Any organization would lose its shit over that. If somehow it leaks, it leaks, and I'll deal with it. Maybe it will be the end for me, and I will have lived the dream." I wait for her to look at me. "I will never regret it, no matter what."

"So, you'd be fine if your playing career was over?" Her question is blunt and hits hard.

I contemplate it to be sure I answer honestly. "Fine probably isn't the right word. I don't want to be done playing yet. I love it, except this, not being able to be with you." I shrug and then wince. "It could be the end anyway if the surgery hits a snag or the pain isn't better." A fist presses down right in the center of my chest, and I want to be done talking about this, so I change the subject. "What are you working on?"

She rubs her forehead. "Dodge Ram with a bad fuel pump. The owner put dirty fuel in it and clogged it up. She's going to have to sit for parts."

"What else?"

She glances around her space. "A blown transmission with a bad torque converter. The guys pulled it today."

The guys. I loathe them and their proximity to her.

"You still drive that old truck?"

She smiles. "She still runs like a dream."

Talking cars with her was the only way I could get her to talk to me at first. In the science lab, I made a kid move so I could sit next to her. She didn't say a word for the first two weeks. When I found out she worked on cars, I had my in. Her face lights up just as it did back then.

"Those old beaters still your favorite?"

"Of course. Although, Mustangs are becoming a close second," she says, biting her lip to hide a smirk—those lips I want to tackle with my own.

"Mustangs, huh? Why?"

"Just something Grandpa said."

"Hmmm." I study her face, the slight lines next to her bright eyes. "How is the old man?"

"Ornery as hell and still the absolute best."

I love that man. Besides my brothers, he's one of the best men I will ever know.

"Have you told him?" I know how close they are.

"No." She twists her earring again. "I figured we'd just keep things between us for now. I won't lie to him, though."

"Good." I stare at her, wanting to memorize every detail to carry me through the night. "When can you have dinner with me?"

She smiles. "Umm, my schedule is more open than yours."

"How about Wednesday? I'll call you. But I'm calling each night unless I'm on the road."

She nods. "Ok."

"If I charter a plane, will you come to have a real date with me sometime? It might only be for a night, but I want you here."

She rests her chin on her hand, thinking about it. "One thing at a time. We'll see how the first date goes."

"You know, I'm pretty confident it'll go really well."

"Still humble, I see. Do you ever get told no, Mark?"

I grin. "Lucky for us, I'm good at getting what I want." She rolls her eyes, but her mouth cracks, and I love that smile. "Text me something when you get home."

"Ok."

"I'll talk to you tomorrow."

"Hey, Mark."

"Yeah." I wait.

"Just so we're clear, all those things that happened the other night, I don't do that with guys I'm only dating." She works hard to hold back a grin. One that's just for me, and dammit, if that doesn't sound like a challenge.

Heat from the memories and the sass in her tone consume my entire body. This part of Lex is brand-new to me, and I am in deep shit. Deeper than I've ever been.

"Then, as of this moment, we are officially done dating. We are in the full honeymoon zone. I'm sending a plane."

Her head tips back, and a laugh spills out, making every minute of torture worth it. All the time we've missed out on, the heartache, it's over now. And I'm going to make her mine all over again.

Chapter 10

LEX

I climb in my truck and toss my backpack on the passenger seat as a strong wave of nausea hits me, along with the massive dose of failure. How many times have I been here? I worked so hard for it to be different this time, but pressure and anxiety don't play games. They aim to win, and today they did. Again.

I place a hand on my stomach and rest my head on my steering wheel. I went in, trying not to let past trauma predict my current ability, but I failed. My throat constricts with shame as the acid rides high, threatening to force itself out. I thought I was ready, but the minute I stepped into the classroom, every bit of my confidence quickly dwindled to nothing.

I crack a window, holding my elbows out to the sides, hoping the rush of cold air will wash away my dismay and the pool of sweat that's collected in my pits. I inhale and push it out, trying to calm my body and mind. *In and out.*

I sit breathing, giving myself a few minutes.

When I know I won't puke, I lift my head, turn the key, and my truck rumbles to life. I use the drive across town to ready myself to walk into the shop where Grandpa and Slade are waiting with expectation. They're anticipating a certificate that's supposed to give people written proof that I know what in the hell I'm doing. Neither of them will be disappointed, and both will be understanding, but I'm sick and tired of the sympathetic look on their faces.

I jam my truck into park and grab my stuff, already loathing the next however many minutes this will take.

I swing open the metal door and step into the familiar noise and smell, but today, it's a swift kick to the last bit of my slowly dying self-esteem. I bypass the board to check what's on the floor, heading back to the office to snatch a bottle of water, then into the tiny kitchen where I can make a piece of toast. Skipping breakfast wasn't the best idea.

As I drop a slice of bread into the metal toaster, Slade's large frame steps into the tight quarters.

"How'd it go?" He leans back against the counter, crossing his arms over his chest.

Not wanting to talk about it or really talk at all, I focus on the bright orange bands warming my bread. "I left."

He doesn't say anything, and that's almost worse. With my frustration and humiliation building, all I want is to be alone.

"You can try again," his uncharacteristically soft tone jump kicks me in the throat. "Don't give up. If you want it, you'll do it."

I scoff. "Yeah, right. Wanting has nothing to do with it." The intense ache in my throat grows. I can't do this. I can't talk about this right now. Too many things are sitting on my chest, and the weight of it all is about to break me. "Look, can we not talk about it?"

"Sure. Don't be hard on yourself."

So easy for him to say. Someday, it'll be him running this shop because he can actually do it, and be one more dream I have to kiss goodbye.

"We've got one needing new brake pads and rotors if you want it."

Out of the corner of my eye, I see him do something with his arms, and then I catch sight of a flock of balloons. I suck in a breath, turning to see the guys shoved together in the doorway. Wind has a fist full of balloons, and Trig holds a large, rectangular box, both smiling ear-to-ear.

I can only stare at them as my double-reinforced safety system malfunctions, and tears form in my eyes without permission.

"We knew you'd kick ass, so we got you cake," Carson says with a sly grin, beaming like a proud big brother.

My body is taken over by an inferno from within as my skin pricks with chills. I suddenly need air, but I can't move.

I glance at the box with the plastic window, waves of pink icing showing through, and I swipe a single tear away. Someone clears their throat, and all four men begin to look uneasy, shifting their weight and scratching their necks.

"Oh, shit!" Carson's head swivels as he searches the other men. "Darlin', you can't cry. Please. We don't know how to fix that."

"Shut it, Carson. You can't fix untied shoelaces," Slade jabs. "I bet your mama still ties your boots."

The guys try to hold in their snickers, but it makes me smile just a little. I swipe at my nose as Slade glances in my direction while the others stand there wide-eyed. It's possible their big feet are inching themselves backward.

Needing to put us all out of our misery, I step forward to peek at the white cake box in Trigger's hands. Inside is a sheet cake with light pink and purple flowers and 'Goodbye Barbara' written in dark purple script.

I stare at these rough and tough guys holding a cake for . . . Barbara. A laugh rams up my burning throat and bursts out. Their rugged, shocked expressions cause more tears to fill my eyes and trickle down my cheeks. There's nothing but silence and my laughter as I bend at the waist, the pressure finally easing.

Somehow, these guys and Barbara's misplaced cake lift my tired and worn heart off the dirty tile floor. "Please tell me you didn't steal that cake," I demand when I can finally meet their nervous smiles.

Wind hits Carson's shoulder. "I didn't know I had to order in advance, you jackasses. It's all they had." Carson's cheeks turn a bit red with his confession.

Trig raises and lowers one shoulder. "Well, Barbara said 'fuck off' and left her cake, so it's ours now."

Laughter fills the small kitchen as Slade drops his heavy arm around my shoulders, hugging me to his side.

"You guys are the best," I say, trying to hold back tears again when Grandpa squeezes into the room. One look at my face, and he knows. Trig hands me the cake, and I set it on the counter as each one lingers, expecting a large piece. I slice and hand them out, keeping my head down and on the task, wishing I deserved their confidence.

As the kitchen clears out and the sound of power tools fills the background, I re-toast my bread, needing it to calm my stomach and disappointment. Maybe new brakes will cure my piss-poor attitude and dwindling dignity.

I carry my toast across the hall to the office and take a seat behind the desk as the old man strolls in and sits in the chair across from me.

"Want to talk about it?"

"No," I grumble, ripping off a piece of toast.

He leans back in the chair. "What happened?"

I look at him from underneath my eyelashes, needing him not to push or I'll break.

"I thought we weren't talking about it?"

"I changed my mind." This is not the time for his stubborn streak to appear. "You were ready. We spent three months preparing and reviewing all the questions. You knew all the answers before we even started. You had this."

I take another small bite, and my phone buzzes in my back pocket, but only once. I want it to be Mark, especially today, but I know it's not him.

Over the last month, our phone conversations, or 'dates' as he likes to call them, have become fewer and far between. It's been two days since I've talked to him, except for our five-minute conversation before he fell asleep, and I'd be surprised if he remembered my test was today.

MOM: How'd it go?

I put my phone back in my pocket, not having the energy to try to formulate a response, and she knows I hate texting.

Grandpa sits unwaveringly. I rest back in the chair, ready to get this over with.

"You know what happened. What always happens."

"Pal, you had this."

I appreciate his vote of confidence, but he didn't have to take the test. I inhale, trying to reel in my annoyance. "The questions were different. At least they appeared that way."

He crosses his arms over his flannel covered chest. "Did you talk to the instructor?"

I push away the other half of my toast. "No. What was I going to say?"

"You could have asked if they had assistance. They have services—"

I stand, my shame and embarrassment morph into anger. "Grandpa, I tried. I couldn't do it."

"Alex, there's a way to do this if you—"

My patience runs out. "It took me ten minutes to try to read the first question, and I only made it through the first couple of sentences. I couldn't even get to the bullet point on the first one. I don't want assistance. I don't want someone or a computer program reading the questions for me like I'm some inept person. It's humiliating and demoralizing."

"There's nothing to be ashamed of. You've worked your ass off to get to where you are, and I don't care if it takes you an hour to read one. The point is you know the answer to every single one of those damn questions. Hell, you should be teaching the class. Don't let this keep you from doing it. We'll figure it out."

I drop my head in my hands, feeling so completely inadequate to do anything.

"Pal, don't give up." His voice softens, and it kills me.

"I can't fucking read! I've tried. I've worked my ass off, but in situations like that, it never gets better."

"You've worked harder than anyone I know. You should be proud of that and how far you've come."

I scoff. "Yeah, I'm real proud. I'm excellent at covering it up, pretending I'm capable of the most basic elementary skill. When it comes down to it, I can't even take a test filled with words I use every damn day because I can't recognize them."

"You cannot help how your brain is wired, just like people that are blind cannot help that they can't see."

"It's not the same."

"Pal, it's exactly the same. Until you recognize that and quit believing otherwise, you're going to limit yourself and keep from having and doing the things you want."

My jaw and teeth ache from clamping it shut before things come out that I don't mean.

He stands, ending his lecture. "I pulled the new brakes inside. She's all yours when you're ready to quit sitting around and feeling sorry for yourself."

I want to punch something, but instead, I shove my hands into my hair and squeeze. How many times have I been here? This was my entire childhood. Trying and failing. Trying and failing again. It wasn't until I was in high school that anyone even paid attention to the fact that I was compensating for my inability when words became more than I could memorize.

Being diagnosed with a severe reading disability was a relief to understand why I couldn't make sense of all the words on a page, but the constant humiliation has never faded. I'm great at covering my weakness. Today's technology and phones have changed my life, but there are times like today when I want so badly to accomplish just one thing. To know that my time and effort are worth it and that I can do it.

I feel completely incompetent, and it takes me right back to all those years of school where I fought for every single passing grade. I wondered how in the world I was ever going to graduate. I spent hours upon hours with tutors and reading specialists, and eventually, Mark helped me with all my schoolwork when he wasn't practicing. Even then, shame ate at me every time I couldn't keep up with the most basic standards.

I contemplate calling Mark to tell him I walked out, needing him to listen and not make me feel worse like he always used to, but what's the point? He's likely with a trainer, being interviewed, or doing some other great thing with no time to deal with my inability.

I need to get to work and focus on the one thing I'm good at. I'll replace a set of brakes and rotors while I try to release failure's chokehold and the reminder that this is all I'll ever be able to do.

I park outside the apartment building and grab the box of cookies I picked up from the bakery on my way home. After spending all afternoon replacing the brakes on a Honda Civic, I pulled myself together and out of my pity party. Spending the evening with Bree will only help push those thoughts and emotions further into the background where I need them to remain.

Dinner with Linda and Bree is a monthly ritual that started years ago. There was a time when playing with Bree was the only thing that gave me hope that I might someday be happy again. Her big, joyful eyes and squishy, happy face were the only things to remind me that I'd done the right thing when everything in me felt like it was all wrong.

The once chubby baby is now a smart, joyful girl who beams brighter than the sun, and that's exactly what I need tonight.

Holding the cookies, I make my way to their unit. I knock, and two seconds later, the door flies open, and the nine-year-old with pigtail braids grins up at me.

"You're here! I finished the model you gave me, and I've been waiting to show you."

The last time I visited, I brought a vintage Volkswagen Beetle model, thinking the little art lover would have fun piecing it together and painting it.

"Really? I can't wait to see it."

I step inside the small two-bedroom apartment and inhale the scent of tomato sauce and garlic.

"Hey, Alex," Linda says, peering through the cut-out in the wall that joins the living room and kitchen. Her dyed dark hair is pulled back with gray roots showing, and her early-aged skin is covered in a thick layer of makeup.

"Hi, Linda." I scan the small place that's orderly as usual, inspecting for any sign of things being . . . off.

"Come on." Bree takes my hand and tugs me toward her bedroom. "I painted it pink."

She bounces down the short hallway and into her room.

"Look!" She picks up the fragile little Beetle bug and holds it in her hands like a prized possession.

"You did an amazing job. You can hardly tell it's not the real thing."

She laughs and turns it in her hands, giving me a three-sixty view.

"I love the color choice."

She beams. "I wanted to show you when we brought the flowers, but you weren't home. I asked Mom if we could send you a picture, but she said we shouldn't bother you."

"You can send me pictures anytime. I'm never too busy."

She sets the model down. "You look sad. Want to see something really funny?" She rummages through her backpack.

Leave it to kids to see all the things you think you're good at hiding. "I'm not sad, I'm just . . . " I wonder what she sees while I choose my words carefully. "Something didn't turn out how I hoped it would." *And I miss Mark like crazy.*

"Look!" She holds out a piece of paper in front of me filled with squares where she drew pictures inside. "I'm making a comic strip. It's starts here." She points. "This girl has twelve brothers and sisters, and she's the youngest. Her name is Baker. Get it, Baker's dozen."

She tips backward slightly, laughing at her own wit. "She loves to bake and here." She points again. "She's having them try chocolate dill pickle cookies." She giggles, showing the dozen gagging and running and telling Baker she's fired from the kitchen.

I laugh as she runs through the whole strip, describing every elaborate detail. "You're amazing. You know that?"

She grins, but then it falters a little. "I wish I had brothers and sisters. All my friends do. Mom says she's just grateful to have me." Her sad tone and soft-spoken wish punches me straight in the gut.

I put my arm around her. "I don't have any brothers or sisters." She leans into me. "But I have really great friends. Slade's so grumpy he's like having a big brother."

Her smile returns as Linda hollers that it's time for dinner, and I'm grateful for the excuse to leave this conversation.

In the kitchen, we sit at the tiny four-person table. Linda serves spaghetti and garlic bread while she fills me in on her current work issues, managing the staff at a fast-food chain. Bree stands next to her chair, rocking back and forth as she sucks noodles between her lips and chatters away about school and her dance class.

"Can you come to my dance show? You have to see it. It's going to be the best one yet," she promises, bouncing on her toes, her arms waving dramatically.

"Honey, your show is at the end of the year," Linda interjects. "Let's check with Alex when it gets closer."

I smile. "I'll definitely be there if I can."

Bree grins, showing off her slightly crooked teeth. "Want to see my new dance leotard? It shimmers and has flowers all over it." Before I have a chance to answer, she's gone.

Linda laughs. "She's been counting down the days for this dinner."

"I'm sorry I missed last month. She's always a bright spot in my day." *Especially today.*

"Well, she's been asking to stop by the shop to see you, but I know these past months have probably been . . . difficult." She sets her napkin next to her plate. "You doing all right?"

My gut pinches tight again, but I remind myself that this little girl is the only thing that matters, and I don't owe Linda anything. I don't want to talk about my certification test, and my relationship with Mark remains only between us for now. Besides, I'm not ready to share the news with Linda. If or when the time comes, I'll have to be sure I'm ready for the fallout.

"I'm ok. I'm busy at work. It's my favorite place to be, so I can't complain."

Linda smiles to reveal her darkened and yellowed teeth. "Alex, you always impress me with your resilience." *You should've seen me earlier.* "You're brave." She pauses, lining up her fork and knife on her plate. "I wish I could've been like you. It would've saved me from making the biggest mistakes of my life. Ones I'll never be able to forgive myself for."

My eyes linger on the tired woman sitting across from me, believing she's lived a whole life full of heartbreaks and challenges I can't even begin to understand. I'm certain she lives each day with regrets she'll never outrun and will haunt her for the rest of her life.

"I'm not brave." I set my fork on my plate, feeling the weight of that admission, especially after today. "I've let fear get the best of me. I've hurt people and not been truthful."

She stares at me across the table. "You recognize it. That's pretty brave to me. You aren't hiding and scared to face . . . yourself."

Her eyes fall to the table again, and I can see the emotion well up behind her eyes.

I smile, trying to defuse them. "Yeah, well, it's clear I have issues just like everyone else."

Bree bops back in, showing off her new dance outfit, and we break out the cookies I brought, all of us needing a dose of sugar.

"Do you think you could watch Bree for me Wednesday night?" Linda asks hesitantly, gathering our empty plates. "I have to cover for someone on the evening shift."

"Please," Bree begs, pressing her hands together over her heart. "We can watch a movie and make popcorn."

"Sure. I'd be happy to." I stand to help Linda clean up the kitchen. After I dry the dishes, Bree shows me her art project from school before I say good night.

At home, I shower and crawl into bed. I stare at my phone, seeing a missed call from Mark. I think about calling him back, but chances are he's already asleep. He's always in bed early to be rested and at physical therapy first in the morning.

I want to talk to him and tell him about my day. He was the one person who never tried to fix it. He always helped when I asked and stood by when I needed space, but he never pushed. He never treated me like my struggle to read needed to be corrected. He was ok with me just the way I was.

I worry that might be another thing that's changed. We haven't talked about it, but I know he hasn't forgotten. It's why he doesn't text me but always calls. The problem is our conversations are becoming sporadic, and it's apparent his schedule doesn't leave much room for anything other than football.

I tap on an app and scroll. My screen fills with his face and interview clips of him being asked about practice, the upcoming game, and his shoulder. I scroll further, landing on pictures of him inside the stadium with a woman cozied up beside him. She poses with pouty lips and in skimpy clothes—the image of self-assured perfection.

It's the same stab right through my chest seeing him with smart, beautiful, successful women. The caption says she's the daughter of the Liberties owner. That should be comforting, but I can't help the insecurity that grabs hold, telling me she fits by his side so much better than I ever will.

Maybe we just don't fit together like we used to when he was the high school quarterback and I was the girl who could barely earn a passing grade. I can't help but wonder if that's why eight years went by. He's no longer a kid looking to make it out, but I'm still the girl with nowhere else to go but here.

Chapter 11

MARK

Finishing up physical therapy, I head toward the conference rooms for a team meeting. Seeing I have a few minutes to spare, I pull out my phone and dial Lex, hoping to catch her. Ever since she left me in Vegas, I've feared the day when she tells me this isn't going to work and disappears again.

Trying to date Lex hasn't turned out how I wanted. I'm worried she's feeling the distance between us as much as I am. I thought our nightly phone calls would be enough. But instead of nightly, they've become sporadic, and that distance is growing.

My life is tied to the game. We're on the cusp of playoffs, and the interviews, sponsorships, and press functions are constant. It's all on top of hours of practice, physical therapy, team meetings, and studying for games. Then, there are never-ending foundation meetings and requests, and I rarely have a moment to myself.

It all comes with making it to the top and leading my team into division finals. But I need Lex, and I'm desperate to know she's still with me. We talked about her visiting, but when it comes down to it, she'll spend most of her time sitting around, waiting for me.

I'm realizing I'm not sure I know how to do this—manage my job and a relationship. Football has been everything. My entire life has revolved around this game and every opportunity it's given me. But now, I have to figure out how to try to balance both.

Her voicemail picks up as my teammates pass, heading into the conference room. I end the call, that nagging worry increasing as if it's a living, breathing thing growing inside me. I finally have her back in my life, and there's no way I'm going to screw this up, but it's quite possible I already am.

I find my seat and try to focus on the upcoming game as Coach gets things rolling. Over the next hour, the pressure of it all builds until there's a giant rubber band looping around my rib cage with each and every order and expectation.

My body temperature creeps to a thousand degrees, and I want to crawl out of my skin. I've given this team and this organization everything I've got for the past six years. I've held off on surgery to be able to stay on the field and carry us this far despite the pain, possible further damage, and time I spend in therapy every single day.

Each game, I jog out of the tunnel, wondering if I'll make it—if my shoulder will hold together. But right now, I'm worried about holding together a whole lot more than just my shoulder.

As the meeting ends, I'm agitated as hell and standing on the edge of losing my shit. I want to go home, talk to Lex, and get my head straight.

"Hey, man. Are you watching the game later? I think this might be the end of the road for them," Carlos asks, getting up from the table.

"I may catch some of it."

"Come on, man. We need to be ready to take on the Vipers. Some of the guys are coming over, and your arm could use every advantage we can find."

This kid tells me this as if I don't know I need to be prepared or understand what's at stake.

"Thanks, but I've got to take care of some things." *Like making sure I hear the only voice that matters.*

"Is that code for hooking up with Rochelle?" he snickers.

I frown, turning to face him, not even trying to hide the fact that I'm pissed. "What?!"

"We saw her slide into you the other day and how you were chatting her up. She's hot and clearly into you. Come on. We all know how you are."

I don't know what he's talking about, but my limited amount of patience just blew into oblivion.

Rochelle is the team owner's daughter, and there's no way in hell I'd ever be stupid enough to get involved in that, even if I weren't married.

It's no surprise that people want to speculate and turn it into something it's not and will certainly never be, but I'll be damned if I'll let this rumor start.

"I don't date within the organization. Never have."

"Ahhh. You sign with another team next season, and you no longer have an issue. I've heard she's . . . "

I don't hear the rest of what he says, clenching both hands into fists, and I quickly release my right as pain shoots through me. I grab my notebook, turning away from him and his wiseass. "I'm done dating. How about you keep your mouth shut and make sure you know the plays?"

He laughs, holding his stomach like it's the funniest thing he's heard. "Y'all," he calls out to the remaining guys in the room. "Sandberg's on hiatus. He says he's done dating."

An eruption of scoffs and hushed comments fills the emptying room.

"Carlos, you need to make sure you know how to run and catch a fucking football at the same time. Otherwise, find a knitting circle who gives a shit about whatever it is you think you know."

I may have done my fair share of hanging out with women over the years, but it was definitely not in the way these guys think it was, and I'm not proud of letting them believe otherwise.

I stomp to the locker room, ready to take the field with these jokers so I can go home. My time here with the Liberties may be short-lived. My contract is up after this season, and I've been ready for a change, but never more than today.

I hold my phone like a lifeline, willing her to pick up. It rings and rings. Then it's that damn automated voice I'm getting really sick of. It's been days since we've talked. Clenching my jaw, I squeeze my phone, not caring if it breaks. This is Lex disappearing, and I know it. I've been here before.

I contemplate screwing it all and arranging a flight, needing to see her.

While I ponder the consequences I'm not sure I give a shit about, I turn on the Vipers' game, hoping it will calm my impatience and temper before they drive me to complete freaking insanity.

I watch the first quarter while icing my shoulder and trying to keep myself from obnoxiously dialing Lex every five minutes, but I'm tempted. Her name on my screen waves itself in my face, daring me.

I give it until halftime, and then my finger takes over, tapping her name before I can stop it. I hit the speaker button, waiting for that loathsome message, but as my thumb violently hangs over the end button, I hear her voice.

"Hey. Can I call you back?"

My instantaneous relief quickly vanishes when I hear music in the background that isn't the normal country music she listens to at the shop.

"Yeah. I don't care what time it is."

"Ok. It shouldn't be too long."

We hang up, and I sit by the phone waiting. I want to know where she is, and I'd know if we'd actually been able to talk the past few days.

Half an hour later, I've watched none of the third quarter while I stew about where Lex is and what she's doing. I don't want to have to wonder. I want to be wherever she is, doing whatever she's doing, not sitting here making shit up in my head because I can't be.

My phone vibrates, and I snatch it up, having lost all sense of calm and coolness that used to be my MO.

"Hi. I was contemplating sending out a search party."

"Sorry."

There's the rumble of her truck, and I realize she's still not home. "Where are you?" I try to sound casual, but after my day, I'm having trouble keeping anything together.

"Um . . . I was helping a friend out."

"A friend?"

"Yeah. I was babysitting."

"Babysitting?"

"Yeah. Don't sound so surprised like I'm incapable of watching a child."

I run a hand through my hair, relieved she wasn't hanging out with Slade or any other of the guys she works with. "It's not that, I just . . . " I decide to let it go because I miss her so much. My unwarranted jealousy has nothing to do with her or even the guys she works with. It's all me. "The past days have been . . . " My agitation and frustration dip as I realize how much I sound like a sad, lonely puppy dog, and it's ridiculous. "Not talking to you isn't working for me."

When all I hear is road noise, my nerves perk right back up.

"I've had some things going on and haven't always been alone." Her somber tone revs up my worry again. I need it to back the hell off.

"Tell me what's been going on. I miss you. I've missed talking to you and want to know everything."

"It doesn't really matter now."

Something is wrong. I can feel it. "What's wrong? I want to know. Please."

There's a long pause, and I listen to the rumble of her truck. "I . . . didn't pass my test."

Shit. I run a hand over my face. I forgot about her test. I grip my hair, wanting to rip it out. "Lex . . . Baby, I'm so sorry. I for—"

"How's your shoulder?" she deflects, and I know she doesn't want to talk about it, but I'm not standing for it.

"Lex, tell me about the test. What happened? I'm so sorry—"

"Mark, please." Her soft voice is a jab to my gut. "Can we just . . . " She pauses, and it's filled with defeat and disappointment. I remember this part of Lex so well. "How's your shoulder today?"

I close my eyes, knowing I'm a complete asshole, but letting it go for her. I've got to do better. She is everything to me, and I've not been showing it. I want to punch myself in the face.

"It feels like it's being mauled by a tiger." She sighs as if this conversation is taxing, and my frustration with everything rears its red-hot, ugly head. "What's up, Lex? I need you to tell me. Something. Anything."

She takes a second before she responds. "I don't know. Maybe you should tell me. I know you're busy and have a lot on your plate, but it's been over a month since Vegas. This trying to date, or whatever you want to pretend it is, isn't working."

Her tone is stiff but not biting. She's telling me straight up, and I can't even be mad about it.

"Lex, I'm doing the best I can. I think about you all the time. I need to get through these next few weeks—"

"Were you thinking about me when dark hair and long legs had her hands spread across your chest and her boobs pressed against you? Or was that just a stunt to make sure no one thinks those wedding rumors are real?"

I let my head fall back onto my headboard. Here's to every single stupid decision I've made coming back to bite me square in the ass.

"That wasn't what it might have looked like. Her father owns the Liberties. I didn't have much of a choice. She showed up on the practice field for a photo shoot."

"Mark, it doesn't matter."

"Like hell, it doesn't, but you don't want to hear what I have to say." I've hit my limit as the pressure all around me folds in, and I can't breathe.

There's silence except for the sound of her engine that's drowned out by the complete desperation filling my ears.

I try to pull in air, but it's difficult. "Lex, tell me what's going on. Tell me what you're thinking because I can assure you no woman is taking up any of my time or mental space except you." The pounding of my heart is so loud it's all I can hear. "There never has been."

After a few seconds, the engine quiets, and I wonder if she's home.

"Mark, it's not the pictures. It's everything. The reality of all of this is hitting, and I don't know how we're supposed to do this. Maybe—"

"Lex, don't. Please. I need—"

"To get through the season, I know." Her voice is soft and gentle, but my head might actually explode. "But then what? You don't even know. It's like we're trying to wish this into something it's never going to be." Her voice is even softer now. "I just walked away from that. Trying to make a relationship into something it wasn't."

"This is not the same. That asshole wanted you to be someone else. He didn't even know you. All I want is you. Just you."

"The season will end, and then what? You'll have surgery, recovery, training . . . My job is here, and I can't just work anywhere." Her voice cracks, and I feel like I've been punched in the throat. "This isn't . . . "

I can't even speak as something somewhere deep inside me begins to crack. Any more, and I'll crumble into a thousand pieces.

Her voice cuts through my spiraling panic. "Maybe you should finish the season and—"

"No." I've never been a quitter. I had to fight for my very life more times than I can count, and this feels no different. I didn't surrender then, and I sure as hell won't now. "I'm not giving up. Not now, not ever. I won't be without you again. Ever."

She sniffs, and her voice is so quiet I barely hear her. "We aren't together now."

Smack. I felt it all the way through the phone. There's nothing but silence as my chest burns with fear.

It takes me a second to come to, and when I do, I'm consumed with rage. Not at Lex, but at the situation. At life and how much time has been wasted, and now, when she might actually be able to be mine, she's slipping away all over again.

"When this season is over, I'm coming for you. Lex, I love you, only you. We'll figure this out, and we will be together."

I hang up, unable to stand to hear her cry or ask any more questions I don't have the answers to.

I shove the cool ice pack off my shoulder and lay flat on my bed, needing air in my lungs and my body to relax. This can't happen. I don't care what I have to do. She and I will be together.

She doesn't have to believe it. I'll show her.

Chapter 12

LEX

"Go home. I have no idea why you even came in. You looked like you crawled out of hell this morning. We don't need whatever you have passed around here."

I lean over the toilet and heave again while Grandpa yells at me from the doorway. I brace my hands on my knees, steadying myself before I stand.

I could argue with him. I don't want to go home and lay in bed thinking about Mark, but a nap does sound good, and I don't need Grandpa breathing down my neck.

"Fine. I'll go home for a while, but if I feel better, I'm coming back. I promised Glen I'd have his bike done by tomorrow afternoon."

The garage is full, and we're short-staffed this week since Carson is on a hunting expedition. Grandpa steps out of the way so I can grab my keys.

Twenty minutes later, I climb the stairs to my room and into a long, warm shower. Feeling queasy again, I dig out my comfort shirt and pull it on before crawling into bed. I lie there thinking about Mark.

I watched his last game and saw his first win of the playoffs, moving his team a step closer to the Super Bowl. I couldn't help but be filled with pride and wish I could have been there.

It's been my dream to be there, standing and waiting for him, as I did after his games in high school. I sent him a voice message and told him how proud I was of him, but I haven't heard back.

He told me after the season is over, he's coming for me. I want him to come for me, or hell, I'd go to him, but his current schedule doesn't have room for visitors.

I close my eyes and pull the covers over my head. This is his job, and it's been his life. It's no different from the garage being mine. I just want to know that at some point, he and I will actually figure out how to be together.

Two hours later, I wake with a warm streak of sunshine on my face. I stretch as my stomach rumbles with hunger. I stare at the ceiling for a few minutes and then pull myself from bed to find something to eat that sounds good.

In the kitchen, I grab some crackers and a glass of water, taking a seat at the table. I scroll my phone, unable to resist the habit of searching for Mark. I listen to a new interview, and his smile makes my lips turn upward. The man takes handsomeness to a whole new level.

A light knock on the back door disrupts me from stalking my own husband, and I click off Mark's face. Krissy stands on the other side of the door. I open it, returning to the table.

"Hey."

She's dressed casually in jeans and a sweatshirt, and she's cute. She has that effortless, adorable gift that's annoying to the rest of us who have to work for every ounce of appearing only slightly put together. Her short, dark bob frames her face, and her long, fake eyelashes almost touch her eyebrows.

"I stopped by the garage. You missed me irritating the hell out of Slade by pretending to flirt with Trigger."

I smile. "Did Slade start barking orders and make Trig take stock in the parts room?"

Krissy laughs. "Yeah, I felt bad, but I don't think Trigger minded. He stuck his head out and winked at me when I left. He made sure Slade saw it. At least Carson wasn't there."

There's something in that mumbled comment about Carson, but I let go for now. "Poor Trig. He bought himself a week of all the crap jobs." I take a bite of a cracker.

"Slade said you're sick, so I thought I'd stop by and check on you." She presses the back of her hand to my forehead. "You doing ok? You don't look so bad."

"Yeah. I took a nap and showered. I'm feeling better. I don't know. It's weird."

Krissy surveys the kitchen. "Want me to make you something? I can warm up some soup if you have it, or run and get some. It's my day off."

"It's ok. I'll eat a few crackers, and if that stays down, I'll make a sandwich."

"I haven't seen much of you lately. We miss you coming over to watch the games with us."

My Sunday afternoons are usually spent at Slade's house, eating and watching football. With everything going on, I haven't wanted to watch Mark with others around and try to pretend not to feel anything.

Not telling Grandpa, Slade, or even my mom about Mark has been difficult. I don't keep things from them, but with our current state, it seems easier. I don't need them getting their underwear in a bunch over it, and I don't need anyone telling me what I should or shouldn't be doing. Mark and I have to figure this out on our own.

"I know. I'm sorry. There's been a lot going on. I'm sure Slade told you about the ASE test, and I've been putting in more hours at the shop."

"And now you're sick?" She joins me at the table, eyeing me questioningly.

I shrug. "I haven't been sleeping well, and I think it's finally caught up with me."

"Huh." She rests her chin in her hand.

"What?" I cross my arms over my stomach, needing her not to assess me.

"Can I be nosy for a minute?"

My brows pinch together because that's a loaded question. "Maybe."

"How long have you not been feeling well?"

"Ok. Nurse Kris, I don't need you to Google some crazy diagnosis."

She laughs. "Humor me." I roll my eyes, resting back in the chair. "Slade said you've looked like shit for a while."

"Wow. That's kind. Remind me to thank him." She squints her eyes. My head falls to the side, unimpressed. "What?"

"Trouble sleeping, persistent nausea, tired, high emotions . . . "

"I'm not emotional." *Well, not in front of anyone.*

She laughs. "Look, I'm going to ask a question you don't have to answer."

I huff, crossing my arms over my chest.

"Is there any possible way you're . . . pregnant?" Half of her face scrunches as she says that last word, almost wincing.

I sit dumbfounded by her question. *Pregnant?* I almost laugh. Almost, but then the word hits me again. *Pregnant. A baby. Could I be . . . pregnant?*

I don't know what Krissy is doing or thinking or possibly saying because everything around me stops and fades to nothing while I sort through a self-evaluation.

I'm on birth control. I may have missed some pills here and there, but did I forget around when Mark and I . . .

Last period? Hmmm. Unknown.

Symptoms? Everything Krissy listed. Plus, my jeans have felt a bit tight.

Am I pregnant . . . with a baby? No way.

I suddenly hear my name and snap to.

"Alex."

"Huh?"

"Did you hear anything I said?" Krissy is staring at me, wide-eyed. "I didn't mean to offend you or cross a line. I . . . It's just your symptoms seem a little suspicious. It could be the flu. I know this is none of my business—"

I hold up my hand, not having a clue what to say while trying to gather my thoughts about what I need to do to get an answer immediately. *Is it even possible I'm pregnant?* "It's fine, really." My mind moves 100 mph, thinking through the possibility and needing to be sure.

"I'm sorry. I shouldn't have said anything." She bites her lip. "Slade is going to kill me."

I stop her right there. "You're not telling him you asked me that. I'm calling patient confidentiality or whatever. The guys don't need to know about this."

She frowns. "Ok. I'm sorry. I'm ridiculous sometimes, but see so many women . . . "

I hear nothing but my own internal dialog that's rambling nonsense. *It's been how many weeks since Vegas?* I grab my phone, tapping on the calendar and counting. *One, two,* . . . Almost nine weeks. I press my fingers to my forehead. It's been nine weeks. *Ok. Just breathe.*

I stand ready to sprint to the nearest drugstore. "I told Grandpa if I was feeling better, I'd head back since Carson is out this week. I should put on some work clothes and get back there."

She slowly gathers her keys and purse, watching me the whole time. "You sure you're ok? I can stay and hang for a while if you want."

"I'm sure. The garage was full when I left, so we need to keep the rotation moving."

She hugs me goodbye as I shove her out the door. I fly up the stairs to pull on leggings and a sweatshirt, hightailing it to the nearest place that carries the only kind of test that won't be difficult for me to complete.

I set the timer on my phone for five minutes. My finger hovers over Mark's name, wanting him to hold my hand through this, but common sense prevents me from tapping it.

He is one game away from the division championship, and our conversations have been short and a bit strained, both of us waiting for the season to be over. The time ticks down, and . . . *I don't care.* I jab his name before I can second-guess it. I need to hear his voice as I wait for the most important results of my life.

My heart thrashes in my chest, and my fingers grip my phone so tightly my hand shakes. It rings and rings as the timer counts down.

Pick up. Pick up. Pick up. Please pick up.

Just when I think it's one more time we'll miss each other, his voice comes through.

"Hey, one second. Ok?"

A storm of relief pours over me. I hear shuffling and other voices in the background, and then he's back.

"Hi. Sorry, I'm getting ready to step into a meeting."

"Hi." That's all I can say as the pressure builds with anticipation of what might be happening. I want him here, holding my hand, but the cellular connection will have to do. My throat suddenly itches with emotion, and I can't speak.

When I don't say anything more, I hear concern fill his voice. "Lex, are you ok?"

"Yeah." I clear my throat, trying to get a grip. "I needed to . . . " *What? I needed to what?* "I just need you to talk to me for a second."

"Lex, what's going on?" he whispers this time. My heart squeezes, wanting to tell him exactly what's happening, but I'm worried I'll destroy his focus and concentration at the biggest time of his career.

I check the timer. Three minutes and thirty-four seconds left. "Do you have a few minutes to talk to me?" I press my eyes shut tight, knowing I sound like a lunatic.

"Uh . . . I have five minutes until my ass needs to be in a seat." I hear him say hi to someone. "You kind of have me freaking out, though, so I need you to tell me you're really ok."

"Yes. I'm ok." I let out a gentle laugh to reassure him. "Things are just a little . . . overwhelming, and you always make me feel better."

"Really?" I know he's smiling, and I wish I could hug him so much. "Because the last couple of months, that's not what I think I've been doing. I've wanted to call you, but . . . "

He doesn't even have to say it. I know. "Well, that might be true, but I haven't liked the not talking to you thing at all."

I have no idea what I'm doing. I've never been able to get myself not to love him or want to be with him, no matter how much I try. Now, there's this and . . . I need him.

"I want to date you for real, and I'm going to." His tone is nothing but pure determination. "I didn't want to keep calling and disappointing you. I can't stand it."

"I'd be ok with dating you for real."

"That so?" That mischievous tone makes my skin tingle. "Seeing that you're already my wife, I'm not planning on taking you home either." His voice is low and sexy, and my quivering stomach flips over at the certainty of his statement.

Liking that promise a little too much, I check the timer again. One minute, forty-seven seconds. "Are you ready for the game?"

He laughs. "Yes. I'm ready to take it to the end, and then . . . " He pauses. "Lex, I meant what I said."

I squeeze my eyes shut tight, a lump forming in my throat and tears welling in my eyes. "I know."

"Do you?" His voice is soft and tender.

"Yes."

"You have no idea how much I want you here with me, for you to be a part of this with me. I don't even care anymore. If I win this next game, I'm getting you tickets, and—"

"It's ok. I'm watching." I bite my lip, forcing the tears to retreat.

"I know I'm asking a lot, but if you'll come, I want you here. I don't care anymore about what happens after this season."

"Mark, we both know that's not true. Finish this season out and—"

My phone vibrates in my hand, and this is it.

"Lex, I've gotta go. I promise I'll call you. Things are going to be ok. I'm working on it."

I grab the magic life-changing stick and hold it up so I can see the results. "Mark," I exhale.

"Yeah?"

My voice cracks despite my best efforts. "I love you. I've always loved you."

There's the briefest moment of silence between us. Then he says the only thing I need to hear.

"I love you, too."

Chapter 13

MARK

LEX: *voice message* *Hey. I wanted to tell you good luck today. I wish I could be there.* Pause. *Remember that time when we stood in the middle of our high school field, and you'd just lost the game to the Panthers? I told you one day you'd make it all the way. Mark, you did it. I knew you would. You should be so proud of what you've accomplished. I am. I'm proud of you. Go get'em today. I'll be watching.*

SEAN: Good luck today, bro. I expect to see you in two weeks.
ANDIE: Two weeks, Mark. We want to see you two face off.
SHANE: Don't get your ass sacked. Stay on your feet and protect your arm.
MAGGIE: I'm so pissed I'm not there. Get those boys running circles.

Eight. I was only eight years old the day I was yanked from our trailer and taken to the hospital with a concussion, dislocated shoulder, internal bruises, and a slice above my eyebrow that took twenty stitches to close up.

I lay on the hospital gurney, listening to the nurse through the thin curtain talk to some lady from Child Protective Services. I didn't know where I would sleep or end up or if it would be worse than what I'd just been taken from.

I was terrified and tried to ignore the unknown, envisioning some superhero breaking into the hospital and stealing me away. The ones from the comic books I'd hide behind a box shoved in the closet. I imagined them taking me to a place where I never had to be afraid or worried again. It isn't what happened.

All I knew was watching my mom cut a line and snort it or drink herself unconscious. Each time, I was terrified she'd never wake up. Or sitting next to my dad while he drank and injected himself with whatever he could get off the street. He introduced me to pain.

He dragged me through our small trailer and threw me against the wall enough times I no longer felt it when it happened. I'd become numb to the only world I'd known, but then I was tossed into a new one where I had no idea what to expect. It was almost more frightening than going back to the only life I knew.

It took years before I could sit in a room and not wonder where the next blow would come from or fear that I'd wake up and find myself right back there or somewhere worse. Trusting people wasn't something I did. That was until two boys just like me moved into the group home I ended up in, and we found football. It changed everything.

Now, I stand surveying the stadium filled to capacity with fans, expecting me to help my team claim the division title. I close my eyes, listening, and remembering lying in that hospital bed, thinking I didn't even have a chance.

I jog to my place on the sideline and listen to the tones of the anthem, taking it all in.

Then, there was a girl who believed in me. Who told me I'd make it all the way and then stepped away so I could—the same one who's waiting for me now.

Her call yesterday shook me. Whatever was going on at that moment, she needed me. It reminded me that she might need me just as much as I need her.

I pull my helmet on and jog out onto the field as the fans roar with excitement and expectation. The adrenaline and anticipation never get old. It's exhilarating and addicting, and there was a time when I survived on it. Like an addict waiting for his next hit, I longed for the next game, the next win.

I want to win this game and take my team to the Super Bowl, but these past few months, that high hasn't been as effective. It's not the only thing I long for anymore.

I want this surgery to be effective, and I want to be able to get back out on the field next season, but Lex isn't just a season. She's the rest of my life.

I hit the thirty-yard line, ready to call plays and do the job I was born to do despite where I started. But it's time I figure out how to be a husband. I don't know shit about how to do that, but I know it involves sacrifice. It also requires being together, and that's exactly what I plan to do.

"It took you a while to get up after the sack in the third quarter, and then strategy moved to short, quick passes before you left the game. Your shoulder has been a recurring issue. Did it contribute to the outcome of today's game?"

With my arm in a sling and feeling like it's no longer attached, I look around the room, wondering how much longer I have to endure this. Most times, I don't mind the barrage of questions, but today, after losing this game, I want to get out of here.

There was a moment in the third quarter when everything went silent, and my world almost went black. It was the moment I'd feared for the past two seasons—the moment when my shoulder finally had enough.

The pain that tore through my arm was like no other, and I knew I was done. I'd given it my all this season, but now it's over, and the pain is just as unbearable as the disappointment. I can't help but think this was my last shot at making it to the end, and that thought has a knife piercing straight through my chest.

"There were a lot of things that went into the outcome. Our receivers weren't able to make their routes. We gave away yards that we couldn't get back. My shoulder issues are only one of the many challenges we faced."

"You're a free agent going into the next season, and we understand you'll be considering all opportunities. With the Kingsnakes losing their veteran quarterback, the rumor is they might be interested in picking you up. Are you looking to move or hoping to stay with the Liberties?"

"I'll be weighing all opportunities, and we'll see what next season brings."

"Are you concerned about the impact your shoulder will have on negotiations with other organizations or if you'll return next season?"

I have so many concerns at the moment I don't even know where to begin. My usual confidence has taken a nosedive this afternoon, and having to answer this question isn't helping.

I force my lips upward, feeling like it's tearing up my face. "I'm taking one thing at a time and looking forward to stepping out on the field next season."

The reporters laugh at my dodge, and I take that as an opportunity to step away from the mic, allowing the next person their chance to relive our loss.

I join my teammates in the waiting area with their families and friends. Stepping into the area with a smile on my face has never been a problem. Today, it's more apparent than ever that the one person I want to see isn't here.

I find an isolated spot in the corner, trying to block out the excruciating pain radiating from my shoulder through my back and down my arm. The pain has been bad, but after taking the hit, any amount of movement brings a wave of dizziness followed by feeling like I'm going to pass out.

As my teammates hug their wives and girlfriends, I try to remove my phone from my pocket, needing to talk to the only one who can remind me I still have something to fight for.

I tap her name, putting the phone to my ear.

"Hi."

I close my eyes, her voice is a balm to my sorrow-filled soul. "Hey." I hear laughter and yelling in the background. "Where are you?"

"I'm at Slade's. The guys are here. We watched the game."

She's at Slade's, her best friend, when she should be here where I can hug and kiss her and have her tell me it's all going to be ok.

I suddenly want to chuck my phone across the room, but I can't because my freaking arm is shot.

"I'm sorry about the game. Are you ok? That hit was . . . " Her voice is soft and quiet like she's hiding in a corner.

"I'm pretty sure my arm is packed with ice and being airlifted to the surgery center."

"Where are you?"

"Waiting for my team to get done hugging and kissing their families so I can go home." I didn't mean to spit that out at her, but I did, and I'm met with silence. "Shit, Lex, I'm sorry."

"What's going on?" The background noise is gone.

"Nothing." But it's not *nothing.*

I want you here. I want to know that my shoulder will be fine and that I can play again, but I also need you with me.

"What happens now?" Her tentative question hits me square in the chest.

"I'm going home to pack my stuff, and then I'll be in Phoenix, prepping for surgery. After that . . . " I have no choice but to be honest. "I don't know. It depends on how the surgery goes and my therapy schedule."

There's a long beat of silence, and it's full of disappointment and broken promises.

When she speaks next, her voice is different. The tenderness is replaced with a stony intonation I've not heard before, and I hate it. "How long will you have to stay?"

"I'm not sure. I've rented a house. Shane's coming to stay a couple of nights to help me get in and out of the surgery center. Then, his family is coming to watch Sean play for the division title."

"Sounds like you've got it all taken care of. I hope it goes well."

"Dammit, Lex. Don't say it like that."

"Like what?"

"Like we're casual friends catching up and wishing each other well."

"That's not what I want us to be, but that seems to be exactly what we are. You're having surgery and living in a new place, a new house. I don't even know where that is or when we might actually see each other." She pauses. "I don't think this is how it's supposed to be between husbands and wives. Hell, that's not how it is with friends."

"I don't know how to fix this. I thought . . . " A teammate calls my name and waves me over. I nod but turn away.

"You thought what?" Her question is clipped.

"I'm not sure I was thinking clearly about the reality of our situation."

A beat of silence is deafening, and my already throbbing body is one unit of pressure away from bursting.

"What does that mean? Have you changed your mind about—"

"No." I cut her off. "Lex, no. Never." I take a breath, knowing if there's one person I can be vulnerable with, it's her. It was always her. It's been a long time since I've done that, trusted anyone enough, and I've kind of forgotten how.

I turn, facing the brick wall, my chest flowing in and out too quickly as my gut churns with pain and fear.

"Lex." I push her name out like I'm being strangled with my own damn hand. "I'm . . . scared."

I let it hang there, trying to gather the balls to give her all of it.

"I don't know if this is it. If I'm ever going to play again. I don't know how to do all of this. I don't know how to be what you need me to be. Who I want to be for you. For us." I suck in air through my closing windpipe to admit that last of it. "I'm terrified. Not just to go into this surgery, but I'm even more scared that I'm losing you."

I rest my head against the wall, the rough brick is cool against my hot, sticky forehead. I wait for her to say something. Anything. It takes some really long, quiet seconds, but then I finally hear her voice. The one I've held onto, tucked away for years. The one that gives me hope when all is lost.

"Can I tell you something?"

"Always," I release the long breath I was holding, then bring in oxygen that eviscerates my throat.

"I'm freaking scared out of my mind." She says it so quietly like it's a secret.

A little laugh escapes while I blink that shit away that's making it hard to see. I need her so much. "Yeah?"

"Yeah. We have a lot to talk about. If I plan ahead, maybe I can sneak away from the garage and come see you?"

"Yes. I can't stand this. I'll have appointments and therapy after surgery, but I'll be recovering. If you can't, I'll come as soon as I can. I promise." Friends and families begin to disperse as we're ushered to the bus. "I have to go. They're loading the bus."

"I know you'll be busy and out of it, but can you text me when surgery is over."

"You want me to text you?" I tease her, inhaling a full breath for the first time in weeks, and it feels good.

"Yeah, a thumbs up or something, so I know you're still alive."

I smile, a portion of my anxiety falling away. "Baby, I'll text you something."

There's that pause again, and I can imagine the slight pink tint to her cheeks, and it warms my cold insides.

I'm not ready to hang up, but I have to. "I gotta go."

"Hey, Mark."

"Yeah."

"I miss you, too. So much. I'm not going anywhere."

I'm still scared shitless about a lot of things, but I hang up with a renewed sense of hope that somehow this might actually work out. It has to. It just has to.

Chapter 14

LEX

I stare at my phone, resting my hip against the vanity. Mark said he's scared. I could hear it in his voice, in the way he snapped at me, and it only means one thing. He's absolutely terrified.

I know how he feels about hospitals and medical facilities and the memories they stir. I want to make it all better for him, but I can't, and I hate it.

I run a hand over my stomach. It's definitely not the time to drop a teeny, tiny baby bomb on his mountain of anxiety. But, as soon as he's out of surgery and I know he's ok, I'm telling him about our baby. *Our baby.*

My lips tug upward as I open the bathroom door to head back out to join the guys. I stop in the kitchen to grab a bottle of water and find Slade cracking open a beer.

"You all right?" he asks, tossing the metal cap in the trash.

I grab a water from the fridge and twist off the plastic lid, trying to act like everything is fine. Normal. I'm secretly married, pregnant, and unsure of exactly what happens next. Plus, Mark is freaking out and heading into surgery to see if he'll ever be able to throw again. I'm fine. *Just* fine.

"Yeah." See, that sounded . . . fine.

He takes a pull from his bottle, his eyes staying on me. "You feeling better?"

"Yes." I take a sip of water. I barfed three times today, but what's new?

"You sure? You were pretty antsy out there watching the game."

Watching Mark hit the ground, his arm twisted behind him and writhing in pain, is not something I ever want to see again. My heart and my stomach hit the floor, one on top of the other, and didn't pick themselves back up until I saw his face as he was helped off the field.

I knew it meant he was done, and everything he'd been suffering for just went out the window.

I pick at the plastic label. "I'm fine. It was a close game."

He stares at me like I'm full of crap, and I am to the very tip-top.

"He'll be fine. I'm sure he's got the best of the best at his fingertips." Slade's cool, smooth tone hits a nerve, and my spine stiffens. He lifts his bottle but stops halfway to his lips. "You know, it might be time to actually do something about it. This shit has been going on long enough."

I glare at him and his big, burly bluntness. "Really? I might suggest where you can shove your opinion."

I see a hint of a smirk, and I'm tempted to throw my water bottle at him. I love him, but this man is the absolute last person I'd take any sort of relationship advice from. What sucks is he's not wrong. I plan to do something about Mark and me. He just needs his shoulder repaired first.

I lean against the counter, crossing my arms over my baggy sweatshirt. "You know, I might be willing to listen to you if you'd dated someone in the last, I don't know, ever."

He glares, that hint of amusement remaining, and somehow, it's as if he sees right through me. This is what happens when you work with each other every day, and they actually care about you. They call you out and make you face your fears, regrets, grief, heartache, and all the other suckass things we'd like to avoid. Forever.

I hug myself tighter.

He drops his bottle to his side, gripping the neck with two fingers. "I don't have to date to know when someone's being stupid."

I let my head fall to the side. "I'm not being stupid. Just sometimes, things aren't as easy as they seem." *Like, ever.*

He adjusts the hat on his head. "Seems pretty simple to me. I thought you might need a brown paper bag in there. How much longer are you going to keep this up?"

"Slade, there's so much—"

"None of that is a factor anymore. You're letting it be a factor." He points his bottle at me. "It's time you quit hiding behind the past."

While I want to punch him, that annoying little internal voice pulls out a pen and my list of fears to cross reference with Slade's accusation. *I'm not hiding. I'm married. Ha!*

I want to be totally and completely pissed at him, especially today, but Slade and I have been friends for too long. This is him caring, *and* part of me knows he's right. *Damn him.*

I had my reasons for letting Mark go before. I'm not sure they're even remotely valid anymore. That's what I need to find out. But like I told Mark, I'm terrified out of my mind.

"You know, I could say the same to you," I smirk, twisting the cap back on as his eyes burn holes into me. "Maybe it's time to let the past go. You might even be able to find a smile in there somewhere if you did."

He grunts, his fingers scratching at his neck. I just turned the uncomfortable tables and pointed them back at him. It's me caring about him, too. He's big, overprotective, and grumpy, but he's the only kind of brother I'll ever have.

"Who's letting the past go?" Krissy steps into the kitchen, pulling a bag of chips from the pantry.

Slade lifts his bottle, but his squinty eyes remain on me.

"Oh, I was just telling Slade that it's time to let his rough and rugged, I-have-no-feelings persona go and think about taking a dip into the dating pool."

Krissy's head tips back, laughter bursting out. "Date? Him?" She points at him, and I might be dead wrong, but I think I see a hint of red behind that dark, trimmed beard. "Slade would have to let go of all of his strict-ass rules, routines, and requirements. Women want a man with a sense of humor and who . . . let's go and laughs now and then. No one would put up with all that gruff grouchiness. Seriously, I'm pretty sure he sleeps in a garbage can."

"I don't want a woman," he growls. "I'm perfectly happy alone."

"Ha. Keep telling yourself that, bro. No one who walks around grumbling and cursing as much as you do is happy."

I can't help but laugh as Krissy dumps the chips in a bowl. It feels good and a little like hope bubbling up.

"Are you staying for dinner?" she asks me. "We decided on pizza."

I shake my head. "No, I have to leave in a few. I'm having dinner with my mom."

She widens her eyes at me, grabbing the bowl off the counter. "Bummer. We could set up a dating profile and list him." She tips her head in Slade's direction. "Big, grouchy, hard-ass mechanic seeking mannequin."

I put my hand over my mouth to hide my laugh, but I can't.

Slade looks at her from underneath his dark eyelashes, thoroughly unamused. "Krissy, I think it's time for your ass to move out."

She laughs and leaves the kitchen, the bowl of chips on her hip. "Ok, well, at least then *I'll* be able to date and sleep around and not have you scare them off or listen to your lectures every five minutes."

His head tips back, and he runs a hand over his face. "She's going to kill me."

I push away from the counter. "Maybe it's time you let her move out. It's going to happen one of these days." I point my plastic bottle at him this time. "And then *you,* big guy, as scary as it is, just might have to get a life."

I grin and leave him grounding out a string of foul words that have something to do with him owning the house and already having the life he wants.

I say goodbye to the guys and Krissy, spending the twenty-minute drive thinking about Mark, everything Slade said, and the little one growing inside me.

I pull in front of the row of townhouses, and my phone buzzes next to me.

MARK: Link attached. *Rental in Scottsdale*
MARK: *voice message* *So you know where I am. FYI, I'm down with a sleepover. FOREVER.*

ME: *voice message* *Is that a formal invitation?*

My lips turn up. He's trying. I'm trying. I want it all to be enough. I want it to be so much more than enough. I want us to be a family the way I've always dreamed.

I climb out, knowing he and I have a lot of talking and sorting out to do.

I enter my mom's kitchen through the back door and immediately sense that maybe I should have stayed at Slade's.

"Oh hey, honey." My mom turns and greets me before she's right back to work.

I slump, asking the question I'm certain I already know the answer to. "What's the occasion?"

I move beside her in the small, brightly painted kitchen, tossing a mixed salad. Her highlighted hair is twisted up, and she's wearing a short, flowy dress. A vase of fresh flowers sits in the middle of the table.

I wouldn't be suspicious, except this setup seems all too familiar. The past few times I've been over for dinner, we've ordered takeout since she's gotten off work late, and I can't remember the last time I saw her in a dress.

She moves on to slicing a loaf of bread and turns toward me, resting her hip on the counter.

"Well, I want you to meet someone."

Her blue eyes brighten with a smile. I want to groan and roll my eyes, but I stop myself. Somehow, I knew this was what this show was all about. I've been here before, so many times.

Growing up, I always knew when a new man was sniffing around. A new wardrobe was purchased, nice dinners were put together so I could meet him, and my mom wore the same bright smile until it didn't last.

The men were always nice and successful, but my mom never seemed to be the one they were looking for, no matter how hard she tried to be. Each time it didn't work, I had to watch her fall apart and piece herself back together until the next one came along.

At fourteen, when she announced she was moving to Florida to follow the Financial Advisor, I'd had enough of the ups and downs and moved in with Grandpa.

"Really. Who is he?" I set the salad bowl on the table, trying to hide my complete lack of enthusiasm, but I do a sucky job.

She bites her bottom lip as if she's already in love. My stomach and its newfound self-rule rises high in complete rebellion. I could gag, literally, but I hold it back. I don't want to meet this man or any man. I'm too old for her short-lived love affairs.

I lean against the counter, resting my hands in the front pocket of my sweatshirt, not wanting to deal with this tonight. I want to go home and see if I catch Mark.

"I met him at work. He's a contractor and has been working on the addition to the recreational center. He has a son about your age."

I raise a skeptical eyebrow. "How long have you been seeing each other?"

"We've been out on a few dates. He brought me these flowers this morning," she points to the ones on the table, beaming at the gesture. "He's excited to meet you."

Yippee.

She slices the bread while I stir the stroganoff on the stove.

"I think he might be the one," she says softly as she sets the basket of bread on the table.

My eyeballs hit their limit and roll to where I'm pretty sure I see my brain deciding it's time to snooze this one out. "Mom, don't you think it's a little soon to know that?"

She huffs, "Actually, I don't. It's different this time."

Hmmm. Seems like I've heard this before. "Mom, that's what you said with Ted and Rick."

She stiffens into defensive mode. "Alex, can't you be happy for me? I understand you ruined things with Seth, but this is important to me."

Oh, hell no. It's like smelling salts waft through the air, and my brain snaps to as my spine lengthens, pushing me away from the counter. "This has nothing to do with Seth. He and I weren't right for each other. It was my fault for not seeing it sooner."

"I don't know how you'd even know that. You've hardly dated anyone." She shakes her head. "You know, I worry about you. Someday, Grandpa isn't going to be there to take care of you anymore. What are you going to do then?"

I pull back at her words. "What?" This. This is not what I need right now . . . or ever, but especially not right now. I don't need a talking-to about how I'll never make it on my own and need someone to take care of me.

She gestures around her kitchen. "Alex, all of this costs. It takes money to survive. What are you going to do? Run the shop? It's a business, and you have to be able to . . . "

She doesn't finish her statement as anger ignites and shoots through me, exploding like a rogue firework. "Read."

She runs a hand down the front of her dress. "That's not what I meant." Her voice is soft, and her shoulders slumping with regret.

It sure as hell sounded like that to me.

"I just mean it takes a lot to run a business, and I'm not sure you understand all that's involved."

I don't even know what to say. I let my hand fall to my stomach inside my pocket, thinking about the tiny being that's growing and changing.

When that little stick showed double lines, it was the absolute best moment of my life. There already isn't a single thing I wouldn't do for this baby. Taking care of it, loving it, and supporting it is my first priority and always will be.

I have things to do, preparations to make, and a man to talk to about . . . everything. What I don't need is her telling me I'm incapable of it all.

My mom exhales. "When your dad took off, I had no choice but to figure things out. It was a terrible time, and I had no idea how I was going to make it. I never want that for you."

I force my eyes from the floor, shoving resentment aside. "I might not be good at very many things, and I may have trouble reading and writing, but I know Grandpa's business from the inside out. I've never needed a man to take care of me, and I don't need one now."

I grab my keys on the end of the counter. "I'm not staying for dinner. I hope this works out for you."

"Alex, wait." My mom reaches for me, and I stop. "I love you. I only want the best for you."

I shake my head. "No, you don't. You've always wanted what's best for you."

I don't wait for her to respond, heading for my truck with steam billowing from my body. The closer I get to home, the more unsure of myself I become. She targeted and picked at every single one of my insecurities.

She doesn't even know about Mark or the baby, and I won't be able to hide it much longer. I need to talk to Mark. He has a say in all of this, and I want him to, but I have to be able to take care of this baby.

I know my limitations, but I also know I can run Grandpa's shop. There are aspects I may need help with, but I know what those are and how to get the help I need.

I bypass Grandpa, asleep in the recliner, and go straight to my room. I don't need him seeing my red face or rehashing what happened.

I cross the room to plug in my phone, but catch a glimpse of myself in the mirror and stop. I pull my shirt up and unfasten my jeans, which are getting a little snug. I place a hand over where my baby is growing. The tiny bump is beginning to make its presence known. I can't help the smile that takes hold as the salty taste of tears falls on my lips.

I've never wanted anything more. I've dreamed of being a mother. The fact that Mark and I did this together only makes it that much more of a miracle.

I long to tell him, but that means I finally have to face those fears I've let dangle around me since I left him in Vegas. All the questions I pushed aside while he finished the season have now been dragged front and center, demanding answers.

I don't know how Mark will react to the baby news, but I'm not afraid to tell him. I'm more afraid of figuring out how to make it work between us. Or really, that it won't. To find out too much time has passed and we're not who we once were. Or that my past actions will ruin the second chance I never thought I'd get.

Chapter 15

MARK

If there's a single place I loathe with every inch of my being, it's the hospital. The stringent smell, the lights, the crinkly beds lined with plastic, the squeaky clean shine of every sterile, cold surface. All of it.

Shane parks my rental car, and we walk through the back doors of the surgical center so that this little adventure into hell doesn't become public entertainment. My nerves are already on edge, and I don't need my paperwork and gown change to be videoed and blasted to every news outlet.

"You all right?" Shane asks as we follow a nurse down the hall into a registration cube.

"Are you going to make me dinner tonight? I'm thinking a grilled steak with a baked potato and a nice cold beer."

The young woman, clicking away on the keyboard and entering my information, stifles a laugh as she hands me back my insurance card.

"I may order you something if you can keep your dramatics to a minimum."

"Dramatics? They're slicing my shoulder open, rearranging a bunch of stuff, and then going to try to put it back together so it works again. You could be a little more sympathetic."

Shane groans. "I've been there." He taps his knee.

"Yeah, well, look how that turned out."

He side-eyes me, the sympathy just rolling off him.

"I think you're all set. Can you verify everything is correct?" The woman reaches across the desk with a white plastic bracelet in her hand.

I verify the information before she secures it to my wrist, and we're off to the next station.

A nurse ushers us to a small, private, curtained corner and scurries around, rapid-firing instructions I'm sure as hell not listening to. The less I know, the better.

She hands me the dreaded gown and then disappears.

I toss the gown to the side and remove my shirt, sitting on the edge of the gurney.

"She told you to put that on," Shane says, trying to fold himself in the tiny chair.

"Yeah, well, I'm doing them a favor. They won't have to deal with all that fabric while they're slicing and dicing."

"Mark, your charms won't get you out of their protocols."

"Maybe they'll get me extra pain medicine and out of here sooner."

Shane rolls his eyes. "The last thing you need is extra painkillers." He shoots me a pointed look. He's right about that, but I'm not admitting it because anything that will knock me out and make me numb sounds pretty damn good right about now.

I stare at him as he flips through the paperwork. I shiver. *Why do they have to keep it thirty degrees below zero in these places?* If you're here, you're already uncomfortable enough.

"Stop staring at me. You have the best surgeon in the country. You need to relax. If you bounce your leg any harder, you'll fall off the bed."

I realize at some point, my big grumpy-ass bro has become a little mother hen. "Your bedside manner is horrific. Why didn't you send Maggie?"

"I didn't want her to have to deal with your overstimulated hyperactivity. Now, what the hell is wrong with you? Are you nervous? You're twitchy and higher-strung than usual."

"Uh. Hell yes, I am. This place is like a visit to an Arctic prison cell where you get tortured and released. I need this to be over and my shoulder to work again."

My phone buzzes, and I pull it from my pocket, needing a distraction.

LEX: *flex arm emoji* *football emoji* *racehorse emoji*

ME: *racehorse emoji*?

LEX: Mustang

ME: Huh?

LEX: *Laughing face emoji* *Heart emoji*

"What's that dumbass grin on your face for?" Shane barks from the corner of our little curtained square.

"None of your business. If you were nicer, maybe I'd tell you." I turn my phone off and tuck it in the plastic drawstring bag the nurse left for all my personal items. "When are Maggie and the kids getting here?"

"Not soon enough. Liv can dote on you like the damsel in distress you are."

Shane reads the care instruction packet as if it's the first time he's ever been in charge of someone, and it somehow makes me feel extra special.

"Ahhh. My little Liv. I can't wait to see my favorite little girl."

He cocks an eyebrow at my claim to one of his girls. Maggie's youngest sibling had Shane wrapped around her pinky from day one, and she's had a firm grip on his heart ever since.

"So, when surgery is done, we're going back to your place, and then I need to have you at the doctor's office at 8 a.m. tomorrow. They'll discuss your therapy schedule."

I've heard all this before. I tune him out, trying to ready myself to be wheeled back and knocked out. Maybe the whole knocking-out thing won't be so bad. Then, I can dream of Lex, and the only thing I want to do when I finally get to see her.

"Seriously, what is up with you?" Shane's staring at me.

"Nothing. I hate all places like this."

"No, you have this stupid goofy look on your face. What's going on? What have you done?"

I'm saved by a nurse rushing in and telling me it's time. I settle myself on the gurney, and Shane pats my shoulder as she wheels me into the hall, telling me things I'm not listening to. In the operating room, they hook me up, and then, thankfully, I'm out.

I blink. I blink again. Everything is fuzzy, and my mouth feels like someone shoved a sheet of sandpaper into it. My mind is cloudy, and I'm floating in some kind of hazy funk.

Lex. I need to talk to Lex.

I try to sit up.

"Hey, lay still." Shane's huge form comes into my view.

I reach for my arm, wanting to be sure it's still there.

His large hand falls on mine, and it weighs a hundred pounds.

"Everything went well. Even better than expected. The doctors said you'll be good as new." His voice is low and muffled.

"Lex." My tongue sticks to the top of my mouth. "I need my phone."

Shane's hands hold me in place while I try to wiggle free.

"Mark, you're all drugged up."

I shake my head, and the room spins. "No, Lex. I need to . . . "

"Just relax."

Frustration fills my sedated mental capacity. "I need to text her. She's waiting."

"Ok. We'll do that later. Do you want some water?"

He holds a cup with a straw in front of me, and I sip the cold water, giving me life. The only thing I want is Lex. I need her to tell me it's going to be ok. To hug her and kiss her. And then kiss her some more and more and . . .

"No. I want my wife. I need to call her." My good arm flaps around, searching for my phone again, but Shane prevents me.

"Mark, relax. You don't know what you're saying. We'll be out of here soon enough, but not if you're high as a kite."

I let my balloon-filled head rest back on the stiff pillow. I surrender, all the pain I've lived with now missing.

"Can you get me out of here?" I ask the big warden who won't get my phone.

"Soon. Although, I can tell dealing with you will be a real treat."

"You're a real jackass. You're fired."

"You can't fire me. I volunteered to take care of you."

"Call a nurse. I'd like someone else, please."

He laughs. "Sorry, I think you're stuck with me until Maggie and Liv get here."

"Well, just so you know, you suck at this job."

"Noted."

"Lex is going to be pissed when she knows you didn't let me text her. She's waiting for a thumbs up so she knows I'm not dead."

"All right, buddy." I don't care for his condescending tone, and I want to punch him. "She'll be waiting a long time," I hear his strict ass mumble.

I close my eyes, wanting to drift away. "You just wait and see."

Chapter 16

LEX

The impact gun vibrates in my hand, tightening the lug nuts on a Ford Explorer. Two tires down, two to go. I roll and lift another to place it on the axle, realizing I won't be able to do this much longer.

A wave of nerves rolls through my already volatile stomach with the need to know what I'm going to do when I reach that point.

I called and made my first doctor's appointment. They informed me that at twelve weeks, my little wild colt is about the size of a plum. I ended the call with a short list of dos and don'ts that I'm certain will grow along with my changing body.

I've started prenatal vitamins and sadly waved goodbye to coffee while my tiny bump is getting harder to hide. Thank goodness for coveralls, but things like lifting these tires won't be happening with a bulging belly.

Hopefully, it will push Grandpa to teach me more about the business side, which I've only been introduced to. It will be an opportunity to learn what I need to know in order to take over the shop one day.

Before that can happen, I have to tell Grandpa and my mom that not only am I married, but I'm having a baby. I've kept this most exciting and life-changing news a secret, wanting the miraculous joy for just myself until I can share it with Mark. But a significant amount of pressure is building inside me with all the things that are about to change.

Time is ticking. All of my pants are too tight, and most of my shirts aren't loose enough to hide my little bump. At least the morning sickness has mostly subsided, and I'm feeling more like myself, but I have to talk to Mark.

He sent me a fist-pound emoji, which I assume was supposed to be a thumbs-up, so I know he made it through surgery. When he's done sleeping off the drugs, I'm spilling the big news. I can't stand it any longer. We can't be some lingering thing out there waiting to happen someday. This baby is growing and won't wait for us to get it together.

I tighten the lug nuts on the last tire, and start the alignment process. When I'm finished, I move the Explorer to the parking lot and return the keys to the board. The shop is quiet, except for the low country music, while everyone breaks for lunch.

I head to the kitchen to warm my leftovers, but I hear the distinct voices of Grandpa and Slade coming from his office.

My steps slow to a crawl as I hear Slade say something about 'buying the shop.' I stand in the short hallway, unable to move, listening as they talk about a payment plan and future growth opportunities.

My stomach drops to my steel-toed boots, and my lungs quit functioning. Before I can think about it, I'm standing in the doorway.

The faces of two of the men I trust most in the world snap in my direction.

"What?" It's the only thing my brain can formulate.

"Alex," Slade straightens, a big hand running over his face. "I was going to talk to you." His deep voice hits my ears and bounces right off.

My eyes shift to Grandpa. He leans back in his chair, exhaling, his chin dropping to his chest.

"Are you selling the shop?" I can only suck in little bits of air, and my question comes out as a whisper. I want to drop to a crouching position in case I vomit, but I keep myself upright.

When he doesn't immediately answer, my eyes flick back to Slade. "You're buying him out?" Something is happening in my throat, and it might actually be swelling shut.

Slade's hands shoot out in front of him. "We're just talking."

I switch back to Grandpa, needing a direct answer to a direct question. "Are you selling?" I choke out.

When his eyes finally meet mine, I think I have my answer.

"We're only talking, but Pal, there's a whole lot more to this shop than the fixing part."

"You don't think I know that?" Fire consumes my tight airway.

"I know you know that, but . . . running this shop will be your entire life. I don't . . . "

I drop my gaze to the floor, my eyes burning, but I won't cry. I won't do it. Not here. Not in front of them.

"Alex." I hear Grandpa's chair creak as he moves forward, but I can't look at him. "I don't want this shop to become the only thing you ever have. The only thing you think—"

"You know what this means to me." I force out.

This garage. These guys. The customers. They're not only part of my dream; they're my livelihood. They're supposed to be my future.

"Alex." It's Slade's voice this time. "You wouldn't be going anywhere."

I can't face him—my best friend.

I swallow, needing my throat to open. "I finished the rotation and alignment. Keys are on the board. I have to go."

My lunch stays in the fridge while I grab my keys to figure out what in the hell I'm supposed to do. Somehow, I'll have to overcome the pain of knowing two of the most important people in my life have so little faith in me.

Hurt and betrayal rage within me while panic takes hold of every part of my body. This was my plan—my future. That shop is all I've known and the only thing I've ever wanted to do for my whole life.

I sit on the edge of my bed, trying to breathe and calm my heart pounding against my ribs. I drop my head in my hands as my stomach climbs into my throat, and I debate running for the toilet.

I grew up in that garage. It's where I felt safe and useful. It was the place where my inability didn't matter—the only place where I excelled.

Never in a million years would I have thought Grandpa would sell. I guess it was my fault to assume he'd trust me with the business he's spent his life building. It's just that now . . .

My body crumples further. I know Slade will always have a job for me, but even the thought feels like a kick in the face. I can't pretend that everything will be fine when all I thought I knew, everything I was counting on, was pulled out from under me.

I run a hand over my small protruding bump as tears finally make their escape. I can't keep letting valuable days slip by without having a plan for how I'll take care of this baby. I'm a mother now, and this baby is the only thing that matters. I have to start acting like it.

I suck in a breath through my hiccups, wiping my tears and snot on the cuff of my sleeve. I can't keep letting my insecurities rule and running from the things that scare me. I can't keep hiding from life and ignoring my responsibilities, willing everything to work out.

I lay back on my bed, letting it all go.

Eventually, I force myself up, wiping the salt-crusted tears from my eyes, and they snag on the threadbare t-shirt I've worn every night since I returned from Vegas.

I inhale long and deep. I wasn't able to keep up with his life when he left here, and that likely hasn't changed. I don't belong in a world of the elite and sophisticated. I'm just a girl who works in a garage, piecing broken things back together.

But I can't raise this child with half of my heart because the other half resides with someone far away.

I stare at Mark's name on my phone, daring myself to push the call button. I count down. *Five, four, three* . . . I will myself to do it, but then something inside me, maybe the tiny being, screams at me.

Eight years ago, I took the easy way out. I can't do that again. This baby is so much bigger than my fears of every unknown and uncertainty.

I back out of his contact and pull up the flight information instead. This time, I will talk to him face-to-face. I won't run away, and I won't hide. It's too important.

Five minutes later, my flight is booked, and I pull my suitcase from the closet, tossing in the few items I'll need for this quick trip.

I lug my things down the stairs and into the kitchen, dialing Linda. I leave a voicemail letting her know I won't be able to make it to dinner tonight and ask her to tell Bree that I'll stop by soon. Thoughts of them stir an uneasiness in my chest that I have to squash for now. I can only handle one thing at a time.

I grab the keys to my truck and glance around at my home—the place I've always felt safe and comfortable. But maybe that's just it. Comfort is no longer a luxury. It's time for me to take control and go after what I've always wanted, no matter how scary it might be.

Chapter 17

MARK

I step in from the garage and stomp into the kitchen, tossing my phone on the counter.

"Stop pouting. What did you think was going to happen?"

I ignore Shane's poke and head to the refrigerator. I came home from surgery, fell into bed, and stayed there until Shane barked at me to get up so we could get to the doctor's office.

My phone buzzes on the counter, but I ignore it, grabbing eggs and a pan.

"Seriously. What the hell is your problem?" Shane takes a seat on a stool.

I ignore him. My shoulder is screaming at me for refusing the narcotics and sticking to Tylenol and Ibuprofen. I don't need his loud-ass attitude on top of it.

I knew this would take time, and the pain and waiting game would be excruciating, but leaving the doctor's office with my physical therapy schedule in hand was the last straw.

Without Lex, every single thing I've worked for, all the time we've been apart, has been for nothing. I have to see her, or I might completely lose my shit and kiss my very limited sanity goodbye. Forever. I told her I was coming for her, but it's clear I'm not going anywhere if I want my shoulder to heal quickly and properly.

I wonder if I can squeeze in one night if I leave today?

Shane grabs an egg from my hand and cracks it into the warming pan.

"Nothing. I'm fine. This therapy schedule is intense."

When Shane doesn't say anything, I peek at him as I stir the eggs. He leans against the counter, arms crossed over his chest, and not buying a single ounce of my bullshit.

"You need to chill out. Your surgery went even better than expected. You'll have the best therapists to get you throwing again even sooner. Shit, you're going to be out of that sling in a few days. What did you want to happen? Be able to jet off to some exotic paradise and live it up for a few weeks."

I drop the spatula and stare back at him, calculating if I can get to Ohio tonight and return for my first appointment. "No, jackass, but I have something really important I need to do. When are Maggie and the kids getting here? I've had enough of you."

"Like what?" Shane challenges.

I reach for a plate, ignoring his question. "When did they say I can drive again?"

"Two weeks."

His eyes bore holes into me as I work one-handed, but he could throw darts at me. I'm not giving.

"Does this have something to do with some dumbass thing you did in Vegas?"

I'm not always great at keeping my cool when someone pushes my buttons, but Shane's not getting this out of me. He can put his nonexistent mustache and Magnum PI skills away and settle the hell down.

"Anyone ever tell you that you suck as a caregiver? I just had surgery, and you sit here pestering me while I make *us* breakfast."

"Maggie likes how I care for her just fine."

"Hold on." I rest my good arm on the counter and gag. "I need her here now. You're unbearable. When are they getting here?"

He sighs, and if my shoulder didn't hurt so damn badly, I throw my hands in the air at his surrender.

"Not soon enough. I've hit my limit in dealing with your diva ass."

His phone vibrates on the counter, and he reaches for it as I finish up the eggs and dump them on plates. I grab my phone to message the charter service to see when I might be able to schedule a flight.

I see a missed call from Lex, but bypass it to pull up the charter website.

I don't know how I'll explain leaving to Shane, given that Maggie and the kids are flying in for Sean's game, but I'll deal with that later.

"Maggie said they've boarded, and I'm picking them up in a bit. Thought I'd bring them here until Sean is home from practice."

I scroll my phone in between bites, needing privacy so I can make a call. "Fine."

There are a few beats of silence while we eat.

"You do what they say, and you'll be fine." My thumb halts movement over my screen, and I meet his eyes. "The doctor said it looked really good. Just stick to the plan. When you're ready, Sean won't let you slack."

I let out a slow breath, wishing football was my biggest worry right now. I am worried. My entire life has been the game, and I'm not ready to be done. But the woman of my actual dreams is waiting for me, and I can't afford to mess it up.

"I've got a lot of work to do." I've got to figure out how to actually be with my wife.

"Well, good thing you know how to work harder than the rest. Quit stomping around and get to it."

Get to it. I grab my phone and head to my room, needing a plane and time. I may only have a few hours, but I'm going to do what Shane said. I'll work hard. I'll work harder than I've ever worked in my life because none of the rest of it matters if Lex isn't a part of it.

Chapter 18

LEX

My Uber pulls up to the address Mark sent me. A couple of cars sit in the drive, and I double-check the link he sent, instantly realizing maybe I should have thought this through. I tried to call him, but he hasn't returned my call. A surprise visit probably wasn't the most brilliant plan, but under the circumstances, there's no such thing as perfect timing.

My driver clears her throat, peering at me in the rearview mirror while I remain glued to the worn fabric seat.

"Sorry," I whisper, apparently having lost all confidence along with my voice on the two-and-a-half-hour flight.

I gather my backpack and small suitcase as my nerves form a protest line. Willing myself to ignore them, I open the door and step out, taking a second to adjust my sweatshirt.

This is what I came to do. I can do this. I need to say the words and ignore his handsome face and charm, deny access to all memories of him and his declarations, and not let him pull me in. No touching.

NO TOUCHING until we face reality and understand where we go from here.

I inhale the dry, warm air as the car pulls away from the curb, leaving me stranded. I stare at the white stucco house with a clay tile roof. I can remain stuck on the sidewalk and request another car to come get me, or I can do what I came to do.

It's you and me, baby. Let's do this.

I haul myself up to the door and stab the doorbell with a shaky finger, not giving myself a chance to chicken out. *Maybe I should call him.*

I pull my phone from my pocket, but the door swings open, and a woman with long, dark, curly hair smiles at me. My lungs deflate like two blown airbags and a cool sweat breaks out in all my dark places. I contemplate running.

I swallow, recognizing her as Sean's girlfriend, and she's even more beautiful in person.

I didn't think this through. I didn't think about Mark having guests or remember his family would be here. *Shit!*

"Hi. Can I help you?"

I shift my weight, wondering if I could play the 'sorry, wrong address' card, but then I hear Slade's obnoxious voice call me a pansy-ass. The thought of him catches in my throat.

The fresh wave of hurt shoves me forward.

"I, uh . . . I'm looking for Mark." I try to suck in air as my anxiety hikes to a ten, and my pulse bangs against my eardrums.

The woman's eyes run over me, taking note of the suitcase at my side as a tiny bead of sweat rolls down my spine. Then her eyebrows raise with something that resembles . . . amusement.

"Mark, huh? Come on in."

She pulls the door open further, and I hear what sounds like a full-fledged party. There's laughter, yelling, and kids' voices coming from somewhere further inside.

I step into the entryway, expecting her to find Mark and tell him I'm here, but instead, she waves her hand, gesturing me to follow.

"Mark's around here somewhere. Come on, but watch out for flying things and crawling littles."

I follow her through the sparsely decorated bright white space and enter a large open kitchen and living room filled with people and kids. I instantly recognize Sean off to the side, holding a crying baby. A woman stands rocking another baby back and forth while kids run loose everywhere.

"Alex?" I hear someone say my name and realize it's Sean. His brows are pinched tight, eyes zeroed in on me.

"Hi," I squeeze out through my quivering vocal box but then go back to surveying the space being overrun by children, Styrofoam darts, pizza, and ice cream.

A boy soars by with a large Nerf gun, turning to shoot across the room as he dives to the floor. A little girl hops up on a stool, shoving a spoonful of melted ice cream in her mouth as Shane's large body pops up from behind a couch. A teenage boy sits in the middle, scrolling his phone, completely unfazed by the chaos.

Shane sends off a round of darts, a couple targeting the petite woman's behind as she turns to shield the baby.

"Shane, you're going to pay for that," she warns, and I see one side of his mouth hitch up as the kid fires a round back at him. "All right, boys, that's enough!" she yells, but her eyes are set on me.

Shane freezes, staring at me as darts bounce off his chest and fall to the floor. The room suddenly turns quiet, except for a spoon clinking against the bowl and a snorting noise coming from one of the babies.

The heat of a million suns takes up residence underneath my skin, and sweat may roll down my face at any moment.

"I think . . . I'll wait for Mark outside." Needing immediate air, I don't wait, turning to make the short trek back out the way I came, but I take two steps, and WHAM!

Something wet and sticky explodes and runs down the front of me. The smell is so strong my nervous stomach heaves, and I gag.

"Teddy!" A chorus of voices erupts behind me, but all I can do is try not to make it worse with vomit.

Then I hear him. "Lex?"

That voice. The one that instantly makes me melt into a giant pile of goo, believe that the world is good, and that everything will be all right. I need earplugs. I can't read or write well, but for this task, I need to not be able to hear.

Just his voice makes me want to fall into him and stay there forever, continuing to put off reality, but I have to be strong.

I remain frozen in place, distracted by Mark's voice instead of whatever is all over me.

Then, he's in front of me. His arm is in a sling, wearing an open button-down shirt, and that face I've never, ever been able to resist. *Crap! Don't look at him.*

"Shit! What the hell is that?" His face scrunches with repulsion, and I try not to heave.

"Mark, you said shit." I hear the little girl from behind me.

"Sorry, Liv. I'll give you a dollar later. Teddy, do I even want to know?" he asks, peering around me.

"Probably not," a young voice says. "I'm sorry . . . whoever you are."

"Are you Mark's girlfriend?" the little girl asks.

The silence is deafening as I try to breathe and not puke all over the floor.

I break my 'No Looking at Mark' rule a second time in desperation. "I'm going to throw up if I have to stay like this."

"Shit. Right."

He grabs my hand. Now, two rules have been broken. I will my body to not to react to the tingles rippling through me at the warm security of his hand around mine.

He takes me down a dim hallway, passing a few doors until we reach the last one. He pulls me into the room, kicking the door closed behind us. He faces me, staring, while I try not to breathe through my nose or touch any part of my top half.

Holding my breath doesn't work because when I inhale again, the strong acidic smell overwhelms me, and my stomach cramps again.

"Shit!" Mark rushes forward, gathers my sticky, rancid-soaked sweatshirt with one hand, and tugs it up over my head.

I gag again as he yanks me free of the shirt that smells close to death. I straighten, trying to swallow down the bile in my throat and wiping my eyes with the back of my wrist, hoping they're clean.

When my blurry eyes clear, I find Mark's eyes on me and the size of truck tires.

"What is that?" His voice is so uncharacteristically soft my skin pricks to life with goosebumps.

I close my eyes, needing a moment. Silence lingers a second before he asks again.

"Lex, what . . . is . . . that?"

I stand in my mostly clean bra, frozen in space and time. I should cover myself, but the reality is he's seen it all before and more. Not that this isn't exactly why I'm here.

I pull in air, and only a trace of the smell still lingers around me. I stare at him as his eyes flick to my little bump and back up to meet mine.

"A baby." It comes out in a rush, like a secret finally flowing freely. It's the first time I've said the word out loud, and it's to the man I want everything with. A warm wave of love washes over me, and it generates a tickle in my throat.

"Nooooo," Mark says slowly, not trusting it.

His dark eyebrows retract back to a normal level as he stares at my stomach in deep thought. I cross my arms over myself, feeling a bit exposed.

Then a full grin spreads across his face, and I can't look. That bright and freaking contagious smile has a way of melting all my defenses and resolve, and that CANNOT happen.

I glare at him, needing to activate all reserves.

He lunges for me, and before I can react, I'm pressed up against him as he holds me tight. He feels and smells so good.

"Lex! We made a baby. I'm going to be a dad."

He sounds so wistful it almost brings tears to my hormonal eyes, but I scream at them to retreat. I can't cry. I need answers.

He pulls away, and his hand glides against my cheek. "Lex, we made a baby. This is the best news of my life! How did this happen?" He laughs in disbelief. "Why didn't you tell me?"

His question sounds pained, and it pierces my reinforced exterior. "I don't know. Maybe I forgot a pill or . . . it didn't work." He stares at me, his face shining with complete awe and elation. "I'm not sure when I was supposed to tell you."

"How about any of the times we spoke on the phone?"

"Our five-minute conversations when you had a free moment didn't really seem like an appropriate time to tell you the most important news of my life."

He pushes out a long breath. "Our lives. I can't wait to tell Sean I beat him to it. He's going to be so pissed." That damn boyish grin takes flight, and he leans in to kiss me.

I drop my chin, taking a step back. I look around the room, spotting a suitcase lying open with clothes shoved in. "You heading somewhere?"

He laughs. "Yeah, to see you. Couldn't get a plane until the morning. It was only going to be for a night, but this is so much better." He studies me, his smile falling. "What's wrong?"

My throat thickens, but I swallow it away. "We need to talk."

"Clearly."

I reach for a shirt on the floor and pull it over my head, needing to get this out. I grip the hem with both hands, hoping it will give me strength.

"I think maybe . . . we got ahead of ourselves. This baby has to be my priority, and I don't know how—"

He takes a quick step forward. "I know these months have been unfair and difficult, but I didn't have a choice."

"I know," I say, softly and meaning it—or at least what I think I know about his life. "But we haven't seen each other for months. I . . . My life is in Ohio. It's the only place . . . " I can't say the words. The burn is too deep and raw when I'm already trying to hold it together. "I don't see how we make this work."

He closes the distance between us, pushing the sticky strands of hair over my shoulder and out of the way. "That night in Vegas, there wasn't a single thing that didn't work."

"I'm not talking about sex, Mark."

He shakes his head. "That was so much more than just sex, and you know it." He hesitantly reaches down to put his hand on my stomach. "There's no better proof of that than this."

Well, just freaking great. His handsy ass is going to pierce all my reinforcements. A tear slips down my cheek, and I quickly swipe it away. He puts his hand on my hip and tugs me to him. I surrender, needing to feel the safety in his arms that's never faltered.

"I want you, and I want this baby more than anything. You've . . . " His voice is so soft it's almost a whisper. "You've made my only remaining dream come true." He kisses my temple. "Don't push me away. Nothing else matters anymore but this."

I step away, breaking the connection. "I heard you that morning in Vegas, and I've heard you every day since."

He frowns. "What? You heard what?"

"You don't have time for this. Us."

His head cocks to the side an inch, but he's looking way too calm, and it has my walls going right back up brick by brick. "My season is over. I need my shoulder to heal and see what I can do, but from this point forward, my focus is on us."

"There is no us. Talking on the phone a few times a week isn't a relationship. We're living in what used to be, not where we are now." His head drops to the floor. "We didn't think this through. After all this time, marrying me on a whim? Mark, you came back thinking I was about to marry someone else. Would you have even done that if you hadn't somehow found out I was getting married?"

He huffs, running a hand through the longer hairs on the top of his head, and I can see that I hit an emotional nerve.

"I would have *never* left all those years ago. If I'd known you were going to ghost me, I would have stayed."

Jab. Jab. Jab. The truth is excruciatingly painful. *But you couldn't stay. I couldn't let you. It would have destroyed you.*

I swallow down the aching lump choking me. "You and I . . . everything is different, and we won't even know in all the ways because we're never together." He doesn't move, and I can't tell what he's thinking. "I'm going home, and you'll go on with your life wherever that ends up being."

He laughs. He freaking laughs. "Like hell you are. We can go back to Ohio, but we're going together to get your stuff. You're my wife, and you're carrying my child. We're going to be together. Forever."

My hands move to my hips. "And I don't get a say in this?"

He rubs his face, and his shoulders sag. "Lex, why are you doing this? You showed up in Vegas. You came to me. *We* got married. You were there and a willing participant. Everything that happened that night wasn't a mistake. It was . . . everything to me."

His confusion and torment are evident, and I'm responsible. My insides are being torn apart. A lot of me wants to go to him and pretend this will all turn out the way I've always dreamed. The other responsible part knows that life doesn't work that way, and that's only become even more apparent over the last twenty-four hours.

He steps closer again, sliding his hand against my cheek and leaving it there. "Please tell me what's going on inside your head. I used to be able to read you and know exactly what you were thinking when you get quiet. I can't do that anymore, and I hate it."

I step away, needing space. I lower myself to the edge of his bed, knowing I need to tell him something. I just don't know what that something is. I'm confused and lost in all of this.

"I need a few minutes to think. Everything is . . . " I don't even know. My eyes sting with frustration, but I blink it away.

His troubled, dark eyes meet mine, and he nods. "I'm going to kick everyone out. We both need a few minutes and then we're going to figure this out. Together. No more running, Lex. Not from me."

He waits for me to agree, and I nod. He leaves the room, closing the door behind him. Maybe to give me privacy or maybe so I can't escape. I want to. It'd be easier, but I know that I can't run away from this, and I can't run away from him.

My feet and brain are tired. I'm tired of running but always staying still. I've been running in place for the last eight years, trying to get this man out of my head and my heart. It's never worked.

I glance around his messy room. Clothes hang on the top of the bathroom door, and there's a pile on the floor. Two of his dresser drawers are half open, with clothes shoved inside. Empty glasses are on his nightstand, along with an iPad.

My vision blurs. He used to say that once he left the group home, he'd never keep a tidy room again. Even with tears cresting, my lips turn upward at the sight.

I dab the wetness away with the hem of his shirt, catching a whiff of whatever was blasted all over me. I go into his bathroom and turn the shower on. Then peel my clothes off to scrub myself clean.

When I step out, drying off, I remember my suitcase is still sitting by the front door. I move to his dresser, pull out one of his t-shirts, and slip it over my head. Unlike the one at home, this one smells like him and isn't full of holes.

I lie back on the bed and stare up at the ceiling. Everything is changing so fast. My brain is moving a million miles a minute, just as it had the morning I left him in Vegas.

I roll over and climb into his bed. While he breaks up his party, I need a nap. I've never been more tired in my life. If I have to be near him and keep a clear head, I need energy and strength.

I rest my head on his pillow and pull the covers over me. His bed is huge and soft and immediately warm. His scent envelops me. Mark the man. My eyes drift shut, thinking the only thing that would make it better is if he were in it with me.

Damn. I'm in so much trouble.

Chapter 19

MARK

I step out of my room and close the door behind me, needing just a freaking minute. I'm in shock and awe and . . . *Holy shit!!*

I have no idea what to do or think other than try to calm the hell down. I run my shaky hand through my hair and leave it there, trying to slow my racing mind.

I lean against the wall, taking in air, and all I see is Lex's stomach. The bulge where there used to be none. I push out a slow breath of complete astonished disbelief.

I need to get it together more than ever before. I need a plan and quick because there's no way in hell I'm losing them—the two most important things that have ever happened to me.

On a mission, I return to a quiet, clean kitchen. Shane and Sean are sitting on the couch like two vultures eyeing their prey. I take a seat across from them in a chair, my mind reeling with questions I have no answers to.

"Anything you want to tell us?" Shane's low grumble irritates my nerves, standing at attention and waiting for orders.

"Not today." My mouth doesn't know whether to grin like the Cheshire Cat or let out a long string of 'fucks.'

Two pairs of eyebrows raise in my direction, but I don't give a shit. The only thing I care about is figuring out how not to lose my wife and baby. *My baby.* My throat swells with a burning itch at the thought of the tiny life. The one Lex and I created.

I swallow it down quickly, remembering the wardens watching me.

"Anything we can do to help?" Sean's concerned tone is a punch to the gut.

I shake my head, hoping they can't see my elation and fear. It's a messed up duo, and I need the former to sack the shit out of the latter. "Not today. I need time with her."

They stare for some long moments as if I might throw them a bone, but I'm not budging. Sean stands and slaps my good shoulder while Shane eyes me with suspicion before they exit. My two brothers. They'll be the first to know I'm going to be a father, but not tonight.

Tonight, I need to go back in there and talk to Lex. I have to convince her that I'm so far in this I can't see straight without her, but I can't do that until my brain puts itself back together.

I slouch in the chair. *I'm going to be a dad—someone's father. There's a real live baby growing inside Lex's belly, and it's my child. My baby. I'm going to be a DAD!*

I stand, running my hand through my hair, wanting to find the nearest mountain and scream it at the top of my lungs. I want to post on social media. I want to wear one of those ridiculous shirts that says 'Rad Dad.'

I have so many questions, but right at this very moment, the only thing I need to do is convince my quiet-ass wife that she has to stay with me. I just have no flipping clue how to do that.

Lex is pushing me away. I don't know what happened back then or what's happening now, but I have to find out. I have to get this mildly mute woman I love to actually talk to me and tell me what in the hell is going on.

She didn't show up in Vegas on some kind of whim. She came because she wanted to. She married me for the same reason. She kept herself from me all those years ago, but I won't let her do that again. I don't care what I have to do. I'll fight.

I carry myself back to my room, ready to do whatever is necessary to get to the bottom of this. When I open the door and step inside, Lex is curled up in my bed, sound asleep.

I stare at her, all my anxious determination melting. *This.* This is all I've ever wanted, but now, she's here, and it's so much more than I could've ever imagined.

Under those covers is a tiny baby. Our baby. I quietly remove my jeans with one hand, then gently slip out of my shirt and replace my arm in the sling. I stack pillows and lie down, careful not to touch or disturb her or my shoulder.

Watching her sleep, my mind soars with possibility, but I try to contain it, knowing the woman next to me has a huge say in what happens next. I just need to make sure that whatever that is, I'm a part of it.

I feel quick movement next to me, and I jolt awake to a dark room and the outline of Lex sitting straight up next to me.

"Hey. You ok?" I carefully push up on my good arm, wincing at the burn radiating from my shoulder.

Her long hair brushes against my skin. "Yeah, I didn't know where I was for a minute."

She rubs her eyes and lays back down next to me, pulling the covers up, her face to the ceiling. Pain shoots through me, trying to get comfortable again. When I get there, I stare at the outline of her profile.

"I don't know what I'm doing." Her voice is achingly soft.

She's talking, so I'm keeping my big mouth shut to see what else she might offer.

"I came to tell you about the baby and . . . "

There's a long pause. Nothing but darkness, and it takes everything in me to wait. Waiting is not in my nature, but I need her to talk to me. Just when I think she's not going to say anything more, she lets out a long breath.

"I can't keep loving you from afar. It hurts too much. I'm not even sure if I'm just loving the memory or if there's love for the man you are now."

Her brutal honesty is a bullet to my chest that sends shrapnel soaring, but it's what I need. It's what we need if we even have a chance.

I think for a moment, knowing it's my turn now. "For the last eight years, football is all I've had. It had to be. I didn't have anything else. I know how unfair these past months have been. I've made promises and broken them. I'm sorry. I'm having trouble figuring out how to be both what you need and do my job."

She rolls on her side, her face inches from mine, and I want to grab it and beg her to stay with me. She tucks her arms between us, setting up a clear boundary. I've never hated her arms so much, but I'll tolerate them for now.

"This isn't just about me. I get that." Her voice remains soft, but there's an ache to it. "That might be the hardest part. I wish I could be pissed at you or hate you, but . . . in all the time we've been apart, you've built a life for yourself. This life. An amazing life. I don't know how I can fit into that. How *we* can fit into it."

Her admission about being scared comes flying back at me like a rogue missile. I need to know all the things she's afraid of, and I will blast those assholes to pieces. If my job and what it requires is one of them, then I know how to take that one out.

"I'll quit. I'll retire." I cross her clearly drawn line and push a strand of hair away from her eye. "This is the only thing that matters now. You and our baby. I haven't shown it or acted like it, but I suck at living without you."

"I think you've done just fine." Her voice is so soft, but I don't miss the slight quiver in it, making my own throat grow tight. "You can't quit."

"Like hell, I can't." I tip her chin up, wanting her to look at me. "I would've given it all up back then if I'd known—"

"Don't say things like that. This is everything I wanted for you."

"But I've been walking around this whole time with my heart missing."

She pulls away, creating more room between us. "Mark, we don't even know each other anymore. I don't know your life or what you're doing most of the time, and you don't know mine. We've changed. Everything about us has changed."

"We can fix that. We just have to give it a chance."

"How? You don't even know where you'll be playing next season, and when you do, what will that change? You'll still be living your life somewhere, and I'll be back home."

My skin is suddenly hot as a wave of panic rolls through me. I don't have the answers to any of her questions, and I won't make any more promises I can't keep.

"Lex, I can't lose you. Not again. I don't know how we'll make this work, but we will." I inhale, my throat stinging with heartache. "You have no idea how much I've wanted to be with you. I hate this. I want you in the stands at my games. I want you in my bed every night. I want to see your face and kiss your mouth and never have to be without any of that again."

There's nothing but silence, and my panic turns manic until I hear a sniff. I'm done with personal space and risk the pain of reaching for her.

"Mark, I'm so scared to screw this all up. I can't do that to this baby."

I tug her flush against me, holding her tight. She scoots closer, resting her head on my good shoulder. "It's going to be ok. I don't know how quite yet, but it will. I promise."

I lay in the dark, her body next to mine, searching for answers and coming up with none. The severe pressure in my chest rivals the joy of her small bump tucked safely up against me.

There's not even a choice in this. Only one thing can be, and that's for the three of us to be a family. I'm not sure how we do that or what that looks like, but I'll do whatever it takes for us to be together.

Chapter 20

LEX

I wake up, my cheek pressed against the soft white sheets filled with the masculine smell I've craved since our one night in Vegas. His warm, muscular body is pressed against mine, and his hand is splayed across my stomach. I smile despite all the remaining unanswered questions that drift around us.

I lay still, needing to memorize the feel of every single inch of his body, but before I can, his fingers move, and his hand is gone. He groans as he stretches. Without the distraction of his warmth, the burning ache of hunger roars through me.

I roll on my back to peek at him, and I'm met with that grin. The one that makes my insides quiver and want to pull the sheet over my head and hide.

"What?" I ask, his face way too handsome and smug.

"Now, I know what it's actually like to sleep with you." I shove him gently, and he grabs my wrist, holding it to his chest. "I like it. Not that I don't like *not* sleeping with you."

I hide my face in the pillow, and he laughs.

"It's all going to be ok," he whispers, kissing my temple.

When he says it, it seems possible.

My stomach rumbles, and my hunger drowns everything else. "Mark," I whisper. "I need food."

He pulls away. "Shit. When was the last time you ate?" He sits up as if it's an emergency, holding his arm close.

"I don't know, but this baby might be eating my insides."

He climbs out of bed, and I can't stop my eyes from taking in the full view. Mark stands only in his boxer briefs, tugging on gym shorts one-handed, his other arm slung across his body. His lean muscles bend and contract with his movement.

A mischievous smirk takes over his mouth when he catches me, and I promise he flexes his abs, that dark writing on his ribs causing my heart to squeeze tight.

One black eyebrow hitches upward. "Like what you see?"

I throw a pillow at him and miss. "Not even a little, you punk."

He steps closer, leaning down so close I can see every hue of brown that makes up his dark eyes. His lips hover above mine, and I. Can't. Move. His eyes trace over my face, and it would be so easy to close the inch between us. The weight of years of longing rests on me, but the magnitude of everything we stand to lose holds me back.

His eyes flick to my lips, and the intense heat I see causes a similar wave to roll up my spine.

"Liar." That cocky grin returns, and he grabs my hand, pulling me up with him. "Come on. I'm making you breakfast so we can feed our baby."

I tug him to a stop. "*You're* making me breakfast?"

He turns to face me, slipping his arm around me and pulling me against him. My hands slide around his back, and his skin is warm and smooth. *Damn him and his playfulness.* "Baby, one of the things that's changed in the time we've been apart is I've become an excellent cook."

I raise an eyebrow. "Really?"

He smiles. "It's just one of the many talents I've discovered that I'm looking forward to sharing with you, but given my current one-armed state, I'll let you help."

I roll my eyes. "Good to see your confidence has remained intact."

He laughs and takes my hand, linking our fingers as if he's afraid I'll disappear on our short journey to the kitchen, but I like it . . . a little too much.

In the kitchen, Mark pulls out a toaster and then opens and closes cupboards, pulling out pans and plates while I watch.

He starts singing, and I smile, taking him in. This Mark is exactly the same, but can clearly work a kitchen, even with an arm tied down. He catches me watching and winks. My empty stomach leaps and twirls.

This guy. *Ugh. Somebody help me.*

We work side-by-side, him stirring the eggs and me doing all the non-cooking duties. In minutes, I have a plate with toast, eggs, and a glass of orange juice.

I take a bite, and a moan escapes my lips.

"That good, huh?" He smiles, slipping onto a stool beside me at the enormous marble-topped island separating the kitchen from the living room.

I bump his good shoulder with mine. "So good, or I'm that hungry."

He rolls his eyes, and we eat in silence while I shovel every last bite into my mouth. As I slow my binge, I take a moment to check out his space, including a sliding glass wall leading to a pool, hot tub, and small yard. The sun and blue sky filter in as the leaves on the palm tree sway gently in the breeze. All of it reminds me of how far I am from home.

Mark finally breaks the silence, and his tone is less playful than it was minutes ago.

"How long can you stay?" His question is filled with hesitancy, and we're back to reality.

"My flight is this afternoon." I knew this would be hard, but the words are like glass in my throat.

"Cancel it."

I meet his serious gaze. "Mark, I can't. I have to get back to work while I can, and . . . I have to tell Grandpa and my mom about you and the baby. My first doctor's appointment is next week."

Thoughts of Grandpa and Slade's conversation cause my full stomach to squeeze tight, and I set my fork down.

He turns, his knees bumping into me, straddling my stool. "What do you mean, while you can?"

I run my finger down the glass, contemplating whether I want to get into this with him. If I want trust in whatever kind of relationship we have, then I have to be open and honest.

"At some point, I won't be able to lift and maneuver around the cars. Grandpa may not let me do anything but change fluids and hand back keys once he finds out. Plus . . . " I swallow, resting back in my seat, making room for the hurt and disappointment to expand. "He's selling the shop to Slade." Saying it out loud feels like getting the wind knocked out of me, and my throat constricts.

"What?!" We've been apart a long time, but Mark knows how important that place is to me. "Your grandpa is selling the shop? Lex . . . What the hell?"

I twist my glass, trying to keep the deep-searing burn of it locked up tight. "Yeah, well, at least I know Slade will keep me on, and after the baby is born, I'll have a job."

He's quiet, and I know he's thinking.

"Lex, I know you wanted to run that shop and how much you love working on cars. I also know you are hell-bent on being self-sufficient, but I make millions of dollars. Job or no job, you and our baby will never have to worry."

I turn toward him, slipping my legs between his. "That's just it. I don't want that. I don't want to be the woman who got knocked up and expects you to support me. My mom—"

He cuts me off, his tone tense, and I know he remembers. "Nothing about this is the same, and it won't ever be."

I force my eyes to his. "This is important to me. I have to be able to support or at least contribute enough."

He rests his hand on my bare thigh, his thumb tracking back and forth. "I know. Can you stay for a few days? I'll get through my first therapy appointments, check in with my agent, and then I'll go back with you. Maybe only for a day or two, but I want to be there when you tell your grandpa."

"Really? You want to go back with me?"

A sweet smile pulls at his lips. "Yes. Lex, I meant what I said last night. I'm going to give this everything I've got. You and our baby are all that matters, and I'm not missing your doctor's appointment."

I don't even try to prevent the smile that creeps across my face. "Ok. I'll have to let Grandpa know I won't be in."

"Ok, you'll stay, and I can go back with you?"

I nod, and he sighs in relief, running his hand through his hair.

I gather our plates, taking them to the sink to rinse them as he grabs the pan. He places it in the sink, but instead of moving away, he slips his arm around me, his hand resting on our growing baby.

He closes around me, his lips pressing against my neck. "Thank you for staying."

The sincerity in his voice almost brings tears to my eyes.

"Thank you for wanting to go back with me."

"I don't want to be anywhere you're not. I mean it. I want to know you again like I used to. I want to be together."

I twist in his arms, turning to face him. "Me, too."

He rests his chin on the top of my head, his hand spreading over my lower back. "Can you please never wear anything else?"

I laugh, standing pressed against him as his hand slides to my butt, dressed in only his shirt. If only he knew of all the nights I slept in one similar, holding on to the only piece of him I had left.

His lips find my forehead, and he leaves them there, holding me tighter. "I'm terrified I'm going to screw this up." His admission is so achingly soft the words bleed through me.

Careful of his arm, I slide my arms up his back and rest my head against his chest, listening to the steady beat of his heart. "I feel like we've done everything backward. I think we need to take things slow and promise that no matter what, this baby comes first."

"I promise, but it's not just the baby. You come first, too."

I hold him tighter. "I don't want to get in the way of everything you've worked for."

Mark pulls back, causing me to look up at him. His dark eyes filled with intense longing. My no-touching rule has gone out the window, but I will myself to stay strong.

"I've waited for this for so long, and now you're carrying my baby. Our baby. There isn't anything more important than that." His thumb finds the side of my small stomach and runs up and down. "We can take this as slow as you want. I just want us to do it together."

I push up on my toes, holding on to his waist. That's the only thing I want, but I'm scared reality has different plans.

Mark's hand slides up to my neck, and he presses kisses down the side of my face to my jaw.

Damn him and his soft lips and hard muscles. Every centimeter of my body wants to go with it, but my brain knows better. We may be married, but we have a long way to go in our renewed relationship.

My back presses into the counter, and I allow myself a few more seconds to savor the feel of his mouth moving over my skin. Some kind of manly groan comes from his throat, and his hand slips under the hem of my shirt as he trails kisses back up my neck, biting and teasing.

His lips whisper against my skin. "You smell exactly the same. I've missed it every day."

I suck in oxygen and try to come to my senses as his fingers grip my hip. "This doesn't feel like slow." It comes out way breathier than I want it to.

He halts his pursuit, a grin pressing against my neck. "I might've lied. This could be a problem. I like you way too much, and I've missed you even more." His warm hand glides over my body and spreads across my spine. I cling to him as he hugs me, keeping him close, his head tucked into my neck. "My love language is physical touch, and your skin is my weakness. If you're within reach, baby, I can't be expected to keep my hands to myself."

Oh, goodnight. I melt into him further, unsure if I even care anymore about what the consequences might be.

He pulls away, leaving me thirsting for more. I hate him and his smooth ways. I inhale, trying to slow my racing heart.

"I have PT today, but I've been waiting for a real date for pretty much forever. Go to dinner with me tonight."

What. The. Hell? I've always known Mark is a tease, but I might actually kill him. I frown, trying desperately not to let him see the effect he has on me, but I suck at it, and it's likely more of a glare. "If someone sees, won't that be a problem?"

He smirks, and I want to kiss it right off his face. "Nope. I'm done with that shit. Can I take a pic of you right now in my shirt and blast it everywhere to let the world know you're my wife and we're having a baby? I want everyone to know exactly what we've been up to." My cheeks fill with fire, which only makes his lips turn up further. His hand slides against my face, still grinning. "Baby, there's nothing to be shy about."

I'm not sure he's right about that.

I swallow, shoving him just a little, and he laughs. I push my lips to the side, thinking about what that would mean. "I don't know if I'm ready for that. We at least need to tell Grandpa and my mom first."

His face softens and turns more serious. "Yeah. I need to talk to Shane and Sean. We'll tell them all first, but it will change things for you." He watches me. "People are going to want to know who you are. I need to be sure you're safe."

I lean into him again and rest my head on his good shoulder. I'm still trying to imagine what it will be like for the whole world to know I'm Mark Sandberg's wife. I can't. I never thought it would happen, and I'm still getting used to the idea.

"So, will you go to dinner with me? We can start there. Just dinner."

The way he says 'just dinner' as if it's a formal agreement has me biting my lip. I don't buy his attempt at keeping things cool for one second, and by the sly smirk on his face, he doesn't either.

"I know you're a big hot shot now, but do we have to go somewhere fancy?"

He laughs and pulls my head up, cradling my face with his hand. "How about somewhere quiet with a basketball game and whatever food sounds good to you?"

I smile. "Ok."

SLADE: Where r u?
SLADE: We need to talk.
SLADE: U r pissing me off.

Chapter 21

MARK

SEAN: Uh . . . Hello. Are you going to give us something?
SHANE: Bro? Seriously, something, or I'm coming over and find out what the hell is going on.
SHANE: Mark, if you're having one of your diva meltdowns, just tell us.
SEAN: We'll give you 24 more hours to sulk, and then I'm dragging your ass out of that house.
SEAN: Unless you want to tell us something about why Alex showed up at your house.
SHANE: 19 more hours, asshole.
SEAN: 18 and a half.

> ME: Listen, dickheads, I'm good. Keep your panties on. I need a few days.
> ME: I love you.

SHANE: What have you done?

I tug my hat lower and slide my fingers through hers.

I really hope I don't regret this.

We step into a small brewery with an industrial vibe and lead her to an open table in the back corner. I pull out a metal stool for Lex, then move the other closer to her, keeping my back to the room.

The place isn't crowded, but most of the tables and seats at the bar are occupied. A game plays on the large mounted screens, but the only thing I'm interested in is sitting across from me.

I watch Lex's fingers move to her silver stud and twist, round and round. Twist. Rest. Twist. Rest. Twist. Her blonde hair falls in waves over her gray T-shirt as she surveys the small space.

"What's wrong?" Her blue eyes meet mine, but she's somewhere far away. She doesn't say anything, but her chest rises with a deep breath. "Whatever it is, tell me."

She glances around the space again before her eyes dart back to mine. "I don't know if I'm ready for this."

My heart stutters, but I will it to stay calm. "Ready for what?"

"I don't know how to do this."

"Do what?"

Both slender shoulders rise and fall. "Be normal with you . . . like this. What if someone recognizes you?"

I lean back in my seat as relief kicks my heart back into rhythm. I turn, glancing around the room and the bar area where everyone is minding their own business.

I didn't think about how intimidating this might be to her and how dealing with my lifestyle will take some getting used to.

"Do you want to go?"

She stares at me, pulling her bottom lip between her teeth, and then shakes her head.

I lean closer to her, tipping her chin toward me. "It's just you and me. My life is big sometimes, but not tonight." I grab menus from the napkin holder, handing her one.

She ignores the menu; her body is still rigid and tense. I grab her hand underneath the table. "Lex, if anyone recognizes me, I'll deal with it."

She nods, searching the room again like she's waiting for someone to pop out, then focuses on her lap. I watch her, wondering what's going on.

"So, you don't care if people see us together?"

"The season is over. When we're ready, we'll let the whole world know. It will change things, and I want to be sure you're comfortable with that. It's too late to change my profession, and unfortunately, that involves people being all up in my business."

"I'm not very good at being social, and I still can't . . . " Her eyes flick to the menu in front of her and then back to me.

She shrinks before my eyes, and I know exactly what's going on. I saw her cower in high school when other kids teased and mimicked her when she was forced to read out loud. They laughed and whispered as they passed her desk while she tried to complete a test. But she fought, barely scraping by and trying so hard not to let it show or let anyone see her struggle. I see the effects of the trauma remain.

"Lex." Her gaze stays glued to the table, and I wait. "Lex, look at me." It takes a second, but she finally drags her eyes to mine, shame written all over her face. "You have nothing to worry about. You're the smartest, most capable person I know. The rest of us had it easy, but you figured out how to survive and learn despite the challenge. Baby, you're incredible. Anyone worth a shit will see that." Her head falls to the side, still full of doubt. "Besides, I'm really good at talking. I'll say enough for the both of us."

That earns me the slightest smile, and she reaches for my hand resting on the table and slipping her palm beneath mine. "I need to call Grandpa. I left after hearing him and Slade talking. Not my most mature move. I didn't tell him where I was going. I'm still so . . . "

She swallows, her eyes glistening. I'd like to have a chat with Cal.

"I thought the shop would be mine. I guess I was stupid to think that, but I still can't . . . " She pauses, and I know it's coming. The key to the box where she keeps everything she thinks about herself.

Her chin finally tips up, but barely enough to meet my gaze. "I can't do all the things it would require. At least not easily, and accuracy and efficiency are important."

I hate that she believes that to be true. "Lex, it wasn't stupid. I bet your grandpa would even tell you that."

Her head drops again. "Maybe. Probably not when he finds out I'm pregnant." Her hand moves to her stomach.

I can't help but smile. "One way or another, you're still going to get to do what you love. That I can promise." She holds back a weak smile while I make it my mission to see that she gets to. "Speaking of the little surprise nugget, I want to tell Shane and Sean about us and the squirt."

One blonde eyebrow raises. "Squirt?"

"Yep. Baby Sandberg. Then I'll need to talk to my agent, but we get to decide when and how this news spreads, ok?" Her eyes roam my face as she studies me. "What?"

One side of her mouth curls up slightly. "Nothing. You're like this hot elite baller but also this businessman calling the shots."

I rest back on my stool, my mouth creeping into a fat-ass grin. "You think I'm hot?"

She rolls her eyes as her cheeks turn pink, and I love that I still make that happen. I tug her wrist to my lips, and she's forced to lean closer as a ruckus breaks out behind us.

A band of guys, loud and clearly loaded, bound through the doors and up to the bar. A quick glance tells me these guys are here to have fun, but not a group I want to get caught up in for a meet and greet.

I turn back to Lex, her eyes set on the frat boys. "Let's get out of here, go by the store, and eat at home."

She hides a smile, telling me she likes the idea. I grab her hand, pull my hat low, and make for the door. Just as I'm about to pass the large group, two more guys push through the glass door and almost step right into me. They stop in their tracks.

"Hey, aren't you . . . "

I pull Lex closer, trying to step around them, but there's no room.

"We heard you were training here during the offseason."

I meet the guy's eyes, making it clear I'm not interested in chatting. In normal circumstances, I'd stop for a second, take a few pictures, and move on, but not tonight. Lex's hand wraps around my forearm.

"Thanks, man. We were just leaving. Hope you guys have a good night."

"How's the shoulder? We're all waiting to see who takes you on next season." A few more chime in, and Lex presses into me. I slip my arm around her, tucking her into my side.

I give a friendly smile, hoping it will make him move aside. "It's healing and feeling good," I say as my arm rests in its sling.

"Yo, it's Mark Sandberg."

Fuck. This is not how I wanted tonight to go. The entire band of brothers turns our way, all yelling at the same time, throwing out questions, and pulling out phones. We're stuck right in the middle.

I hold up my hand. "Hey, guys. We need to get going. I appreciate you and your support. Hope you have fun."

I move to step around the two guys again, and they reek of liquor. They move to the side, but not enough that I don't hear the comment.

"Boys, Sandberg's got himself a new flavor of the week. Young and fresh."

Lex's hands loosen their hold on me, and they might as well have reached in and grabbed hold of my insides instead. Past decisions will always come back to haunt you. Even though mine aren't as they seem, it doesn't make any difference when they pierce the one I'd never want to hurt.

I firm up my grip on her hand but turn to address the group, not knowing who decided to be an asshole. "There's only ever been one." I press my hand into her back, moving her forward through the small space to the door. "Don't believe everything you read, guys."

We step into the evening air, and I follow Lex to the car. Her downcast face and quick steps tell me what they said got to her. We climb in, but I sit there trying to figure out exactly what to say, but nothing comes.

Lex starts the car as I ask Suri for directions to the nearest grocery store, also needing her to provide insight on how to handle this. It's the shame I carry. I made years of bad decisions while trying to forget the only one I've ever wanted. Payment for my dumb ass behavior was just collected, and the currency was a kick in the gut of the one I love.

While Lex sits next to me, staring out the window, I want to punch myself in the face. I know it wasn't anything like how it appeared, but the media knows how to sell stories, and at that time, I didn't care.

The challenge is getting Lex to see that appearance isn't even close to reality when the only thing I have to offer is my word.

If I were captured by international spies and they needed a torture device to get me to talk, all they'd have to do is sit Lex in front of me and have her give me sad silence. I'd carve my own heart out with a spoon and serve it to them on a platter so I didn't have to suffer the agony for another second.

We left the brewery and ran through the grocery store, going our separate ways so she could grab a few items she needed while I gathered food for dinner. The whole time, I was met with calm and quiet, and my skin shrunk two sizes.

Now, she's in my room checking in with her grandpa, and if she tells him where she is, I wonder if he'll give her even more reason to be hurt. Fear is clawing at my every nerve, waiting to see her roll out with her suitcase in tow and give me the big 'have a nice life.'

I pull the chicken off the grill and step inside, leaving the large glass slider open to let the cool evening breeze in. I place the chicken on our plates of rice and salad, and Lex steps into the kitchen, looking just as despondent as she had when we got home. Her hair is damp, and she has on an old T-shirt that stabs me in the chest, seeing it's not mine.

She tugs at her ear. "Sorry, I took a shower. I couldn't stand those pants one more second." Her hand runs over her stomach but quickly falls away.

I stare at her. *Say something, you idiot.* "Did you talk to your grandpa?"

She bites her lip. "I panicked. I'm not sure what I want to say yet or how I feel and I don't want to get into where I am. I was a coward and voice-messaged him to let him know I'd be home in a few days. The guys are probably cussing me sideways for leaving them high and dry."

"It's understandable, given what you learned." Her eyes drop to her bare feet, but she doesn't say anything. I lift my plate. "Can you grab yours?" I gesture to the other plate. "I thought we'd eat outside."

She watches me for a moment before following me. I cross the patio, passing the pool to the small rectangle of turf. I sit, setting my plate in front of me, but Lex stops ten feet away, staring.

I can't read the look on her face, and my heart picks up pace again. "I thought . . . ." *Shit, maybe this was a terrible idea.* I inhale, needing my body to settle down and find some shard of confidence that has left me high and dry for being such a complete dumbass. "I thought we could eat like we used to."

Her head falls to the side while her light blue eyes search my face as if she's trying to dissect my thoughts. Then, after a moment, she brings her plate and takes a seat next to me, crossing her legs.

We take the first few bites in silence as the sun sets behind the neighboring houses, casting a golden glow over the backyard and pool. The air chills, and I hand her a blanket that she spreads over her lap.

I let the silence linger, trying to work up the courage to address my poor past choices, but it was how I survived.

"The food is really good. Thank you," she says quietly.

I watch her take another bite, and the tension that's gripped my body relaxes a little. "Yeah? It wasn't what I had in mind, but I guess it's not bad."

She side-eyes me, pushing some rice around her plate with her fork. "I like this better. This reminds me of hanging out with you on the field after everyone else went home. Those nights are my favorite memories."

My mind flashes back to our high school football field, where we lay on a blanket in the dark, stared up at the sky, and shared secrets. That's where I fell in love with Lex, where she let me see her soul, and I gave her mine.

"Mine, too. Knowing I'd get to make out with you got me through each game."

She rolls her eyes and backhands my stomach. She brushes my sling, and I rub at it like she hurt me.

Her eyes grow wide. "I'm sorry. Are you ok?" I grin, hoping I'm getting her back. "You jerk. I thought I hurt you."

I move our plates to the side and pull her closer to me, making sure she's covered with the blanket. I slide my arm around her, and she rests her head on my shoulder as we watch the sky darken, just like we used to. I stare into the dusk, trying to find the words to express what I need her to know.

"Lex, those nights, those memories are what got me through all these years. They were all I had left of you. Just visions, but as time passed, they were slipping away. I started to wonder if they were even real or . . . if I'd made it all up. I missed you so much." My throat tingles, and I clear it.

Her hand slides over my stomach, and she pinches my shirt between her fingers.

"When you didn't call and then changed your number, I couldn't understand. I was angry and hurt, and for a long time, I tried to figure out what happened. But I couldn't. I didn't understand how I could've been so wrong."

"Mark—"

She starts, but I cut her off, needing to get this out while I can. "I did stupid things trying to get you out of my head. I convinced myself that if I kept pushing forward, trying to move on, I'd forget you. I slept around in college and drank myself silly but after a while . . . It didn't work, so I gave everything I had to football. Once I made the draft, a whole new world opened up to me. Women started throwing themselves at me everywhere I turned."

Her hand releases my shirt, but she leaves it there, limp on my stomach.

"So, I went out, trying to find someone to make me forget. I kept trying and trying, wanting someone, anyone, to erase how you felt in my arms, how you smelled, laughed . . . How safe I felt to be me when I was with you."

She must feel my heart pounding and rests her hand over it.

"Lex, what that guy said tonight, it wasn't like that. I'm not proud of some of the things I've done, and I did some stupid shit, hurt a lot of feelings, but it wasn't what it looked like. I promise."

"Mark, you don't have to explain anything to me. I don't deserve it."

I pull away, needing to see her. The calm gray dusk falls around us, but I can make out her grief and . . . something else unfamiliar.

"I want you to know. To understand. I hate that my actions have some dick saying things like that about you." I hold her face, forcing her to look at me. "I went out with a lot of women. A lot of different women, but that's it. We went out. I wasn't taking them home. I need you to know that. I couldn't. Every time I even thought about it, I knew I'd only be thinking about you."

Warm dampness seeps under my thumb, and I brush her tears away. "I'm sorry I hurt you. I didn't know—"

"Mark, stop." She drops her head. "Please. Stop."

My dinner stirs in my stomach, and a burn crawls through my chest as it tightens. "Lex, I'm sorry—"

She pushes away from me. "Mark, stop! I don't care what that guy said."

My breath catches in my throat, and I can't speak. I don't know what is happening, and I have to swallow hard to keep my dinner down, the cold spike of panic thrusting it upward.

Her head hangs as she swipes tears away. "Don't. Stop apologizing. I can't—"

"Lex, I know what that guy said tonight hurt you." I breathe, trying to steady myself.

She sniffs, her head hanging low. "It killed something inside me every time I saw or thought about you with someone else, but I deserved it." She wipes her nose on her wrist. "It's my fault. I . . . I wanted to go with you, and I wanted you to stay, but you couldn't. You had to go, and I had to . . . I wanted everything for you. I couldn't let anything hold you back. I wanted you to be happy and achieve everything I knew you could."

Her sad, shiny eyes meet mine in the dark. "I made a choice, and I couldn't take it back. I thought you were happy. You looked so happy. I forced myself to be fine. I pretended to be someone else so it wouldn't hurt so bad. I didn't want to be me . . . with anyone else."

A fist slams into my throat, and I'm done with the distance between us. I pull her to me, wrapping my arm around her shoulders to hold her close. "I'm so angry with myself that I didn't come back." My lips brush against her temple.

"I would've only held you back. You would've never left again."

"I wouldn't have," I whisper, unable to breathe through the ache ricocheting through my chest.

"I know." Her lip quivers. "That's why you had to go, and I had to be sure you wouldn't come back. I wouldn't let—"

I press my lips to her salty cheek, wanting her mouth. I know if I start, I won't stop, so damn scared she's going to disappear again.

We stay like that, linked together for a long time, eventually lying together, staring at the sky. Lex pulls the blanket up and rests her head on my chest.

Everything seems precarious as if I'm walking a tightrope. One wrong move, and when I turn, she'll have fallen away. Tonight, though, feels like a monumental moment in finding each other again and gaining back some of what we lost. The trust and connection we once had. The devotion. I want it all.

I speak softly into the dark night, taking a risk and knowing the answer determines the stability of our new foundation. "Do you trust me?"

Her body stiffens slightly, and I know my question caught her off guard. "Can I?" Her question is simple yet profound.

"Yes, with everything. I may screw up a lot of things, but I won't mess that up. I promise."

She snuggles into my chest, and her voice is so soft I almost don't hear her. "I know."

My entire body warms at her faith in me. There was a time when I deserved it. That time isn't now, but I'll do anything to earn it back, which begins with never making her question it.

"Mark." She says my name softly, tentatively.

"Hmmm."

"I know I lost yours when I disappeared." She links her fingers through mine and pulls them into her chest. "I'm not going anywhere this time. I won't ever leave like that again. I promise."

I inhale a long, deep breath and let it out, needing those words probably more than any other. I press my lips to her forehead. "Good. I'm not about to let you go. Ever." She tips her chin up and places a gentle kiss on my neck. Heat radiates through my body, but I push it aside for tonight. Lying here with her is all I want.

"Lex, I'm a little worried about your grandpa kicking my ass."

She laughs, and it's the cure for my weary soul. "You should be more worried about not signing his posters that night you showed up. I haven't heard the end of it."

"What?" I laugh. "You told him I was there?"

"Yeah, I was kind of a mess, but he was worried about his posters."

"I'll make sure I sign them this time. Maybe even throw in a football if he doesn't kill me for making him a great-grandpa."

Lex reaches up to push my hair out of my eyes, which is way past needing to be cut. "Thank you for going back with me."

"I want to do all of this with you."

She pulls her bottom lip between her teeth, making me want to kiss her, but I can tell she's thinking. We agreed to take things slow, and there's nothing slow about what's going through my head at the moment.

"What happens then?" she asks.

"Babe, I don't know." I stare at the sky, hoping it will give us answers. She rests her head next to mine, her hand flat on my chest.

"One step at a time. Your grandpa might chop my balls off and leave me to bleed to death. Then we won't have anything left to discuss."

She buries her face in my neck, suppressing her laugh. "Well, you might be right."

Chapter 22

LEX

I turn the key in the ignition, and my truck rumbles to life. I yawn, buckling my seat belt. I huddle close to the steering wheel, bracing myself from the cold. The winter sky is black, and I already miss the warm, dry air we left behind.

"If it weren't yours, I wouldn't believe this old girl still runs."

I turn and smile at Mark. "I told you she's got good bones."

"Babe, that was, what, ten years ago?"

I grin, surveying my restored F-150. Her crisp black lines are everything my teenage heart longed for, and the woman in me still loves. "I'm good at what I do."

I throw cockiness back at him, and a smoldering, sly smile spreads wide across his too handsome face. After these past few days with him, playing it cool is becoming increasingly difficult.

He pulls my hand to his lips and kisses the back of it. "That you are."

"I'd restore trucks every day if I could." His eyes stay locked on mine in deep thought, and I have to look away, or I might do something in the airport parking lot that I'm pretty sure isn't allowed. "You ready?" I ask, linking my fingers with his as he continues to study my face.

He tries to smile, but I see through it. "As I'll ever be."

His unusual nerves make me smile. I lean over to press my lips to the edge of his jaw, purposefully avoiding his lips.

I reign in my hormones with some kind of superhuman pregnancy strength and put the truck in drive. I'm not sure I've ever seen Mark nervous, but his quietness makes me wonder. I'm not worried about telling Grandpa. Mark shouldn't be, either. The old man loves him. In high school, Mark practically lived at our house when he wasn't at practice or making curfew at the group home.

It's sharing the news with my mom and the guys at the shop that will be . . . interesting. Then there's the little thing of talking to Grandpa about Slade buying him out, which reawakens a deep ache every time I think about it. That's the conversation I'm not sure I'm ready to have.

I glance at Mark, and my breath catches in my throat at the reality of him being here, next to me. No longer the boy I fell in love with, but a man who I'm beginning to see is so much the same inside, but with a confident, sexy swagger that comes from growing completely comfortable with himself.

These past few days, waking up next to him makes this feel real again, and I don't want it to end.

Three nights ago, when we lay in his backyard sharing painful truths, it was as if we were finally coming home to one another. Like the old us was meeting the new us, and I don't want to lose that progress or get lost in the separation we'll face again when he has to leave.

Mark told me the carousel of women wasn't as it appeared, and I believe him. He said he wanted to forget, and I understand that, too. Hadn't that been what I'd tried to do with Seth? And no matter how hard I tried, Mark was always there, blocking my heart from ever being given to another.

I can't blame him for any of it, even if it had been what it seemed. It hurt like hell seeing him with other women, but I was the one who didn't show up. I was the one who stayed away and made him believe something that wasn't true.

I did it to give him a chance. To save him from being dragged down and never having the life he deserved. But as I lay there with him, learning the pain I caused, which I could see extended beyond what he admitted, I wondered if I did the right thing.

I tried that night to tell him. All of it, but Slade's stupid, growly voice kept reminding me that the past belongs right where it is. I weighed the truth, unable to force it out, and despite how much Slade hurt me, maybe he's right. What good would it do?

Telling Mark the truth means hurting him all over again, and I'm not sure I'm willing to do further damage. It's over now, and he and I are trying to move forward.

I squeeze his hand, needing to remind myself that the present is what matters. He squeezes mine back, that slick smile causing a warm sensation in my core that sends pulses to the rest of my body.

Fifteen minutes later, I pull into the driveway of the simple, white-sided, two-story home. My home. The small front porch, bare shrubs, and dead grass are all the same, just as I left them, but everything else in my life is totally different.

Parking my truck right next to Grandpa's, I turn to Mark. "You ok?"

He surveys the house. "I feel like I'm sixteen again, heading in to tell your Grandpa I got you pregnant." I smile, and he catches me. "What?"

"You're cute when you're nervous." I unbuckle and scoot closer to him.

"Baby, I'm not nervous. It's the best news of my entire life." He slips his hand behind my neck, pulling me close and resting his forehead against mine. "Buckle up, sweetheart. After this, we're telling the whole world."

My stomach jumps into a rolling somersault. "You're making this 'taking things slow' stuff really difficult."

That small, sly grin returns, and this man knows exactly what he's doing. "That was your idea, not mine. Slow isn't really in my vocabulary." His lips are an inch from mine, his breath whooshing across them as his eyes dare me.

My entire body hums with need. "Huh, I never noticed." It comes out as a pathetic whisper, and I might see the beginning of a smug smirk, but it's gone too fast as he pulls away and opens the door.

He doesn't have any idea what is going on inside me with all these hormones, and right now, I might kill him. I sit for a second, letting those bad boys slither back into place while he casually climbs out. I help him grab our suitcases, but if his shoulder wasn't still a bit fragile, I'd punch him.

It's possible I stomp to the back door, and he follows but stops, taking a deep breath as I unlock it. *He's not nervous, my ass.* I might not feel so bad if Grandpa wants to rough him up a little.

Inside, I hear the rumble of the TV, and I have no doubt Grandpa's eating fast food and watching the news. Mark pulls our bags inside, and the old man hollers.

"Either you're finally home, or whoever is robbing me is a real dumbass thinking there's something of value in here."

I smile and head for the living room, ready to face the man I've missed these past few days, even though the massive bruise on my heart remains.

I round the corner to the small room with a couch, and Grandpa's recliner shoved into the corner. The brick fireplace sits unlit, but the TV flickers as Grandpa takes a bite of a double burger.

"You shouldn't be eating that," I say as he wipes his mouth.

"I'm too old to care. It tastes good, and my chef left without notice. If this pushes my arteries into overdrive, that's your damn fault."

I let my head fall to the side, happy to see we're falling right back into our rhythm even though I haven't handled things in the best manner. "I'm sorry I just left. I was hurt, and . . . there was something I had to do."

"So, you said in your message. Anyone ever told you your verbal skills are lacking?" I bite my lip, knowing my quiet nature irritates the hell out of Mark, but I also know these two men, my favorite ones, love it.

He sets down what I have no doubt is a milkshake and rests back in his chair. Anyone who thinks only women eat their feelings is a fool. Rather than cake and ice cream, these jokers mop up their tears with beer and grease.

He raises a gray, bushy eyebrow that needs a lawn mower taken to it as he casually shuffles his fries around in the carton. "Want to talk about it?"

I find my earring and give it a couple of twists to calm the swirl of emotion flowing through me. "Actually, I need to tell you something." This man is not soft by any stretch of the imagination, but as his gray-blue eyes find mine, I see a tentativeness there that's as rare as a Ford GT. "But—"

Mark finally rounds the corner and steps beside me, sliding his recently freed arm carefully around me. His large hand stops to rest low on my hip but mostly on my butt. Him and all his touchy-feely tendencies. I might as well light myself on fire.

Grandpa's eyebrows shoot higher. He doesn't say a word, and I know the stubborn old goat is going to make me say it.

"*We* have something to tell you," Mark says, evidently having ditched his nerves in the kitchen. He grins like he just won the Super Bowl.

Damn him and that smile and his hands and every last stitch of manly self-assuredness.

Grandpa rests back in his chair, eyeing us as my pores prickle with sweat. Are nerves transmitted through contact? I inhale slowly.

"When I played in Vegas, Lex showed up, and I asked her to marry me." Mark just throws it out there like it's no big deal or surprise.

I watch Grandpa's face, and the man should've joined the CIA because he doesn't even flinch. I'm not sure he's even breathing.

Mark continues, unfazed. "She said yes, or actually ok, and I wasn't about to let her leave without making her mine forever."

Mark's fingers stretch to my hip, pulling me into him while I wait, watching. The only sound in the room is some news anchor droning on about gas prices.

Eventually, one rough hand reaches up and scratches at his day-old whiskers as his eyes move to mine. "You're married . . . to this one?" He points at Mark.

I bite my lip and nod. "Also," I say softly, needing to get it out. "I'm pregnant."

The news suddenly flips to a commercial, and the room vibrates from the increase in volume. Grandpa's blue-gray eyes zero in on Mark and stay there, and his body presses closer to mine as if maybe his carefree attitude bolts. *Ha.*

The silence would be deafening, but the commercial blares on instead.

Eventually, Grandpa leans forward in his chair. "You got my granddaughter pregnant?" he asks Mark like we're sixteen again, and my insides wiggle just a little at his tone.

Mark's arm pulls me even tighter, my shoulder pressing into his chest. "Yes, but I was sure to marry her first." His voice is clear and confident, and I press into him this time, wanting to wrap him up and also kiss him like never before.

"The two of you are married and having a baby." Grandpa's finger wags between us.

I stare at him, wondering what in the hell is going on. I know he didn't go deaf, but then again, the blaring TV filters through, making me question.

"Grandpa," I say, getting his attention. "Mark and I are married. I've been with him these past few days in Phoenix, and we're having a baby." The words I'd never in a million years thought I'd say roll right off my tongue.

"Well, hot damn!" Grandpa jumps up like a spry fox. "Congratulations, boy. Hell, it took you long enough to get your ass back here." He lunges forward and wraps Mark in a bear hug while I stand speechless. "I'm going to be a great-grandpa. How about that?" He claps Mark on the back, and I wonder if he remembers I have a role in this.

Grandpa beams at me and pulls me in for a hug with what might be tears in his eyes. Mark stands to the side, grinning like he just stole the last cookie from the cookie jar. I knew Grandpa wouldn't be mad or disappointed, but I didn't expect him to start prancing around as if he won the Mega Pot.

Grandpa leans back, holding my face in his hands, and those tears cause pools to form in my own. "My brave girl. It was always the Mustang."

"What's the deal with Mustangs?" Mark asks, eyeing the two of us. I think he might be catching on.

An ornery smile pulls at my grandpa's lips. "Damn. I've got to tell the boys. They're going to . . . Sandberg and a baby. Ha!"

"Hold on, Grandpa." I grab his arm. "I'm stopping by the shop in the morning, and then I have my first appointment, so you're keeping your big mouth shut until then."

His elation falters. "Pal, you can't be on the floor pregnant. If anything happened . . . "

Mark's hand presses into the small of my back, and it's comforting.

"Grandpa, I can't sit around tagging and handing back keys. I'll go crazy." My eyes drop to the floor. "I know we need to talk about Slade buying the shop—"

He cuts me off. "Not tonight, but you should know we were only talking. We would've told you that if you'd stuck around."

"We have a lot of things to figure out," Mark says, breaking the tension.

"What time is your appointment?" Grandpa asks, smiling again. "I want a picture of my grandbaby."

"Ten," I say, and his gaze drops to my stomach, hidden under my sweatshirt.

He gestures to my midsection. "How long have you been hiding that?"

Memories of Mark's reaction flood the forefront of my mind. I lift my sweatshirt to reveal my snug T-shirt underneath.

His eyes grow wide at my little bulge. "Well, shit, Pal. No, hiding that anymore."

"Thanks, Grandpa."

"You plan on telling your mom?" he asks, moving back to his chair and taking a bite of his burger.

I pull Mark to the couch, and he sits next to me, throwing his arm over the back while keeping his other tucked securely to his body. "I'm going to see if she wants to have dinner. Mark can only stay until Friday."

"I'll be sure to disconnect my phone and sleep at the shop until you give me the all-clear."

I roll my eyes at him. "She's preoccupied with a new man, so hopefully that will help."

His body shakes with laughter, and Mark's eyes meet mine.

I eye Grandpa. "What's so funny?"

"I want to be there when she finds out you're married to Sandberg. She was all hung up on Mr. Shiny Shoes."

"She doesn't know anything about Mark, and I'm fine keeping it that way for as long as possible."

"I don't get it," Mark says.

I turn toward him. "You know how my mom was. She wanted me to find someone to take care of me. When she finds out you're one of the highest-paid players in the NFL—"

"So, she's going to be ecstatic," Mark smiles.

I frown. "Uh . . . yeah, probably, but I'm not telling her what you do. I'll be surprised if she knows who you are. She'll tell me my life is over, and someday when she figures it out, well then . . . she can think whatever she wants."

Mark kisses my forehead. "There's going to be a lot of people who think a lot of things. She's not going to be the first or the last."

Great. My stomach lurches. People have always had a lot to think and say when they find out I read at a first-grade level and worse when I feel pressured.

Grandpa slurps the end of his shake. "I'm going to have fun watching how this all turns out." He points at Mark. "I fed your growing ass for years. I have two posters that need signing. Tickets to a game for all my pain, suffering, and worrying about your hormonal teenage tendencies would be sufficient compensation."

Mark laughs. "Any team I should stay away from during negotiations that wouldn't fit the bill?"

"Don't even think about taking my granddaughter or that baby anywhere near the city." He gives Mark a look that says he means business, then moves right on as if Mark never went missing. "That brother of yours has got a good thing going on after the trade. You going to the big game?"

Life has been crazy these past weeks, and I haven't watched the remaining playoff games, but I know that Mark's brother, Sean, is playing in the Super Bowl.

Mark shifts next to me, and his hand drops to my shoulder. "Yes. Shane and his family will be there, and I have the awards beforehand." His chin dips to look at me. "Maybe you could come with me." His eyes hold an unusual hint of shyness that I don't understand. Mark is *never* shy.

"To the awards?" I ask, thinking about what that would mean. It would mean being on full display in front of the entire world.

"Both," he says quickly.

Grandpa must sense my apprehension and jumps in. "Pal, there isn't going to be a whole lot you can do around here."

I slump. "I can't go the next six months without a paycheck."

The old fart snickers at my comment, like the idea of needing money is absurd. Mark's hand squeezes mine.

I inhale and let it out, resting my head on his shoulder and settling back into real life.

Trying to let it all go for tonight, I relax into Mark and yawn while he tells Grandpa about his surgery and expedited recovery plan.

I listen as he talks about his agent gathering information, but for now, everything is speculation. Any solid interest will depend on his progress over the weeks ahead. I run a hand over my stomach and focus on the warm body next to mine, trying not to think about what it all means.

Mark sets his suitcase down in my small room and sits on the foot of my bed. I close the door as he looks around, taking in every square inch. I unzip my tight jeans, and it's instant relief.

"This is my teenage fantasy come true." That mischievous grin appears as he watches me peel off my jeans and toss them in the closet.

"What? Watching me struggle with my too-tight pants." I grab a scrunchy and twist my hair into a low, loose bun.

"You have no idea how many nights I laid in that small, horrible bed above Shane, pondering the risk of sneaking out and crawling in this bed with you. You taking off your pants sweetens the entire vision."

He stares, taking me in, and I will my face not to flush, surveying my small, safe space—its light gray walls, white duvet, and curtains. An old wooden dresser with a mirror sits along one wall with a nightstand beside my bed. In the corner is my tiny bathroom with a shower.

"It's pretty much the same. My walls were lavender when I moved in, but Grandpa and I painted them that summer." I pull my sweatshirt off, leaving on my long T-shirt that's stretched tight. "It's a little strange to have you in here."

He reaches forward and pulls me between his legs, his hands resting on my hips. His forehead presses against my stomach as memories of a younger us flash through my mind.

Mark tugs my wrist, pulling me down, and I straddle his lap. One hand dives underneath my shirt and runs up my spine. I shiver, and a smirk skirts across his lips before he inches me closer, my chest pressing into his.

I let out a long, slow breath. "How's your shoulder?"

"Not a problem at the moment." It comes out ragged.

He stills, our lips inches apart, and he studies me, letting me decide. "I think I might actually die of starvation if you keep this charade up much longer."

"Charade?" I ask with innocence.

His fingers slide down my back, digging into my hip. "Is this how things are now, Lex?"

"I don't know. You seemed to enjoy torturing me earlier."

"Torture?" His eyebrows hitch up, but the sexy stare remains. He leans down close to my ear. "Hmmm. So, we're talking revenge, huh? I don't know that I can be expected to behave myself when I'm currently reliving every teenage desire."

I run my hands up his arms, wrapping them around his cut biceps. "Oh, but you're so much stronger now than you were then."

"Not when it comes to you." It sounds like a promise, and I bite my lip, trying to suppress a smile. His thumb runs across my cheek, his eyes suddenly turning serious. "Baby, I'm running very close to my limit, and I can't be held responsible for what happens when I hit it."

A shot of adrenaline zips through my body, and my need for him reaches unbearable heights.

I press my forehead to his, squeezing my eyes shut tight. "I could get lost in this with you." It comes out as a whisper. I could, but I wonder how long it would take until I woke up. The small bump between us deserves more than that. It deserves to come into this world with a strong, stable foundation between us.

His lips brush against my cheek. "I'm all in. There's no going back. Ever."

I don't know a lot at the moment, but I know he means every word. I slide my hands around the back of his neck, holding him close as I run my lips over his jaw to the corner of his mouth. His body tenses, and I know it's taking every ounce of his strength to hold back. Payback really sucks.

His hands run up my sides, pushing my T-shirt—

"Sandberg!" His hands freeze around my ribs at Grandpa's loud bellow from the bottom of the stairs. "I don't care who you are now and how much money you make. She's still my granddaughter, and this is my house."

Mark huffs and almost sounds painful. "Yes, sir." He drops back on the bed, holding his shoulder and running a hand over his face. "I knew he'd bust my balls."

I lay down beside him, giving us space. We lay there in the quiet, and I stare at the ceiling, floating back down to reality.

I remember all the nights I cried myself to sleep, thinking he'd never be mine again. I can't ever go back to that. As the blissful fog clears, my mind starts sprinting, heading absolutely nowhere fast.

After a minute, Mark rolls on his side to face me. "Tell me what's going on up here." He taps my temple. "You got pretty quiet downstairs."

The past couple of days, when it was just Mark and me, the real world felt far away. Being back home, the reality of our situation is roaring to life again.

Hmmm. There are so many things. Where would I even start? There's the fun of sharing the good news with my mom, which will suck the life out of me. Or not knowing how my guys, my best friends, will react. I have to face Slade and the fact that he's probably about to blow his lid since I've been ignoring him. The recent confirmation that Grandpa won't let me on the floor. *And* I only have two more days with Mark, and then we'll be back to being apart.

If that's not enough, there's also the little thing of having him here that calls up the secrets I still hold, and the weight of them is growing enormously heavy.

Mark moves closer, his arm curling around my middle. "Lex, tell me. I know your brain is in overdrive."

I take another second to figure out where to begin. "When it's just you and me, it feels like everything is going to be ok. Coming back . . . all the unknown is smacking me in the face. I need to tell my mom, and I know how that will go. The stuff with the shop. You heard Grandpa. I'll be sitting behind a desk tagging keys."

"Babe, one thing at a time. You don't have to figure this all out by yourself anymore."

I turn toward him, resting on my side. "Mark, you're leaving." I grip his shirt, needing to ground my racing mind.

He tips my chin up, forcing me to look at him. "Come with me. When I start negotiating, we'll see what the options are and decide together. If you can't work anyway . . . "

I close my eyes as the desire to run away with him and the fear of doing that war within me. "Mark." My voice sounds as small as I feel. "This is where my life is. The thought of leaving . . . it's terrifying."

His strong arm hooks around me and tugs me closer, my body pressed to his. "I know, but I'll be there. We'll figure out how to navigate things together. I don't want you to be afraid to be with me."

"I've never felt safer than when I'm with you, but I'm not made to sit around waiting for you to come home. These past few months, you were busy every moment."

He pushes a strand of hair behind my ear. "It's not like that in the offseason, and I'm talking to my agent about cutting back as contracts expire."

"Ok, but . . . " I hold my breath, taking a second to shuffle through my pile of insecurities and pick one. *Screw it.* I need to quit being a coward.

"It's not only that. Mark, it's the rest of the world. Your world. The one that doesn't understand me or my limitations. I've seen players' wives and girlfriends. They're ridiculously beautiful, poised, and professional. Your world is big, bright, and loud; those women handle it all gracefully. I'm none of those things."

I pause, forcing myself to be brave and let go of everything that's had a chokehold on me since I stepped out of the hotel in Vegas. "You're the best quarterback in the NFL. I'm just a girl covered in grease who works with men who burp and fart like it's what they get paid to do. People look down on me for what I do, and that's before they realize I'm practically illiterate."

The Ford dually stalled on my chest, finally turns over, and drives off.

When he doesn't say anything, I risk a peek at him. His black brows are tipped in slightly, his eyes roaming my face with such fierceness I almost have to look away.

"Lex . . . " His nickname for me comes out like it's challenging to remain calm, and I pull back a little. His hand wraps around my waist, holding me there.

"Lex, *you* are my wife. I want *you* by my side wherever I am. All the time." He pauses, making sure I'm listening. "When it's bright and loud . . . when those blowhards who think they know you want to make assumptions, you hold on to me. I'll handle them and the noise." His hand slides up my back, pulling me close again. "They don't mean anything."

I stare into his big, brown eyes. So earnest and good, and I don't deserve any of it. I tuck myself into him, resting my forehead against his chest, where it's safe, and give him the rest of it.

"I'm scared. Everything is happening so fast, and I feel . . . lost," I whisper. "I don't think I can do this without you."

His lips press against the top of my head, his arms fully surrounding me. "You're not going to. We just need some time to sort it all out."

I want to believe him and time is all we need, but I'm growing a beautiful little time bomb that will blast right into our world regardless of where we're at.

We lie twined together, and my eyes get heavy.

I push up. "I need a shower."

He yawns, grabbing his phone.

I pull shorts and a shirt from my dresser and shower while Mark scrolls his phone. When I open the bathroom door, he's sitting in the same spot, shirtless, fisting a tattered and worn gray shirt.

"What's this?" He holds it out, his eyes a little red.

I stand perfectly still, knowing he knows exactly what it is.

"Lex . . . " he breathes out, his head dropping and his voice shaky. "Dammit."

I cross my arms over my chest, suddenly feeling very exposed. He wasn't supposed to see that. "It was all I had."

He stands, anger and confusion filling his sharp features, still gripping the holey, threadbare shirt. "Why? Why did you leave me? I waited every day to hear from you."

My voice catches in my throat. I don't know what to say. Nothing will make it better.

I shake my head, staring at the floor. "I couldn't."

He steps closer. "What does that mean?"

I search for the only part of the truth I know for sure and force myself to face him. "I would've rather lived without you than have you stay here. Nothing here would've been good for you."

His warm, rough hand slides against my cheek. "You were here. I would've stayed. I would've come back."

"I know! That couldn't happen," I say, honestly, because it couldn't. It would have destroyed him, slowly, one day at a time.

"I don't understand." His shoulders drop, his tall frame sagging, and I hate myself a little more.

I step into him and slide my arms around him, wanting to protect him just like I had then from anything that could hurt him. He suffered enough to last a lifetime. Only I'm afraid I might've hurt him the most.

I run my thumb across the black script on his ribs. "I meant it when I said it. Every word." It's the best I can do. I rest my head against him, holding him tight, but he doesn't say anything. "I'm not wearing that shirt tonight."

His arms come around me, wrapping me up. "You're not wearing that damn shirt ever again. You're coming with me."

Chapter 23

MARK

I blink and gently roll my stiff, sore shoulder. I blink again, the early morning light barely filtering through the white curtains. I stretch, brushing against the warm, soft skin pressed against mine.

Her clean scent surrounds me as I force my body to come alive. I glance down at her peaceful face against my bare chest. I carefully move a small strand of hair and tuck it to the side. *Everything I could ever want.*

When I found my old shirt lying in a pile on the floor, so worn and filled with holes, it almost broke me. All this time, she kept it and wore it, but why? Why, when she could have had me? We could have been together.

She said she couldn't let me stay and be dragged down. Being back here, maybe I understand that. Everything here brings back memories, too many disturbing old wounds and scars. My moments with Lex I've lived a million times over in my mind, but some horrors have the power to suck me back into the depths of hell.

It only took the plane hitting the tarmac, and I was back to being six years old. I was home from school with a fever, sleeping on the couch with my mom passed out beside me, likely high or drunk by noon. My dad came home, lifted me off the couch by my shirt, and threw me into the shower because I smelled. He held me under the burning hot water while I screamed, my skin turning red and scorched, which only made him do it longer. My mom remained lost in some kind of paradise while more of me was burned alive.

I close my eyes, inhaling long and slow to ease my racing heart as I swallow the memory and force it back into the past. I slide out of bed, careful not to wake Lex, and pull on shorts and a shirt. I grab my phone and reach for the door but turn back to look at her.

Her back is to me. The early morning sun filters through the window, casting light over her. Her long blonde hair is fanned out behind her, and one bare shoulder peeks out from under the white sheet. The vision I've longed for.

I hold up my phone and snap a picture. Last night, I asked her to come back with me, and I want that more than anything, but I know I can't push.

I close the door quietly, heading downstairs and into the kitchen. I find Cal at the table with a cup of coffee and the newspaper.

He peers at me over his glasses. "Took you long enough."

I reach into the fridge for a bottle of water and join him at the table. I scratch my chin. "I had to be prepared to say goodbye for good. I wasn't sure I could do that." He nods, understanding. "You could have told me she called it off."

He eyes me, his head falling to the side. "I could have. Have you told her?"

I shake my head. "It took me eight years. I'm not sure it matters."

"What now?" Those same blue-gray eyes of one of the few men I trusted and respected as a young man stare into me, waiting for an answer.

"I don't know." I shrug my good shoulder. "I want her with me. I can take care of her and our baby one hundred times over, but you know she's determined to be able to take care of herself. I respect that, even love her more for it."

He folds his paper. "I can't have her on the floor, and she's going to be pissed."

"You selling the shop?" I ask straight up, needing to know what we're dealing with.

He sits back in his chair and wraps his older and more wrinkle-worn hands around his mug. "That shop would be her whole life. It would consume her and . . . " He inhales as if debating if he wants to say more.

I cut to the chase. "If you need a buyer, I'll buy you out."

He leans forward, resting his arms on the table. "She's been hiding in that shop since the day you left. She thinks this is all there is for her, and

I've let her believe that." He rubs his forehead. "She's worked hard and fought to be able to do the most basic things you and I take for granted. I should have gotten her more help or shown her how smart and capable she is. Shit, she works circles around every one of my guys. Fixes things no one else can figure out."

He exhales long and slow. "If I handed it over to her, there wouldn't be more capable hands, but she's meant for more than this. She's meant to have a life, a partner, a family, and to do a hell of a lot more than change oil and rotate tires. I've failed her, but I won't fail her in letting her think that her only worth is wrapped up inside that brick building."

I let it all sink in. "Cal, running your shop is her dream."

His eyes meet mine dead on. "It's the only dream she's allowed herself to have. It's the only dream she had left."

It's a jab to the throat. "She's scared, and I won't—"

"Then you show her she doesn't have anything to be afraid of."

Right. "I don't know how to do that."

He rests back in his chair, crossing his arms over his chest. "Son, I don't know anything about love. I was never enough for the woman I married, and she hightailed it out of here to sniff out greener pastures." He pauses, rotating his mug. "Alex has been grasping onto worn-through memories for years. She sacrificed her own heart to save yours."

His eyes meet mine again. "I'd guess there aren't many people who can say they've ever had someone love them quite like that. Hell, she'd still be sitting here suffering if it meant you were out there living, but she's had enough of that. If she has you, she'll be all right."

His words hit me square in the chest, and my lungs falter.

Cal gets up, places his mug in the sink, and moves to the door, turning back to me. "I don't care what you two decide. You don't leave her." His head drops a second, but when his gaze returns to mine, tears crease his eyes. "Those months after you left, she had to force herself to keep going. Figure out how to live without you. She had good reasons, but not anymore. You take care of my girl and that baby."

"I will," I promise with everything I am.

"I know you will, or I'll fucking kill you." His eyes tell me he means every word. He nods, closing the door behind him.

I sit for a moment, everything he said floating around in my head. I'm not sure what to do with it all. Thoughts of her suffering for me ignite a flame of anger that I have to dampen right back down.

I stand, running a hand through my hair, and move to the living room to start my shoulder exercises.

I don't know how to show Lex she can come with me and still do what she loves. Cal's garage isn't the only place she can do that. Shit, I'll buy her a building, and she can set up her own shop. I won't let her hide here, thinking she's not good enough or this is all she's capable of.

After two reps, I rest, and a pair of fantastic legs appear beside me. I wrap my hand around her ankle and slide it up her calf, tugging her to the floor.

She settles beside me in an oversized sweatshirt, looking sleepy. "Did Grandpa leave already?"

"Yeah, a little bit ago."

She yawns. "I should've known you'd get up early."

"I can't afford to slack off, especially not right now. Teams are watching, and I want to have a say."

She tucks her hair behind her ear. "When will all that begin . . . teams getting in contact?"

"I need to touch base with Rob. He's got his ear to the ground and listening for rumblings, but my guess is a few weeks. After this season officially ends, organizations will hit the ground running toward next year. They'll finalize their budgets, know where they stand in draft picks, and how they want to spend their money."

She pulls her hands inside her sleeves and tucks them in her lap. "Did you mean what you said about me going to the awards and the game with you?" Her shyness in asking if I meant it has me thinking about everything Cal said.

"Lex, yes. I didn't want to pressure you, but I really want you there." I lift her chin. "There'll be cameras and reporters, but I want to hold your hand and have you by my side. And when the season starts, no matter where I'm playing, I want you and our baby on the sidelines before the game and waiting for me after. I want you with me always. Everywhere."

She rests her head on my shoulder and inhales. "It's a big day. I need to go to the shop, and then we'll see the baby for the first time." I brush my lips against her forehead and leave them there. "Then we're having dinner at my mom's."

"Tonight?"

She sits up straighter. "Yeah, I messaged her, and she said she's looking forward to it. The last time we tried, it didn't go so well. She wanted to introduce me to her new boyfriend and told me about his son." She rolls her eyes. "Hopefully, it will just be us."

"Does she know I'm coming?"

She turns her body toward me. "Mark, she doesn't know anything about you. I never told her. I couldn't stand to hear—"

"Maaamaaa, just killed a man . . . " I start singing "Bohemian Rhapsody."

I get two verses in, and Lex shoves me. I roll back, pulling her with me, her laughter the only joy I'll ever need. "So, she's going to think what?"

She bites her lip and shrugs. "I don't know. It doesn't matter. I just need to tell her. She already thinks I'm incapable of doing anything worthwhile or taking care of myself."

"You don't believe that, right?" I ask, needing to know that she doesn't believe that.

Her eyes drop to my chest, and I don't like that she doesn't answer me right away.

"Mark, I've tried really hard to increase my fluency, but I still struggle, especially under pressure. It's embarrassing. I get flustered and can't concentrate. The words just . . . I've learned to compensate even better than before. There are so many more tools now, but . . . "

Her eyes fill with the same humiliation I remember. "People will always look at me like I'm stupid or uneducated or like there's something wrong with me. That will never change. No one will ever hire someone who can't read. Even if I wanted to, I'd never make it through college. I'm only good at one thing."

I stare at her, knowing I can't fix a lifetime of assholes in one day, but I can start working on it. "You're more than capable of doing it all. There are programs and organizations that aid and educate people about dyslexia and its challenges. There's more awareness now, but it's still misunderstood and underdiagnosed."

She stares at me, her brow scrunched together.

"You have nothing to be ashamed of." I kiss her furrowed brow. "But you're going to keep fixing up those pieces of shit and turning them into gold." Her lips curve upward into that sweet, beautiful smile, and I pull her closer. "All those jerk-offs who don't understand haven't seen you under a hood."

She wraps her arms around me and hugs me tight.

My phone buzzes, and I reach for it. "It's Shane."

She stands. "I'll let you break the news while I make breakfast."

I answer as the water in my stomach bubbles with excitement to tell my brother the best news of my life. "Hey, bro."

"Times up, asshole," Shane grumbles. "This MIA, give me a few days shit is done. What the hell is going on?"

"Has anyone ever told you that you'd make a good drill sergeant?"

He groans.

"I told him to lead with 'How are things going?'" Sean's voice comes through the line.

Perfect. I can tell both of them at the same time, and Sean will reel Shane's overprotective gruff ass in.

"Shane, you can hang up. I like Sean's approach better."

"I'm not a kiss ass. Where are you? Sean said you're not home."

"Sheesh, I didn't know you two were becoming my keepers."

"You need one," Shane jabs.

"Dude, you're living three blocks from me," Sean says in defense. "I don't have time to worry about you right now. Could you tell us what's happening so we can quit thinking the worst?"

"My two little worrywarts."

"Mark!" they both yell.

I sigh "Fine. I'm in Ohio."

"Shit," Shane mumbles.

"I'm at Cal's with Lex."

"*And*," Sean says, and if I know my brother, he's smiling.

"And . . . those rumors about me getting married were true. Lex and I are married. We told Cal last night, and now I'm telling you."

There's nothing but complete silence, except the sounds coming from the kitchen where Lex is making breakfast.

"That was months ago," Sean says like he's processing.

"Yes, we've been taking things . . . slow."

"Mark," Shane barks out. "You better not screw this up."

I laugh. "I'm not going to. Trust me."

"When do we get to welcome Lex to the family?" Sean asks. "I'm looking forward to seeing her without vomit slime all over her."

"I'm not sure. I'm here for another day, and then I'll be back. PT will hopefully be releasing me for light training soon."

"You've got to get out of the city," Shane says, Papa Bear acting like he's three steps ahead of me.

"I know, man. I'm working on it." I take another breath and let it out, readying myself to tell the most miraculous part. "There's one more thing." Both my brothers wait. "We're having a baby."

Nothing. Dead silence. *Still* nothing. I check the phone to make sure I didn't lose them, and the call timer ticks away.

Then . . . Shane's low laugh comes through. "You've got to be shittin' me. Ha. *You* are going to be a father."

The shit-eating grin that covers my face could light up a city.

"You jackass. How in the hell did you beat me to this?" Sean laughs. "Damn. After the game, we're celebrating. Bro, I'm so happy for you."

"Thanks. I'm hoping Lex will come with me. I can't wait to see you guys." These guys. My best friends. My brothers. My family.

"Can't wait, man," Sean says.

"Get ready for Maggie to blow up your phone," Shane laughs again.

"I'm ready. I'll see you boys soon."

We hang up, and I find Lex in the kitchen eating toast and eggs.

"How'd it go?" She pushes a plate toward me.

"I blew their minds, but they can't wait to welcome you to the family."

She smiles. "I like the sound of that."

"Me, too." I just have to make sure she stays.

ROB: New York is getting antsy. You need to meet with them. See what they're offering and sign or let them know you're entertaining other offers.

ME: How long do I have?

ROB: They want a meeting ASAP. I can meet you there tomorrow.

ME: Call me.

Chapter 24

LEX

I park my truck in my usual spot along the side of the old building I thought one day would be mine. I take a deep breath, gearing up to face my guys inside. Particularly the tall, heavily tattooed, and bearded one who's probably spouting steam since I've ignored his messages.

I glance at Mark, who's been preoccupied with his phone all morning. He received a text from his agent, but his quiet nose-in-his-phone state is making my crazed nerves wage a battle over which worry takes top priority.

He sets his phone on his leg, coming back up for air. "You ok?"

I pull the keys from the ignition and wipe my sweaty palms on my unbuttoned, mostly unzipped jeans. I tried that elastic hair tie around the button trick, but even that didn't give me enough room.

"I have no idea what Grandpa told them. I haven't missed days of work . . . ever. I left them without a word in the middle of projects, so I'd be pissed if I were them. Plus, Slade's texted me a couple of times—"

"He didn't talk to you about possibly buying Cal out." Mark's irritated tone almost makes me smile.

"Are you ready? These guys are like my brothers."

"Yeah, I'm ready. You have no idea how much I hate that you work with a bunch of dudes. I'll happily tell them to keep their eyes and hands to themselves."

I laugh. "You're ridiculous."

"Hey. I know exactly how you look when you're talking cars, let alone working on them. Your tank tops and flannels. Shit, the work boots. Lex, you're stunningly beautiful, but when you're in the middle of all that . . . I'm getting pissed just thinking about anyone else seeing you—"

I lean over and kiss him, hard and fast on the lips, then pop my door open. "Let's go. Sitting out here won't make it better."

Mark doesn't move. "Are you sure? I think you should come back over here." His voice is low and sexy.

I bite my lip to suppress a smile and shove myself out. He meets me, grabbing my hand. "You know, I wouldn't mind kicking someone's ass or watching Cal do it. I know that man has still got a few rounds in him."

I laugh, knowing he's probably right. I haul open the heavy metal door, and there's a whoosh of the same heavy scents and noise that's filled my days since I was old enough to help out.

I was six years old when Grandpa had me on a stool watching how to change fluids and replace hoses. This is my place, and these are my people. The idea of it not being mine causes my throat to ache and constrict, and I stop inside the door.

As if Mark can sense it, his arm slips around me. I peer up at him, reminding myself of all I have to gain if I let this go. His strong jaw is set as his beautiful, dark brown eyes roam the space like he's taking stock. A few long strands of black hair rest on his forehead, and I want to reach up and push them back in place. His powerful, muscular body stands tall in defense.

He asked me to go with him. Looking at him, I wonder what's holding me back.

"Well, look who it is?"

Wind's voice breaks through my perusal of my brilliantly handsome husband. I notice all the noise has died down except for the radio, and the guys are standing, staring.

Carson leans against the hood of a Dodge Caravan and crosses his meaty arms over his broad chest. "Is this show and tell? I forgot to bring Taylor Swift."

Ok. So they're mad. I knew they would be. I can handle it. I'd be pissed, too.

Mark's fingertips dig in, and I know at least Slade, standing in the far back, notices our closeness.

"Is that Mark Sandberg?" Trig leans over and whispers to Wind as his hands fidget with a socket wrench.

"Taylor Swift? Really? That's your comeback?" Wind asks.

Slade shifts, widening his stance as he grips a greasy carburetor. His cold, hard eyes are dead set on me. He. Is. Pissed.

Great. I've seen him with Krissy, and his bark is always worse than his bite.

"We heard what Slade did." Carson disrupts the weird stillness.

I hear a growl, and I don't even have to look at him to know Slade's nostrils are flaring wide. It's possible there's fire, but I don't peek to confirm.

Wind settles his hands on his hips. "We aren't on speaking terms if that makes you feel better? What he did, not talking to you, that was horse shit."

I bite my lip, trying really hard not to smile. These men are seriously worse than a bunch of old ladies with nothing but gabbing to fill their time.

I hear the squeak of Grandpa's office door. He comes down the hall and stands just inside the shop.

I bite my lip. "So . . . "

"Like, you didn't even tell us you were leaving." Trigger's sad baby face is a punch in the gut. The budding race car driver with the need for speed is tender-hearted and too sweet for his own good.

"I know. I'm sorry. I . . . There was something I needed to do, and it was kind of urgent." I rub my forehead, feeling like a big, fat, lying excuse-maker. I don't even have to look to know Grandpa is sporting an ass-eating grin. That man just rolled in here to watch his daytime drama.

I glance at Mark and . . . To hell with it. These are *my* guys, and they're giving Slade the silent treatment for me. "I called off the wedding because I couldn't marry someone unless it was him." I point at Mark. "So, that's what I did. I met him in Vegas months ago, and we got married." Not one of them moves a muscle, except for maybe their jaw when their mouths fall open just a little. "I needed a few days. I needed to be with him because . . . I'm pregnant."

It's as if I can see thought bubbles translating what I said into the English language or whatever the hell it is Carson speaks. I suck at reading, but that man makes up words with his southern drawl no one can understand.

"You married him?" It's Slade's low, forced tone that breaks the silence. I meet his eyes and severe frown. "And you're having a baby?" His eyes flick to Mark and then back to me.

"Yes," I confirm.

I know this man. It takes a moment, but I see a glimmer of a smile behind his thick beard, and my chest expands with relief. We aren't all good yet, but we'll get there.

"I'm sorry I—"

Wind holds up his hand. "You're pregnant, like with a baby? Fuck. How the hell did that happen?"

Carson snickers. "Let's see, Wind. When a man and a woman—"

"Ok." I hold up my hand this time.

"Is his name really Wind?" Mark whispers.

"Congrats, darlin'." Carson beams. "About damn time you snatched back the one that got away."

A bubble of laughter rolls out of me. Of course, they all know about Mark. Well, maybe not Trig. These men couldn't mind their own business if they were paid a million dollars. Man, do I love them.

I pull in air, and the muscles around my ribs relax.

Trigger surveys the room like he's missing something. "Wait, you're married?" He's dumbstruck, making me wonder if Slade was right about that little crush.

"All right, you blockheads," Grandpa steps forward. "It's no wonder you never have a woman. Man!" He shakes his head. "Alex married this guy and is carrying my grandbaby. That's all you need to know for now."

"I need to know if she's got ten minutes to help me figure out what's wrong with this dumpster on wheels," Carson winks and kicks the tire on the van.

I smile. "I've got ten for you, Gorgeous."

The guys laugh and whistle, and my body relaxes as my nerves settle. For now.

Mark pulls his phone from his pocket. "I'm sorry. I have to take this." His hand slides further around me to pull me closer, and he kisses me on the corner of my mouth.

I smile against his lips. "Do you want to pee on my leg, too?"

"Whatever it takes." His face breaks into that perfect, sexy smirk. "Just making sure we're all on the same page. You're mine." He swats me on the butt and then steps outside, and I return to the now amused stares.

Heat rushes my cheeks. "What? Just out with it."

"Never seen you smile like that before," Wind says in a highly uncharacteristic, wistful tone.

Carson steps forward and wraps me up. "We're happy for ya and so glad you're back. Please don't ever leave us again. These guys don't have a clue as to what they're doing," he teases as they throw jabs back at him. "And Slade has been like a starved bear on the prowl," he whispers. "We've thought about locking him out but then worried he might rig something to blast the door open." He raises his eyebrows and widens his eyes in warning.

Slade starts toward me as Carson retreats to the Dodge and Grandpa heads back to his cave.

"Nice to see you're ok." The big man tosses out, his crossed arms a clear boundary between us.

I stare at my shoes. "I'm sorry I didn't text you back."

"Was that payback?" His bright green eyes bore into me.

I don't know what to say, so I save my words for the moment.

He doesn't wait for an answer. "I'm sorry you found out like that. It was only a discussion. I would have talked to you about it." He pauses. "It's not because I don't think you can run this shop." It's just like Slade to always cut straight to it. "I know you could and do it better than me." That has me peeking up at him, wanting to know if he really believes that. "This is yours for the taking. I wanted Cal to know I'm interested, but I should have told you."

I exhale slowly, gathering the right words. The ones that hurt to admit out loud, but I trust him with them. "It's terrifying to think that the one thing you're capable of might be taken from you, especially when . . . "

His stiff stance eases. "You and that baby are going to be just fine. I can see that." A sudden burn consumes my throat, and I blink a few times. "I'm proud of you for finally going after what should've always been."

This big, growly man hits me right in the chest. I step forward, push to my tiptoes, and throw my arms around him. His big arms scoop me up, and I'm surrounded by the strength and stability of one of the men who helped me keep going when my heart wasn't sure it could.

"I'm real happy for you. Just don't disappear like that again. Krissy's been asking about you every day and blaming me. I'm surprised she didn't kick my ass out of my own house. And these nags . . . I can't take one more minute of their nonverbal assaults."

I laugh. "I'm sorry."

"Krissy's going to flip her shit when you tell her."

The metal door bangs closed, and Slade releases me, his eyes flicking to Mark as he steps up beside me.

"Mark, this is Slade," I say, standing between the two men. One, my best friend. The other, my husband. "Slade, this is Mark."

It takes a second, but eventually, Mark sticks out his hand. "It's nice to meet you." His words come out stiff, not in his usual playful tone.

"Congratulations." Slade returns the shake.

Slade looks back at me. "You be careful out here on the floor."

"I will. I can't stay long. I have a doctor's appointment."

He nods, stepping away. "Good." Reading my mind, he says. "Don't worry. We'll figure something out."

I offer him a soft smile, but telling me not to worry is like asking me not to breathe right now.

I turn to Mark; his eyes are locked on Slade's back. Something about the expression on his face recharges the churn in my stomach. "Everything ok?"

He rubs his forehead, his eyes not meeting mine. When he doesn't immediately answer, my intestines decide to join the party and do a little jig. The kind that makes me want to run for the bathroom.

The noise in the shop resumes, and he grabs my hand, pulling me to the door. His gaze drags to mine, and I'm not sure I want the answer.

"That was Rob. I have to leave tonight. I'm meeting with the Liberties first thing in the morning."

I stare at him. I don't know what to think or say, so I don't say anything.

I knew he'd be leaving. I just didn't think it would be today. It wilts the joy that's been blossoming. I close my eyes.

It's not goodbye.

I pull in a slow breath, shoving down the looming panic that he's leaving and absolutely nothing will be ok. We'll be back to two people who love each other but live completely separate lives.

Chapter 25

MARK

My knee bounces next to hers as she absently scrolls her phone, with an empty pee cup resting between her legs.

She's shutting down on me. I can feel it. She's right here but miles away. The timing of this meeting in New York couldn't be worse, but according to Rob, I don't have a choice. I either need to sign with the Liberties or let them know I'm seeking other offers.

I know what I want. I want out of the city and an offer from a decent-standing team I can take to the Super Bowl, but I have to hear what they're offering. The Liberties organization has been good to me, and I need to give them the courtesy of telling them no to their face and explaining why.

The door swings open, and a woman enters with a car seat slung over her arm. A baby with soft pink cheeks in those footed, zip-up jammies is tucked inside.

A warm sensation crawls through my chest at the idea of that being us. Lex and I. My stomach squeezes with pressure and the deep desire to get this right. I don't want to be in one place and Lex in another. I don't want to watch my baby grow from afar. Being gone so much during the season will be bad enough. When I get home, I want them there, where we can be together.

My knee bounces harder, and it gets Lex's attention. She side-eyes me, but that's it. Her silent, retreated tendencies are about to send me into a grown-ass meltdown.

"Alexandra."

Thank God. A technician waits for us, and we follow her back to a small, darkened room.

"I'm April. I'll be performing your ultrasound today." The woman zips around the room, keeping pace with my nerves. She gestures to the table. "You can climb up here, and Dad, you can have a seat."

Dad. More sitting is the last thing I need, but I put my ass in the plastic chair as the pressure of it all pushes past my limit.

Lex sits on the table, still looking like she doesn't need me, and it stings.

April pulls her file while I try not to be suffocated by my anxiety. "So, you're around fourteen weeks. This is your first ultrasound?"

"Uh, yes. I know I'm a bit behind." Lex's hand reaches for her ear. *Ha. Gotcha.* I catch her and her nervous habit. Feeling a little less alone, I scoot my chair closer.

The technician smiles while I'm about to jump out of my skin.

"Well, let's see who you have in there. Hopefully, the little one cooperates, and we'll get some good pictures," April says, holding Lex's file and a pen. "Do you want to know the gender when it's visible?"

"No," I blurt out, and Lex's head snaps in my direction. Then, the corner of her mouth tips upward, but just barely. We didn't discuss it, but this baby is the absolute best surprise of my life, and I want to keep the surprises coming.

Lex lays down and pulls her shirt up to her ribs while April squirts clear goop on her stomach. My eyes dart to the small screen on the wall, waiting, but all I see is black with white streaks as she rolls the wand back and forth.

My heart bangs against my ribs, threatening to beat all the way out of my chest. I move to the edge of my seat, having no idea what I'm looking at but knowing it's something.

April takes her time moving the wand around from one spot to another, only the sound of my pulse filling the silence. April's long, quiet perusal forces me to my feet, and Lex's instincts must be on high alert because she reaches for me.

I grip her sweat-slicked hand, and when her eyes meet mine, they're alive with fear. I bring her hand to the middle of my chest and hold it there. Her eyes flick between mine as her hand tightens its grip. I try to smile, wanting her to know everything will be ok when I have absolutely no clue that it is.

"This is your first ultrasound, correct?" April asks, again in confirmation, but still in that calm, chipper tone.

"Yes," Lex answers, her hand squeezing mine even tighter. I've been scared before, but this moment shreds all those fears to dust.

"You see this right here." April gestures to the pointer on the screen. "It looks like . . . " She moves the wand around some more. "You're having twins."

Some kind of noise comes out of my mouth that might sound like I was being held underwater and yanked back up for air.

Uh . . . what? I feel a little woozy. I might need that chair after all, but Lex's hand falling limp in mine, spurs me to remain standing.

April rolls closer to the screen and points. "See right here. This is Baby A." She taps away on her keyboard, telling us she's taking measurements.

I squint, seeing it. The head and tiny, little feet, and two hands. I look down at Lex, and a tear falls out of the corner of her eye.

"Is it ok?" Lex asks, her voice shaky.

"It's measuring a tad on the small side, but that's not unusual for twins. Let's see if we can hear the heartbeat."

It only takes a second for the screen to fill with color and the room with the whoosh, whoosh, whoosh. Something deep in my chest blooms so full it's possible it might explode; everything inside me splattering this chilly, dark space.

I lean down, kissing Lex's forehead as something warm drips from my cheek. She smiles, and her hand slides around my neck to hold me there.

"We're going to do the same with Baby B," April says.

I can only watch as baby number two fills the screen. *Baby. Number. Two.* I see its head, hands, and feet. We listen to the strong heartbeat, and for the second time, it's like I've learned how to breathe again.

Two babies. Twins. Lex and I are having twins. Dos. Double. Bambinos.

April puts her wand away and wipes Lex's belly off. "Congratulations. Your babies are looking healthy and strong." She hands Lex a long strip of black-and-white pictures as she pulls her shirt down and hops off the table.

We follow April down the hall to another room, where we're bombarded with pamphlets and forms about genetic testing, cord banking, breastfeeding, and vaccinations.

Her face falls, and her shoulders slump as she collects one piece of literature after another. It's a posture I remember, and I slide my arm around her, taking the forms and letting the doctor know we'll review it all and get back to them.

Lex's stoic face has me only partially listening as the doctor talks about birth plans and options. All I want to do is take our reusable bag, crammed full of every imaginable tidbit about childbirth, and get Lex out of here so I can understand what's going through her head.

After making her next appointment, we hit the cold winter air, and I grab her hand. "I'll drive."

She hands over her keys, not arguing. At the passenger door, I stop her from climbing in, turning her to face me. I don't quite know her like I used to, but I recognize this part of Lex. When she feels like the world is closing in or the fear gets too big, she shrinks, closing herself within. I need to be inside the iron-barred gates she's dropping into place.

I pull her close, my arms wrapping around her back. She tucks her head into my chest, and I hold her tight. "I'm not going anywhere. Ever." I want her to hear me and believe it. "It's you and me. It's always been you and me." Her fingers dig into the back of my coat like she's holding on for dear life. "It's going to be you and me and our babies."

Babies. Two babies. I didn't have any kind of example of what it means to be a good parent, but these babies will get all of me—the very best I can give them.

I know she needs a second, so I release her, and she climbs in the truck. I drive us back to Cal's house with nothing but dread, knowing I have to leave her when we just got the best overwhelming news of our life. We had a lot to figure out before, and now it's doubled.

It's been sixty-four minutes of nods, 'yeses,' and 'nos,' and she's given me nothing. I place the last of my stuff in my suitcase and sit beside her on the end of the bed, my patience sputtering on fumes.

Grabbing her hand, I entwine her fingers with mine, wanting her to feel the connection. "I need you to talk to me. I can't leave like this."

She rests her head on my shoulder but doesn't say anything. I've kept my nerves mostly under control, but they start to count off one by one, taking a nosedive off a ledge. The distance between us feels far and wide, and I can't handle it. Flashbacks of eight years ago singe the edges of my mind, and I have to fan them out before they burn me alive all over again.

I wait with as much calm coolness as a mildly dramatic person can have for her to give me something.

"I don't know where to start," she whispers.

"Start anywhere. I don't care. I just need something." I kiss the back of her hand. "A sign, smoke signal, pigeon carrier with a clue. Anything that will help me understand what's going on in here." I kiss her forehead.

Her chest rises slowly, then falls with an exhale. "When the technician didn't say anything at first, I . . . " She doesn't have to finish that sentence because I know. "What if something happens to them? Like I do something I shouldn't and . . . " She sits up straight, pulling away and shifting to face me. "Them, Mark. Them. Two. No wonder I'm huge already, and I have a long way to go."

"You're not huge. You're perfect and sexy as hell. If you want, I'll show you just how much I think so."

Her head falls to the side, pure sadness taking over, and it's enough to split me in two. "How am I going to have two babies in here?" She gestures around the room. "I mean, I thought that with one, but now, two of . . . everything."

She swallows, gulping down a mountain of emotions.

My stomach drops to the floor and bounces up into my throat at her thinking about the babies being here. Some miraculous force holds my mouth shut, knowing this isn't the time to point out that I think that idea is total and complete shit.

"I don't even know what I'm supposed to be doing. It'll take me an entire month to try to piece together all the papers and information they gave us. Who's going to teach them to read and help them with their homework? What if they have the same issues I do?"

Her voice quivers, but I force myself to sit tight, giving her space to get it all out. "And my job. I can't work. Grandpa will pay me to sit and deal with customers but . . . Eventually, the guys will have to roll me around in his awful, old chair that probably won't even hold me. I'm having dinner with my mom, and she'll add to the list of all the ways in which I will never be able to care for these babies."

A tear makes a slow track down her cheek, and I catch it with my thumb and push it away. "All these damn hormones," she groans. "And you're leaving. We aren't any closer to knowing how any of this is actually going to work!"

Her chest rises and falls quickly, having shoved it all out.

"Shit, Lex. That's a lot."

She puts her hands over her face and falls back on the bed. She sniffs, and I lie down next to her, slipping my arm over her and moving close.

I tuck a strand of her long hair behind her ear. "When the technician kept rolling her magic wand and not saying a damn word, I don't think I've ever been more scared in my entire life. She should be fired for that long period of silence." Lex fists my shirt and buries her head into my chest. "We can't control everything. All we can do is love and protect them as best as we can."

"Mark, we're having two babies." She tips her head back. Her eyes crease with tears, and her lips turn up into the sweetest smile. "We made two babies."

"When you showed up, and I saw you were pregnant, I thought it was the best day of my life. Baby, today, it doesn't get any better than this." I slide my hand into her hair. "You have no idea how much I don't want to leave right now."

She snuggles into my neck. "I don't want you to go."

"Come with me. I'll go to my meeting, show you the city, and then we'll head back to Phoenix. Next weekend, we'll go to Charlotte for the awards and the game and celebrate with my family."

She rolls back, her eyes searching mine as if she's thinking about it. "I can't go with you, at least not tonight. I need to talk to my mom and find out what Grandpa will allow me to do. I have to . . . deal with some stuff." It sucks, but I understand her need to stay. "Maybe . . . I can meet you in Charlotte?"

I smile. "How about I pick you up on the way?" She rolls back into me, sliding her arms around my back, and we lay there for the last bit before she has to take me to the airport.

Our drive to the airport is filled with silence and so many unanswered questions. Her comments about where all the baby stuff will go at Cal's eat at me, but I have no idea where my home will be and no permanent place to offer her.

The late afternoon sun beams down, warming the cold Midwest air as she pulls her truck into a parking spot and climbs out. She comes around to my side, and I scoop her up.

"You said you trusted me." I press my lips to her cheek and leave them there. "Lex, I need you to trust me. I have to do this, but baby, I'm not leaving you." I release her, and her eyes are everywhere but on me. "Look at me." I hold her face in my hands. "I know I keep saying we'll figure this all out, and we will. I have to know where I'm going, but I want you and our babies with me wherever that is. I'll do whatever it takes to make that happen."

She doesn't respond but only hugs me tight, and I can't allow myself to think it means anything other than it's what she wants, too.

"I'll call you tonight. Ok?"

She pulls away just enough to push up and press her lips to mine. I hold her, making sure it doesn't feel like goodbye, but I'll be back. Because I will. I'll see her in a week, but once I get my job sorted out, I'm coming to get her and my babies for good.

Chapter 26

LEX

Why didn't I reschedule?

I want to go home, take a long hot shower, and crawl into bed, needing it to still smell like him. But no, I'll just pile a little more onto today.

When Mark told me he had to leave, it was like getting hit with a truckload full of disappointment. I understand why this is important, and he has to hear what they are offering, but I just got him back. For these past few days, we were a team, but here we are apart again.

I pull up in front of my mom's townhouse, reliving seeing my babies on the screen and hearing their heartbeats. *Twins. I'm having twins.* I keep saying it, trying to get it to stick. I saw them. Both of them. Their little hearts squishing in and out and in and out, but I can't get myself to believe it. Mark and I are having twins.

I run my hand over my stomach. I really wanted Mark here for this. I wanted my mom to see that I have a partner and I'm not as totally and completely inept as she thinks. But he's not here. I'm pregnant and alone, and that's all the ammunition she'll need.

I could have rescheduled and tried to wait until Mark could be here, but I have no idea when that might be. At the rate these babies are stretching my midsection, hiding them is pretty much over. So, here I go, needing my steel-toed boots to guard my insecurities and pride.

I hike up my unzipped jeans, fix my sweatshirt around me, and prepare myself to shock the hell out of my mom. Maybe she'll be so stunned she won't add her lists of worries and concerns to mine.

I open the side door into the kitchen but stop dead in my tracks. My mom is at the stove stirring a pot with a man wrapped around her.

Oh, for real. I want to retreat and never return to whatever is happening here.

I inch the door closed, but the damn thing squeaks. My face scrunches painfully tight as my mom and her new man turn.

"Oh honey, there you are. I was getting ready to call you." My mom prances across the room and pulls me into a hug. "Bob and I were . . . " She blushes, and my stomach revolts at the sight.

"Alex, this is Bob, my boyfriend."

Bob, the *boyfriend*, who looks like he belongs in an old western, steps forward and sticks out his hand. He's short and broad with a bit of a potbelly that stretches the pearl snaps on his shirt, which somehow goes with his jeans and work boots. He smiles, but it's covered with one of those thick, full mustaches that hide a large portion of his face.

"Alex, I've heard a lot about you. I'm glad we're finally meeting."

I shake his hand, wanting to make like an opossum and play dead. Maybe then I can go home.

"Come on and sit down," Mom says, ushering me to a seat. "I hope you're hungry. I made your favorite."

I watch my mom flit around while Bob joins me at the small table. "So, Alex, your mom says you work in a garage."

I avoid eye contact, not wanting to talk to this man about my profession or anything else. "Yes."

"I'm a car guy, myself. My son and I fixed up an old Corvette."

"Alex bought an old truck in high school and flipped it," my mom says like she's talking about a house. "She still drives that old thing around. You can't even tell it belonged in the junkyard."

"Oh yeah," Bob perks with interest. "What make and model?"

"F-150."

"No kidding. What year? I had one of those when I was in high school."

Mom takes a break from Betty Crockering and wraps her arms around Bob's neck.

Why? Why did I do this to myself? I want to jab my eyes out with a dull fork and use the candle to pour the hot wax into my ears so I don't have to endure another second of this.

I've spent too much time with Mark. His dramatics are contagious. I bite my lip to prevent my smile.

Do I want my mom to be happy? Of course, I do. I've just been down this road and met too many of 'the one' to want to extend my limited amount of social energy on a strange man who's temporarily hanging around.

When I don't respond, my mom jumps in. "We'll eat in a few."

Bob checks his watch. "Yeah, Brad should be here any minute."

Uh. What now? My hand slides over my babies. "Brad?"

My mom smiles that sickening, sweet smile. My gag reflex is in full working order these days, and I for sure might upchuck the limited contents of my stomach.

"Bob's son. We thought it would be fun for you two to meet. He's about your age and really into cars."

I have no idea what my face does, but it definitely feels like, 'Oh, hell no.'

I'm not doing this. I'm not sitting here while these two adults try to play house or matchmaker or whatever the heck this is when I have major stuff to worry about.

I stand, and my mom's eyes grow wide. "I'm sorry, but—"

The door opens, and who I assume is Brad steps in. *Well, let's just give Brad a key.* I contemplate making a run for it, but he's blocking the doorway.

"Sorry, am I late?" he asks as the awkwardness seeps through the room like one of Wind's massive bombs.

Brad is taller, broad, and lean, with blond hair and light eyes. He steps further into the small kitchen, allowing my eyes to flick between Bob and him. They don't look anything alike. If I cared, I'd ask clarifying questions, but I remain standing and silent.

"You must be Alex," he says as if he's heard a thing or two about me and offers his hand.

I want to ring my mom's neck.

I shake his hand with my burning hot one, and I don't even care if I leave sweat behind. If I weren't married to the absolute and literal sexiest man alive, I might think he's mildly attractive.

Mark. Why in the hell isn't he here with me? I clench my jaw. We could have gotten in, told her we're married and having babies, and gotten out. TOGETHER.

Mark would have turned this little dinner party into a comedy hour, but all I can do is try not to lose my ever-loving mind. I have to put a stop to this, whatever it is, so I can go home and not do this again. Who knows? Maybe next time, she'd invite the preacher. We'd be one big, happy family.

Brad sits as my mom offers him a drink. I sit reluctantly.

"Alex was telling me she restored an old F-150," Bob says as if he and I were actually conversing.

"Really," Brad says, sipping his iced tea. "What year?"

"77," I say, not adding detail.

"Sweet. So, that's yours out on the curb?"

"All right, who's ready to eat?" my mom cuts in. "It's tomato soup and mac and cheese. Alex's favorite."

I don't tell her it hasn't been my favorite since I was ten because, at this point, who cares? She places the food in front of me while Bob and Brad discuss something happening on a job site. My mom joins in as I stir my soup and pick at the mac and cheese with my fork.

"Alex, Brad said he would love to come by the shop sometime and see what you're working on."

I drag my eyes to hers, shining brightly with hope and possibility. I want to squash it like a bug. *She has GOT to be kidding me.*

Brad clears his throat. "I'm sure she's got plenty keeping her busy and doesn't need spectators."

I glance at him, appreciative of his perceptiveness.

"Oh no," Mom pooh-poohs. "She'd love to. It's like pulling teeth to get her out of that garage. She'd love it."

Bob must have a fraction of insight and jumps in. "Sweetheart, I think we can let these two figure things out for themselves."

What the fu . . . My mouth moves without my permission as my body heats to the temperature of a blow torch. "Figure what out?"

It must be the shock of my voice, but all utensils still.

My mom takes over. "We thought it would be nice for you two to get to know each other. Now that you're single, Brad has friends and . . . "

Brad's eyes grow wide, but I can't tell what that means, and I don't care to know.

My inability to handle uncomfortable and difficult situations kicks in, and my mouth moves. "I'm not."

My mom chews and swallows, appearing pleased with herself. "You're not what, honey?"

I set my fork down, a thick layer of sweat coating my completely clothed body, and if I were anywhere else, I'd be stripping, especially these pants. "I'm not single."

"Oh," she perks like a dog waiting for a bone.

My heart joins in on the freakout party and begins to race. My phone buzzes in my pocket, and I pull it out, needing the distraction and not giving a single crap if it's rude. Being pawned out to my mom's new-forced-stepson's-friends feels like permission to flip the bird in the form of looking at my phone.

I see a notification that Mark posted something new. I click on it.

What. Did. He. Do?

A picture of me in bed fills my screen. You can't see my face, but my hair is sprawled out over the pillow. My naked shoulder is peeking out of the covers, and the light filtering through the window is just enough to create yellow rays of warmth.

The caption reads: *The rest of my life.*

I bite my lip, hiding the smile that breaks through.

"Alex, what is it?" my mom asks.

I pull my attention away from my phone and back to this mess. "Nothing."

My mom's brow creases as her eyebrows tip inward. "You said you're not single. Are you and Seth . . . "

The picture released to the whole world, or at least Mark's five million followers, fills my mind again. I'm done with this.

"Actually, I'm married." I let it hang, but not for long. "I married my high school boyfriend, who I've never been able to get over, and not only that, I'm pregnant . . . with twins."

My mom's mouth falls open. Bob chokes on a macaroni noodle and coughs, so I know he's getting air, while Brad makes some sort of snorting noise. I offer him a shrug because what else do I do when he looks highly amused by my verbal vomit?

Mom wipes her mouth with her napkin. "You're married and . . . pregnant?"

"Yes."

My mom studies me like she thinks I might be joking as her fork stabs around her plate, not catching anything. "Where is your . . . husband? Do we get to meet him?"

We? "He's out of town. He has an important meeting."

Her fork finds the pasta, and she frantically shuffles it around. "A meeting. And what does he do?"

I could throw it in her face and tell her that Mark is one of the highest-paid professionals in the league, but I decide it's not worth it. "He . . . works seasonally . . . travels a lot," I stutter out. Based on her instant dismay and stiffened posture, I have second thoughts about withholding information.

"Seriously, Alex. Does he have a name?" Her head drops with disapproving dread as she finally sets her dinner weapon down.

Whatever. I'm done with this. She'll find out sometime anyway. "Yes. Mark Sandberg."

Tiny particles of pasta, soup, and tea spray the table from the two opposing ends. I want to grin. I *really* do, but I keep that crap under wraps, just waiting to see what's next.

As Bob and Brad wipe their mouths, my mom's face moves into a frown, studying them. "He travels a lot. Huh?"

I could say something, but why? Here it comes, from the woman who has had such great relationship success that started with my dad giving her duces when he found out she was pregnant.

"And twins." Her voice rises an octave as Bob and Brad keep their heads down, eyes on plates, clearing their throats and sipping tea, trying to recover. "Does he know?"

I'm happy to revert back to my usual comfortable minimal word usage. "Yep."

"And let me guess, he'll be there for you through the whole thing. He loves you and wants to take care of you." *Here it comes*. "But yet, he's not here."

I'm not going to lie. That last little jab is a hit to a purpling bruise. I put my hands in my sweatshirt pockets and rest them against my stomach.

"Not every man is a liar," I say, knowing Grandpa, my guys at the garage, and Mark are living proof.

Both Bob and Brad perk up at my declaration.

"That's true," Bob says, sitting up tall in his chair, almost as if he's . . . defending me.

My mom acts like she was bitten but recovers at lightning speed. "Sure. That's true, but Alex is . . . naive." It's like I'm not even here.

My mom lets out some kind of nervous laugh and stands, flitting around the kitchen like a gnat.

When I find the energy to deal with the awkwardness, Bob studies me intently. Brad looks . . . confused, maybe.

Bob's surprisingly kind eyes meet mine. "You've known Mark Sandberg since high school?"

I can't help but smile at his astonishment.

Brad leans closer, whispering, "Like Mark Sandberg the . . . "

I nod.

"Wow. Congratulations," Brad says.

My phone buzzes again.

SEXY BABIES' DADDY: Landed. How's it going?

I almost laugh out loud when I see Mark apparently snuck in and changed his contact name to something so ridiculously fitting.

SEXY BABIES' DADDY: I miss your*Lips emoji*
SEXY BABIES' DADDY: Your *Smiley face emoji*
SEXY BABIES' DADDY: Your *Leg emoji*
SEXY BABIES' DADDY: Your *Peach emoji*
SEXY BABIES' DADDY: I'm *Skull emoji*

My mom catches my smile. "What's so funny? Is that him?" she asks with venom, certain he's the scum of the earth.

My phone buzzes again. I glance, unable to decipher it quickly.

SEXY BABIES' DADDY: *SpeechEasy App link.*

She makes an annoyed throat-clearing noise.

"Yes." I set my phone on my leg, slightly rejuvenated. There are so many things I could say, so many things I could tell her, but I won't. She doesn't know Mark. She really doesn't even know me, and that's her problem.

"These babies and Mark are the best news of my life. I'm sorry you don't see that," I say quietly.

She turns from scrubbing a pan at the kitchen sink. "You may think differently when you're raising them alone and trying to scrape by. Alex, what are you going to do? Have you thought about this? How will you support two babies on what little you make at the garage? Daycare will eat up everything you make, and it's not like you can get a better job."

I breathe in through my nose and hold it, squeezing my stomach muscles tight. I knew it would come to this. I just freaking knew it.

Bob and Brad both set their forks and napkins down. "I think we'll head out," Bob says, pushing his chair back, but remains seated when she ignores him.

"I'm sure you think this guy is going to show up. He'll be there holding your hand and caring for the baby when it cries at night or is sick." She lets out a disappointed huff. "How are you going to do this? You can't even . . . "

It should hurt, but it doesn't. It normally would, but today, I feel sorry for her that she thinks the entire male population is a bunch of lying deadbeats. I have people who love me. A whole handful of men who've stayed and supported me. Men who don't give a flying fuck that I can't read and think no less of me because of it.

I put my phone in my pocket and sit back in my chair. "Mom, I'm sorry that's what you believe. No matter what I say, it won't make any difference. I have a disability, but it doesn't impair my ability to judge someone's character or their capacity to love me."

It's the first time I've used that word in relation to myself and not felt complete shame. "I will take care of these babies, both of them and regardless of what you think, Mark will be a part of it." I stand and glance at Bob, who seems like he might actually be a decent guy. "I hope for you that someday you'll meet someone who changes your mind."

I move to the door and turn back. "Bob, it was nice meeting you," I say softly, not wanting to be a total jerk.

He nods and winks at me. "You too, honey. Congratulations. You take care now."

Brad hops out of his chair like a jack-in-the-box and meets me at the door. "I'll be heading out, too."

The cold, moist air feels good against my hot skin. I exhale a long breath, and it billows in front of me. Brad closes the door, and we walk down the driveway together.

"I'm really sorry about that," I offer quietly, pulling my keys from my pocket as I quickly walk to my truck.

He holds up his hand. "No need to apologize. I wish you the best. *The* Mark Sandberg, huh? I knew he was from here, but man . . . " He stops at my truck, rubbing his chin. "Your mom clearly has no idea who he is." I smile, shaking my head. "That'll be something when she figures it out." I nod, my smile growing a little wider.

I know my mom loves and worries about me. I also know deep down she wants the best for me. She just uses her past decisions and experiences to predict my future. We aren't the same, and Mark is not my dad.

Brad surveys my truck. "You do good work." He gestures to it. "I know a lot of people who'd pay good money to have a truck restored like this."

I glance at my old truck. "Yeah. It's my favorite kind of work."

"You've clearly got talent. It was nice meeting you." He steps away and smiles a nice smile. "If Mark ends up being an asshole . . . " He gestures with his fist.

I laugh. "He's not."

"Good," he winks, and I see Bob in it. "For the record, neither is my dad."

He opens his car door and climbs in, and I get in my truck, wondering if I'll ever see him again. He was nice. Ironically, he and his dad made it a little more tolerable. Two more guys that don't belong on the list of dickheads. Maybe I won't mind if Bob the Builder sticks around.

I step into the house and toss my keys on the counter, ready to find my bed and stay there for the foreseeable future.

"Pal, is that you?" Grandpa hollers from the living room.

I pour a bowl of cereal, add some milk, and carry it with me to the couch.

"How'd it go?"

I shove a spoonful in my mouth. "She was working to set me up with her new boyfriend's son's friends."

"No shit. What in the Sam Hill is wrong with her?"

I raise an eyebrow. "I don't know. She's your daughter."

"Yeah, well, I blame your grandma. She left us both, seeking the high life." He rubs his forehead. "I know she's difficult, but she loves you. Doesn't want you to struggle like she did."

I nod, knowing it's true, but it still sucks she can't see how different we are and trust me to live my own life.

"How'd your doctor's appointment go?"

I set my bowl on my lap and finish chewing. "I'm having twins."

Like a slow-motion instant replay, the old man's entire body shifts in my direction. "You're shittin' me?"

I shake my head. "I have the pictures and two strong heartbeats to prove it."

"No wonder you're huge."

"Grandpa!"

He pops his footrest back in and sits up straight. "Where is that boy? I need to congratulate him on the good work."

I shove another bite in my mouth. "Thanks. I clearly had nothing to do with it."

"It wouldn't have happened in any way without him."

I roll my eyes and take another bite. "He had to leave. He's meeting with the Liberties in the morning."

He settles back in his chair. "You didn't go with him?"

"What, and follow him around like a lost puppy dog?"

He crosses his arms and gives me that look over his glasses like he doesn't appreciate my sass, but it's his fault. He taught me. "You've been apart too long. Maybe it's time you actually be together."

"What, are you tired of me?" I joke, but he clearly doesn't think it's funny.

"I'm a selfish man, and I've gotten far more time with you than I ever deserved. I'd keep you here with me forever if I could, but it's not meant to be that way."

I set my bowl on the table between us, leaving the milk. "My life is here. I can't sit around while he trains and figures out where he's playing next season."

"Why not? That's what wives do."

"Did you really just say that?"

I see his wrinkled mouth try to hide a smug grin, wanting to get me riled up. After our little moment passes, his serious tone takes over. "Pal, you've got two babies coming who need a mom and a dad."

This stubborn, hard-ass old man is sensible. *What the hell is happening to my life?* "What about my job and the garage?"

"I'm thinking about selling to Slade." He says it. Just like that. "And before you get your panties in a twist, listen." He pulls his glasses off and sets them on his leg. "Pal, this shop isn't meant to be the rest of your life. It was your beginning." He pauses. "I know you love to work on cars, but you're too good to be stuck there. I know you think you can't work anywhere else, but you're limiting yourself. Anyone would see your work and hire you on the spot. I've let you think otherwise for too long."

I look at my grandpa. Rough and tough and hardened by life. "I don't know if I can just give it all up and hope this will all work out."

He nods, understanding. "You're not her, and he's not your dad or any of those men. That young man has been in love with you since day one. I saw it then, and he's even more in love with you now. My eyes may be old and worn, but I see that clear as day." He shifts in his chair. "Can you really live and do all this without him?"

This joker knows I can't, and I kind of want to be mad at him for pointing it out and making it sound really that easy.

He blows out a breath. "You can work on cars anywhere in any fashion you want, but I think . . . the rest of your life will be pretty full of something so much better and more fulfilling."

The tears in his eyes get to me. I'm up and reaching for him, hugging him tight.

"I'm so proud of you."

"I love you, Grandpa."

"I love you, too."

I release him and move back to my spot on the couch. "I'm going with him to the awards and the game."

"You shit. Where's my ticket?"

I smile. "Maybe next year."

"Ha. I might be dead by then."

"Not your ornery ass."

He puts his glasses back on, focusing his attention back on the TV. "Did you tell him?"

My body stiffens, and I know exactly what he's asking. All the cereal turns into a giant rock, sinking to the bottom of my stomach. "No."

"What you did matters."

I inhale and push it out. "I don't know. I'm not sure anything good will come of it."

Grandpa hits that power button on the remote and stands. "That will bite you in the ass. I'd think long and hard about it."

Like I haven't for the last eight years.

"I'm going to bed. I could use you at the shop in the morning for some light stuff."

I nod, wanting to push thoughts of what he said out of my mind, but they linger there with bright red warning lights.

I climb the stairs and peel my clothes off, knowing I have some major shopping to do. I hate shopping, but Krissy doesn't, so she'll make it tolerable. I shower and pull the sheet back to slide into bed, where I find a folded Liberties shirt. One I saw Mark wear.

I take my shirt off, tug his on, and then FaceTime him.

"Hey, baby." His beautiful, handsome face fills my screen. He's sitting in his bed in Manhattan, and I'm in mine. "Nice shirt."

"I like it." I lift the soft cotton material to my nose and inhale. "It smells like you."

"How'd it go tonight?"

"About as good as expected."

"That good, huh? I'm sorry I wasn't there."

I sink down in my bed and pull the covers higher. "Me, too. Her new boyfriend was there."

"No way."

I nod. "It gets better. His son joined us. She wanted me to get to know him and his friends."

"Lex, I'm sorry."

I shrug. "It's ok. They actually seemed nice. Although it was awkward to tell her I'm married and pregnant in front of them. Then she went on to rant about men and me and . . . " I sigh, releasing the last bit of stress from the night. "It's over. She knows and can stop trying to pawn me off on strange men."

"Yeah, that shit ends today."

I smile. I could tell him more, but what's the point? "When we left, Brad told me to let him know if you were an asshole."

"I bet he did," he grunts.

I shouldn't like to see him jealous as much as I do. "You're a sneak."

He pulls back, feigning innocence. "What? Me?"

I glare. "You trying to drive the world crazy or just me?"

That mischievous grin takes over, and I want to kiss him so much. "You have no idea. My phone is blowing up with people wanting to know who you are and guessing what it means. Rumors are flying."

"You're such a drama queen."

"The only kind of drama I'm having from now on is the good kind. The you kind. The baby kind. I'm obsessed."

"You're insane." I bite my lip. "Hey," I say quietly. "You still want me to go with you this weekend?"

His face softens. "Yes. So much. I'll pick you up."

"Ok."

"You'll need a dress." I groan, and he smiles. "Preferably a very sexy one that shows off lots of skin and our growing babies."

"Seriously. Are you trying to get the entire female population to hate me?"

He laughs. "No, I told you. I want to let the whole world know I did that, and I'm damn proud of it."

"Ugh. You and Grandpa. Do I have any role in this?"

He smiles. "You played the most important part. You came and found me."

"You came and found me first," I yawn.

"I did. The best, most terrifying decision I ever made." I study him, missing him terribly, and thinking about everything Grandpa said.

"Will you let me know how it goes tomorrow?"

"Yes. I'm getting out of this city and somewhere with some room for us to grow."

Us. Room to grow. A warmth rolls through me at the thought. It sounds nice. Like a dream. A dream I've clung to for so long it's hard to let myself believe it could come true.

"Hey." Mark's voice is soft and tentative. "Did you see the app I sent you?"

I remember the text he sent me. "Uh yeah, but it was during dinner, and I haven't opened it. What is it?"

He scratches his jaw. "It's a new text-to-speech app. It's supposed to be better than the current apps on the market. It's more efficient and has new features. It can read documents and images, so if you take a picture of something, it will read it to you."

I blink, staring at him. "You got that for me?"

"Yeah. I thought you could try it." He suddenly sounds unsure. "It's probably filled with bugs and isn't foolproof just yet, but I thought it might help with the babies and . . . "

My throat and eyes burn, and he must see it.

"Baby, you don't have to use it if—"

"Thank you," I swipe at my cheek and sniff, my chest aching with . . . how much it means to me that he would think of this. "I can't wait to try it. That's . . . Thank you for thinking of me. It's amazing. How did you even find it?"

A gentle smile appears, and all I want is to wrap him up and never let go. "I've got connections." His smile spreads a little wider. "But," he leans out of the frame and then returns. "For now, I thought we could go through these together." He holds up the stack of pamphlets from my doctor's appointment that he apparently stuck in his bag when I wasn't looking. "I want to know everything that's happening."

At one time, it was history books and classic literature. Now, the man is going to read me prenatal pamphlets.

Another tear falls as he selects one and holds it up. "How about cord banking?" His eyebrows arch upward. "Sounds cool."

I smile through my blurry visions. It doesn't even matter how things turn out for us. I'm so damn lucky to be doing this with him.

Chapter 27

MARK

"You all right? You sure this is what you want?" Rob sits across from me, a cup of coffee halfway to his lips.

I roll my neck. "Yeah. I need a change."

"Rumors are still circulating about the Kingsnakes being interested since Kenny is retiring. I've heard Packard isn't working out in Seattle, so I'll make some calls and see what I can find out. Houston's a mess. They're looking to make trades but have only a few draft picks to work with and flimsy management. I'm not recommending it, but it sounds like they're being aggressive."

I rub my forehead. "What do you think?"

Rob, my long-time agent, stares out the window at the pedestrians charging by. I know he isn't happy I just pissed away a hell of a deal. Despite my healing shoulder, they offered a five-year contract, $200 million, with no franchise clause. It doesn't get much better than that.

When Rob heard me say, thanks, but no thanks, I thought he was going to have a stroke right there at the full conference table, but he's stuck with me so far. The management I've worked with over the past six years was speechless. They were even more stunned to find out I have a wife and twins on the way, but that information helped them understand my decision and wish me well in finding a new team.

Now, I have to find an organization willing to take me on with a half-healed shoulder and the reputation of walking away from an impressive offer.

Rob weighs his head from side to side. "We've got a hefty hill to climb. I'll start knocking on doors and put some feelers out there. I need you to get fans invested and rooting for you. Next weekend, you need to be lighting up social media."

"Lex will love that."

"This is part of your life, man, and you're good at it. She'll get used to it. Nice tease, by the way. People are scouring the web, wanting to know anything and everything about your mystery woman. That post is creating a firestorm, and fans are going crazy."

"I've seen. I need them in my corner, or I don't have a chance."

"Lay the charm on thick. Your fans only expect this kind of surprise from you, and they're eating it up. Teams will pay attention. You add in some good content about how your arm is healing, showing you're ready for next season. The calls will come. The question is, will the money be there?"

I hope he's right. I've needed this game some days like I've needed air. I love it, and I'm not ready to walk away.

"I'll do my part, but I need you to find me the best deal in a place where we can be a family."

Rob nods. "I'll do my best. You know I will." He pushes his mug to the side. "Keep your head up. I may not have liked your decision, but I respect it. You're going to be a fantastic father. That's what makes a man. Not big deals." He stands. "Congratulations again, buddy. Tell the same to your wife. I'm looking forward to meeting her and congratulating her myself."

I stand and shake his hand. "Thanks. Sorry again for keeping you in the dark."

He chuckles. "I expect nothing less."

He slaps me on the back. "I'll be in touch. Have fun next weekend."

We're greeted by the frigid wind and part ways. A plane is waiting to take me back to Phoenix. I need to be in the best shape of my life and have my arm working better than ever.

Rob said we have a hill to climb. I've got mountains. I need a team that wants what I have to offer and to convince my wife that the only place to be is with me, wherever that is.

I rest back on the bench, my lungs burning. The early morning breeze flowing through the open door is cool against my damp skin.

"You sure you should be working out this soon?" Sean's voice comes out of nowhere, and I sit up, wiping my face with the hem of my shirt.

"Where the hell did you come from?"

"I'm on my way to our last practice. I thought I'd stop by and see if you made it back. I heard you turned down a goldmine."

I stand and move on to lunges. "There's not a chance in hell Lex and my babies are going to sit around the city while I play ball."

"Babies?" Sean's brow scrunches.

I grin, but it takes effort. "Twins."

"You bastard. Does Shane know?"

I shake my head, pushing my breath out as I lunge again. "Just found out a few days ago. I've been busy turning down millions and trying to get in desirable shape. Rob says I need to parade around this weekend, showing I'm good as new."

"Twins. That's . . . incredible." His wide eyes and loss for words are like all my thoughts, spinning around in the dark, trying to find which way is up. "What's with the sharp attitude? This is amazing news."

I push up and take a rest before the next set. "Too much in my head. This sitting around waiting to see if anyone wants to pick me up is torture. I've worked too hard to be here."

"But you walked away from the deal."

My temper spikes, and I fist my hands. "I know, and I'd do it again. I'm ready to move on, and that's not the place for Lex. I need her with me. I want to see my babies grow."

Sean leans up against the weight rack. "Where is she?" I side-eye him. He freaking knows where she is. "So, you getting out of New York will change that?"

"I fucking hope so. It's all I've got!"

Sean crosses his arms. "Why don't you tell me what's really going on?"

I drop my head, my temper flaring into the red zone. I breathe through my nose, knowing he's not here to piss me off. "What are you talking about?"

"You look like you want to punch something. I know walking away from that deal had to hurt, but you did it for the right reasons." He pauses, but I give him nothing because I don't know what he's looking for. "Lex isn't here, and that's clearly a problem."

"Bro, what do you want from me?" I hiss.

Sean, the annoyingly sensible and calm one, doesn't even flinch. "I want you to tell me why you're pretending to be He-Man and melting down like a teenage drama queen." I grab a dumbbell, but he steps in front of me. "Stop. You're gonna break what they just fixed. Out with it, or I'll call Shane, and you'll have to deal with his gruff, no-nonsense coach tone. You know he'll drag it out of you literally if he has to."

No, thank you. The last thing I need is Shane barking at me and telling me what to do.

I sit on the bench and rest my head in my hands, trying to figure out where to start. "This is what I want. I want a chance to start over with Lex."

I stare out the garage door. "Football is all we had. It's all I've had, and it's what got me through. I possibly just kissed away my career. Pissing into the wind, hoping she'll come with me wherever I go." I wipe sweat from my brow. "I'm not ready to be done, and she's hell-bent on taking care of herself."

"And that surprises you? When we were in high school, she worked in that garage and studied harder than anyone else. She did it despite how difficult it was for her. Who else have you ever met that was that determined?"

Memories of finding Lex in the garage before school zip through my mind. She'd be fixing something or sitting at the workbench trying to piece through a history book. She was determined never to let anyone see her struggle and worked night and day to get a full-time spot in the garage.

"Uh, us . . . but we didn't struggle every day to read the playbooks or have people constantly treat us like we were stupid or didn't belong. We *were* the football team. She still struggles with reading and is a woman working in a man's world. Cal said she's convinced no one will ever hire or work with her."

My shoulders slump, feeling like I've already lost. "That garage is her dream. Taking it over and restoring cars is all she wants to do. She trusts the guys she works with, and they know how good she is." My teeth grind together at the vision of Slade's big arms around her. "How can I ask her to give that up to follow me? We saw how people treated her in high school, and you and I both know the world hasn't changed that much. I couldn't stand it."

When Sean doesn't say anything, I decide I might as well be out with the rest. "She's scared. She's never been outside of that town and away from the people who see her as equal. I'm scared I'm not enough to take her away from all of that. I sure as hell wasn't enough back then, and now . . ."

I meet Sean's sympathetic eyes, feeling my own begin to sting. "What if this is it? What if I'm done?" I swallow the burn in my throat. "What if I have to go back and live there haunted by flashbacks and memories I left locked up in that town?" There, I said it. "I feel like a giant, selfish asshole, given all I've been able to do."

I put my head in my hands, trying to release the pressure in my chest that's only continued to build since leaving that meeting. "Sean, I have two babies counting on me. I can't screw this up."

He remains silent, sorting through all I just tossed out, and then drops onto the bench beside me, his arms on his legs. "You won't screw this up. You're already putting them first. That's what you did walking away from that deal."

He bumps my shoulder. "You need to chill out. Do what Rob said. Get that pretty ass face in front of the cameras this weekend and win votes. He'll find you something. Probably something amazing. In the meantime, you need to work on getting your girl. Show her she can do what she loves wherever you are."

It's the same damn thing Cal said. I run a hand over my face. "How in the hell do I do that?"

He shrugs, which is incredibly helpful. "I don't know, but you're smarter than you've ever let people see, and you know Lex."

"Wow, jackass. Do you want to be paid for that advice?"

He laughs and steps toward the door. "You love her. You'll figure it out. You don't have a choice, and we don't let anyone back us into a corner."

He's right about that. He stops at the door of his truck. "Quit pushing it. Give me the game and some time with Andie and Ax, and then I'll work your ass to the ground. We'll get you there, maybe even on the field with me, but not if you mess up what they fixed."

He climbs in his truck and disappears.

"Dammit." I toss my water bottle in the trash. He's right.

I grab my phone and head into the house. I can't control anything. I can't pull a team out of thin air, and no offer will come if I can't pass a physical or my arm is jacked up.

I lean over the counter, pushing out a long breath. One thing at a time. First, I need to get Lex through next weekend and the media storm that will follow. Then, somehow, I'm going to show her we can live these dreams together. Or . . . I'll walk away from the one thing I've survived on so I can be with the only ones I can't live without.

Chapter 28

LEX

"She won't start?" Carson rubs his forehead. "I replaced the timing belt, but the damn thing won't fire."

"Did you check the sprocket alignment before you put the cover on?" I try to lean over to get a closer look.

"This piece of shit," Carson says, tossing his wrench down. "I thought I had them aligned."

I lean over the fender, squishing my babies, and as much as I hate it, I know my hands-on days are over for now. My back hurts, I drink enough water to hydrate a city, and peeing is becoming a constant interruption to every task.

"Let's remove the inspection plate." I hold out my hand, and Carson hands me a screwdriver. I bump the starter until I see the sprocket alignment marks. "The lines have to match up exactly. They're off a tooth." I straighten, arching my back. "You have to take it apart. Get them lined up, and I bet she starts."

Carson curses under his breath but removes the timing cover.

The metal door squeaks and slams as Krissy enters.

When I called and asked her to go shopping with me, I broke the extra wide news. We haven't seen each other, and she definitely hasn't seen my double-size belly uncovered in all its growing glory. I'm convinced it's expanding by the minute.

Her eyes widen to the size of rims, and then her glossy lips turn up into a show-stopping smile. "I still can't believe I was right."

"Right about what?" Slade returns with a new filter in his hand.

"I was right about this one being pregnant, but can you even believe it's twins?" She rubs her hands together. "I'm throwing you the most badass baby shower you've ever seen." Her mouth drops open. "We've got to have it here. I'll talk to Cal."

"Need some help with that," Trig winks at her.

Slade growls. "She doesn't need your help with anything."

Krissy grins at Trig, knowing it will drive Slade bananas. "You any good at planning baby parties?"

These two flirt like love-sick teenagers just to piss Slade off.

Trig leans up against the Toyota he's working on, looking brave. "I'm good at a whole realm of things."

Carson's hand falters on the screwdriver. He mumbles a few choice words, looking like he's about to take out the SUV in front of him.

"Take all that mushy shit somewhere else," Wind yells.

"They're not taking anything anywhere," Slade dictates. "There isn't a single thing having to do with babies the two of you will be involved in . . . together."

Krissy ignores him, keeping her attention on Trigger. "I'll be in touch, and we can plan," she winks. "We need double the party."

Trig grins.

Slade points at him. "I know you think this is funny, but I'm about ready to take your ass out."

"All right. We're leaving," I say, waving goodbye. "Don't get any blood on the vehicles."

Krissy laughs and blows Trig a kiss, which just about sends Slade through the roof.

"Kris, if you don't want to find all your shit on the lawn, I suggest you knock it off."

She laughs, "It's too easy, Slade. Maybe you should get out there and find yourself a woman, and then you won't be in such a pissy mood all the time."

"Yeah, man," Wind adds. "If you ever find someone who can tolerate your stoic, boring, ritualistic lifestyle. You need to have a little fun."

"And you need to mind your own fucking business," Slade shoots back.

I grab my coat, leaving the guys to their grunted comebacks.

"Where are we heading?" Krissy asks, pulling the door open, not giving a crap about the large masculine pot she stirred.

I shrug. "I was hoping you'd know. I need a dress."

She raises a perfect eyebrow. "A dress or a *dress*?"

"Is there a difference?"

She laughs. "Let's go. We'll figure it out on the way."

Twenty minutes later, Krissy thrusts me into the dressing room of an uptown boutique I've never set foot in and hands me an armful of dresses. I take them, wondering what I've gotten myself into.

As if she knows I'm not undressing, she pops her head inside the curtain.

"Scoot. This might take us the rest of the afternoon. You need a whole new wardrobe, plus a killer dress. Those won't take another second of that." She waves her finger toward my completely unzipped jeans held up by luck and a tight tank.

I shimmy out of my clothes and tug on item after item, hoping it will work for this weekend, but still feel like me. I'm not into playing dress up or wearing bright colors or flowers or things that make me look like I stepped out of a Target ad.

I pull on a navy and white striped three-quarter length sleeved dress that hugs my body and is not completely terrible.

I step out, searching for Krissy, my arms at my side.

"Oh, that's really cute. It hugs all the right things." She comes closer to inspect. "This would work for a casual party or dinner." My stomach fists at the thought of going to one of these highfalutin sponsor parties that Mark mentioned. "With your blonde hair, you look like a cute little pregnant beach babe."

"I feel like a sailor."

"You're a cute one, and I think you could get by with some sneakers." That ups the appeal. "Try on that fitted, black T-shirt dress. I bet it would go with a cute jacket or one of your flannels. Totally you."

I try the shin-length, tight-fitting dress in my preferred color wheel.

"Yep. Definitely a winner. We should see if they have this one in other colors."

And this is how it goes for an hour. Eventually, we move on to fancy dresses, needing one good enough for the awards, where I'll be surrounded by supermodels wearing designer gowns.

I groan, taking a seat in the wooden chair in a horrible emerald lace dress. "Krissy, I'm done."

"Not now. We're so close." She steps inside with two more dresses. "Up, I'll unzip you. One of these is it. I have a feeling."

"You said that about the last eight dresses."

"You can't show up in a tank and unzipped jeans. The women will be showing the goods in shimmery gowns." I slump down in my chair. "What's wrong?" She leans against the side of what has become the dumping ground of unwanted clothes.

I could tell her I'm tired. It wouldn't be a lie. I'm exhausted. I haven't slept well and have been up all hours of the night staring at the ceiling. It's given me a lot of time to imagine what this weekend will be like.

I want to see Mark. Each time I talk to him, I miss him more. I can tell he's stressed about turning down the Liberties offer, which I can't help but feel guilty about. Now, we're headed into bright lights, and I'm not sure what to expect.

"This weekend will be . . . a lot. The cameras and attention. Mark is used to that, but I'm not." I pick at the ugly dress. "I'm not made for fancy clothes and crowds."

"But you'll be with Mark, so it really doesn't matter if you fit in. You fit with him."

She makes it sound so simple. I let my head fall to the side. "Yeah, for the weekend. Then what?"

Krissy hangs the last two dresses up and takes a seat on the floor across from me, leaning back against the wall. "What do you want to happen?" Her soft tone eases the swirling in my stomach.

I raise and lower one shoulder. "He wants me to go back to Phoenix with him, and part of me wants to. To see what it would be like. I want us to have time and a chance to really be together, but I can't just sit around while he trains and . . . "

I inhale and let it out slowly. "He gave up an amazing deal because he knew I'd hate New York, and even though he'll never admit it, he's worried about finding another team. I feel like a total jerk. I've never wanted him to give anything up for me."

"Alex, he walked away from the deal. It shows how much he loves you and wants you to be happy. He took a really big risk because he wants you with him."

She pulls her knees to her chest. "I don't know a lot about relationships, but I know they're scary. Sometimes, we have to risk it. The world out there is terrifying. Change is terrifying, but regrets are a thousand times worse than the fear of the unknown. Those suckers we hold on to forever and torture ourselves with what-ifs."

"So, just go back to Phoenix? Leave the shop, my job, the guys . . . Grandpa. What am I supposed to do?"

She smiles. "Spend time together. See what life is like with his training schedule. Go out to dinner and hold his hand. Make out anytime you want. Go on vacation." She shrugs. "You have a few months before you'll have two babies that will need all of you all the time. Maybe put your feet up and love on the guy you've waited so long to be able to."

She grabs a hanger, twisting the hook around and around. Her tone shifts down to a sad whisper. "I don't think it'd be that bad to have someone who'd do anything to be with me."

I stare at her and her downcast face. I don't know all of her and Slade's story, but I know enough to know those words are filled with pain. And . . . she's right. It's pretty damn amazing what he did for me.

I lean over and hug her tight. "Ok. Hand me those dresses. Please, God, let one of them be good enough."

"Good enough? Honey, it needs to be drool-worthy." I groan, and she swats me in the butt with a shirt. "The entire football community is waiting to get a glimpse of you. If women are going to hate you for stealing Mark's heart and having his babies, then you should look fabulous while you're doing it."

"What in the hell is that? A coffin?"

I drop an oversized suitcase in the middle of the living room and unzip it. "Want to get in and test it out? If it doesn't work, I have another in my truck?"

"Who taught you to be a smart ass?" Grandpa asks, settling in his recliner for dinner and news. "Damn, girl. Did you purchase an entire department store? You better tell Mark he needs to charter a cargo plane."

I perch on the edge of the couch. "I forgot my phone, but I'm heading to Linda's for dinner." One overgrown eyebrow raises as he stuffs the corner of his sandwich in his mouth. "I need to talk to her, but I also want to tell Bree I'll be gone for a little while."

"Really?" he mumbles through a mouthful. "You're telling her?"

I shrug. "After this weekend, it'll be no secret."

He nods, taking another bite. "You're going back with him?"

"Mark and I need time, and I can't sit around drooling over what the guys are working on."

Grandpa takes a sip of his drink. "Pal, I want you here, and I'll miss you like crazy, but this is what you've waited for. Don't waste it. I want you to be happy."

A burn rises in my throat, and I swallow it down. "I'll be back for my next doctor's appointment, but I need you to check in on Bree and make sure—"

He holds up his hand. "I've got it. Maybe I can bring her to the garage. I've got a lot to teach her."

"After tonight, I need you to—"

He pulls his sandwich away, cutting me off. "It's time for you to let this go and finally live your life. I'll make the rounds."

I smile, knowing if there's anyone I trust with this, it's this old stubborn fart.

"Have you told him you're infiltrating his space?" He lifts his sandwich and takes another bite. I shake my head. "That boy could use some good news."

I smile. "I've gotta go." I stand, needing to find my phone, but pause before heading upstairs. "I'm going to miss you like crazy, too."

I leave him to his obnoxiously loud newscast while I break the big news one more time to a woman who once needed help. She needed help, and it changed everything.

I find my phone on the floor at the bottom of my bed. I scoop it up. I glance at the time, noticing I'm going to be late.

SEXY BABIES' DADDY: Tomorrow. Noon. *Airplane emoji*

My stomach leaps into a flip, thinking about spending the weekend with Mark and telling him I'm going back to Phoenix for a while. The flip-flop is followed by a swell of nerves that ripple through me. Being with Mark this weekend will be one thing. Having all eyes on me will be another.

ME: **Kissy face emoji**

I shove my phone in my back pocket, along with my anxiety. I have somewhere I need to be and a more pressing matter to deal with. A little matter that had major consequences and maybe still does. It's like a swirling whirlpool that's churned for years and has the power to spin out of control and pull the weak under.

I made a choice, and even now, looking back, I wouldn't change it. I close my eyes, reliving the moment I stood in the stands, watching Mark celebrate his first college win. Tears ran down my cheeks, everything in me wanting to slide over the rail and onto the field. I wanted to run to him. To hug him and kiss him and let him know I was there. I wanted him to know I'd always be there, but I didn't. I couldn't so that he could be free.

SEXY BABIES' DADDY: Voice Message: *Just so you know, there will be a whole lot of that happening this weekend.*

Excitement and anticipation for my trip are overshadowed by restlessness and worry about what lies before me this evening. I used the ten-minute drive to pull myself together. Taking a big, deep breath, I barely have a chance to knock when the door swings open.

"Alex!" Bree's arms fly around me, and she hugs me tight only for a second before she steps back, her little brow scrunched. She doesn't say anything as she tries to comprehend what's different. I bite my lip to keep from smiling. The bubbly, confident little girl is now speechless, her mouth hanging open.

"Ummm . . . " Her eyes light up with wonder.

"Hi. Can I come in?" I ask as she continues to study me.

She moves back inside, and I follow as she closes the door. I survey the small space, ensuring things are as they should be.

"Mom, Alex is here," Bree yells like she's looking for backup.

Linda appears, pulling down the hem of a fuzzy sweater. "Sorry, I just got home. I'm running—"

She stops mid-sentence, staring at me in my new clothes. A plain heather gray shirt with extra room in the middle to stretch over my bump and an old flannel hanging open over the top. Thanks to Krissy, I now have jeans that fit, and when I put them on, I realized I was an idiot for waiting so long.

"So . . . " The two ladies stare at me. "I have some news."

"Looks like it." Linda's dark, colored-in eyebrows raise, and she smiles softly.

"I uh . . . I guess I should start with a couple of months ago, I got married."

Bree's eyes bug out. "You did?!" She bounces on her toes, clasping her hands together.

"Yes."

Linda's head falls to the side slightly, her brow scrunched. "You married Seth?"

I shake my head, needing to keep paddling through this and not get sucked into the current of avoidance. I want to head straight for it, but I can't.

I focus on Bree's confused face. "Actually, I couldn't marry Seth because I've been in love with someone else for a very, very long time."

She pushes her lips to the side. "So . . . you didn't love Seth?"

Kids' blunt questions have the ability to make you feel like the biggest jerk in the entire world. I glance at Linda, and she's watching me and listening carefully. "I cared about Seth, but not in the way I should if I was going to marry him."

"But you love someone else like that?" Bree asks. Her gentle curiosity makes me smile.

"Yes. I've loved him pretty much since the day I met him, which was a long time ago." She smiles, and I notice she's missing a tooth. "And we're having twins." I run a hand over my stomach as her eyes grow wide again.

She claps her hands and hops in place. "You're having twins! I can't wait to babysit them." I drag my eyes to Linda, who's as still as a statue and growing a bit pale. "Mom, can you believe it? Alex is having twins!"

Linda shakes herself free enough to offer a small, fabricated smile. "That's . . . amazing news." She squeezes Bree's shoulders. "I'm . . . going to check on dinner and make sure it's not burning."

She scurries away to the kitchen as Bree grabs my hand.

"Come on. You've got to see my art project. I finished it today." She tugs me down the short hallway to her room and lifts a small, misshapen clay pot. "I used a purple glaze, and my teacher put it in the kiln." She holds it up, supporting it underneath with her hand. "I'm going to put all my colored pencils in it. Mom said I could get new ones. If we make something else, I can make something for the babies."

"That's very thoughtful. They'll love it, I'm sure." I sit on the end of her bed while she sets it back on her small desk and shuffles a few things around. "Hey, Bree," I say, wanting to make this quick.

She turns around, her dark braid falling over her shoulder as her fingers squish some kind of peapod fidget toy.

"I'm going to be gone for a little while, but I want to remind you that if you ever need me, you can call me anytime. It doesn't matter day or night, ok?"

"Where are you going?" Her sad tone spears my chest.

"The man I married . . . he doesn't live here, so I need to spend some time with him, but I'll be back."

"Will you be back for my dance recital?" She peers up at me with so much hope that my throat grows a little tight.

"I'll talk to your mom and find out when it is. I'll do my best."

She plops down beside me. "Are you moving?"

It's the question I ask myself a thousand times a day, and all I can do is answer her honestly. "I don't know. Right now, I'm . . . taking it one day at a time."

She's quiet for a long moment, her lips pressed together, thinking hard. "If your husband doesn't live here, you should probably be with him. Your babies really need a daddy. I wish I had a daddy."

I put my arm around her, hugging her close and resting my chin on her head. "I know, sweetie." I let out a long, slow breath. "It doesn't matter where I am. We'll still be best friends."

She peeks up at me. "Always?"

"Always and forever."

She beams. "If you have to move, maybe I could come visit you sometime."

My stomach kicks me in the throat at the idea of explaining all of this to Mark, and suddenly, the past doesn't seem so far away.

Linda peeks her head around the doorway. "Dinner is ready." Her tone is soft and uncharacteristically cool.

We follow her to the kitchen, where dinner is waiting on the table. We sit, and Bree bounces in her seat, filling all necessary dinner conversation with school, dance, and everything under the sun while Linda contributes little. When dinner is finished, she reminds Bree to finish her math homework. She hugs me and leaves us to do the dishes.

I hand Linda the plates, and she sets them in the sink, but instead of rinsing them, she turns to me.

"I didn't know you were still in touch with him," she says, continuing to avoid eye contact.

"I hadn't been, but then . . . " I stop, realizing I don't need to explain this to her. "It's been eight years, and I was done trying not to love him anymore. We're going to be together. Always."

Saying the words gives me confidence I didn't know I had. "I'm going to tell him. I wanted you to know."

She grips a towel tight in her hands. "Telling him won't do anyone any good."

I shrug. "Maybe not, but I won't lie to him. I've hurt him enough and won't do it again. Ever."

"You haven't lied to him." She fidgets with her watch. "I don't want him . . . I don't want him involved. I can't—"

"I did what I did for Bree and Mark." I pause, needing her to hear me. "*You* need to make sure that this doesn't . . . change things."

She still won't look at me, and a low boil simmers in my belly. "Linda," I say, waiting for her to pick her head up and meet my eyes. "You need to focus on Bree. This is about her." Like I've shocked her back to life, her eyes clear, and she nods. "I'm leaving town for a bit, but Grandpa will be checking in, and if you need help with Bree, he'd love to have her."

She doesn't move.

"Ok," I say, pushing away from the counter. "I'm going to hug Bree again and then head out. Please take care of her."

"Alex." She stops me, swiping at an eye filled with fear.

I nod. "Just . . . take good care of Bree. That's what matters."

I tell Bree goodbye, hugging her tight but not lingering, ready to go home.

I climb into my truck and turn the ignition, taking a deep breath as my gut sinks. I need to hear Mark's voice and be reminded that things are different now. I grab my phone and tap his name.

"Hey, baby. I can't wait to see you tomorrow." His voice is low, and he sounds tired.

"Me, too." My throat swells, and it's all I can manage.

Mark is going to get all of me, which means telling him exactly what happened eight years ago. It won't be this weekend when he's celebrating with his friends and family, but I will tell him.

I glance back at the small apartment, worrying for the joyous little girl with too much good and innocence inside to have darkness enter her world.

"You ok?" Mark's concerned tone has me getting it together.

"Yeah."

"Are you having second thoughts about coming with me this weekend?"

I bite my lip. "No, I just . . . miss you."

"Just a few more hours."

Just a few more hours, and then I'll step foot into a whole new world, suddenly on display, but I'll be with Mark. It's what I've been waiting for, and it's time to find out what life is actually like together.

Chapter 29

LEX

"Where are we going?"

Mark's arms slide around me from behind. "One of my major sponsors is throwing a party. That's tonight, and then the awards are tomorrow. There's a huge expo, but I'm thinking we take advantage of our time alone." His lips find the sensitive, ticklish spot right behind my ear. "Shane, Maggie, and the kids are coming in tomorrow, and we'll catch up with them at the game. Andie's with Sean, but she'll be there."

He pushes my hair away, trailing kisses down my neck.

I can definitely get on board with this part of the plan, especially when my nerves are about to sprout nerves.

When I met Mark at the airport, I climbed aboard the chartered plane, and my excitement to see him veered right into the lane of anxiety.

His hands glide over my belly. "Tonight will be pretty low-key. We'll make an appearance. Talk to a few people, then—"

I pull away and spin around to face him. "I have to talk to people." I'm kind of joking, but not really. Just the idea of hanging out with his family makes my palms sweat, and my heart skip to a different beat.

He snatches me back, my body fully pressing against his. "Not if you don't want to. We can pretend you're mute."

"Mark, I might actually be a little too good at that."

"Hmm." His lips hover over mine.

He's not making this easy. I want to know exactly what I'm stepping into, but his hands are sliding into my hair, and if I let him, he'll take me somewhere far away. It's all clouding my brain when I should be preparing for battle or at least a high-profile presentation, which I. Would. Never. Ever. Do.

But I can't think about anything at the moment other than his hands, gentle and tender, as he tips my head to just the right angle. His mouth moves slowly over my jaw to my ear like we have all the time in the world. His grip shifts to my hips, taking a firm hold and walking me backward.

"I've thought about this every night since I left you." His lips brush against mine, teasing.

I want to be all in this right now, but my brain is rapid-firing questions that need answering.

My legs bump the edge of the bed, and I hit the pause button. I press against his chest. "Mark," I whisper.

He pulls away just enough to rest his forehead on mine, his hands slipping under my shirt and around my back.

"I need more details, so I can reel in my freak out. I'm on the edge of panic." My heart is racing, and my stomach is quivering with the unknown.

He kisses my forehead and then releases me, flopping on the bed. "Come here," he holds out his arm.

I sit and scoot into the place next to him. He slides his arm around me and pulls me to his chest. "It's going to be ok. Some friends messaged me. They're going to meet us there. Guys I haven't seen in a while. There will probably be a bunch of fans."

"But they, your friends, don't know about me . . . about us?"

He doesn't say anything, so I tip my chin up to peek at him. He grins like he loves this. "Nope."

I groan. "You punk. You think this is funny."

"Baby, there is nothing funny about this." He cups my cheek, holding my face, forcing me to look at him. "You are the only thing that's been just mine. The most important thing that the rest of the world never knew about and didn't get to see. Only me."

"Yeah, well, you're about to blow the concealed lid wide open. Maybe you should keep me hidden forever."

He laughs. "There isn't a chance in hell. It's you and me from now on. No more hiding."

I rest my head against his chest, needing his amused calmness to work its way into me. "I should probably start getting ready."

He holds me tighter. "In a minute. I just want a minute like this." His hand spreads over my stomach, my legs tangling with his. "Besides, I'm worried I might lose you in all the clothes you brought."

It's my turn to smile. "Yeah, maybe. Krissy went a little crazy, but at least I'm not walking around with my pants unzipped and hanging open."

"That doesn't sound like a problem to me."

I try to roll away from him, but he laughs and tightens his hold.

I grab ahold of his shirt. "I was thinking I wouldn't go home after this."

Silence. Complete stillness. Even the rise and fall of his chest halts. Finally, when I'm getting nervous about his oxygen level, he speaks.

"Are you serious?" His voice is soft. "You're coming back with me? What about . . . " He doesn't finish his thought but slides away, propping himself up on his elbow.

"I can't sit and watch the guys work while I do nothing. It's driving me crazy." I stare into his brown eyes, which are rimmed in gold. "More than that, I'm just really tired of not being with you."

He laughs. "Really?! You're coming with me?!"

I nod. "Unless—"

He holds my face, bringing his close to mine. "Thank you," he whispers against my lips.

"We need time," I whisper back.

He presses a soft kiss to my lips. "It's all I want." His hand slides up my thigh and over my hip to my butt.

I stare into his eyes, the heat and longing matching my own. I bite my lip, forcing restraint, but I don't know how much longer I can take it.

I let out a slow breath as he watches me with a hint of a smirk, knowing exactly the effect he has on me. *Damn him and his sexiness.* "If you want me to go to this sponsor party thing with you, I need to get ready."

"Why?"

"Because I'm not stepping into your world in leggings and a sweatshirt."

"I really, really like this look." He pulls my sweatshirt up, revealing my growing belly, his hand gliding over it. "I can't believe how much they've grown."

I hold his hand in place, to what I think are little kicks I've noticed more each day. The most amazing and crazy feeling in the world. A pure miracle. Two of them. "Can you feel any of that?"

His eyes grow wide and shoot to my stomach. "What?! You can feel them."

I nod, smiling. "I think so. One of those pamphlets said it's possible to start feeling them around fifteen or sixteen weeks." He squints his eyes, trying to concentrate. "If I lay still, I can feel them go crazy after I eat."

"I want to feel them."

I guide his hand to the other side, where I feel movement. "Soon, you will. They're growing by the second. I'm going to be as big as a house."

"Want me to get you one of those motorized scooters?" I shove him, and he falls back dramatically, laughing. "You'd be hot zooming around. I'd hit on you."

"Mark, a ninety-year-old woman would think you were hitting on her by just smiling at her."

"I can't help it if my charm gets misinterpreted."

I roll my eyes and try to get up, but he holds me there. "I need to get ready."

"Stay here." He pops up and rummages through his suitcase. He returns and sits beside me on the bed, holding out his fist. "Open your hands." I frown at him, and his grin stretches its limits. "Trust me."

I side-eye him, cupping my hands. Three silicone bands fall into my palms.

I try to sit up, and he helps me as I inspect them—gold, silver, and black.

"I thought about getting you the real deal, but know you won't be able to wear it, so I got these. Just the last piece to ensure everyone knows you're mine."

I grip his shirt and pull him to me, pressing my lips to his. "Thank you. This is perfect. I love them." I slip the black one on my finger and hold out my hand. "What about me? Do people get to know you're mine?"

He hops up again and comes back with a matching black band. "I knew you'd choose black. I got the same." His face turns serious as he leans in and cups my face. "Lex, you are the only one I want. The only one I've ever wanted. I don't want you to be anyone else. Ok?"

I tip my head, pressing my cheek into his hand, a truckload of emotions rolling through me. My throat is thick and dry, and I try to swallow. I nod, unable to speak with the way that he's looking at me. So honest and sincere.

I've tried to pretend to be someone I'm not. It didn't work so well. I guess I'll have to be ok with letting the world see me.

I reach up and run my fingers along his stubbled jaw. I can do this because the only times in my life I haven't been scared or felt less than or ashamed is when I'm with him.

Mark grabs my hand, weaving his fingers through mine. I follow close behind, wrapping my free hand around his forearm. I'd really like to crawl inside his T-shirt and hide, but it's snug across his shoulders and chest. There's no room for me in there.

He stops before we reach a giant man wearing a polo with security across the back. I hear the steady beat of a drum, and distant music fills the air. Cars file past us, stopping only long enough to let people out.

Mark moves us to the side, keeping his back to the arriving people and hiding me. He tips my chin up. "You ok?"

I survey my surroundings without moving my head. His eyes are filled with earnestness and dead set on me. "Um . . . sure. You're not going to leave me, right?"

He shakes his head. "Nope. You're stuck with me. Forever."

I bite my lip to hide my nervous smile.

His large hands find the sides of my growing belly and hips. "You look incredible. I'm going to have to thank Krissy when I meet her."

I peek at my form-fitting black dress and low-top sneakers. My stomach is getting so big that I have to lean a little to see my feet.

He lowers his mouth to my ear. "This pregnant with my babies thing definitely works for you." He kisses the corner of my mouth, and heat surges from my head to my toes.

If offered, I'd be totally down with heading right back to the hotel.

He takes hold of my hand. "Let's do this. Just ignore all the people taking pictures." I whimper, and he grins, making me want to hit and kiss him at the same time. "You trust me, right?"

I nod, not even having to think about it. Mark takes my hand again, interlacing our fingers and holding tight as he pulls me toward the entrance. The bouncer, recognizing him, lets us walk right through. We stop for Mark to pose for pictures in front of a backdrop advertising his beverage of choice.

Women on their way in call out his name, trying to get his attention. I can't even blame them. He's beautiful. His smooth olive-tan skin and dark hair with those few strands that never want to stay in place. His perfect white teeth, under that devilishly handsome smile, but it's different from the one that's only for me.

He winks, and I smile back. He's always been a bit of a rebel, but with a gooey center, I'm beginning to believe he's held aside only for me. I want that to be true. I want to be the only one who gets that part of him. It's selfish, and I'm undeserving of that kind of reserved intimacy, but I want it.

I want it so badly that a slight ache forms in my chest at the thought of it not being true. The ache quickly slides into a growing pit in my gut, where the truth resides, and I wonder if the past should remain where it is. Tucked far away from the one I aim to never let it touch again.

After a few rounds of clicks and flashes, Mark leads us through the crowd of people to the bar under a large metal awning. A band performs on a small stage, and a few hundred people are spread around high-top tables, laughing and having a good time.

Mark slides his arm around me, putting me between him and the bar while he orders water. I raise an eyebrow.

"I only have a beer now and then. Usually, only with Shane and Sean."

I nod, understanding and incredibly proud that he only drinks when his brothers are watching. I push up on my toes to kiss him. Just a quick peck, but he grins like we made out.

I bite back my own, quickly feeling eyes on us as if we're rare tropical fish in a pretty aquarium. People who've been drinking do a remarkably terrible job of being sly. Whispers are unguarded, phones are popping out, and people are shuffling around to get closer.

He braces his arms on either side of me, bringing his head down closer to mine. "Just ignore it. It'll get better in a few minutes."

This is a brand-new side of Mark that I've never seen. He's calm, cool, and collected. The cockiness is still ever present, but it's self-assured and sexy as hell. "Does it ever get old?"

He shrugs, unbothered. Confidence pours from him, but it's different from the unshy, bold guy I fell in love with. He's a man who lives his life with everyone watching, and he's totally comfortable with himself. The allure is real, and my skin tingles with desire.

"I'm used to it, but you and this . . . " His hand slides over my belly. "It's going to cause a stir. That part is new for me, so we'll see. I have no problem telling people to back off if it becomes too much."

Mark's hand moves around close to my butt as he settles against the bar.

"Maybe we should cool the PDA. I feel like everyone is watching us."

He leans close, kissing my cheek. "That's because they are watching, and I'm all about PDA. Only with you."

I think about that. I tortured myself, scrolling through pictures of Mark with other women, but they weren't anything other than him standing next to them, with an arm around their shoulders.

He pulls away, leaving his arm around me. "You're here with me. I didn't believe this would ever happen. I'm taking every advantage of it and making it perfectly clear where I stand."

I roll my eyes. "You're full of yourself." *But I love it.* I take hold of his shirt. "Did I ever tell you that you're trouble?"

"Yes, many times, and I know you're non-dramatic ass secretly loves it." He leans to kiss me but stops when we hear a loud, deep voice bellow.

"Sand-berg."

Mark turns his head, and I see one huge dude walking toward us with a posse in tow. His hair is pulled back in a ponytail, and his smile is blinding. He looks familiar, but I can't place what team he plays for. The giant man nears, and he and Mark slap hands, moving into a man hug.

Mark is tall. He's 6'4", and I barely meet his shoulder with shoes on. This guy is taller. He's huge and greets Mark with a smile that matches his size. I watch as his eyes shift to me. He stares while Mark hugs the other guys.

I stand like a suspect in an interrogation room who won't talk. I'd like to sip my water and pretend I'm completely normal. I want to be unfazed by all this, but I'm certain it will slip from my sweaty hand, and I'll make more of a scene than I already am by just being here . . . with Mark.

The big dude continues to eye me but then bumps Mark on the shoulder. "Who's this pretty little thing you've been trying to hide?"

I want to roll my eyes, but the jolly giant's smile tells me he didn't mean it in a gross, dickhead way.

Mark's arm slips back around me, and there's that damn smirk again that has me ready to get back to the PDA.

"This, boys, is my wife, Lex. Lex, this is Macgowen, Cush, Frank, and Jacobs."

"You, bastard. You're married?" Macgowen grabs his shoulder. "When and why the hell wasn't I invited?"

I can only watch these men interact. It's been a very long time since I've seen Mark in his element, and these guys appear to be his friends, ones I've never met. It reminds me of all I've missed.

"A bit ago," Mark answers. "We wanted it to be private." He kisses my temple as his hand spreads over my stomach, then his eyes flick to mine. A smile appears like he's the holder of the last secret. "We're having twins."

Macgowen's eyes grow wide. "No shit. Sandberg is gonna be a dad." The other guys let out a loud round of manly cheers, all congratulating us. Macgowen moves forward and sweeps me into his massive arms, hugging me. I don't know this man, but I go with it before I fall into awkward, overstimulated uncomfortableness.

When he releases me, I scoot right back next to Mark, and as if he knows I need it, his hand rests low on my hip, keeping close contact.

They talk shop on the latest trades and moves, and Mark's posture stiffens. He restrains from providing details about his status and quickly changes the subject. It all tells me he's more stressed about it than he's been letting on.

"How about you, Lex? What do you do besides putting up with this handful?"

All eyes in our small circle are on me. My babies and I want to puke up my few sips of water.

Here it comes. The furrowed brows. Then, the comments, followed by the jokes. As if this is my lucky day, a few more people push into our group.

I recognize the guys as some of Mark's now former teammates. The woman with them is, of course, the daughter of the owner of the New York Liberties, Rochelle Gibson. The same woman, I suspect, was very much after Mark, and by the way she eyes his arm around me, my suspicion is spot on.

Her long, dark hair is slicked back into a tight ponytail, and she's wearing a dress that covers about as much as one of my bandanas. I wonder if she's ever worried about something slipping or popping out. Probably not. She's tall and beautiful but in that too-perfect kind of way.

Mark ignores the newcomers and answers Macgowen's question for me. "Lex is a mechanic."

The group eyes me. "Really?" Macgowan says. "What do you work on?"

Mark laughs. "The shorter list would be, what doesn't she work on?"

"I grew up in a garage," I add, wanting these people to know I can actually speak.

One of the other guys in the group, Cush maybe, says, "I test-drove a McLaren 720."

I can talk cars all day and all night. So, ok then. "The Brits know how to make a sweet-looking car. All luxury and style. But do you want to drive a computer or a vehicle?"

"All right, now," he says as the guys laugh, but the condescension I was waiting for isn't there.

"Who's this?" One of his former teammates asks, gesturing to me with his chin.

Mark's body goes rigid, his fingers digging into my hip.

Something tells me this cocky jerk isn't one of Mark's friends, and with the way the chick next to him is staring at me, I'm certain they don't have anything nice to say.

For some reason, I don't find myself intimidated. Maybe it's the confident man standing next to me. Perhaps it's because I've dealt with people like this before. People who look down on me as if I can't possibly have anything to offer. Either way, it's new, and it feels damn good.

Chapter 30

MARK

Who in the hell invited Carlos?

We were teammates, but we're not friends. He's a partier, can be a hothead on the field, and overall, I don't care for his wiseass face. He's a showboat with the attitude of a peacock—loud and egotistical.

Right now, he needs to quit eyeing Lex like he's TMZ's newest employee. The ugly smirk that tugs at his lips has my hand curling into a ball, and I want to punch it off his face.

"What's up, Carlos?" I ask, not answering his question and getting his attention off Lex. Rochelle doesn't flinch, keeping her dark dagger eyes aimed straight at her.

"Ahhh. I think I should be asking you. Heard you left the team. Just walked away. That was a ballsy move." He sucks his teeth. "How's the shoulder?"

I let my head fall to the side. This dick is trying to get a rise out of me. "Ah, now, Carlos, I appreciate your concern, but none is needed. I know what I'm doing."

He laughs, scratching his nose.

"I don't know. Seems to me you left some pretty great things behind in New York," Rochelle says, her eyes moving from me to Lex. "It's a shame. You can't fix that kind of mistake."

I can tell she thinks she's included, and I want to laugh, but I've burned enough bridges recently. I can't help the small sliver of dread sinking like a rock in my gut. It's possible I walked away from the game altogether that day in New York. That it was the end, and I didn't even know it.

I pull Lex in front of me and surround her because I have no doubt she'll try to shrink away under their intense scrutiny. It's not happening on my watch. Plus, I need her close to remind me why I'm doing this and what's most important.

"I did leave some really great things behind in New York. Lots of good memories, a great team, and an organization that supported me." I kiss the top of Lex's head, needing her to hear this. "But it was time to move on. My life isn't there anymore." *My whole world is right here, tucked between my arms.*

Rochelle smiles, but it's one of those fake, taunting smiles to inform me that I'm an idiot. "We'll see how long it lasts this time." She gives Lex another unimpressed once over, and I'm done here. "Unfortunately, it'll be too late."

I want to respond, but for the first time in my life nothing comes out. The fear of it being the end growing too fast for my cover to keep up with.

Maybe Lex senses it because she shifts in my arms. "When Mark wants something, he gives it his all, nothing less." She runs a hand over her round stomach. I'm not sure if it's subconsciously or if my girl has grown a pair in the last eight years, but I freaking love it. "He knows what he's doing." She tips her chin up and kisses the corner of my mouth, making me smile. "I have to find the bathroom."

"You good?" I ask in her ear.

She nods, and I watch this amazing woman weave through the crowd. Her faith in me has never changed. It's never faltered, and it's everything I need.

The Lex I said goodbye to years ago was quiet and shy. The woman she's grown into is still reserved, but there's a humble tenacity that's new, and it's breathtaking.

"I like her." Macgowen bumps my arm, stepping in front of Carlos and blocking him out. "I'm happy for you, man. It was time for you to settle down. Hang in there. Teams will show up. You've got too much left to give."

I hope he's right, but things are pretty bleak at the moment. Carlos and Rochelle sniff around for a bit before they head off to find another group to piss on. I talk with Macgowen and the guys about the Pro Bowl, wondering if this will all be the last of it for me.

The band moves from one song to another, and my eyes roam the area, searching for Lex. When the song finishes, and she hasn't returned, a prickle of panic rolls through me. *Was this all too much for her? Did Carlos and Rochelle make her second-guess things? Did she leave? Shit.*

I check my phone. Nothing. My stomach hits the concrete, and I set my glass on the bar. "Sorry, guys, I've got to—"

"Hey, man." Frank rejoins the group. "Your wife is outside," he laughs, shoving his phone in his pocket. "I was making a call, and a bus broke down. It's holding up all the traffic. Cars are backing up, and drivers are pissed. One lane and no way around. She was heading over to check it out."

My lungs expand with relief, washing the fear away. "I'm going to see if she needs help."

"*You,* help . . . with a bus?" Macgowen chuckles. "All right, man. I like this look on you. Find me at the game."

I slap his hand, unable to help the shit-eating grin on my face. I push my way through people who call my name like they know me. I don't stop for photos or autographs, wanting to find out exactly what Lex is getting her hands into.

When I step past security, I see her. She's standing on the driver's side tire, her long blonde hair pulled over her shoulder, peering into the popped hood of the black luxury party bus. Her tight dress, hugging every glorious curve, and her growing belly clearly getting in the way.

I snap a quick pic. The sight of her working does crazy things to me, and I will never ever get enough of it. Seeing her at work with my babies in tow brings it to a whole new level.

A horn blares, and I'm pulled from checking out my wife. Drivers of backed-up cars sit waiting, phones in hand or pressed to their ears, while Lex inspects the bus.

I don't know much, but I know she shouldn't be standing on a tire, leaning over, and reaching in.

"That your lady?" the security guard asks me, following my gaze.

"My wife." I step away to get her off the tire.

"Does she know what she's doing?" he asks, and I turn back. "If this line gets any longer, we'll have a safety issue on our hands."

"Where's the driver?" He points to an overweight man sitting on the curb with his phone to his ear and a cigarette hanging from his lips. "Oh, she knows what she's doing. Better hope she doesn't need parts."

I approach the bus, careful not to startle her.

"What the hell do you think you're doing?" I keep my tone smooth, although everything in me is poised to snatch her off the worn tire.

She doesn't take her eyes off whatever she's inspecting. "They had an issue. I'm taking a look."

"I can see that. How about you get down?" She doesn't move. "Like . . . now."

"Just give me a minute." She pulls on something, and I move closer, gripping her around the middle to be sure she's steady.

"No. Right now, Lex. If you fall . . . "

She straightens and peers down at me. "I need to check the—"

"Get down, babe. The driver doesn't seem to be concerned his bus isn't working, so—"

"He didn't even know how to pop the hood." Her tone tells me it's the craziest thing she's ever heard. "I had to show him."

"Great. Now he knows and can call a tow truck. You have to get down."

"Get a tow truck in here, how?" She looks around with a huff. "Clive needs these cars out of here."

"Who's Clive?"

She points, and the gatekeeper smiles. "Give me a minute to check a few more things, then—"

"Lex, you're carrying our babies. You've lost your pretty mind if you think I'm letting you stay up there, balancing on a piece of worn rubber, or a ladder, or anything else that puts you four feet above the ground. Get down."

She takes my hand, and I help her down while a horn blares in the distance.

She brushes off her dirty hands. "Fine, then I need you to help me."

I look around. More people have gathered, waiting for their ride out.

"Me? You want me to help?" I stare at her. "Remember that time I tried to help you line up the transmission on your truck? You told me under no circumstances was I ever to lay my hands on car parts again."

Her mouth turns up into a beautiful smile. She's in her happy place, and it makes my heart explode with a kind of joy I've only recently been reminded exists.

"Yes, I remember. I meant it, but desperate times call for desperate measures, and I don't have Carson or Wind here, so you'll have to do."

She walks over to the man I now know as Clive, and he follows her, carrying his stool.

All these men are standing around completely helpless while she's ready to work. Part of me is excited to get in there. I'm going to watch my girl kick this party bus's ass, and I actually get to assist *in* the ass kicking.

Wait. "Why didn't you say Slade?" A flash of him hugging her skates through my mind. Slade, her best friend. Everything seemed platonic from my angle, but I was very aware of his laser eyes on Lex, which were full of irritation.

No man gets his jock strap in a wad over unanswered calls unless feelings are involved. I would know. I never cared if a woman returned my call, but Lex better damn well, or I'd lose my shit. It makes me curious if there's anything more than friendly feelings happening on his side.

"Huh?" She points to the stool, expecting me to climb up, so I do.

"Why did you say you don't have Carson or Wind here? You didn't include Slade."

She side-eyes me as I step up. "Slade would just push me out of the way and do it himself."

Great. Manly Slade could just get in there and fix this beast himself. That answer doesn't give me anything, but if Slade has feelings, I really don't care. He had eight years to make a move and didn't. Now, Lex is mine and always will be. It really sucks to be him.

"Now, come on. Roll up your sleeves, Sandberg. Get in there and get this fixed, or I'll climb up there and do it myself."

"You know, I kind of like it when you're bossy." One eyebrow raises. "Maybe we should work on engines together more often."

"You know there's more in there than the engine, right?" She is giving me rare shit, and I love it. Lex talking cars and engines is damn sexy, and I want it all day and all night.

I hear a group hoot and holler my name, recognizing Macgowen and the guys. They've now joined the group of useless spectators.

"It seems like an electrical fault. I need you to check the battery cables for any looseness or corrosion."

"Uh. Where's that?" I stare at all of inner parts, having no idea what they are.

She moves to the side and pushes to her toes, trying to get a look. "Over here." She points. "Wiggle each of those cables to see if they're loose. Look for corrosion. It's white or green and powdery."

I find the cables, and they don't move. "They all seem tight, and I don't see any residue."

"Ok. Follow the cable down to where it connects to the body and do the same." I lean further, moving my hand along the cable. "You should feel a bolt, and it should be securely attached."

My fingers find the bolt. "There's a ring."

"Yeah, it should be connected to the bolt. See if it moves."

I jiggle. "It's loose."

"Great. We need an adjustable wrench."

I straighten. "Clive," I holler. "We need an adjustable wrench stat." Lex snickers. "What you are you laughing at? I'm going to fix this drunk mobile, and then you have to take back your 'I can never put my hands on a car again' rule."

I get both eyebrows this time. "That so."

I lean down my lips an inch from hers. "You're so beautiful when you're doing what you love."

She bites her lip, her eyes flicking between mine. "Not even close to watching you play." Her voice is achingly tender, sending a warm ripple through my chest.

A throat clears, followed by a gravelly voice. "Hey, this is all I've got." The driver stands, holding an emergency kit with a handful of silver tools.

Lex selects one. "Let's see if this will work." She hands it to me. "See if you can get this around the bolt enough to tighten it." I take the wrench and angle it to fit it onto the bolt. "You'll have to keep the cable from twisting and make sure it's snug."

It takes me a few minutes, but little by little, the bolt tightens.

Lex tells the driver to try to start the truck. I hop off the stool as he climbs in the driver's seat.

She gives the go-ahead, and it roars to life. The gathered crowd cheers.

Lex grins, and I can't help but lean over and kiss her, holding it for just a second before kissing her again.

"We did it," she says against my lips.

"Damn straight we did." I wrap my arms around her, kissing her one more time. "You ready to get out of here? I wasn't expecting this to turn into a work trip for you."

"That was fun. Besides, you getting those million-dollar hands dirty is pretty hot."

"That so."

"Totally." She yawns and rests her head against my shoulder.

"Maybe if no one picks me up, I'll work with you. I can be your assistant."

She laughs. "Let's not get ahead of ourselves. Your little jealous streak works just fine." She grins, and I want to kiss it right off her mouth.

"I'm not jealous. I stole your heart a long time ago. It's been mine ever since. Always will be."

Her arms slide around my back. "You're so sure of yourself."

"Baby, being tentative would've gotten me nowhere. You said it. When I see something I want, I play to win. With you, I played for keeps."

A warm flush creeps up her cheeks, and we can't get back to the hotel fast enough.

Clive gathers his stool while the guys praise Lex for not letting them die stranded on a sidewalk.

As we wait for our car, she slides her arms around my waist and rests her head on my chest. "You're going to be fine, you know that, right?"

I frown, unsure of what she's talking about.

She tips her chin up. "They're coming . . . the teams. Everyone knows what you can do. They always have."

I press my lips to her forehead, inhaling her and hoping she's right.

ROB: **Picture attached of Lex on the tire, reaching under the hood of the party bus.**
ROB: I'm assuming this wasn't intentional, but definitely a way to get peoples' attention.

Chapter 31

LEX

I blink, hearing the soft tones of Mark's voice. I blink again. My back is pressed up against his warm body.

"She told me what to do. All these men, standing around completely useless," he whispers.

I frown, wondering what he's talking about and who he's talking to.

"That was definitely not the plan, but I'll take it. Yeah. Ok." He chuckles soft and low. "I'll let her know."

I roll over, stretching my arms over my head. My body is stiff like I laid in the same position the entire night.

I don't even remember falling asleep. The car dropped us off at the hotel, and Mark ordered food while I changed into a shirt and shorts. The last thing I remember is eating and him teasing me for folding my pizza before taking a bite.

I haven't slept well in weeks, but apparently, I didn't even move last night. I groan, and the weight of Mark's strong body moves over mine, making room for my belly.

He braces himself on his arm. "Good morning."

I yawn, heat crawling up my body from my toes. "Hi."

"I had to make sure you didn't fall asleep with pizza in your mouth. I was scared you'd choke."

I rub my forehead. "Sorry. I was so tired. I haven't slept well for a while. I guess . . . "

He kisses my neck. "I like that you were able to sleep with me." *Me, too.* His hand glides up my thigh to the hem of my shorts. His lips move over my cheek. "How come you haven't been sleeping?"

His question comes out soft and curious, *but* I'm not sure I want to think about it when I'd much rather get lost in what he's starting.

When I don't answer, he pulls away, his eyes meeting mine. I hold his face, running my thumb over his jaw, needing my head to stay clear. I guess we're going there.

"I'm scared." I drop it and let it sit there. And it does, for a few long seconds while he watches me.

He pushes my unruly hair behind my ear. "What are you afraid of?"

That's the big question. The one I spend endless hours tossing over and over in my mind, and the list is overwhelming.

I think about Grandpa, the garage, the guys, and all the life I've lived in that little circle. My circle. The thought of leaving is sometimes too much to handle. Then there's Bree, and that pit begins to open again, but I yank it shut. But it's the two little beings counting on us to make sure everything is right for them that have me staring at the ceiling into the wee hours of the morning. The idea of not being able to share all of it with Mark causes my throat to swell.

I swallow, taking a second to let the fear claiming the number one spot float to the surface. The one tied down with uncertainty and the unknown. "I don't think I can do this by myself . . . away from you."

His forehead falls to mine. "You won't have to. I'm right here."

I bite my lip, trying to reel it all in. "For now, but we don't know where you'll be or what that will even look like for us. I lay in bed at night thinking, and I can't stop. There are so many things we have to do and decide beyond that. We need two car seats. Two. And they won't fit in my truck. Am I going to breastfeed? Do I want to? How will I work when I'll be feeding one and then the other all day and night long? Their little crib thing probably won't even fit in my room, so I'll be sleeping on the floor in the—"

"Shhh." Mark hushes me and kisses my forehead. "I'm sorry, Lex." He rolls off me and pulls me close. "I've been so caught up in my own shit. I'm sorry I haven't thought about what you're going through and what they need."

"I just . . . " I start, but I don't really know what to say.

"Baby, what do you want?"

I let out a slow breath and close my eyes, gripping the fear tight.

He tips my chin up, forcing me to look at him. "Tell me what you want. How does it look when you close your eyes?"

Oh, man. Seriously. One tear breaks loose, and he pushes it away with his thumb. *Damn hormones.* "I don't know. Everything I thought I wanted . . . it's all changing, and I don't know what any of it means or what to do."

Mark's eyes roam over my face like the answer to his question lies underneath. He's warm and safe, and when I'm with him, I believe everything will be ok. Maybe that's just it. Somehow, with Mark, I'm ok being scared.

My mind scurries back through all the things Grandpa said about living life and not wasting time. He said he was selling the shop to Slade, and it's not meant to be my future. I think somewhere deep down, I want it all to be true. I don't want to waste another second, and it's difficult to imagine anything other than a future with Mark.

Little flutters in my belly make me brave, so I risk it and tell him what I see. "When I close my eyes . . . I see us with our babies building a life together."

"I'll give it up and move to Ohio." His solution is quick and firm.

"Mark." I pull away from him. "That's not—"

"No, listen to me. I've played in the NFL. I've made millions of dollars doing what I love . . . for years. How many people get to say that, Lex? But all I've ever wanted was to be with you. Now . . . " His hand moves under my shirt and lays flat against my stomach. "*They* are the only thing that matters. I won't miss this. I won't miss being with them. With you. I can't do that again. So, if you need to be in Ohio, that's what we'll do."

"No." I don't even have to think about that. "No, you can't come back to Ohio."

He smiles. "If you're there, then that's where I'll be."

"Mark, you escaped. You made it out of the place that reminds you of—"

"Then you'll come with me." His grin widens.

"I want you to keep playing as long as you want to. You love it. It's why I—"

He pulls me to his chest. "Then come with me. After the babies are born, we'll figure out how to get you under a hood."

"But these babies are coming, and you'll be training and heading right into the season with a new team. You won't be able to be up all night helping me. You'll be gone all the time." *And I'll be left in a new place alone with two babies.*

His chest contracts as he sighs, knowing I'm right. We lie together in silence.

"Ok. Come on. Get up." He throws the sheet off.

"What?"

"Let's go." He's up and moving.

"Where?"

He stands in his boxer briefs with his hands on his hips. His long, lean muscles cut through his skin. I need him to get back to what he was doing before I let my mind get in the way.

I'm so tired of thinking. "How about you come back here first?"

He doesn't move. Only his eyelids drop into a bit of a squint. "Extremely tempting." My entire body lights with fire. "But the next time I make love to you, I'm going to do it over and over again. There won't be anything between us preventing it or clouding it. Withholding myself from you has been enough torment to last me a lifetime."

Someone help me. I pull the sheet up over my face, and it's possible I groan.

He rips it off. "Get up. We're getting breakfast, and then we're going shopping."

"What? Now?" I stare at him, enraged at my brain for interrupting . . . things.

"There has to be a Target or one of those big baby stores or something around here. We can't figure everything out today, but we can at least start with car seats and the other gobs of shit these babies will require. We'll make the list and then order it."

"Krissy is throwing me a baby shower."

One side of his mouth tugs up. "Even better. People who make millions less than I do can buy it." I throw a pillow at him, and he catches it.

I climb out of bed but walk to him, throwing my arms around his neck and pushing up to my toes to get closer. "Thank you."

His hands find my waist. "For what?"

"For letting me be scared."

"It's ok to be scared for now, but this is all going to work out."

"Yeah. You think so?"

"Yep. It has to."

I let my forehead fall into the crook of his neck. "Maybe I'll quit and follow you. That'd be the easiest."

"Not a chance in hell. I saw you yesterday dealing with that big-ass bus. In fact, social media is blowing up with pictures of you working."

I pull my head back to see him. "You were working on it."

"No, it was me doing what you told me to do. I was talking to Rob earlier. He wanted me to let you know he's available if you need an agent."

"What?"

"Women and girls are screaming for you to post more. They want videos of how to fix things."

"Videos?"

"Yeah, they want more. I mean, when have you ever seen a woman fixing a broken car?"

I think about that for a minute but come up with nothing.

He smacks my butt. "Let's go. We have shopping to do before you have to put on that sexy dress." He heads for the bathroom but stops in the doorway. "Plus, since we made it through all the pamphlets, we'll grab one of those tell-all books so we understand everything we have to look forward to. I want to know all about the birthing part." He raises and lowers his eyebrows.

"Mark," I warn, but he laughs while I decide that's the one part I'm perfectly fine knowing absolutely nothing about.

He laughs that ridiculously contagious laugh, and I'm so glad his punk-ass can't see me smile.

This man. I didn't know it was possible to fall in love with someone who already has your whole heart. But Mark, the man, I'm pretty sure I'm falling for him in a way I didn't know existed.

Oh, man. Falling isn't even close to what's happening. This man is wrecking me. Totally and completely . . . for good.

Chapter 32

LEX

Mark slides out of the black Audi Q5 and reaches for my hand. I grip it as if I'm stepping out onto a teetering ledge. My palm is slick with sweat, but it doesn't faze him. He takes a firm hold, linking our fingers like he's afraid I'll bolt.

He's smart because I might. I seriously might tuck a hand under these babies and hightail it right back to Ohio, where I can slather myself with grease and linger among car parts, not having to be seen or known.

But then I look at his beautiful face. He smiles and nods to fans, and even though I'm paralyzed and sick with fear, this is where I want to be.

For years, I've longed for this, and here I am, in this surreal world, standing beside him as cameras flash in the distance. People are everywhere. As if Mark knows I need it, he pulls me close, his lips pressing against my hair, which hangs in long, loose waves like a shield around me.

"Just breathe. We'll walk through, and then inside, it'll be better."

My stomach rejects his calming attempts as it rolls with nerves. Beautiful people surround us dressed in designer suits, gowns, and jewelry, likely costing more than my entire lifetime earnings. Mark raises a hand at someone yelling his name and moves us toward the red carpet.

Just before we enter the danger zone, he pulls me to the side, hiding us behind the giant, shiny archway.

"It won't take long to get through here. I won't leave you." He smiles, but it doesn't have its normal deescalating effect. "You are absolutely breathtaking."

I want to scoff, but I don't. My eyes fall to the dusk blue form-fitting lacey dress. The V-neck and cap sleeves are flattering, especially with the new bra Krissy made me buy to hold my growing boobs. Given my hormonal state and the impending hot flash, I'm grateful it's knee-length. It's the nude heels I'm wobbling in that I want to chuck in the nearest waste can along with my lunch.

I glance around at all of the stunning and sophisticated people filing in. It's not just the biggest names in the NFL. It's photographers, reporters, businessmen, and women. It's intimidating as hell.

"It's all a bit much," I say, trying to meet his eyes.

His hands find my belly, and he steps closer. "They are all just people. So many of these guys have had hard lives. They may make millions now, but you can't even imagine where they started."

I know he's trying to help, but I feel so completely out of place. I peek at him from underneath my eyelashes. "Mark, I can't read, and I fix cars, that's it. It's a little different."

He pulls back, almost like I've struck him. His hands fall from my waist as his face morphs into . . . something. He takes a couple of steps away. Then he's pacing just a few feet from me. I glance around, feeling the slight tinges of panic rising.

He turns and walks back toward me but with an attitude. He's freaking James Bond—gorgeous trained assassin. His jaw is set, and his eyes are...

"Are you mad?" I whisper, grabbing the lapels of his tux so he can't leave me again.

"Hell yes, I'm mad." His eyes roam the crowd behind me. "Are you out of your mind? Look at you."

I glance down at myself, seriously concerned about what's happening here. He looks like he's about to throw a hissy fit right here at the entrance of the fanciest place I've ever been.

Mark can be dramatic, but it usually only comes out when someone strikes a nerve. Apparently, I struck a live one.

His hands take a firm hold of my hips, and he waits until I look at him.

"Lex, I don't give a shit if it takes you longer to make it through a paragraph or if reading isn't your thing. Half the people here likely haven't read a book in their entire life, and spell-check has saved their careers. You're brilliant. You're crazy smart. You use your brain and hands in ways these people wouldn't even begin to comprehend. You take things that ordinary people like me will never understand and make them new."

His toes meet mine as he slips his arms around me, holding me against his body. "And baby, when you're doing it, it's the most stunning thing I have ever seen." He pauses, his stare intense. "I can assure you, there isn't a person in there that can top any of that."

I slide my arms up his back and hug him tight. "I'm sorry. This is all really overwhelming." He squeezes me tighter. "Thank you for saying that and getting pissy in my defense."

"I'll throw down for you in a heartbeat, but I won't have to. Everyone will see just how amazing you are. You don't need anyone telling them that." He kisses my cheek. "How about we let these reporters grill us about all the things we aren't going to tell them?"

I groan, and he grins. "Does it ever get old? Baiting them?"

He slips his hand in mine and tugs me straight into the madness. "Nah. They love it."

We follow the line, moving from one backdrop to the next. Mark stands tall next to me, grinning ear to ear for the cameras. I hang on to him, trying to keep it together as he whispers ridiculous stories about past interviews that have me laughing so hard I think pee might start running down my legs.

"Mark." A woman, tall and slender, catches his arm. She has a microphone in hand, and this is the part that I've been dreading.

"Seems you've been busy teasing your fans during your recovery. Care to take this opportunity to set the record straight and put all those longing hearts to rest?"

She shoves the mic toward him, and he pulls me closer.

"I've been resting and letting my shoulder heal. I'm feeling good and looking forward to getting back out on the field."

"It appears you've been using your time wisely." Her eyes move to me and then back to Mark.

"My time has been very well spent if I do say so myself." I pinch his side, and his grin spreads even wider. The reporter laughs. "My wife and I are excited for this next season for lots of reasons."

"Wow. You heard it here first, ladies. Mark Sandberg is officially off the market and, dare I say, quite the proud papa."

Mark doesn't say anything, making the reporter squirm. He only grins, and I resist the urge to roll my eyes.

Unfazed by his game, she moves along. "Everyone knows you're a big supporter of underprivileged youth. We're all familiar with the organization you set up with Shane Carter and Sean Greyson. Tonight, you're up for the Walter Peyton Man of the Year Award, and we were all surprised to learn that you—"

Mark cuts her off. "My goal is to fund and support causes I'm passionate about. Kids deserve to have equal opportunities no matter their background."

I've followed Mark's work with Shane and Sean. Their organization helps kids in the foster system have access and assistance to participate in sports and other extracurriculars they might not be able to otherwise.

"Well, you certainly seem to be doing that. Good luck tonight." She drops her mic and thanks us for stopping, and off we go to the next reporter.

Mark answers questions about his recovery and the organizations rumored to be interested in signing him for the next season. A few questions about his non-profit are sprinkled in that he seems to dodge, along with the specifics about our marriage.

It's the fourth stop where things take a different turn.

"Now, Mark. We're all looking forward to seeing where you end up, but female fans want to know when your wife is going to teach us how to change our oil and rotate our tires."

Mark looks around. "Man, word travels fast." He laughs. "She can teach you a hell of a lot more than that. She's brilliant and takes those big metal machines down to frame and puts them back together."

The reporter turns her attention to me. "Pictures of you on that truck tire have taken social media by storm. Young girls and women are no longer asking for your head for snagging this guy but want to see more of what you can do. It's not every day you see a powerful woman getting in there and fixing things."

She points the mic at me, and I know I'm supposed to speak, but nothing comes out. The idea that anyone, let alone young girls or other women, would want to learn from me is . . . inconceivable.

"I . . . I just work in my grandpa's garage. I started on a stool when I was six, and it's my absolute favorite place to be."

"Sounds like you've got a lot to teach us, and we'll be anticipating more."

I smile, but I'm so taken aback it can't possibly look real.

Mark pulls me away, and we've finally made it to the auditorium. He stops me outside the doors. "You have nothing to worry about. These people see everything I've always known."

It's the first time in my life that my disability doesn't feel so much like a curse, but maybe more like it made room for a gift I never allowed myself to see I had.

We're ushered toward seats way farther to the front than I would ever choose—second row, dead center along the aisle. The auditorium fills with people, and Mark knows just about everyone.

He stands off to the side, talking to who I assume is a coach, while I settle in my seat, ready to sit back and watch. My body and mind relax, knowing my part of the show is OVER.

Mark's tall frame folds into the chair next to me, and his hand finds my knee. It's a little sweaty. Nerves and Mark don't make sense.

"Hey, you all right? I can't be the calm one in here."

He leans closer. "You did good out there. No more hiding in that garage."

"Great. The guys are never going to let me live this down." His smile returns, but only halfway, and I lean closer. "I haven't told you, but I'm so proud of you for all the work you've done to help so many kids. It's really amazing."

He stares at me, his eyes moving over my face, and it's possible I see his throat bob.

His hand slides behind my neck, and he presses a quick, soft kiss on my lips as the music begins playing and the stage lights up. Things move quickly as the host welcomes us, and players are ushered on and off to accept awards.

During commercial breaks, people shuffle seats, and then they're back to announcing winners. Mark sits beside me stiffly, his knee bouncing slightly, and I'm not sure what's going on.

His hands rest on his thighs, and I slide mine underneath his. His cold, clammy fingers wrap around mine as the lights dim again.

I lean into him. "Hey, what's up? You're starting to freak me out."

His dark eyes meet mine while the music plays. All teasing and charm are replaced with quiet seriousness. "I love you."

I blink, trying to understand what's happening with him.

The host returns to the stage, welcoming a former player who gives a back story about the Man of the Year Award. Then a video starts, and Mark's face fills the screen as he talks about the organization he created to help promote awareness, aid, and educate those diagnosed with . . . learning disabilities.

My head whips in his direction, but his eyes stay trained on the stage.

My brain kicks into a jog, and my heart quickly joins the race as my eyes coast to those around us, all learning what it's like for those who have difficulties reading, writing, or processing sounds.

The video continues, showing Mark in schools with kids, handing out books, and talking with teachers and faculty about the long-term impact of undiagnosed learning disorders.

My sweat-slicked hands grip the armrests to keep from bolting to the nearest exit. It's always been one thing to share my inability with people that I trust. It's something else entirely to feel outed to an entire room of the rich, famous, and completely capable.

I close my eyes as my ears fill with fog, drowning out Mark's voice. He speaks about early intervention and his organization's assistance to give kids the best chance at success without facing the shame and embarrassment of not being able to keep up.

What? He has an organization that helps kids . . . like me.

I inhale slowly as my stomach rises in my throat, every pore on my body oozing a cool sweat.

"Ladies and gentlemen, please welcome this year's Man of the Year, Mark Sandberg."

My eyes pop open, and I can't breathe. Mark leans over and grabs my face. "I love you. I've *always* loved you." His words are only a whisper but sure and true. His eyes crease with tears as he kisses me.

The imprint of his lips remains as fire consumes my throat, and I hold my breath to keep my own tears from spilling over.

Then, he's gone, leaving me with . . . what? I don't even know.

People stand, shielding me while I try to figure out what in the hell I'm feeling. I'm not exactly sure what happens because I CAN'T SEE, but the next thing I know, he's standing in the middle of the stage.

My pulse pounds in my ears along with applause, and I try to blink my eyes clear, but maybe it's better if I don't. Then I can't see all the people surrounding me.

My tears recede enough I can make him out, shaking hands and man-hugging a huge blurry form.

I try to inhale and let it out slowly as I watch him step up to the mic, wanting to run and hide but also . . . stay.

As the room quiets, I sink further into my seat, trying to get something to settle enough to take in what he's been doing for kids who face the same challenges I do. All this time, he's been working to ensure they don't have to struggle and be left with nothing but the shame I still feel.

My chest seizes again as that shame wars with my love for him and what he's worked to do. My mind stops. *The app.* This is how he knew about the app that I now use every day. I seriously want to punch and maybe yell at him and . . . kiss him and never stop.

He clears his throat and my breath catches, waiting to hear his voice.

He stands tall and strong as his eyes roam. "I'm a fortunate man. More fortunate than most, but I didn't start that way. As a kid, school for me was a reprieve from the world I belonged to. I . . . " He rubs his jaw, and I shift in my seat, sweat pooling under my armpits as I wait to hear his words. "I can't say that I was necessarily good at it, but just being there was better than being at home."

"It wasn't until I was in high school that I realized all I'd been taking for granted. I had nothing. I lived in a group home for years after being hauled away from a trailer park that was more like hell on earth. My dad left me with internal bruises, a dislocated shoulder, and a cut that required twenty stitches. Those were the wounds they could see."

He pulls his shoulders back, adjusting his stance. I can't take my eyes off him. A rare sight of complete vulnerability, and I sit a little straighter, unwilling to miss it. He's laying down the mask, and I won't cower this time, no matter how badly I might want to. I'm finally able to be here for him, like I've longed to be.

I swallow the massive lump in my throat, remembering the stories he shared. Everything that he's done, all that he's survived, and I've . . . missed it. Tears I'm no longer able to contain stream down my face.

He clears his throat. "But even having been through that, I'd taken the most basic skills and abilities for granted. See . . . " He shifts his weight to the other foot. "I met someone in high school who struggled to do what all of the rest of us didn't even know we were doing. We'd get an assignment, write our name at the top, and get to work. Our futures were bright and filled with possibility. We could read, and that meant we could do anything. Literally."

He huffs. "I'd never thought about what it would be like if reading was a challenge or if I couldn't easily show my knowledge in written form. How that would've changed everything, especially for a kid like me and where I came from."

He studies the piece of metal in his hand. "I was sixteen and angry at the world. One day, I walked into the science lab and told another kid to move so I could sit next to this beautiful girl."

His eyes finally hit mine, and there's the slightest pause as his lips pull into a hesitant smile. I know he's reliving it just as I am. The moment the loud, cocky high school quarterback slid into the seat beside me. The absolute last person I'd ever want to be lab partners with or find out I couldn't read.

Mark's eyes move back to the crowd, and he grins. "That one obnoxious adolescent move changed the rest of my life. She had her head down, focused on a closed notebook, and wouldn't give me the time of day."

The crowd laughs, and tears run down my chin, to my neck, and then chest. I remember his young, handsome face asking to borrow a pencil and then teasing me that I wouldn't get it back. Even then, he was a flirt.

"I eventually found my in with her, and by some miracle, over time, she trusted me enough to show me her weakness."

He finds me again, and it's as if my soul aches for how much I love him. How much I've always loved him. How much he loves me, and maybe I'm only just realizing it.

"Man . . . " he shakes his head. "She was good at covering it because this chick was brilliant. Hands down way too good for me and the only reason I didn't flunk physics. She could run circles around the rest of us, but . . . school was excruciating for her because reading was difficult. She couldn't do it, at least not the way the rest of us could. Every assignment, every textbook, and test took her hours and hours to complete, but that time wasn't afforded."

I side-eye those around me, and all eyes are straight ahead, nodding and taking in his words.

He clears his throat again, taking a moment. "The pain, shame, and embarrassment I saw in her eyes every time she tried and failed, with no one's help or caring to understand what made her different . . . it did me in. No person, no child, should sit in a classroom feeling like there's something wrong with them simply because their brain doesn't allow them to see things the way the rest of us do."

Mark goes on to discuss how we can make a difference and change futures. He outlines the resources his organization provides and how critical awareness and education on the topic are essential for those kids who are struggling. Often, it's only because they haven't been introduced to the right tools or had access to the assistance they need.

Tears and snot streak my face for all the years that I've held myself back. I swipe my cheeks with the back of my wrist, smearing it everywhere.

He's been helping kids like me while I've done what? Nothing.

I've sat around feeling less than and ashamed, but he was out there doing the work to ensure others don't have to endure it. I shake my head with anger at myself for letting my challenge keep me from . . . everything.

I sit up, leaning closer to watch him, no longer caring who might see or worried about what they might think.

All this time . . . I've missed so much. I've missed him. His wins and losses. All he's worked for and overcome. He survived horrors, but not only that, he came out the other side compassionate and loving and so damn good.

I've missed knowing his friends and his family. His gigantic growing family that he's built with his brothers. I've missed eight years' worth of time and love we should have had together.

I left him. I let him think I didn't want him. I didn't fucking show up for the man who I know would have given this all up to stay with me.

No more. Never again. I won't miss another second. Wherever he's going, I'm going. He said it. It's always us. And it has been. Ever since the day the cocky sixteen year old boy sat down next to me, I never had a choice.

I don't deserve it, but he's given me a chance, and I'm taking it. I'll never again let him think that I haven't chosen him.

The crowd applauds and rises to their feet as Mark wraps up his speech. He's ushered off the stage, and I'm left in my seat a freaking mess, but I don't care. The only thing I care about is finding him.

The need to see him and tell him is nearly causing panic. I don't want to go another second without him knowing we will never be apart again. I need him to know that I'd follow him to the moon if that means he'll keep on loving me the way he always has.

Chapter 33

MARK

My heart smacks against my rib cage as I shake another hand, and the camera flashes. I need to find Lex. I couldn't tear my eyes away from her tear-streaked face. Her sad, gentle smile is the only thing giving me marginal comfort.

Not warning her was a big risk, but I wanted her to see that it never mattered. I had nothing and came from less. I was my dad's punching bag, his torture doll, the object of his despise. Most days, my mom couldn't stay sober long enough to make breakfast or ensure I wasn't beaten to death.

Until Lex, I was letting my circumstances dictate my future, but she showed me I could do and become anything. Where I came from and who my parents were didn't matter. She believed in me like no one else ever had.

Through high school, Lex and I worked hard together. When I could, I read our textbooks out loud and helped her memorize the material. But I couldn't help her with tests, and it tore me in two every time she failed. She knew the answers, but if you can't read the questions or write the answers, it won't ever matter.

But it was her fight and bravery that only made me love her more. She never gave up. She always tried despite the comments, discouragement, and knowing the outcome. She kept going. Kept trying.

It all showed me how much I had when I didn't have a damn thing. She gave me perspective and, eventually, love. The only kind I'd ever known. The kind I desperately needed.

All this time, it was the hope, the possibility that I wasn't wrong. That I hadn't made it all up. What we had. What we felt for one another. That she really did love me.

Besides football, it's what kept me going. Kept me clean. Kept me from spinning out of control and going down a road I'd never return from.

"Mark." Another person sticks out their hand.

"Yes. Thank you." I thrust my shaky hand out in return, having no idea what they said to me.

I pose for another picture, trying to inch my way to the exit. When I finally break free, I want to sprint, but I leash myself and wind my way to the auditorium doors.

A few people linger as awards continue to be presented. I wonder if she's still inside. I pace a second, my heart racing and a cold sweat breaking out over my body, and then . . .

My lungs kick out a breath. She's twenty yards from me, tucked back outside the restroom. Her eyes are red and puffy. Her face is smeared with mascara. She's gripping a wad of paper towel as her lip quivers and tears fill her eyes.

My feet move subconsciously, and then she's in my arms, her face buried in my neck as she lets loose. She squeezes my neck so tight.

I hold her, not quite sure what's happening but comforted by the fact that she's holding onto me as if she's afraid I'll disappear. My heart slows, trying to return to its normal rhythm.

When her hiccups and sniffs subside, she inhales deeply.

"I'm sorry—"

Her head pops up, and she looks up at me. Her face is a complete mess. I release her to run my thumbs underneath her eyes to remove some of the black makeup.

"Mark, I . . . " She shakes her head, dropping her chin. She wipes her nose with the paper towel. "I'm so sorry." Her voice cracks again. "I didn't—"

"Shhh." I push the sticky, damp strands out of her face.

"I wanted to go with you. I never wanted to say goodbye."

I hold her face. "Baby, I—"

"I came to see you," she sniffs. "Your first game."

"What?" My voice catches in my throat. "When?"

"At Notre Dame. I watched you win your first game."

I step back. "You . . . were there?" She nods. "What? How?" My heart stutters at her confession.

"I had to see you. I had to know you'd be ok." Her bottom lip begins trembling again. "You won, and then I watched you celebrate with all of your friends."

My mind rewinds to that time and spins. "Lex, why didn't you find me? I searched for you. I needed you."

My throat burns with the memory of searching for her and how much I wanted her to be there. *She was there.* My chest explodes with a consuming ache for all of the hurt and time lost but also . . . so much love.

She was there.

She shakes her head. "I couldn't. I just had to know you'd be ok. That you were happy and on your way to doing everything I knew you could." She swipes at a tear. "It's all I ever wanted."

"I would have—"

She presses her finger to my lips. "I know, but you couldn't. Look at what you've done, what you've accomplished. Mark, you did it and so much more. I'm just so sorry I missed it all." A tear tracks down her cheek.

My lungs hitch as my vision blurs. "Lex, I . . . " My wounded heart aches for all that we've missed together.

She swipes at her face with the towel. "I won't miss another second. Wherever you go, I'm going, too."

"What?" Something drips from my cheek and hits the floor somewhere beneath us.

"I'm going with you. I don't care where or when. I couldn't before, but I can now, and I am. I won't miss another thing. Ever."

My heart starts beating wildly again, but it's different this time, and it's all I can hear. "Lex, what?"

One side of her sad mouth tips up. "My life is with you. You were right." She shrugs. "It's always us. No matter what. It's my turn to show you that now . . . if you'll let me." She sniffs while I stand like a damn fool trying to make sure I understand.

"You'll come with me?" She nods. "Like for good?" She nods again. "We can be together, always?"

She pushes up to her toes and throws her arms around me. "Yes, if you can forgive me. I will follow you to the ends of the earth."

I scoop her up, my throat swelling shut. "We don't have to go that far."

I hear another sniff and then a whisper. "I'm never leaving you again. Ok?"

A boulder that's sat on my heart for so long finally breaks free. "Ok."

I toss the key card on the table. Lex heads straight for the bathroom and washes her face. After finding her near the restroom, we nabbed a car and blew off every after-party.

All I want is to be with Lex. Alone.

The silence that's lingered between us is full of promise and anticipation, and it's as alive as an exposed wire connecting the two of us.

I hang my tux jacket and hear the faucet turn off. She stands in the doorway of the bathroom, watching me. Her face is flushed, and her eyes are a bit puffy, but she's still the most breathtaking sight.

One hand reaches up and fiddles with her earring, and I can't prevent the tug at my lips. She's nervous, and so the hell am I. I'm sixteen again, needing her like I'll never need another again.

"Get over here." I toss my head back slightly, beckoning her. Here she is, my wife, already pregnant with my babies, and I feel like this is the first time I've ever been alone with her. Blood pumps through my veins as if I'm connected to a machine set on high.

Everything that's stood between us is finally gone, and there's nothing left but the two of us. Together.

Her only movement is her eyes tracing over me.

"It will get much better if you come over here."

Her head falls to the side, testing me. "Huh. That so?"

"Lex, you're challenging my very limited and mostly non-existent patience. Slow has never been well received with me, and you can be damn sure it's been eliminated when it comes to us."

That has a smile breaking across her face. "Fine."

I let my head fall back. "Fine. That's it. Really?"

I take two quick steps toward her, but she retreats and holds out her hands. "I . . . need to say something first."

"Lex, not tonight, not right now. I don't care. No talking."

She lowers her arms. "Ok, but before you touch me—"

I groan. "Hurry up."

She points at me. "No touching."

"Fair warning, I'm not very good at following rules."

"Shocking." She smiles, moving toward me, but it quickly falls away. Her fingers grasp the top button on my shirt and works it free. Then moves on to the next. "I don't want to go back. I want to start here with you." Her hands stop on the last button, and her eyes remain focused on the remaining slick, round object. "I don't want anything between us. I've never lied to you, but . . . " Her hands fall to her sides, and she shifts back an inch.

I loathe the distance. All I can't think about is feeling her skin on mine. I fist my hands, dying to touch her.

"I need to tell you something."

I break her useless momentary rule, tipping her chin up with my finger. "Does it change anything? Does it change us being together, or what happens after this?"

Her eyes flick between mine for a few long seconds, but before my stomach can determine if it needs to clench, she shakes her head ever so slightly.

I release a slow breath. "Then, not tonight. Not right now. We have time for that. Right now, I just need you, or I literally might die."

That bottom lip gets sucked in between her teeth again. "But it—"

I'm DONE. My hands find her hair, and I crush my mouth to hers. My tongue swipes across her lips, and she responds, hers tangling with mine. Over and over again, I kiss her. Taste her. Her body molds to mine in need. It no longer feels of desperation and longing but of something everlasting. It's so familiar, yet so very different.

Her hands glide over my chest, pushing my shirt to the floor.

My fingers fumble with the zipper on the back of her dress, and I snag it. In one swift motion, the fabric pools beneath us.

Lex pulls away breathless, looping her hand around my belt and tugging me toward the bed. "I'm still mad you stole my pencil. It was my favorite one from the shop."

My hands slide over the soft skin around her ribs.

"Baby, I didn't steal it. I told you I wasn't giving it back."

"What about my heart?" She stops at the edge of the bed. "Taking it and never giving it back. Was that always your plan?"

I hold her face. "You're damn right it was. The first time you smiled at me." My teeth graze her neck. "Every time I made you laugh." My lips find her shoulder. "You in the stands, grease-stained fingers over your heart, and your blue eyes telling me I could." I make my way back up to her lips. "Laying in the grass all those nights, knowing you were the only home I ever needed."

I kiss her soft, slightly swollen lips. "I fell in love with you over and over and over again. Harder, deeper, and now, there isn't a word to describe what I feel for you. Your heart . . . it's mine."

She pushes up to her toes. "You never gave me a choice."

I angle her head, diving in slowly and savoring this moment, knowing it's just the beginning. The new beginning I've dreamed of a million times.

I pry my mouth away, letting my lips brush over hers. "I knew what I was doing."

She pushes me down on the bed and stands between my legs. "You were so cocky and full of yourself."

"I was confident." Her soft laughter turns the fire in my belly into a blaze. "When you finally broke and spoke to me . . . told me about a stolen catalytic converter. I was a goner."

"You didn't even know what that was," she laughs.

My hands coast over her smooth skin from her thighs to her belly and ribs. My thumbs brush along the silk of her bra. "Shane and Sean razzed my ass for weeks when I brought home every mechanic book I could find at the library."

"You did not?"

I grip her hips, pulling her with me as I lie back. "Oh yes, I did. There wasn't a chance in hell I'd miss an opportunity to get you to talk to me again." Her hands hold mine as she straddles me. "And look . . . it worked."

She grins, but then her face falls to an intense seriousness. She stares at me lying beneath her. "All that cockiness has turned into a beautiful confidence." Her eyes roam my face, taking in every detail. "I'm so proud of you." It comes out as a whisper. "Your love . . . I don't deserve it, but I want it so much it hurts. All the time."

I smile. "I was just a kid who didn't have a clue what it meant to be loved . . . until you. We went eight years without this. Loving you from afar really, really sucks."

A bright smile appears. "It really does."

I sit up, my hands skirt up her spine, and find the clasp on her bra. "What's it going to take to make this happen?" I free her of it and toss it. "How big of a garage are we talking about?"

She laughs, her lips brushing over mine. "It's going to take more than a garage."

"Oh, really. Do tell?"

"I'm going to need a four-post lift." Her teeth nip my bottom lip.

"Oh yeah."

"And a workbench." Kiss. Long and torturously slow. "A large tool chest with lots and lots of tools." She trails kisses along my jaw to my neck.

"Got it."

"At least an eighty-gallon air compressor." Her hands run over my stomach muscles.

"Damn, girl. This sounds expensive." She tries to pull away, but I tug her back. She's not going anywhere. "I'll throw in a crappy, old radio for that awful country music."

Her hands pause from undoing my belt as her gaze lands on mine. "Only if you hang out with me when you're not working."

"Fine. Done." I arch an eyebrow. "I'll warn you, if I do that, it's not likely you'll have time for fixing things."

She smiles, her cheeks turning pink, and that's it.

Unable to wait a second longer, I take her mouth fast and hard. A soft feminine hum escapes her, sending my need into the unknown.

She said she never had a chance, but it was me. Her quiet, blue eyes saw straight into me.

Once you find someone who sees you just as you are, all screwed up and flawed, mostly just a bunch of broken pieces held together by invisible duct tape, and somehow, they believe in you anyway, you don't have a choice but to love them fully and completely right back.

ME: I need your help.

CAL: It'll cost ya.
CAL: Again

ME: I'll pay any price.
ME: As always.

Chapter 34

LEX

"And I'm going to take care of you. You'll never question how much I love you because I'm going to tell you all the time."

I blink, hearing his soft voice, almost a whisper.

"We're going to be a family. I'll teach you how to throw the perfect spiral, and I don't care if you are girls. But if you are, you're never leaving the house."

His lips press against the side of my stomach between his hands.

"Now, if you are boys, then we'll raise hell and drive your mom crazy."

I lie perfectly still, listening to him making promises and telling them how things will be. A smile sweeps across my face.

I've known that Mark would never leave me alone in this, but after last night, there's no choice but to be together. It's time for me to move on and forward, and I get to do it with him.

I'm still scared out of my mind, but for years, I've been checking off the days like Grandpa said. But I'm learning that if I want to live, really live, then I have to take a chance—risk it despite the fear. Not just for me but for Mark and these babies. Only then will I allow myself the full potential this life has to offer that, until now, I've never allowed myself to think I could have.

Mark whispers something about them needing to sleep so that he and I can have adult time, and I can't hold in my laugh.

"Hey. We were having a private conversation," he grins, his head resting next to my stomach.

I yawn, completely exhausted, emotionally and physically. "You three are not allowed to make plans without me."

Mark runs his hand over my stomach and presses another kiss to it before sliding up and wrapping his arms around me. "Too bad. We've already made deals."

"They're too young to form verbal agreements."

"The book says they might be able to hear. Sorry, Peyton and Eli's silence counts as approval."

"Peyton and Eli? Really?" He smiles against my cheek.

"You said they're wild in there."

"Imagine that. I wonder who they get that from." I snuggle into him, ready for this to be the rest of my life.

Mark rolls on top of me, keeping his weight off our babies. His eyes hold that devilish playfulness. "Definitely from you." He kisses my shoulder. "Are you ready for the game today? It'll be crowded."

"Yes." I made it through last night, so this isn't nearly as intimidating, although Mark's family is large and growing.

"Shane, Maggie, and the kids are here. Maggie's brother Cole plays for the Stingrays, and he's bringing a friend we've taken in. Plus, some of Andie's friends and family will be there."

I press a kiss to his bicep. "I'm looking forward to meeting all of them."

"I told Shane we'd meet them, but we have some time. Then, I have a plane booked for tonight." He stares into my eyes. "What about your stuff?"

I push the strands of hair off his forehead. "I have to go back for my next doctor's appointment and see the guys. Krissy is having the baby shower." I run my hands over the muscles in his back, pulling him closer.

"I'm going with you if I can, but you need to find a doctor in Phoenix." His lips trail over my neck to my chest.

"I have a to-do list a mile long, but I can't think straight when you are doing that."

He grins against my skin. "Good. We aren't thinking right now. We are strictly on the doing part, and this is at the top of the list . . . every time."

"Fine," I say like I'm put out. "What was it you told me last night? Hurry up."

He pulls away to meet my eyes, and I try to withhold my smile, but I do a sucky job of it.

Slowly, a mischievous smirk creeps across his mouth, and it's so sexy it almost kills me to refrain from kissing him. "You've gotten kind of bossy."

I shrug one should. "Dealing with men every day makes you that way."

The flame in his eyes turns to a raging blaze. "Good thing you won't be dealing with them daily anymore. You could become insufferable."

I slide my hands over his shoulder and up his neck to the soft, short hairs. "Now, I can just be bossy with you." I pull his face to mine. My lips gently brush over his. "So, are you going to get to work or not?"

Mark's hand remains clasped around mine as we sift our way through the stadium. He's posed for dozens of photos and shook more hands than I can count. Seeing him in this environment is . . . different. There's a shield he puts on.

It's like an armor he slips into to be sure nothing sensitive is exposed. His fans get the fun-loving, charming Mark only.

He pulls me to his side. "You ok?"

I nod as we push our way through a crowd, finally making it to the box where we'll watch the game. Mark pulls the door open, and it's filled with people.

"Who's ready for some football?!" Mark hollers entering.

There's a collective cheer, and all eyes are on us.

"You meet your picture quota for the day?" Shane strolls over, and the two exchange a quick hug.

Besides appearing three times larger and manly, Shane doesn't appear to have changed much. He was always on the quiet side but was never afraid to speak up when he was looking out for Mark.

His eyes move to me. "Congratulations on marrying this idiot. Now you're stuck with the lot of us, too."

I smile. "Thanks. You guys certainly know how to do the family thing."

"So do you," he gestures to my stomach. "We need another one. We're shooting for a whole team."

Mark clears his throat. "Twins." He has that shit-eating grin on his face as if he did this all by himself.

Shane's eyes move to him. "You bastard. Of course, you had to go and show me up. Maggie," Shane's deep voice bellows, glancing around for his wife.

The young, beautiful, petite woman slides under Shane's massive arm with a baby over her hip. "Twins. This shithead did that. Why can't we do that?"

Maggie rolls her eyes. "Grizz, don't forget *I* pushed this one out. You'll be lucky to get another shot." She sticks out her hand. "Forgive this, baby-obsessed giant. I'm Maggie. Congratulations on marrying into this nut house and on the babies. That's incredible."

"Yep. See. I know what I'm doing." Mark's chest puffs out further, and Maggie and I laugh while Shane groans, his head tipping back toward the ceiling.

"Does Sean know about this?" Shane's voice is full of irritation.

"Sure does," Mark gloats.

"Shit. Now, he's going to be working for triplets."

"Uh. No, he's not." Andie joins our circle, stopping next to me with a toddler on her hip. "Sean will find himself stripped of . . . .privileges if I hear such craziness." She smiles at me. "It's nice to see you again."

"Who's losing privileges?" A little girl moves to stand in the center of our group. "Teddy lost privileges to liquids and balloons when that one exploded all over you." She peers up at me. "Is there a baby in there?"

She points to my stomach.

"Liv," both Maggie and Shane say at the same time.

Mark squats down to get eye level with her. "There are two in there," he says with awe.

Her blue eyes grow wide, and I hear Shane groan.

"How does that happen?"

"Nice job, moron," Shane grumbles.

"Well, I worked really hard." Andie and Maggie laugh as Mark scoops her up. "How about you show me all the junk food they have to eat in this joint?" Mark walks away, grinning.

"We're never going to hear the end of this," Shane says.

Maggie pats him on the chest. "Don't worry. You did good work, big guy. Look at this little dude." Maggie hands over the baby, but the kid must take after his dad because there's not much little about him. "And if you're lucky, I might let you try again." She winks at him and then joins the kids around the food.

"It's a bit intimidating, isn't it," Andie bumps my elbow with hers. We stand at the back of the room as I try to take it all in. It is a lot, but as I watch Mark carry Liv and fist-bump the boys, I'm really grateful to even be here.

"Sean never warned me about the pranks the first time I met this crew. I found one of those rubber snakes on the kitchen floor in the middle of the night. All three men came charging in half, dazed and confused but ready to fire. There's nothing like this family . . . anywhere. Come on," she tips her head in the direction of the madness. "It's best to just jump in."

I follow her, watching Mark dance with Liv as the boys throw jabs at his ability.

"Hey, you two," he points at them. "Grab a pencil and paper. Take notes cause one day you'll thank me for this." He winks at me.

I roll my eyes. I always knew Mark would make an excellent father, but seeing him like this has my hands sliding over our kicking babies, knowing there is no better man for the job.

Liv puts her hands on both sides of his face. "Why do you call her Lex, not Alex?"

"Ugh," Shane groans. "Don't ask. I had to hear about this so many nights. My Lex this. My Lex that," he says, flexing his voice to a high pitch and making the kids giggle.

"Whatever, bro. You were just jealous." Mark grins, and my cheeks heat with the attention. "I wanted everyone to know that she was mine. I branded her Lex. My name for her and mine only."

"Can we call her Lex?" Liv asks, squishing Mark's cheeks. "I mean . . . she's our Lex now. She's part of our family."

A warm rush spreads through my chest at her, claiming me as part of this amazing family that three abandoned men created.

"Yes," I answer, not giving Mark a chance. "You can call me Lex."

Mark's eyes meet mine before moving his attention back to Liv. "But no one else, ok? Just our family. I don't like sharing, but I will this time."

He spins Liv several times before setting her down and then slides his arms around me as he starts singing "Alone" by Heart. "How do I get you alone?" His off-key tone continues until Shane throws a fry that bounces off his back.

Mark spins. "Hey, bro. Maybe you need to be taking notes. This is how you make magic happen."

Shane mumbles something, and I laugh, feeling right at home with these men.

"Later." A sly smile covers his lips as he grabs my hand. "Come on. Let's sit out here and let Andie have the room to pace," he gestures to the seats in the open air.

"You know, I've never actually watched a game with you."

"Baby, this is going to be one hell of a game. I'm so happy you're here." He kisses my cheek. "I hope it's me down on that field next year."

I hear the wistfulness in his voice, and I really want that for him.

We step into the cool breeze, and Shane and two other guys stand, talking football.

"Hey, man." A tall, handsome, dark-haired guy with piercing blue eyes leans in and hugs Mark.

"How are the Stingrays treating you?" Mark asks.

"We'll see how next season goes. We've got work to do."

"Chip, nice to see you again." Mark slaps hands with the other guy, who's just as tall, with lighter features and tattoos covering his massive arms.

"I'm never going to lose that nickname."

"Nope. You're stuck with it. You might as well put it on the back of your jersey." Mark's arm wraps around me. "Boys, this is my wife, Lex. Lex, this is Cole, Maggie's brother, and this guy is Nick, but we call him Chip."

I shake their hands, but the conversation immediately returns to football. Cole fills Mark in on his losing season with the Stingrays, and Nick talks about possibly being picked up by the Liberties.

"There's lots of speculation about teams wanting to bring you aboard. How's the shoulder?" Cole asks while Nick and Shane discuss training.

Mark pushes out a long breath. "I'm sitting tight. After today, hopefully, things will pick up. I've got to get my arm working again."

"You will. Everyone knows what you can do. Teams will be fighting for you. I've got to figure out how to get my team to quit focusing on my name."

Mark nods. "Give it time. They'll see. Those first seasons are tough. Hang in there. If you have time, come out and train with me."

The big muscle in my chest twinges, wondering what those first seasons were really like for Mark.

The players are announced, and quickly, the game is in motion. Mark and I eventually sit, his hand squeezing my thigh.

"Do you get nervous before games?" I ask.

He eyes me, but only briefly before his attention goes back to the field. "Not anymore. I get my head in game mode, and I'm good. I'm more nervous watching Sean get his ass pummeled."

The crowd roars as the opposing team scores again.

"I couldn't eat on your game days," I admit. I never told anyone that. I'd watch Mark's games but never told anyone but Slade about him, so everyone thought I was just a big Liberties fan.

His hand moves from my leg to my face. "That shit's got to stop. You're not only going to eat, you'll stand down there and kiss me for good luck from now on," he nods toward the field and presses his lips to mine.

The game goes on, and with a minute and thirty left in the fourth quarter, we know it's over. The Kingsnakes are down by ten, and there's no coming back.

Everyone gathers their stuff, and we slowly wind our way through the stadium to the friends and family area.

When the players start to file in, Sean sweeps Andie up, but for a man whose team just lost the Super Bowl, you'd never tell. He has the biggest smile on his face as he kisses his girl.

I nudge Mark. "They're sweet together."

"He is so over the moon for that woman, and she's amazing." He turns into me, linking his arms around my neck. "It's a good thing we got started making babies a little early. Now that his season is over, Sean will be working in a whole other way."

I swat him.

"What?! Look at them. Tell me I'm wrong."

I don't look at them, giving them the privacy they deserve, but bury my face in Mark's chest. "You're ridiculous."

"I want to see him try to outdo twins."

"Oh, for real. Will I have to hear you claim ownership of creating these miracles for the rest of my life?"

When I tip my chin up, waiting for his answer, there's a heat in his eyes that makes my insides quiver and warm simultaneously.

"Baby, all of this is a straight-up miracle." He lays my hand flat across his heart. "But I will own making those two babies in every single way for the rest of my life."

Awe, hell. How in the world will I ever be able to argue with that?

He brushes his lips against mine. "How about we hang out with these crazies, and then we get ready to go home?"

Home. It's currently up in the air exactly where that will be, and the thought makes my stomach squeeze just a little.

His mouth hovers over my ear, and he starts singing again. "Til' now, I always got by . . . "

My head tips back with a burst of laughter. I wrap my arms around Mark's waist and hold on tight. I know it doesn't really matter where we are. As long as I'm with Mark, it'll be the only place I ever want to be.

Chapter 35

MARK

"I have a call into the Kingsnakes to gauge their interest level. With Kenny out, they're on the hunt. I'm pursuing them until you tell me not to. Houston called, but I wanted to talk to you before I get back with them."

I lift my shirt to wipe the sweat off my brow before it drips into my eyes. "Shit! Going to Houston would be stepping back in time, man!" I take a second, needing to cool the defeat beginning to overwhelm me. Rob has always looked out for me, and I know he's trying his damnedest to get things moving. "What do you think?"

Rob's long and forceful sigh has my nerves spiking higher. "I think we should have the meeting. Doesn't hurt to talk and see what they've got going on."

In that long exhale, I detect a hint of resignation, creating a giant wave of anxiety that charges straight through me. I take a seat on a bench along the wall of the gym, needing to shake it loose and calm the hell down.

It's been over a month since the season ended, and the new season has officially begun. There's still plenty of time, but each week that goes by is one less week before training camps, preseason, and when the babies will be born.

Lex has spent these last weeks hanging out while I get to work, but I know she's about to hit her idleness limit. She doesn't have to say it. She's been tugging on that earring non-stop, and I know her hands are itching to work. Hopefully, the surprise I have for her will solve that.

Waking up with her in my arms, making her breakfast while she sits on the counter, and then spending our evenings together have been the happiest times of my life. I'm not about to let her sit around, missing any part of the life she left behind if I can help it.

"Ok. I'm in Ohio next week for Lex's doctor's appointment, so that's out, but let me know. We'll hear what they have to say, but Rob, that can't be it."

"Mark, let's be smart, not rash. This is only the beginning. I need you to reel in the emotions."

"Emotions! Shit, Rob! Time is ticking like a giant ass bomb."

"You knew this would take time. Keep strengthening your shoulder. That needs to be your focus." He pauses, knowing I have a hell of a lot more important things to worry about, but no team will want me if I can't throw. "Let's meet with Houston and get the rumor mill working for us. It might help get organizations moving."

I inhale, needing the tightness in my chest to ease and my brain to slow down. "I have to get settled somewhere sooner rather than later."

"I know. Just hold tight."

Hold tight. Yeah, right. There's nothing about me that's good at sitting around waiting for things to happen. Consistency is what I need. Something to grip onto that I know won't slip or change.

I hang up, rubbing my temples, hoping he's right.

This up-in-the-air stuff is wearing my excessively strained patience thin. Houston feels like desperation, but I may not have a choice. Rob's right. Talking doesn't hurt anything. I need the Kingsnakes' rumored interest to be solid, but interest isn't a signed contract.

My stomach pinches tighter as my nerves gnaw away at my gut lining. All I want is a home with Lex and our babies in a place where she doesn't end up regretting the choice she's making . . . for me.

I grab my bag to get home before I miss the delivery guy. With traffic, it takes me twenty minutes, and I walk into the kitchen to find Lex sitting at the island with my laptop and sheets of paper littering the countertop. Just seeing her lessens the weight of all the uncertainty piling on my shoulders.

"Hey, baby. What are you doing?" I lean down, and she tips her chin up to receive my kiss. Having her here and being able to kiss her any time I want melts all my previous agitation.

Her head falls to the keyboard. "This is all too much."

I grab a water from the refrigerator and a banana. "What is?"

She rolls her head to the side, peeking at me. "Maggie and Andie sent me these lists of all of the baby things they recommend. I've taken pictures with the app, but even it doesn't recognize what half of this stuff is."

I move to stand behind her, picking up the lists. Maggie and Andie would have no idea how this would take Lex hours to piece through and decipher.

"Did you know they make these sleeping bag things you wrap them up in like a tiny straitjacket?" She leans back.

I pull her off the stool, wrapping my arms around her. Her overwhelmed and frustrated tone awakens my protective instincts.

Her round stomach presses into me, and I feel a decent kick at the pressure. I palm the side of her growing belly, waiting for the little kicker to do it again.

"See, they already think we suck at this."

I press my lips to her forehead. "We will probably screw this up way more than not having the right tiny restraint bags." She groans into my chest. "We'll add it all to the registry. Whatever you don't get at the shower, we'll hit the order button, and it'll be here in two days."

She lifts her head. "How can you be so calm? Look at me. I'm huge. The doctor said I'd most likely deliver around thirty-six weeks. That's only fourteen weeks from now, if not sooner."

If only she'd seen my nerves ready to stick their white flags in the air, thrusting me into an epic meltdown.

"These babies need love. They've already got that. All these overly-priced marketing gimmicks might make things a little easier, but they won't give them the only thing they really need, which is us."

She hangs her head back to look at me. "You are way too insightful about this."

"You are having *my* babies. *That* is all I care about. We'll buy them some of those footie jammies and some diapers . . . you'll breastfeed. It'll be fine."

"This no-playing football thing has made you lose your mind, but you're right. They don't need all this fancy shit."

I lean down and capture her mouth. Her arms link around my neck as she tilts her head, and I'm down. My tongue swipes hers, provoking a soft moan to escape her.

She sucks in a breath as my lips move down her neck.

I pause as my brain snags on something. "Maybe we should look at those sleeping bags if they'll help them sleep. Shane said that's the hardest part."

She pushes me away. "See! I knew you couldn't be this calm." I snatch her back, and she rests her head against my chest.

"Maybe that tell-all book has a list of necessities. It has everything else."

"Stop." She holds her hand up.

"What?!" My hands slide over her butt. "We wouldn't know anything about what the babies are doing or what to expect these next months. I sure as hell didn't know there was such a thing as a doula."

She releases me and steps away. "Mark."

I grin, unable to help pushing her buttons. Lex all riled up does funny things to my insides. "What? Hiring someone to be your personal birthing coach sounds pretty nice to me."

"The only birthing coach I need is you."

"But don't you think it would be nice to have someone there who knows what they're doing? I mean, the book says—"

She places her hands over her ears. "By the time you get done with all of your intricate research, you'll be able to deliver these babies yourself."

"I'm a curious creature. I want to be prepared. Those books talk about needing to know what you want so—"

"I want to take those books, shove them in a pressure cooker along with a lit stick of dynamite, and count down until it explodes into a million tiny pieces."

I rest my hands on my hips. "Well, damn. Do you need to be that dramatic?"

She huffs. "I've been living with you too long."

I step behind her, sliding my arms around her and pulling her against me. "I like it when you get all hot and bothered." She groans, her head falling back to my chest, but there's love in it. I rest my chin on the top of her head. "I just want us to be prepared."

She twists in my arms to face me, her brow furrowed, and lips pressed together in determination. I'm tempted to kiss it away, but I refrain.

"Mark. Pay attention. I want to do this the old-fashioned way. I want to go to the hospital and have them inject me with whatever will numb me so that I don't have to feel a single thing. I don't want to listen to you read about what will happen or have someone talk to me about techniques and positions or have any clue about what's going on down there. I'm going to push these babies out, or they're going to cut them out, and you are going to keep your big, fat mouth shut."

"But, babe—"

"Mark, you are one word away from losing a testicle that could prevent us from ever doing this again. Now, please let me just be naive when it comes to this part."

I grin, and her head falls back toward the ceiling. "Have I ever told you that I think it's incredibly sexy when you get all riled up?" I kiss her exposed neck.

"You're annoying."

"You love me." I work my way up her neck to the sensitive skin below her ear, backing her into the counter as I lower myself to grip her thighs and hoist her onto it. I move to kiss her lips, but she pulls away in tease.

"I'm kind of mad at you right now."

"Kind of, huh?" I slip my hand under her shirt and spread my hand over her round stomach. "I think I have an idea of how I can make it up to you."

"Not likely."

I slide my palm against her cheek so I can see her blue-green eyes. There's a rare sparkle of mischief in them that I just put there, and I freaking love it. "What's it going to take?"

She pushes her lips to the side, thinking long and hard. "I want you . . . " She presses her lips to mine. "To . . . " She kisses me again, longer this time. "Make me." Kiss. "That chicken with the sauce again for dinner."

"Oh, really," I say against her lips.

She pulls away. "Yep. I've been craving it all day."

"Huh." My fingers dig into her hip.

"Like right now." She pushes. "Then, after I've eaten, maybe I'll think about forgiving you."

"How about I show you how much I love you first?" I lean in again.

"No." Her tone is firm, and she crosses her arms over her chest, declaring this is serious business.

I laugh. "Fine, but I'm showing you how much I love you later, just to be sure we're all good."

She bites her lip, trying not to smile, and I kiss her to expose it.

My phone buzzes, and I pull it from my pocket.

ROB: Kings want a meeting next week. I know you said you're out, but this is big. Can you make it work?

"Shit."

"What?" Lex moves to peek at my phone, and I show it to her. "That's a good thing, right?"

"Yeah, but it's next week. I'm going back with you for your doctor's appointment."

"Mark, this is huge. You have to go. I'll see if I can move it, or you can go to the next one. I have to find a doctor here, anyway."

I push out a long breath. I don't want Lex to go back to Ohio without me. I want to be there and hear everything the doctor has to say. If I'm really honest, which I don't want to be, there's a part of me that's afraid she'll be reminded of all she left behind and won't come back.

"Tell him, yes, and I'll—"

The doorbell rings, and Lex frowns. I shove my phone in my pocket, not wanting to think about her leaving, and happy my irrational fear is momentarily distracted by what's sitting on the other side of the front door.

"What's that look for?"

I grab her hand and help her off the counter. "What look?"

"That one." She points at my face.

"Come on." I pull her with me, unable to contain my excitement, and hope this will help her see that she can have part of the life she left behind anywhere with me.

"Mark, seriously," she says tentatively as I pull her along. "You know I don't like—"

I swing open the door, and parked in front of the house is a large transporter. On the trailer, ready to be rolled off, is a worn and rusted classic Ford Bronco.

My quiet and modest girl gasps. "What is . . . "

"Your F-150 won't cut it much longer."

Her eyes widen as she takes in the old truck. "You . . . bought this? How did you . . . "

I pull her along, meeting the driver. Lex leaves my side to get a closer look while I sign the paperwork.

She walks around the trailer. "What year? Seventy-one?"

"Seventy-two," I say, waiting to know if she likes it.

The driver unhooks the straps, and Lex turns to me. Her eyes are bright, glistening in the sun.

"You seriously bought this for me?"

"Uh . . . it's here and will be sitting in our garage, and we both know I won't be touching it."

She fists my shirt, holding onto me. "I . . . " She blinks quickly a few times. "I don't even know what to say," she whispers and then throws her arms around my neck. "It's so perfect. Thank you."

"Yeah? You like it? You'll fix it up?"

She sniffs. "Are you kidding? It's exactly what I would have picked. I already have a list in my head of where to start."

Of course, she does. I hold her tighter. "We'll get you everything you need. Ok? You can fix it up and keep it or sell it. Whatever you want. Hell, create your own YouTube channel and show people what you can do." I pause. "I just want you to be happy."

She pulls away, staring up at me. "Thank you. Mark . . . This means everything to me. Thank you so much." She pushes up on her toes to press her lips to mine. "I can't wait to get started."

She leaves me as the driver rolls the truck off the trailer, and the smile on her beautiful face is everything I was hoping for.

She turns back to me, beaming. "It's big enough for the babies."

Chapter 36

LEX

I squat, trying to get low enough to see how bad the undercarriage is as the soft country music plays on my phone. There's rust, but the floor panels don't look as bad as I expected.

I hoist myself up, surveying the classic truck, still unable to believe Mark bought this. It's perfect. It's exactly what I would have picked, and somehow, he knew.

The driver's side door whines with age as I open it, and I see the potential. My hands itch to get to work. The heavy stuff is where I need to start, but it'll have to wait until the babies are born. It doesn't mean I can't plan, though.

This past month and a half with Mark has been amazing. It's been six months since Vegas, and I'm finally getting to know the man I married again.

Mark relies on consistency. He always has. When things are unstable, he's not giving away a single part of his anxiety and fear. It's too risky and scary, so he keeps it all locked up tight. I see all of that clearly now.

I ache for him. I'm filled with sorrow for the part I played in making him feel like he has to guard himself.

I've seen it while he waits to hear from teams. He's good at pretending to be patient and believing the right team will come through, but underneath, the idea of not being wanted or sought after is eating him alive. The thought that the very thing that has kept him going might be over, and it not being his choice, is wreaking havoc on his need to feel secure.

Mark needs security—something he's never had. I'm understanding that now. I need him to feel safe with me and know I'm not going anywhere ever again, but getting him to trust me enough to truly believe it will take time.

I hurt him more than I may ever know, but I'll wait, give it time, and keep showing him until he has no choice but to believe.

The door to the garage swings open, and Mark steps into the garage, rubbing his eyes. His hair is swept across his forehead, and his joggers hang low on his waist. *Oh, man.* Sleepy, Mark, uninhibited by the protective layers of carefree bubble wrap he surrounds himself with, is almost too much. *This will never get old.*

He squints his dark eyes at me, trying to avoid the bright light. "What are you doing? It's one a.m."

"I can't sleep. I was laying there, staring at the ceiling, so I came out here to figure out what parts I'll need."

He moves into the light, more awake now. "I don't like waking up and you not being there." He says it with a bit of force, and it only confirms the scars run as deep as I'm gathering.

"I'm sorry." I smile, liking his groggy irritation. "She's got potential. I'll eventually need Slade out here for a weekend to help me pull the engine."

"Slade, huh?" he grunts.

I glance at him, unable to hide my grin at his jealous tone. "Yeah, he's big and strong and will be able to help me strip it."

"Big and strong, my ass," he grumbles.

I laugh. "You know you're cute when you're jealous."

He stands straighter, his hands on his hips and fully alive. "Baby, he had eight years to make a move, or he did and didn't work. Either way, you're mine. You've always been mine. I'm not jealous."

I eye him, knowing he's full of crap. He's a little jealous, but he's one hundred percent right. I've always been his.

I peek in the back seat. "I'll need to attach safety anchors to the body for the baby seats, but there will be plenty of room." One side of his mouth tips up, and I have to look away. "I need a few more minutes. Hang out with me, and then we'll go back to bed."

He moves to me, sliding his arms around my middle, and pulls me against him.

"I told you if I hang out with you in the garage, especially wearing my T-shirt, you won't get much work done." He pushes my hair away from my neck, his mouth running over it.

"You're trouble." I tip my head to the side to give him better access.

"I never pretended not to be."

I turn in his arms to face him and find his lips. His hands slide into my hair as mine glide over the muscles in his back. It only takes a second, and he's pulling me toward the door, and who am I to fight him?

"It's time for bed," he mumbles against my mouth, and I have no doubt if I weren't pregnant, I'd be over his shoulder right now.

The music on my phone suddenly breaks into ringing, halting our steps. Mark pauses but doesn't release me.

His lips brush against mine. "It's probably a robot."

It stops ringing, and I fall against him as his hands pull at the hem of my shirt. It doesn't get past my bump before my phone starts ringing again.

Mark groans, loosening his grip as I let my head fall to his shoulder.

"I should check it." I tug my shirt down and grab my phone from the stool, seeing that it's Grandpa. My stomach hits the concrete floor.

"Grandpa. Everything ok?"

Mark moves to stand next to me, his comforting hand on my shoulder, while all I can do is listen as my dream come true crashes into reality.

"Ok," I say because there's nothing else. "I'll see you soon."

I hang up, holding my phone and unable to look at the face I'd walk through fire to never ever hurt again.

"Hey, what's wrong? Is Cal, ok?" His voice is so soft and tender that it only plunges the sword of truth deeper with a twist.

I pinch my eyes closed, wanting this to all go away. I want to ignore it and let it be someone else's sacrifice this time and prevent Mark from ever having to relive the nightmares he escaped from.

"Lex . . . "

I hear my name, but if I move, if I speak, everything I've finally let myself believe I could have will disappear.

"Baby . . . " Mark's hands grip my elbows. "You're scaring me. What's going on?"

I force out a breath, needing the tears and utter terror about what's coming to stay at bay. What is it they say? The truth always catches up with you. Or is it the past? Either way, it just snagged my ass, and the only thing I can do is hope that he'll see that I did it for him.

I swallow the tidal wave of dread and fear for what's to come. "I have to go . . . back." I could have said home, but Mark is my home now. At least, I hope he'll still be.

"What happened?"

I move, suddenly needing to get out of the garage—this place where I see everything we're becoming. I move quickly, unwilling to let him trap me there.

Inside, I go straight to our bedroom as he calls my name.

"Lex, stop."

I keep going, flipping on the light.

He finally catches my arm, stalling my attempt to flee. "Lex, you need to tell me what the hell is going on?"

Knowing I can't protect him from this any longer, I force my eyes to his. The severe concern I find there rips my chest wide open.

I inhale as the weight of crushed dreams fills my lungs. "I have to go back. There's . . . " I sink down onto the edge of the bed, hoping the padding will somehow soften the blow. "I have to tell you something." I wrap my arms around myself, preparing for the aftershock.

"Ok." His brow scrunches tight, and his stance is strong and wide. His defenses are in place. I fucking hate it. All of it.

I don't even know where to start or what to say, so I jump in, needing him to hear me and understand. "Please just . . . listen to me."

My pathetic voice sounds weak as I watch his muscles contract.

"Ok." His tense tone makes it already feel like a lie.

I shove out a quick, short breath, my heart beating too fast. I slide my sweaty hands under my thighs to prevent them from shaking. "Remember that day after graduation when we had the party at the shop for you and Shane and Sean, and the newspaper showed up to feature the three of you? Three guys from the system headed off to major universities."

"Yeah." His stance softens, but only slightly.

"Pictures of you made circles around the state for weeks. People couldn't stop talking about it as you left for camp that summer."

I kissed him goodbye, promising I'd be there. I wasn't. It's a fresh, direct punch to the diaphragm every time I let myself remember.

I swallow the painful lump in my throat. He deserves the truth, free of my heartache and suffering.

"Two weeks after you left, I was at the garage working." I peek at him, praying he'll listen. "A woman walked in with a baby. She was looking for you."

The crease between his eyes deepens like he's trying to recall something or make sense of my words.

"Lex, I don't know—"

"It was your mom."

He physically pulls back. "My mom?"

I nod. "She saw your picture in the paper and was looking for you and for . . . help."

I wanted to kick her out and tell her every single thing I thought about her. Then two tiny brown eyes, much smaller versions of the ones staring at me now, peeked at me from the hip of a woman who was strung out and reeked of alcohol.

"She was a mess, slurring her words, and had the shakes." It was the first time I'd ever seen someone like that, and I could have vomited all over the floor thinking of Mark living with that for years.

"I told her to leave and that I had no idea how to get in touch with you. She started to cause a scene and begged me to help her find you. When I didn't budge, the baby began to cry. She was jostling her around, calling me names, and telling me I was keeping her from trying to do the right thing."

Mark steps away from me, his eyes dropping to the floor. "I don't understand." He shakes his head, his voice rough.

"She said she was trying to get clean, wanted money, and needed someone to take Bree." At her name, his head pops up. "Your . . . sister," I say softly. "She stormed out, calling me a liar, and said she'd find you." Despite my protest, my eyes fill with tears. "I ran after her and told her I'd help her as long as she'd leave you alone."

His eyes flick between mine so fast I can't keep up. "You." The word comes out with force. I nod. "What? You helped her?" His tone is filled with nothing but betrayal.

Stab. Stab. Stab.

My shaky hand pushes my hair behind my ear. "She left her with me. Just handed her over and walked away. Grandpa and I worked with a social worker. I made sure your mom got into a treatment program and . . . " I don't finish when I see rage flood his dark eyes.

"Why the hell are you telling me this now?"

A tear slips down my cheek. He's angry, but there are wounds underneath that I've sliced wide open.

"Eventually, she got clean and regained custody of Bree. I've been making sure that there weren't any slips. I wasn't going to let anything happen to Bree like . . . "

What happened to you. My gut squeezes so tight bile creeps up my throat, knowing what Mark went through as a child.

I don't say it, but I can see he knows. His jaw is set, his hands fisted, but he needs the rest.

"I told your mom about us getting married and the babies. I told her that I was going to tell you. She . . . has a lot of regrets."

"Don't. Don't you dare defend her," he spits.

"I'm not. I reminded her that she needed to keep going . . . to stay clean . . . for Bree." I drop my head. "She's been arrested."

I don't want to say the rest, but protecting him went out the window. "She was picked up and is being charged with manufacturing and delivery, and . . . " The last part is going to shove a hot poker into every freshly opened wound. "Child endangerment."

I give him a minute, watching him struggle with it all. "Bree is sitting in a facility right now. I don't know the details, but I have to get back to speak with the social worker. Grandpa tried, but . . . "

I don't continue. There's no point. I can tell he's done listening. His eyes are trained on the floor. He won't even look at me.

"So, you just decided to keep your mouth shut about this? This whole time. You never once thought you should tell me."

"Yes, I was going to, but . . . " What can I say? Nothing. I tried to tell him, but we got caught up and . . . It's all one fat excuse when nothing will make this better for him.

He shoves a hand through his hair, gripping it tight. "But what? How about, hey Mark, I've been hanging out with your shitbag mother, and oh, by the way, you have a sister? That would've been a good place to start!"

I have no defense.

"I want to know why you didn't tell me."

I need a second to think about it. Over these past months, I had a million opportunities, and I didn't take any of them.

"You can't be the woman of few words right now, Lex. I want to know."

A sheen of sweat covers my body. I pull my hair back, twist it around my sweat-soaked hand, and let it fall again. "I know. Just give me a minute to find the right ones."

He waits. His hard eyes stare into me while I think, process, and hunt for the truth. My fingers twist my earring. I don't have to search very hard, and there it is.

I suck in a breath for courage, hoping it will slow my racing heart. "I tried a couple of times, but . . . " I drag my eyes up to his, needing to see him. "I know what she did to you. How much she hurt you, maybe even more than your dad." It's possible the lump in my throat might burst as I think about the stories he shared with me, and I know they weren't even the worst of them. "The absolute last thing I've ever wanted to do was hurt you, and I know this hurts like hell."

He scoffs. "Hurt. Fuck! That doesn't even begin to—"

I stand. I can't be a coward. His shoulders are rigid, and his eyes are wild with anger and pain. All I want is to make it better, and nothing I say will.

I let the rest of it go. My voice is only a whisper. "How could I? How could I tell you about her and Bree . . . when she didn't even try for you." I ached to touch him, hold him, and make him see. "Mark, you deserved for her to fight . . . for you. To put you first, like she did Bree."

He scoffs. "Just like you put me first and disappeared."

I feel the smack all the way from my face to my toes, and I can't even say I don't deserve it. I step away from him, sliding a hand under my growing belly to support it and move toward the door.

He spins, watching me. "Where the hell are you going?" I don't stop, but in two seconds, he's standing in front of me. "Where are you going?"

My skin is hot and sticky, and I'm one second from melting down as I watch my dreams swirl in the toilet. My stomach lurches again, but I force it down.

I will myself to stay strong. "I'm going to give you some space."

"Seriously, is that how this will always be? You just leave every time things get hard." I pull back at his words. *That's not what I'm doing. Am I?*

"I'm pissed. No, I'm so angry I can't see straight, but I don't want space. I want you to stay here and help me understand. I've never left, Lex."

Another punch right between our twins.

"I've never left and never will, but I need to know that you won't either."

It's the truth. His truth. He's terrified I'll leave again. That I won't show up or be here. That *I* won't fight for him. I hate myself for letting him ever doubt my love.

I pull myself up, letting the total and complete truth go. Nothing reserved. "Even if your mom hadn't shown up. Even if I'd made a different choice that day, the only thing I would have done was hold you back and slow you down. Mark, you lived through hell and somehow walked out alive. There wasn't a chance I was going to be that person to you."

I suck in air. "You made it to Notre Dame! Walked on as the starting quarterback." Everything in me rises to the surface. All eight years' worth. "I was only ever going to be in that shop, covered in filth. Just a girl who can't fucking read." I shrug as one tear rolls out. "I could've never kept up with you. I wanted you to soar, not be the weight that tied you down."

The burn in my throat is so strong I'm not sure it won't close up. I let the tears stream down my cheeks, no longer caring to hide them.

"When she showed up at the shop with a baby, asking for help, that was it. I gave up every hope of ever seeing you again. I knew if I told you, if I came to you and told you that sweet baby girl existed, you would've sacrificed everything for a person who never deserved you in the first place." My voice breaks. "She never deserved you."

I wipe my nose on my wrist. "So, I took Bree and cared for her until Linda could again. I didn't know if she'd ever come back, if rehab would work, or if she'd stick it out, and if she did, that she'd stay sober. I've made sure Bree was healthy and safe because that's *exactly* what you would've done."

I match his stance, more convinced of that now than ever. "Right or wrong, I did it for you. Being anywhere near Linda would've pulled you so far into the dark. I would've rather spent my life without you than let that happen."

He scoffs. "So, you left me, made me wonder if it was all a joke, if I made it all up, everything we had . . . to save me?" His voice is softer now, but the pain has never been more apparent.

"Maybe you can't see. Maybe I was dead wrong in what I did. I couldn't even breathe for months after you left. But I kept going, and I'd do it all over again if it meant saving you from ever returning to any part of the life you'd been pulled from." I move one step closer. So close, but I don't touch him. "I love you so much. I did then, and I love you even more now. I don't care what I have to do. I will *never* let her or any part of that life touch you ever again."

There was no one there to protect him when he was just a little boy. Even at eighteen, I'd sacrificed it all to make sure that never happened, and I do it again.

I take a step away. "Now, I have to go back and make sure nothing happens to that little girl."

He stands tall again. "I'm going with you."

I shake my head, wiping my face clean and knowing it's time to do things right, whether that's together or apart. "No. No, you're not."

"Like hell—"

I cut him off and risk it, putting both of my hands on his face so I know he hears me. "You're staying here. You're going to stay here and calm down and have that meeting with the Kings. Then you're going to Houston. *You* are going to sign with a team and play football. All of this . . . it wasn't for nothing. You made it out, and you have turned into the most incredible man. I'm . . . " I can't breathe, and my voice breaks with everything. "I'm so proud to be your wife."

Tears spill over my cheeks again as he blinks, holding his own back. "I have to talk to the social worker, find out what's happening with Linda, and hopefully get Bree. Then, you and I will figure this out."

"So that's just it. You're leaving, and we're what?"

"You and I are us, always, but right now, there's a terrified little girl who needs us to put her first. I don't know what she's been through." My stomach rolls with the possibilities. I step closer, my body pressing against his and needing him to know I'm still here. "This can't pull you under. I can't lose you again," I whisper.

His forehead falls to mine. We stand in silence for a few long seconds before he surrenders and pulls away. I give him a minute and when he doesn't say anything I find my phone to book my ticket.

Chapter 37

MARK

I pull up to the curb as cars and buses zoom past. Silence. There's been nothing but silence for the past eight hours.

I don't know what to say, and I'm sure Lex said everything she wanted to. I feel sick. The bile in my stomach stirs. In two seconds, she'll step out of this car and walk through those sliding doors.

The last thing I want is for her to leave. I need her here. I need her to help me sort through this, to make me understand.

I want to go with her. I want to know that my mother won't steal her away from me again, but Lex is right. I can't go back like this. There's a wildfire blazing within me that's likely to destroy everything in its path.

Every time I think about my mom expecting that I'd help her and then Lex taking the hit instead, it spreads further. At some point, it's going to consume me, and I can't be with Lex when that happens. And I can't let it impact my . . . sister. *My sister. Shit.*

Lex pushes the door open, grabs her backpack, and lifts herself out, belly first. She's leaving with my babies, and I have to swallow down a sob that wants to break free.

I pop the trunk and lift her suitcase out, setting it next to her. She stands, watching the passing traffic—everything but me.

I hate this. I hate it so much, I could scream.

I move into her and slide my arms around her, holding her close to me, but it's awkward and stiff, and I detest it.

"Call me when you get there. Ok?"

She nods. I release her, knowing it has to happen. Her eyes lock on mine for a second. I think she might say something, but she doesn't.

She pops the handle on her suitcase and turns. I watch her, my stomach twisting into a hard knot. My whole life. I'm watching my whole life walk away. *FUCK!*

I run after her, grab her arm, and pull her to me. The sick feeling in my gut eases only slightly. "I'm angry. I'm so fucking angry." I bury my face in her neck as her arms wrap around me, holding me tight. "But I'm not going anywhere, ok?" She sniffs, and the coolness of her tears soak through my shirt. "I need time to sort through this. It's . . . I don't know how to feel about any of it."

I pull away, my hands cupping her face. She won't meet my eyes. "Lex, look at me." Her eyes don't move from my chest. "Please, look at me." They drag up, filled with tears, and I want to make it better, but I can't right now. "I just need time, and you have to . . . " *Go. I hate it.*

I hate my mom. It wasn't enough to let me be beaten while she drank herself unconscious and lived for her next hit. She took Lex from me. She used her, and Lex let her. The woman who didn't care whether I lived or died right in front of her.

Lex helped her when she should have been with me. She kept herself from me. Kept the truth from me. For what? An addict who didn't give a shit about me. Who would've probably sold me to get her next fix.

She let Lex take care of my sister, the one I should be looking after. They should be calling me to come to get her and keep her safe. Lex and I could've been caring for her together all along.

I press my lips to her forehead.

"I love you." Her voice is so weak I barely hear her. She wipes her face, grips her suitcase, and walks away.

I watch her, just beginning to waddle, as she walks through the sliding glass doors. Her hand slides over and under her belly to support it. I bite my cheeks to keep from losing it. I fist my hands, wanting to beat the absolute shit out of something. Anything.

But I can't. I have to figure out how to let this go without it drowning me. I need to do what I've always done. Play the game. The one that's always saved me. I need a team, a contract . . . something to work toward. Something that will help take away a little bit of the rage that's threatening to boil over.

Chapter 38

LEX

"How is she?"

I carefully lower myself to the couch, completely exhausted, and it's seriously becoming a challenge to get up and down. Like a big rig tow truck, I need flashing lights and a backup horn.

Grandpa waits patiently in his chair while I try to get comfortable. The bags under his eyes tell me he hasn't slept much, either. At least my pregnancy insomnia is helping in this case.

"She's . . . ok. She's starting to open up about what it was like those weeks I was gone. She saw and heard a lot. Seems Linda was incoherent most of the time. People were coming and going all hours of the night, and they weren't quiet about it. It scared her."

I try to imagine what that would be like, and I can't. Linda was letting the worst kinds of people into the apartment. By some miracle, I don't think Bree was harmed.

"She keeps asking about her mom and what's going to happen."

"What'd you tell her?"

I push air between my lips. "The truth. I don't know."

It's been two weeks. Two long weeks of complete mess, and my heart breaks for everything Bree is going through. It's also been two long weeks of short, strained conversations with Mark.

I spent the first few days working with the social worker. During that time, Bree was placed in a home with a family. They seemed nice, but relief didn't even describe what I felt when I got the call that I was assigned as her temporary guardian.

When I picked her up from school, she ran to me, burying her face in my side and letting loose the tears I have no doubt she'd been holding on to.

Now, we wait for Linda's court appearance. Given her previous record and the fact she was not only found in possession but also dealing out of the apartment, she's facing a long-term sentence.

Eight years ago, pursuing permanent guardianship may have been a challenge, but now that I'm married to a blood relative, it may be possible. I just need to get Mark to talk to me. I know there's no way he'll let Bree go anywhere other than with us if we have a say.

When I left him in Phoenix, Mark told me that he wasn't going anywhere, but these past two weeks, it feels like he's anywhere but with me. He met with the Kings and then Houston, but no official offers were made. I know that, but not much of anything else. He's shut down completely.

I can't even blame him. I know he's hurting and is trying to sort through all of this. So, I'm trying to be patient, but selfishly I need him.

His consistent calls to check in are reassuring, but he's short and guarded, and I'm beginning to worry that maybe we won't be ok. I want him to remind me that we're still in this together and know that when everything settles, we'll be standing at the end of it.

I kick my legs out in front of me, peeking at my swollen ankles. "I told Bree we'd go get some of her things tomorrow. The landlord won't hold it any longer."

"You take Slade with you. Who knows who she'd been dealing with that's watching that apartment." I nod. He sighs, running a hand over his gray scruff. "Have you heard from Mark today?"

"Not today. He's . . . " I realize I don't know what he's doing.

"Give him time, but not too much. Letting him wallow in that shit won't get him anywhere. It'll feast on him, which is why you did all this to begin with. To protect him."

"I can't make him get over it. I hurt him, too," I huff.

"Well, you aren't doing yourself any favors by not knowing if he can forgive you."

The truth is, I'm not sure I'm ready to know if he's able to forgive me.

When I don't say anything, I hear that whistle as he pushes out a breath through his nose. "You know, when your grandma left, I just watched her go. Didn't even say a word. I thought . . . if she wasn't happy, well, I wasn't going to stand in her way."

He rubs his scratchy jaw. "I've had enough years to wonder what would've happened if I'd actually fought. If I'd asked her to stay. She might have still left, but I think sometimes the people we love need to know we think they're worth fighting for, come hell or high water. Sometimes that means fighting with them, making them see that we actually give a shit if they stick around, or asking them to forgive us when we really need them to."

I stare at him, trying to understand. All I've done is fight for Mark.

"Pal, you didn't give Mark any say in this. Might be time he had one. You need to talk to him. Not talking will get you nowhere you want to be, and you need him. Maybe he needs to hear that." He rests back in his chair like he's finished, but I know this man. His final word is coming. "And you need to not hide from his anger. This won't be the last time you hurt him or piss him off."

There I have it. He's done now. I can't argue with facts.

I have fought for Mark. All this time, I've been fighting, but I haven't been fighting *with* him. I never gave him a say.

I keep thinking if I give him time, he'll lower the guardrails and let me back in, but Grandpa's right. I don't have the luxury of sticking my head in the sand, waiting to see if he'll trust me enough. I need him. I can't fight alone anymore, and I don't want to. Maybe he just needs to hear that.

Chapter 39

MARK

I shove my gear in my duffle and then toss some clothes in. I need this visit to give me something to go on.

I met with the Kings, and even though the meeting was promising, Rob's heard nothing. My trip to Houston was just as I expected. They're rebuilding, and it's a mess, but if an offer comes through, I may not have a choice if I want to play.

I sit on the edge of my bed and scroll through my phone, sifting through rumors. None of which are even remotely accurate. Now, Seattle called, and their private plane will be waiting for me in the morning.

I flick to my contacts, my finger hovering over Lex. I want to call her, to hear her voice, but the last thing she needs is my lingering anger. I know she's tired, and I hear her worry and stress. I want to be the one to take it away. I just don't know how when every time I think about her ghosting me and why, I'm in desperate need to beat the shit out of something.

I hear my door slam. "Yo, bro." Sean's voice carries through my house, and I fall back on the bed.

"Get your ass out here."

Shit! Shane's bark is always worse than his bite, but his directness is not what I need. It might push me over the manic ledge I've been hanging on these past weeks.

It doesn't surprise me that they've both shown up after not responding to their texts and calls, but I'm pretty damn sure I don't want to hear what they have to say.

I drag myself from the bedroom and into the kitchen, where they're loitering. Shane rests against the counter, his large arms crossed over his chest. Sean leans over the island, his stare is softer.

I met Sean at the training facility the day after I dropped Lex off at the airport. When I told him about my mom and Bree, he remained quiet, likely sensing I was on the verge of exploding, and he chose not to pull the pin. Now, he's called in reinforcements, and I have no doubt we'll be here until they're satisfied with my course of action. The problem is I don't have a plan, and I'm not really interested in them helping me develop one.

I pull out a stool and sit, not offering to start this conversation.

"You done sulking now?" Shane's tone is a little gentler.

I set my phone on the counter along with my elbows. "Man, I'm not sulking." I'm angry as hell, and he's an excellent target if he wants to push.

Shane's head falls to the side. "Oh, you're not. You want to tell us why you're here and not with your wife. Why your ass isn't back in Ohio doing exactly what you know you should be doing?"

"I can't do this." I shut him down, standing and they both step in my direction. "What do you want from me? I'm angry. I'm so fucking angry I can't see straight!"

Their demeanor relaxes slightly as if they think we might be getting somewhere.

"I can't go there. I might literally kill someone. One person in particular, and then you two will have to pick up the pieces. All the pieces that belong to me."

"You're sure as hell not acting like they belong to you," Sean states matter-of-factly.

I roll my eyes, shaking my head. "She waltzed her strung-out, drunk ass into Cal's shop and ruined the best, most important thing that has ever happened to me! It wasn't enough to sit stoned out of her mind while my dad beat the living shit out of me. To watch me burn alive as he held my hand over the stove or say nothing while he'd see how many hits I could take before I had no fight left."

My fists ache to make contact with something. "She walked her baked-ass in there and stole the only thing that ever mattered to me. The only thing I've ever fucking needed!" My jaw is clenched so tight I'm surprised it doesn't crack.

I sit back down on the stool, collecting myself before I do something I regret.

"Get up." I drag my eyes to Shane's, and his dare me not to. "Stand up, Mark, and lift your shirt."

I stay seated. One dark eyebrow arches slightly, and I know he's two seconds from lifting me out of this seat, and we both know he could.

"You had those words permanently engraved on your skin for a reason. And you weren't wrong. They weren't a lie. Not even a little bit. Don't you see that?"

The very spot on my ribs feels like a match is being held to it.

Perhaps your love will make me forget all I wish not to remember.

After I read them out loud for our English Lit assignment, she'd asked me if I thought love could do that—allow me to forget. I knew right then that her's could. She repeated those exact words over and over again to me, believing it was possible.

I drop my head, unsure if I'm able to hear the truth.

Shane's now gentle voice filters through. "Those words are exactly what she did. She loved you enough to let you go, so you never had to go back there."

Stab. Right through my heart, twisting as it sinks in. It's the truth I don't want to face. The truth is that she loved me enough to carry the burden so I wouldn't have to.

I shake my head, letting it fall into my hands. "I spent all that time walking around, trying to convince myself she was a liar. Forcing myself to believe that I'd made it all up."

"Stop." Sean's voice is soft. "Stop punishing yourself. She needs you now, and you need to be there."

The fire that was dampened returns, and I burn with rage. "Punish myself?" I scoff. "I was floating around on bought air, messing around with women, and living the high life while she was there taking care of a baby and living my hell so I didn't have to." I stand. "And even worse . . . she had to watch. She had to watch me with those women, pretending like I was living on cloud nine."

I want to ram my fist into a wall a thousand times. "There is no punishment that's enough."

Shane steps forward. "You think this is helping? You think sitting here making a list of all the ways you were wrong will help anything?" I don't respond, and Shane moves to stand a foot from me. "She's pregnant, you asshole."

Shane's patience is gone, and I can feel the heat radiating off him. "I don't care what your mom did or didn't do. What she let happen. Lex is your wife. She needs you more than anyone else. And there's a scared little girl who needs you to get your head out of your ass and make sure she's safe."

His finger jabs my chest, and Sean moves closer, poised to intervene.

Shane is unfazed. "You have a sister who needs you to step up and give her everything you never had. Someone to love her and take care of her. Give her a family. She's probably scared shitless while you're here having your princess pity party." His nostrils flare as he inhales, cooling down.

"You made it out, man." Sean's tone is much softer. "You got out and made it here. Lex made that happen. She saved you from the life that would have taken you down. You could be the one sitting in that jail cell or worse." He pauses, not saying what we all three know. I could be dead. "Now, you owe it to her and Bree to get them out of it. Go get them and give them both the life they deserve."

A burn crawls up my throat that's so intense I can't breathe. "I don't know how to do that."

"Yes, you do." Sean's tone is tight now. "You aren't that kid anymore. All you need is to be the man we know you are. Be the man Lex married and brother you've been to us every single day."

Tears crease my eyes as I stare at my two brothers. The ones I somehow got lucky enough to find, or maybe they found me. I'm not sure. All I know is they're right. Period. There's nothing else to be said.

"Get to Seattle tomorrow. Then have the plane take you to where you really need to be." Shane's coach tone returns, but there's no heat to it.

My blurry gaze pops up to theirs.

"Tell Rob to find a deal. A decent one and take it." Sean states it as if it's a simple task. He knows it's not. "Until then, your ass stays in Ohio."

It's where I need to be. Shit. The problem is, it means I have to go back and face all that I don't want to, all that I've tried so hard to forget, but they're right. It's time I get them out of there, where I know my past won't touch Lex or my sister ever again, at least not without having to go through me.

Chapter 40

LEX

"Anything else you want to grab?"

Bree sits on the edge of her twin bed, pressed against the wall, holding the pink model Volkswagen Beetle and her clay pot filled with colored pencils. Her head hangs, and the bright, lively little girl is missing. The pale tinge to her skin tells me she's sick with heartache and terrified of the unknown.

I lower myself beside her, having to lean back to make room for the giant kicking machines that have invaded my entire midsection, including the space underneath my ribs.

"Are you ok?" When she doesn't say anything, I prod, knowing Slade will be back any minute. We have to return the keys to the landlord, who's impatiently waiting for us to load up what we can. The rest will be up to him. "You know you can tell me anything, right?"

She nods, barely. "I . . . What's going to happen if my mom has to stay in jail for a long time? Are you leaving again to be with your husband?"

It's the first time she's mentioned Mark, and I have no doubt it's because she's smart enough to be afraid of the answer. I wish I knew what he was thinking, but I don't.

The more days that go by without Mark really talking to me, the more I wonder if he ever will. Two days ago, he told me he was meeting with Seattle's team doctors and therapists, but after today, I have to know what's going on. It's not just Bree that needs answers. I need a plan.

I promised Bree I would always tell her the truth, and so I give her the only thing I'm absolutely sure of.

"Remember I told you he travels a lot." She nods, still not looking at me. "He's got a really busy schedule, and when that settles down, he and I will talk about it."

Her slim shoulders slump further, and I put my arm around her, pulling her to my side.

"But I can tell you that I won't be leaving you. Ok? Unless someone tells me I have to, you're staying with me and Grandpa Cal."

One side of her mouth tugs up a hair. "And the babies, too."

I squeeze her tighter. "And these little monsters, too. I'll need your help."

The first smile I've seen in days spreads across her beautiful face.

"All right, you two, I don't think we can fit one more stuffed animal or art piece in the truck." Slade's big, broad frame leans against the doorway.

"I only have three stuffies," Bree challenges.

"Well, they're buckled in and ready to go."

Bree scans the small room, checking it over one last time. She pulls a small picture of her and Linda at her last dance recital off the wall and shoves it in her pocket. "I'm ready." She looks so much older than she should ever have to for only being nine.

Slade steps into the room and offers his hand to help tug me up. "Shit, woman. You get any bigger, and we'll need a crane."

I slap his arm, and he chuckles. "You're mean."

"Want me to drive you to your appointment later? I've got a dolly."

"Slade, if you don't want to lose a nut, keep your mouth shut."

His hand jets out as I get ready to step out of the room. "Seriously, you want me to go with you?" I smile up at him, swallowing what feels like razor blades. "He needs to get his head out of his ass quick before I go remove it for him." Slade's eyes are hard and serious.

"Tomorrow." I manage to squeak out. "He's going to have to give me something tomorrow."

He swings his arm around me. "He's no delicate flower. You need to quit treating him like one. He better give you a hell of a lot more than something."

I hug him. "He will."

"He doesn't deserve you, you know that? Everything you did for him."

We meet Bree at the door, and she steps out as Slade locks it.

"He does." *And so much more.* "He's got to face the evil this place holds. He has to be ready to do that."

Slade doesn't say anything, but I know he heard me. I also know he understands a little something about what it takes to stare down the past.

What I don't know is when Mark might be ready. All I can do for now is believe that he will. The man I married—the one whose eyes I stared into as he declared his love for me over and over again—would stand and take on any force just as he would have when I did it for him.

The receptionist hands me a card with my next appointment on it. I shove it in my pocket.

Two weeks. I no longer have monthly appointments but will be coming every two weeks so they can monitor for contractions and keep an eye on potential early labor. For now, I have to take it easy and call if I start feeling any tightening.

I climb in my truck and sit. I have thirty minutes until I told Krissy I'd pick Bree up. Not long, but maybe long enough.

My moment of positivity and hope I shared with Slade earlier quickly dwindled as I lay listening to the babies' hearts beat. Their little whoosh, whoosh, whooshes crept into my throat, and I about lost it right there on the short exam table.

I glance around my truck. I don't even have a way to bring them home.

Enough is enough. Times up.

I twist the key, and my truck rumbles to life. I fasten my seatbelt, tap Mark's contact, and then the speaker button.

It rings five times, and then the voicemail picks up as I pull out of the doctor's parking lot. I'm tempted to hang up and dial again, but I don't. I let the recording play, having no idea what to say.

The tone beeps.

"Hey. I need to talk to you." I pause, needing air. The pressure of this imminent conversation overtaking my emotions. I swallow hard, trying to keep a clear head.

"I'm leaving the doctor's office. I thought you'd want to know . . . " I blow out a breath as the weight of these past weeks fills my eyes and the fear I've been actively ignoring roars to life. I blink rapidly, needing them to retreat immediately.

"I know you're angry and . . . Please call me." My voice breaks despite my best efforts. "I can't . . . I can't do this by myself."

The truth. I can't do it without him. "I need you here." It's all I can manage.

I don't want to have these babies without him. I don't want to sit and face Linda's consequences alone. I want to tell Bree that Mark and I will never let her be scared again. I want him here with me. I need him . . . for the rest of my life.

"I'm so sorry." I sniff, swiping at my cheeks. "Please . . . just—"

Out of the corner of my eye, there's a flash, and then—blood and pain, and everything goes black.

Chapter 41

MARK

I lace up my cleats and toss my sweatshirt on top of my gear.

I stretch my arm, ready to work. I'll show this crew what I can do.

Sean's words race through my head. Get a decent deal, and then get to Ohio. That's exactly what I'm going to do and Lex doesn't get a say this time.

I warm up, tossing balls to a trainer. The sky is gray, and there's a chill in the air, but the slight breeze is invigorating.

My blood pumps faster as my fingers find the laces. I've missed this. I just need my shoulder to prove my worth.

"All right, let's set it up," one of the offensive coordinator directs. "Show us if you've still got it, Sandberg."

The receiver takes off. I cock my arm, release the ball, and it makes contact. The receiver jogs back and sets up again. He runs to the corner, turns at the twenty-yard mark, and the ball drops right into his hands.

We do it again and again. He runs toward the post this time and into the end zone. I drop back, thrust my arm forward, and it's gone. The ball spirals long and far and straight to my target. *Dime.*

I can't help the grin of pure satisfaction that creeps across my face. There it is.

We run a few more plays, but my shoulder is tiring, and the trainers know it. All I need is strength and endurance, and it will come.

They call me in, and we discuss my therapy and training schedule. They thank me for visiting as Rob stands off to the side, working the GM.

I pull my sweatshirt back on, knowing my shoulder will hurt like hell later, but it's a different kind of pain. A healing one and it feels damn good.

Rob smacks me on the back. "That's the way to do it, kid. Now, you sit back and leave the rest to me." I smile for the first time in what feels like forever. "Drinks on me before they shuttle you home?"

I shake my head. "Nah, I've got to get going." He frowns, but I ignore it. I need a deal, and Rob needs to make that happen, not worry about what's happening in my personal life. Plus, Bree's life will remain private, at least until I have a chance to meet her and understand my role.

The thought has my stomach clenching tight.

"Well, all right. Let's get out of here."

Rob and I exit the facility and walk to our rentals.

He offers his hand. "I took video. We've got something solid to work with. I'll be leaking this ASAP."

"Keep me updated. The sooner we get something locked in, the better."

He pats me on the back and then steps away. "Keep training, Mark. I'll be in touch."

I laugh, alive and ready to get down to business. There's no way in hell I'm going to let my past ruin everything I've worked for. I certainly won't let it steal one more second of my time with Lex.

I climb into the SUV and toss my duffle onto the passenger seat. I dig for my phone to notify the pilot I'm on my way.

Lex's name appears next to a voicemail notification, and my chest swells with the need to see her.

I press the button to start the car and put the phone to my ear. I listen to her tell me she's leaving her appointment. *The one I should have been at.* Her sad, unsteady voice all but begs me to call her. I want to ram my head into the steering wheel for letting her do this on her own. Again.

I back out of the parking spot and proceed toward the security gate. On the line, she pauses and sniffs before she says she can't do it without me. Someone might as well rip my heart out and throw it under the car so I can run over it. I hate myself all over again.

The gate opens, and I drive through as she apologizes. Then, I slam on my brakes as I listen to horns and then what sounds like a blast of crumpling metal before dead silence.

I pull the phone away to check the screen and put it back to my ear. Nothing. I hit dial and call her as the gate tries to close but bounces back up.

It goes straight to voicemail, and my stomach churns with such force I fling the door open just in time for all the contents to splatter against the asphalt.

I spit and breathe, my stomach emptying again. When I'm certain I'm done, I close the door, letting my head fall to the headrest as tears crest my eyes. All I can see is her face. My hands feel the gentle bump, bump, bump as I slide them across her belly.

I hear her voice quiver as she tells me she needs me. Tears run down my face. I blink them away while my shaky hand scrolls to Cal's number. I put the car in drive as it rings, flooring it.

When there's no answer, I hit his number again, my heart hammering as I speed through stoplights to the private airport. There's no plane that can get me there fast enough.

I feared what I would face reliving my past, but I was a fucking idiot. I can't even let my mind acknowledge what I could face when I touch down. The terror is so intense my entire body vibrates. I need someone to answer the damn phone and tell me that she and our babies are all right.

Please, baby. Please don't leave me. Please.

Chapter 42

LEX

I blink as the last bits of light filter through the large window that expands the wall of my hospital room. I try to survey the room, but a throbbing ache prevents me from moving too quickly.

I reach for my forehead, where the searing pain burns. My fingers run over the bumps of the bandage where they stitched my skin back together.

"Hey." My mom pulls a chair over next to the bed. "How are you feeling?"

"Like I've been hit by a truck." My voice is low and scratchy.

"It's good you didn't lose your sense of humor." Her hand falls on top of mine, and her voice softens. "You scared me. You know that?"

I meet my mom's soft eyes. We have our differences, but she's still my mom, and I know now more than ever that she loves me.

"Where's Grandpa?"

"He'll be back soon. He went to get Bree to bring her to see you. I'll take her home and stay with her tonight."

I remember the doctor advising me to stay overnight to monitor the babies. I twist to see the narrow strip printing as it records.

"So far so good." My mom smiles, clearly following my gaze. "They must be two very content babes in there."

I spread my hands over them, so thankful it brings tears to my eyes.

"Shhh." My mom's hand runs over my hair, smoothing it back. "They're fine. You're fine."

"What if . . . " I can't even finish it.

Her hand wraps around mine. "No matter what we do and how hard we try, we can't protect or shield our kids from everything. You did your very best today, keeping them safe."

I swipe at a tear, remembering that I was talking to Mark's voicemail. I try to sit up. "I need my phone. I have to call Mark."

"We can't find it. Grandpa called him. He's on his way."

I rest back, frowning. "What? Grandpa called him."

"Yeah. He should be here soon."

Every part of me yearns for him to be here.

"I'm excited to meet him," my mom says, smiling. "I didn't know you two were so serious in high school. Also, didn't know he was *the* Mark Sandberg." Her eyebrows raise with amusement, but then her gaze falls to her finger, running over a wrinkle in the scratchy sheet. "You know, when your dad left . . . I just never want anything like that for you."

"Mark isn't my father, Mom."

"I didn't think that's who your father was either."

"It's not the same." I don't know how to explain this to her. I know she's never had what I found with Mark at sixteen. I brace my hands on both sides of my belly, feeling our babies move. *Peyton and Eli.*

I let out a breath of relief. "I trust Mark." Even as I say it, I do. I trust him with everything. "He's in this. He's not going anywhere. He'll be here for these babies and me . . . always."

There isn't any part of that declaration I believe to be untrue. I'm not sure how I know. I just do.

"I like Bob," I offer, wanting to move off Mark.

One side of her mouth tips up. "He kind of laid into me after you left dinner that night. I'm not used to having a man tell me I'm wrong."

"It means he cares."

A soft, subtle smile appears. "I think I'm beginning to see that."

There's a light knock on the door, and Slade and Grandpa stroll in with Bree. Her face is pale, and she sticks close to them.

"Hey. Come here." It takes a moment, but she comes to stand beside the bed. "I'm fine. Ok?" Her eyes flick to my belly and the bumps of the monitors. "They're fine, too. Want to feel?"

She bites her lip and slowly raises her hand. I take it and place it on the underside of my belly, where one of them punches me.

Her eyes grow wide, and a small smile escapes.

"See, they clearly don't understand we're supposed to be resting."

Grandpa plops down in a chair as Slade stands at the foot of my bed, assessing me.

"You look pretty good compared to your truck." Slade's large hands rest on his hips.

My truck. "Totaled?"

He nods.

Great. Now, I don't even have a vehicle. I sigh, but it sounds more like a pathetic whimper.

"You and the babies good?" he asks.

"Yeah. I have to stay overnight for monitoring, but we're good."

"The guys were about to camp out in the waiting area. I'm not sure if it was for you or the nurses."

I laugh, and it hurts my head. "These nurses are too nice to have to deal with their loud nonsense."

"That's for sure," he chuckles.

My mom stands, placing her hands on Bree's shoulders. "What do you think, Bree? Shall we grab a pizza, watch a movie, and paint our nails this evening?"

"Sure," she says hesitantly, and I hate that this happened. Consistency has not been her friend lately, and that's exactly what she needs.

I grab her hand. "I'll be there to pick you up from school tomorrow, ok?"

She nods. "Can I call you in the morning?"

I smile. "Uh . . . you better."

She leans over the bed to hug me, and I squeeze her tight. My mom will keep her busy this evening doing all kinds of girly things she'll love that I never wanted any part of.

"All right, girlfriend." My mom takes her hand. "Gentlemen, if you'll excuse us, we have beauty treatments and chick flicks waiting."

"Don't you be turning my house into some beauty salon," Grandpa says, but there's a twinkle in his eye.

Bree giggles, and my mom turns back in the doorway. "I wouldn't dream of it."

Once they're gone, I turn to Grandpa. "You talked to Mark?"

"I just wanted to check on you," Slade cuts in like he doesn't want to intrude on this conversation. "Get some rest. Let me know if you need anything."

I nod, holding my arms out so he knows he's not leaving without a hug. "Thanks for coming and for checking out my truck."

"Anytime, but don't ever do that again."

"I'm going to try really hard not to."

Slade ducks out the door, leaving me with the old man, and I have some questions.

My eyes find him, but he's fiddling with his phone, and the fart isn't doing anything but avoiding me.

"I heard you called Mark." His eyes remain set on his screen. Complete and total avoidance. "I didn't know you had his number."

"Huh." He scratches his gray scruff that's quickly turning into a beard.

"Would you like to tell me how you got that?"

"Not really."

Well, that was quick. "You can either tell me or he will."

He rests back in the odd chair that converts into a bed, crossing his arms over his chest. "He gave it to me."

He's like an old mule that won't budge no matter how hard you kick. "Did he? When?" I know this man won't lie to me.

"Pal, does it really matter?"

"Since you're putting up such a fuss, it seems to me it really does."

He leans forward, his arms on his knees. When he sits like this, he looks younger, and I see the man who showed me how to remove an oil filter for the first time.

His eyes stay trained on the floor. "He called me after his first win in the NFL. Started off shootin' the shit."

He rubs his jaw while an ache forms in my core that expands quickly. He called.

"I knew what he was calling for, and I told him you were good. He started calling me about every couple of months, which stretched to twice a year or so. He never asked about you, but I knew he wasn't calling to ask me about the shop and life in Ohio."

I rub my chest, needing the pain to stop. Grandpa must be able to tell and pauses, exhaling a long breath.

"When you got engaged, I called him. I told him he either needed to get his ass back here or quit calling. You both had lived miserable long enough."

"Why didn't you tell me?"

His head falls to the side. "Pal, you and I both know you were carrying enough pain around, and it wouldn't have done anything but add more. You didn't need that on top of it. One of you had to make the move."

Mark had been calling for years. I can't even process that. "Did he call you about the Bronco?"

Grandpa grins. "I knew you'd lose your shit over that old thing. You're gonna need it now."

I laugh, and one small tear escapes.

"Pal, my old ticker can't handle this. You and these babies . . . " His voice softens, and I see the glistening in his eyes.

"I love you, too, Grandpa . . . so much."

He sniffs and wipes his nose. "How about I go see what kind of cardboard marinated in salt the cafeteria offers while we wait for Prince Charming?"

"You shouldn't be eating that?"

"Shit, girl. After today, nothing's going to kill me. Certainly not ultra-processed and fried beyond recognition garbage."

"Fine. Hurry up. Your grandbabies are hungry."

Grandpa hustles out of the room while I try to wrap my head around Mark calling all those years. He called, and I never knew.

I close my eyes, just needing him to get here.

Chapter 43

MARK

My Uber drops me at the curb, and I jog to the entrance. The bright lights inside illuminate the darkness. I find the separate side entrance Cal specified in a text and charge through the sliding doors.

The security guard sets a sandwich down, doing a double take.

"My wife is in room seven."

His mouth turns upward into a toothy grin. "Congratulations." He punches a button, and the double doors pop open, but he leans over the desk.

"Hey, can you sign this?"

He scrambles for a marker, shoving a white napkin and then a ballpoint pen at me. I want to ignore him, but I step back, grab the pen, and scribble my name.

He grins. "Thanks, man. Can't wait to see where you're headed."

I slide through the doors, searching for room numbers. The small waiting room on my right is empty, except for a large, bearded, tattooed man who stands. His eyes are hard, his lips are tight, and I'm pretty sure his chest expands as he moves toward me. Slade.

Not right now, man.

"Nice to see you made it." His snark makes every hair on my entire body stand on edge. My temperature instantly hits a thousand degrees as he stops in front of me. His arms are crossed, and he reminds me of Shane.

"Where's her room?"

I don't have time to deal with whatever he's trying to bring. I need to see my wife and babies. I need to touch her, breathe her in, and know for myself they're all right. I'm so close, and this joker is in my way.

"You sticking around this time?" When I don't answer, his jaw ticks. "I'm not sure where you've been or what you've been doing, but they both need you. She's taken enough hits for you."

"Look, I need you to get the hell out of my way. I get that you're her friend, but right now, I don't give a shit about what you have to say. I've spent the last six hours with the most horrific thoughts flooding my mind, and if you don't move so I can see my wife, I will take you the fuck out."

If looks could kill, I'd be dead.

He stands unfazed "She wasted away to nothing the first time you left. Suffocating right before our eyes. That may not have been how you wanted it, but it didn't change the fact that I had to watch her try to figure out how to live. Now, she's pregnant and trying to sort this out with Bree, and she'll fight until she has nothing left. That can't happen."

I don't need to justify or explain anything to him, but his standing here tells me how much he cares about Lex and Bree, so I will. I pull in a breath and let it out, trying to reel in my fists and temper, which is about one second away from ballistic.

"I would've never left if I'd known. She's everything to me. Always has been and always will be. I'm not going anywhere unless they're going with me. All of them."

I mean every word. I don't exactly know how to make that happen or what it will mean for my football career, but after today, nothing else matters. I've known it all along, but the truth punched me right in the face about a hundred times this afternoon, and I won't ever forget it.

I release my fists, not realizing how tight I had them wound. "Now, I need you to move. Please." I try for calm, but it sounds more like a passive threat.

He stares at me, hard, like he's trying to see my soul and determine if I'm a lying piece of shit. "A few doors down the hall on the right."

I move past him, ready to finally see my wife.

His low voice stops me. "Call me if there's anything I can do . . . with any of it."

It's possible I see him relax, but I can't be sure. "Thank you," I say, stepping away and moving door to door, looking for the one that holds my entire world.

Room 7. I stop at the cracked door where the TV flickers in the dim light.

I push it open slightly and find her in bed, eyes trained on the TV, hand resting on her large belly. Her blonde hair is in waves around her, and the large strips on her forehead make my own burn.

My lungs kick into action for what feels like the first time in hours, and I must make a sound because Lex's attention snaps to me.

Her eyes roam over my face as mine blur, making her fuzzy.

I blink rapidly, needing to see her. "Baby, I'm so sorry I—"

"Don't." Her voice is achingly soft.

"Lex, please."

"Just . . . not right now."

"I need to—" I push, wanting to tell her everything.

"Does it change anything?" Her voice catches. "How you feel about me? About us?"

I shake my head. "Never."

Her lip quivers. "Then, please . . . just get in this bed with me."

I don't even hesitate, taking a few steps forward to slide in next to her and pull her to me. Her arms curl in, and I surround her.

"You're ok," I say, needing to convince my still racing mind. She nods against me. "The babies?" I whisper, tears filling my eyes as I hear her sniff.

She doesn't answer, and my stomach seizes into a hard knot. If there was anything in it, I'd be looking for the nearest trash can.

Her voice shakes. "They're ok. Both of them." My chest expands with relief as I hold her even tighter. "I had a few contractions, but they settled down pretty quickly. They're monitoring me tonight, and I can go home tomorrow." Her voice is so soft. "Mark, what if—"

"Shhh. They're ok. You're ok." I press my lips to her head, running my hand up and down her back. "I was so scared. Lex, what I heard . . . I've never been more terrified in my life."

Her hands fist my shirt, pulling me closer, but we are already tucked together as tight as we can be. I move my hand to her stomach, feeling the hard monitor.

"I think they're finally sleeping," she whispers. "Peyton and Eli apparently liked all the attention this afternoon."

Peyton and Eli. "Great. Two drama queens on our hands. They totally get that from you."

She tips her chin up to look at me. Her teary blue eyes are soft and sleepy. "I've missed you so much." She blinks quickly, forcing her emotions away.

I press my lips to hers gently. "I've been a complete selfish prick."

She tucks her head in my neck, and even with the stringent smell of antiseptic and plastic, she smells so freaking good.

"Mark." She pauses. "It's a really big mess."

"It's ok. We'll figure it out."

"She's scared. She's not eating or sleeping. She's sick."

I know she means Bree, and I hate myself even more for not being here. I know exactly what that feels like. I should've been here all along.

"Does she know about me?"

She shakes her head slightly. "I didn't want to tell her . . . "

While I was being a self-centered asshole. "How about we do it together?"

Her lips press against my jaw. "Ok." She moves her arm beneath mine to wrap it around my back. "How did it go in Seattle?"

"I don't want to talk about that. It doesn't matter."

"Please. I need to talk about something else. Take me out of all this for a bit." She sniffs again, pressing in further to my neck, and I feel the dampness of her tears.

I tell her about it—the general conversation, short practice, and Rob taking a video to shop around. As I talk, her body fully relaxes into mine.

Today was a wake-up call. I want to keep playing football at the highest level, but I want this more. So much more. There was a time when I'd have given it all up. It's still true. I'll give it all up if I have to.

She said things are a mess. Tomorrow, I'll find out exactly what that means and make sure Lex knows we're in this together. I'll meet my sister and let Cal know I'm moving in.

Then, at some point, I might have to face the woman who cared more about getting high than she ever did about me.

Chapter 44

LEX

I put a hand under my belly to try to help roll myself over in this tiny, crinkly, hard bed. I boost myself up and grab the railing, shoving my hips to the side to let gravity assist.

After lying on that side for so long, my arm and leg are numb. My eyes land on Mark, sleeping in the chair next to me. His muscular arms are crossed over his chest, almost like he's protecting himself, and I really want him to crawl back in bed with me. He spent half the night holding me until a nurse came in to reposition the monitors, and then we decided we needed more room.

Mark stretches his arms over his head. He rubs his eyes, and then those dark brown circles fall on me.

"Hey." His mouth curls into a small smirk. The one that makes my stomach hop, skip, and jump. "How you doin'?" He says it all confident and sexy-like, and I bite my lip, unable to hide the blush creeping up my busted-up face.

He pushes the footstool down and stands to stretch his shoulder better. I can tell by the look on his face it's sore. My mind starts spinning with questions. If he stays, I wonder what will happen to his PT schedule, training, meetings . . . everything that fills his days.

"Hey." He moves to the side of the bed, leaning down to kiss me. "What happened? What's going on in here?" He kisses me again before sitting on the edge of the bed and spreading his hand across my bulging stomach.

He smiles, feeling the kicks from one of our little monsters.

I run my fingers over my sore forehead. A dull headache still lingers, but it's much better than yesterday.

"It's back to real life today," I say, remembering how I savored every moment last night in this quiet room with him. I knew then that it'll be anything but calm or peaceful when we leave here.

He brushes a strand of hair away from my face and tucks it behind my ear. "Yeah. I have some thoughts about that."

I raise an eyebrow and then lower that sucker right back down when a burning sensation tears over my skin.

Mark runs his finger over the bandage. "Hey, be careful." He takes my hand and links his fingers with mine, bringing them to his chest. "We have a lot to talk about, but I want you to know how sorry I am for letting you come back here alone. I was mad . . . no, I was furious with myself for never being here. I should've been here."

"Mark, that's not what I wanted. I wanted you to be free. That's it. I would've done anything."

He presses my hand flat to his chest. "You did." He closes his eyes. "But now I'm here, and I'm not going anywhere. I don't care. If that means football is over, then—"

"No." I try to sit up, but it takes me too stinking long, so I settle for resting precariously on an elbow. "No. We need to get Bree permanently, but you have to keep playing. We didn't go through all of this for you to quit."

Mark helps me sit up, and I reach for him, pulling his head to mine. Somehow, his giving up football makes it feel like we are both losing everything we have suffered for.

"Please. I want to go with you. I want to have these babies and a room for them that's decorated and just right. I want to crawl in bed with you each night and wake up with you each morning in our own house. I want to fix up the Bronco and figure out what old thing I'll make new next."

I take a breath before my guts come spilling out my eyes, but it's difficult. "And I want to sit in the stands and watch you do what you were born to do. I want to watch you play and wait for you when the game is over and be there like I never was."

Saying it out loud feels so incredibly self-centered. "Please. Tell me we'll do that . . . somehow."

His finger comes under my chin, tipping it up to look at him. "I will do everything I possibly can. I promise." He shakes his head. "But I won't leave. Lex, I won't." One tear slips out, and he pushes it away. "Ok?"

I nod, not wanting to accept it.

His lips press to mine quick and soft. "Now, while we're waiting to sort through all the shit that's flung off the fan, I have some things to do."

I wrap my arms around his middle, holding him to me. "Yeah?"

"First, I need to know if you have a preference for the kind of truck we get. I'm calling a dealer today."

I lift my head. "Really. You'll just call them and put in an order."

He grins. "Baby, in case you're not aware, I've made millions. You're my wife without a prenup, so if you want to call and place the order to your specifications, I'm down with that. I'll give you my credit card."

I laugh. "You're ridiculous."

"No, what's ridiculous is that old beater lasted this long."

I push him away. "Beater? She was in mint condition."

He stands. "Not anymore. So, one of us is calling, you decide. Then, I'm calling my trainer to find a private gym and getting his ass out here. While that's happening, I was thinking about talking to a realtor."

I frown, but . . . *Ouch*. "A realtor?"

"Yeah. I told Cal I'm shacking up with you guys, but let's be real. We need our own space that's not over your grandpa's room."

"You're just going to buy a house?"

One shoulder shrugs as he scrolls his phone. "Maybe. Or maybe rent. I don't know. We'll see what's out there."

"And then what happens if you get picked up by a team?"

His fingers stop moving, and his eyes peek out from under his long, dark eyelashes. "I'm not thinking about that."

"Mark, Bree is just getting settled. We can't . . . " I pause, not wanting to crush his enthusiasm. "I think we should start with you meeting her. She'll need time to wrap her head around this. Her whole world has been ripped apart."

His stance softens, and he moves closer to me. "Ok. When are we doing the big introduction?"

"She's at school. I thought I'd pick her up, and then we can talk to her."

He nods slowly. "How do you think she'll take it?"

"She's going to be surprised. She's the sweetest, kindest, brightest girl." I see the uncharacteristic hesitancy and uneasiness overcome him. "She'll love you."

There's one thing we haven't talked about, and avoiding it won't get us anywhere, so I tiptoe into it. "Can we talk about your mom?"

He sits down on the end of the bed, setting his phone aside. "How much trouble is she in?"

"Her court date is coming up. She's being charged with possession, manufacturing and delivery, and child endangerment." I let that sit for a moment. "The DA is on the hunt based on prior convictions."

"And you have custody of Bree?" he asks, turning to face me.

"I've been appointed temporary guardianship for now."

He stiffens. "What does that mean? Does the social worker know about me? That we're married, and I'm her brother."

"I told her." This is where the mess only deepens, and the old wounds will be ripped wide open. "Before I left, I told Linda about us. She knows we're married. I'm pretty sure that has something to do with her using again."

I watch Mark's face carefully as he processes.

"She doesn't want us to have guardianship."

His head pops up. "What?" His eyes search my face. "She doesn't want *us* to have guardianship or me?"

He stands. "What the hell is she thinking? She sure didn't have any issue signing me away. All they had to do was give her a pen." He paces along the large window. "She's nothing but a selfish, self-centered piece of . . . "

He doesn't finish as he turns toward me.

I sit up a little. "She's afraid you'll take Bree from her."

"She lost her all on her own when she decided to deal and put Bree at risk with those . . . " His tone is fierce, and I understand his anger. "I'll get a lawyer. Maggie knows an excellent one. She had to go through something similar with her siblings. There's no way a judge would . . . " He rubs his forehead. "She can't have a say in this. Bree can't go into some stranger's home. Who knows what could happen to her."

My brain has traveled down the same horrible path, but I can't let it go very far.

"She seriously can't have a say in this. Does she?" His anger has turned to worry.

"The social worker told me to sit tight and wait for her court date. She likely won't have much of a say if she's sentenced. We've got a good case, given that you are blood-related, a law-abiding citizen, and I don't think it'll hurt that you're a public figure and loaded."

"How long is this going to take?"

I shrug. "You know the system works at a snail's pace." I shift to get more comfortable, needing to tell him this last piece. "Mark, I know you have terrible memories and feelings about your mom. But . . . those aren't what Bree knows."

I wait for him to look at me. "You need to be careful. Her heart is breaking, and doesn't understand what's happening. I've tried to explain it to her, but Linda is her mom." I don't want to say this last part, but I have to. "And until now, she's been a good mom to Bree."

Mark's chest expands as he inhales, and then he lets it out long and slow. "Ok. I'll watch what I say."

"Come here."

I make room again on the bed and extend my hand. It takes a second before he comes to sit with me. I wrap my arms around his middle and rest my chin on his shoulder.

"I know you want to dive in and make this all better. The new truck. The house. Bree. I love you so much for it. We need to go slow. One thing at a time."

His lips press against my sore head. "I suck at one thing at a time."

"Clearly." I move his hand to my stomach, where our twins are causing a ruckus.

"I knew exactly what I was doing there." His tone is low and stirs my belly.

I push his jaw toward me and find his lips. "You really did. Now, what do you think about heading out there and charming one of these nurses into letting me out of here?"

He pulls away just enough to hold my gaze. "You want me to go flirt with the nurses?"

"I didn't say flirt. Just ask really nicely and smile. I'm sure that's all it will take."

"Is this how it's going to be now? Me being your side piece and working it to get you what you want."

"Well, I'm married to the sexiest man alive."

His lips brush against mine. "Should I take my shirt off, too?"

I hit him with the pillow. "Absolutely not. That is reserved for me and me alone."

He stands. "Oh, possessive, are we?" He grins, but it doesn't quite meet his eyes.

He strolls toward the door.

"Mark." He turns back, holding the door open. "If you wink, I bet they'll also let you snag me a donut or something from their stash."

"Got it. Offer sexual favors to get you a cookie."

It's my turn to grin as I watch the tall, gorgeous miracle, who somehow happens to be my husband, leave to work his magic and get me out of here. And maybe some kind of sweet treat that I need to adhere to my anxiety and temporarily squander it.

Chapter 45

MARK

I drum my fingers against the small kitchen table. I pick up my phone and then put it down. *What in the hell am I supposed to do with myself?*

I've already called the dealership and purchased a brand-new, fully-loaded F-150. I've talked to my trainer, and he's working on finding a gym and making travel plans. Now, I can only sit here and wait for Lex and Cal to get back from picking Bree up from school.

I wanted to go, but Lex thought it was best we didn't ambush her and at least give her the ride home to know I'm here. Although, she's going to walk in here thinking I'm just Lex's husband.

Nerves and I don't mix well, and I've had enough. My skin feels too tight.

What if she hates me? Or she doesn't think I'm funny? Or can't stand my hyper-spontaneous tendencies? What if she doesn't want me to help take care of her? What if she's angry I wasn't here for her?

I pound my fist on the table, then pick up my phone and call Shane.

"Finally, get your head out of your ass?"

"I'm about to lose my damn mind, so if you could take it easy on the shit-giving for the moment, that would be nice."

"What's wrong with you?"

Given my state, I'm down for cutting to the chase. "I'm probably ten minutes away from meeting my sister."

Silence. The one who always has something to grumble says nothing.

"Yo, you're supposed to say something reassuring here. You deal with an army of kids every day. What am I supposed to say to her?"

He clears his throat. "So, you're in Ohio?"

"Shit, Shane. Catch up, please. Quickly. Lex went to get her from school, and they'll be here any minute."

"Just calm your high-strung ass down, or you're gonna need a sedative." He lets out a breath as if somehow its relaxing effect will be infused into me. "You're great with kids. They cling to you like you're the sugar high they've longed for."

"But this is different." I try to think why it's different. "She's my sister. I need her to like me. There's pressure. I've never cared if kids like me. They just do." My knee starts bouncing. "But this one. What if she thinks I'm high-maintenance?"

"You are."

"What if she hates football or thinks I'm uncool or a complete imbecile? What if she's really smart like Garrett, and I can't keep up? Or she doesn't take to me like Liv latched on to you right away? What if it takes years before she sees how cool and fun and smart I really am?"

I take a breath.

"Jeez, Mark."

"I know." I rest my head in my hand. "I need her to want me to take care of her." This is the truth of it, and what if she doesn't? What if she doesn't want me to be a part of her life?

"Is that what you want?" His blunt question strikes.

I don't have to think about it. "Yes. I don't know her, but . . . I want to give her what I didn't have. I understand more than ever why you did what you did for Maggie and the kids."

"How old is she?" I'm certain Shane is rubbing his temples, trying to sort out my meltdown.

"Nine. She'll be ten soon."

He sighs, likely thinking about his family. "Just be yourself. Not the hyped-up life is grand guy. Be you. She'll love you. And show her that she can count on you no matter what. She needs to trust you. One hundred percent. All the time."

I think about it. I can do that.

"What's happening there?" He pauses, and I know what he's asking.

"Her court date is coming up. There's a stack of charges. It doesn't look good for her."

Shane grunts.

"She doesn't want me to be Bree's guardian."

"She shouldn't get a say. What's the social worker say?"

"Wait for the court date. You know how this goes."

"What are you doing about it?"

Shane asks the question I've been wondering all damn day. There's a lot at stake here, and the main thing is Bree's life and safety.

"I need Maggie's lawyer's number. I could use some advice."

"Yeah. I'll get it to you." He's quiet for a second before he clears his throat. "You need to get her to change her mind."

I pull in air and let it out, hearing him say the exact thing I don't want to hear. I don't want to see my mother. I don't want to face or ever ask her for a single thing.

"This isn't about you anymore. You have a little girl who, from the moment she walks in that door and knows you're someone important to her, will rely on you to protect her and put her first. *That* is what you have to do. It's what you're doing for those babies."

"You know what that means."

"Sure do. And you can handle it. You are the best damn quarterback in the NFL. You've fought, overcome, and accomplished things little boys and grown men all over the world dream of doing." He pauses. "Get your ass in there and tell her where to sign. You're not asking."

He makes it sound so simple.

"Who knows? Maybe it'll help relieve some of the anger, too."

I'm not sure that's possible. "Don't let me forget to put a word in for you when Dr. Phil retires."

"Hang in there. You're gonna do just fine with this kid and those babies. When it all settles, bring her out. These kids will show her how to really make you lose your damn mind."

Bree, meeting my family sounds like too much to hope for at the moment.

"Thanks. I'll let you know how it goes."

I hang up just in time to hear a truck door. I stand, and then I sit back down.

Cool. Just be cool. I am cool. I'm the best quarterback in the NFL. What nine year old girl wouldn't think that's awesome? Shit. Probably all of them.

I swipe a hand over my face and pick up my phone, pretending I'm busy. The back door pushes open. Lex steps in, holding a purple backpack blasted with flowers.

Right behind her comes a girl. Her long, dark hair is in low pigtails that hang over her shoulders. She's skinny, her skin tan, but when her eyes hit mine, they're a reflection of my own.

She steps inside, only far enough for Lex to close the door. She stares at me, tucking her chin like she's nervous, too.

"Grandpa had to head into the shop for a bit." Lex breaks the ice, hanging Bree's backpack on a chair. "I told him the three of us would figure out something for dinner."

Lex makes wide eyes at me, probably to tell me to quit being a freak and staring, but she looks like me. It's the craziest damn thing.

"Sooo, Bree," Lex says slowly. "This weirdo is Mark."

Bree's shy mode cracks, and she giggles softly. The sound instantly has my nerves retreating to a more normal level.

"How was school?" I ask like a complete moron, and out of the corner of my eye, I see Lex trying to hold in a laugh. I want to hide behind her and make her talk this child into liking me.

"Ok."

"How about a snack? I think Mark needs sugar. He's looking a little catatonic." Lex pulls open the fridge door, an amused smirk riding across her lips as she peeks inside.

I pull out a chair for Bree, and she slides into it. "Any visits to the principal's office today?" Her eyes go wide, and I force a smile, trying for my best one.

Her lips curve upward as well when she sees I'm teasing. "No, but Brent did, and Mrs. Lawson had to help another teacher with a kid who shoved an eraser up his nose."

I laugh. "I would've shoved a jar of pepper at him and waited until that sucker came blasting out. It would've been like a booger rocket."

Bree falls forward in a fit of laughter. "Eww. That would be so gross. It'd have snot all over it."

"Well, make sure you don't cheat off him. He's clearly not the brightest crayon in the box."

"I don't cheat. I don't have to."

I rest back in the chair, crossing my arms over my chest. "No? You're smart, then? I used to cheat off that one all the time." I point at Lex. "She's crazy smart."

Bree glances at Lex as she rolls her eyes.

"You knew Alex when you were little."

I shake my head. "Not when I was little, but when we were in high school. I liked her a lot, and she wouldn't talk to me."

"She likes you now," she sings.

"She can't get enough of me now." I raise and lower my eyebrows.

Bree laughs as Lex pulls out a chair and places a plate with a sliced apple and some pretzels on the table. "I tolerate you," she says, taking a seat.

"Ha. Is that what you call it?" I wink at her, happy to be crawling back into my own skin.

Bree grabs a pretzel and breaks a piece off before popping it in her mouth.

Lex pushes one of Bree's pigtails over her shoulder, breaking the silence. "Mark and I need to talk to you about something."

Bree sits taller in her seat. "Is it about my mom?"

"Kind of," Lex says softly. I knew it before, but I see it fully now. She's going to be the most amazing mom. My heart squeezes in my chest.

I rest my elbows on the table. "You want to know something totally crazy." I cut in, finding my voice. She nods. "You and I are related." Her small brow wrinkles. "We're . . . brother and sister. Your mom had me many years before she had you."

Her eyes flick between Lex and me. "That makes no sense to me. You're my brother? But . . . you're old."

I pretend to stab myself in the center of my chest. "Ugh, I'm not that old."

"I don't know. You're starting to get a few wrinkles and a couple of gray hairs." Lex jabs, trying to keep things light.

Bree doesn't play along but stares at me.

I take it back down. "I know this is strange, and I'm sure you have lots of questions, but I want you to know I'm stoked to have a sister."

"How come I didn't know about you before?" She's still frowning.

I scratch my jaw. "Well, that's a really long story, but the short of it is, I couldn't live with our mom when I was young. She . . . needed to get help just like she does now and couldn't take care of me." I try to be as gentle as possible. "By the time she got better, I'd already moved away."

Her eyes move to the table while she thinks about what I said.

I cut into her thoughts, wanting to make sure she knows that isn't going to happen to her. "I was thinking I'd stay here with you guys for a while, and we can get to know each other."

She bites the corner of her lip. "Alex said you have to travel a lot for work."

"I do, but not right now." I hesitate and then continue. "I'm looking for a new team."

"She said you play football."

"I do." I lean closer to her. "I'm pretty good, too." I hope for a smile, but she's still processing.

"You mean, you're like one of those players on TV?" One side of her face scrunches up, and it makes me smile.

"I am."

Her face brightens. "Mom watched football when we had cable. She really likes the Liberties." I nod because there's nothing else I can do. I'm not letting that little tidbit of information touch me. "What happens when you start with a new team?" She looks at Lex instead of me. "Will you leave then?"

Lex puts her arm around her. "We'll have to figure things out as we go. We're hoping you can help us."

"Really?"

"Yeah. Plus, these babies aren't going to stay in here much longer. So the three of us have lots of work to do."

I watch Bree lean into her and see the bond that they have. A small wave of anger flares for not being here, but I'm really glad I get to be now.

"Good thing your shower is soon. You need lots of stuff," Bree says, taking an apple slice.

I groan. "Don't get her started on baby stuff, or she'll go into meltdown mode."

Bree smiles.

Lex leans back in her chair, her eyes meeting mine. Somehow, it's going to work out. It has to. This right here . . . is my family. All four of them.

"Can you come watch me at dance tonight?" Bree's bright eyes peer up at me.

"Uh . . . I'm not sure that's a good idea," Lex cuts in, and Bree frowns. "See, the thing about your brother, he's kind of a big deal to a lot of people, and if we're not careful, it causes a scene. Plus, his head expands three times its normal size."

I raise and lower one shoulder. "Hey. I'm a likable guy and good at what I do. People love me."

Lex points at me as Bree grins. "See, big head, but when he goes places, people tend to surround him, but he'll drive us. Ok?"

"Wait." Bree holds out her hand, revealing her chipped fingernail polish. "You're like . . . famous."

I smirk. "Bree, I'm super famous."

She grins, and it reaches her eyes. "This is incredible. I have a brother, and you're famous." Her hands cover her mouth. "I can't wait to tell my friends."

I lean forward. "Bree. You and I are going to get along just fine."

She giggles as Lex groans, and that only makes her laugh more.

"All right, you two," Lex says, but there's love in her eyes. "What are we having for dinner? We have to eat early so we can get you to dance."

I rest back while they discuss dinner. I know what I have to do and who I need to see to make it happen.

Chapter 46

MARK

The fluorescent lights cast a horrendous haze, and the buzz matches my vibrating insides. I could vomit. It might make me feel better, but it would show weakness, and there's no room for that today.

I hear the shuffling of feet and the clank of metal. My heart pounds so hard it pulses in my ears. I rest my hands on my thighs underneath the table, wiping the sweat on my jeans.

A shadow forms in the doorway, and I'm not sure what I was expecting, but it's not the woman slinking into the small, abrasive room.

The officer pulls out the metal chair, and my mom slides in, not raising her eyes from the floor. I stare at her. Her thick, gray roots are a distinct contrast to the rest of her dark brown hair. Her eyes are sunken in, and her skin a strange tint of gray.

I try to reconcile this woman to the one from my horrific childhood—the one who drank or drugged herself into becoming nonexistent.

Somehow, in the place where I thought I'd feel rage, I find pity or empathy, maybe. For the first time, I wonder what demons possess her that this has been her chosen or destined path. Who would choose this?

I want to believe it wasn't a choice. Maybe it'll make this easier to bear.

My eyes wander over the woman who birthed me but provided nothing more. Strangely, I'm overcome with gratitude for the life I've found and that I didn't end up in the pit of hell chained to substances and a prisoner to my own self-destructive habits.

"It's been a long time." I will my voice to hold strong and steady. She doesn't move or even acknowledge I spoke. I fold my hands together on top of the table, unwilling to play the silent game. "I never expected to see you again. I sure as hell never expected to have a sister." Nothing. "Where's her father?"

I want to know if there's anyone I need to worry about. I know we don't share one since mine ended up dead in a ditch after a heroin overdose not long after I was taken away.

Still nothing. My temper revs. "You can either tell me, or I can hire someone to find out. Either way, I'm going to make sure she's safe."

Her eyes tip up to mine, harsh and cold, but her chin stays tucked. "He's . . . not involved."

I want to ask what exactly that means, but if he's not a concern, then I really don't care. "I heard you don't want me to be her guardian."

"You'll take her from me. I can't . . . handle that. She's not yours."

"You think having her sent to some stranger's home where who knows what can and will happen to her is better? Because let me tell you, I've done that, and that shit you hear is real. If you're dreaming of a life that destroys her, keep this up."

Her head finally comes up. "She's all I have."

I scratch my jaw. "Then you put her first. If you love her, and I've heard you do, you put her first."

"I've always put her first. That's why I left her with Alex when I tried to find you."

"Is that what you were doing when you decided to get back into the business? Is that what you were thinking when you were cutting, lining, injecting, and selling yourself on the other side of the wall from her? How about when you were bringing every kind of danger into your apartment? Did you even think about what could happen to Bree?" Nothing. "What if they'd come looking for you when they didn't get paid on time or were desperate to score their next hit? What if they took Bree?"

I sit back in my chair, my skin prickling with sweat. "Does any of that sound like putting her first?"

"I know I wasn't any kind of mother to you, but I've been a good one to Bree."

"That may be so, but right now is when it matters. You and I both know you aren't getting out of here any time soon." I lean forward, needing her to hear me loud and clear. "Don't punish her because you can't handle the fact that you never once did anything to protect me. You can punish yourself all you want, but don't you dare punish that little girl."

She doesn't move, but a single tear drips down her rough, sunken-in cheek.

I take a breath and let it out. "Lex and I are a family. We could have been a family years ago. You won't take that from me again. Let Bree be a part of that. I'll fight if I have to, and I can guarantee you won't win."

A new confidence blazes within me. I wait until she meets my eyes. "You put her first before. Do it again."

I'll give her that. She let Bree go before when she knew she couldn't be who she needed to be.

I take a second to reel myself in and ask what I've wondered since the night Cal called Lex. "Why are you here? Why now?"

She stares at the wall behind me. A damp streak is still evident on her cheek. Just when I'm about ready to give up, her soft voice surprises me.

"Seeing you, facing you, has been my single greatest fear. And also my biggest dream come true." She sniffs as another tear escapes. "I'm weak. Fear won out." She finally meets my eyes. "I know what I am. What I did to you and what I didn't do for you."

I want to tell her she has no idea because she was stoned out of her mind, but I keep my mouth shut.

"There is no punishment that will ever be greater than the regret and guilt I carry for . . . " Her voice breaks. "Not being any kind of mother to you. I've lived with that every day and watched you become everything you never should have been because of me." She leans forward, bringing her cuffed hands to her face. "I . . . I'm sorry. I'm so sorry."

I want it to mean something, but it doesn't right now. There's a flicker of hope in me that someday it will.

"I have an amazing family," I say softly. "Filled with so much love, it's unbearable sometimes. Let me give her that."

"I can't let you take her away from me." It's a knife to the gut. "She's all I have."

"Let me give her what you can't."

She wipes her face with her hands. "She'll forget about me."

I choose my words carefully, knowing their meaning will strike, but I need them to. "Believe me, she couldn't forget about you even if she tried." She blinks her tears away to lock eyes with me. "Let her hold on to the good memories."

I give it a second, and then I stand. I take one last look at my mother, unable to think about how things might have been different. I move to the door, but I hear her say my name and stop as it rips something wide open in my chest.

"Do you think there's a chance . . . you could ever forgive me?"

There's a burn in my throat that's so severe I have to breathe through it.

I stare at the woman who dragged me into this world, knowing it was most definitely not by choice. I tell her the only truth I know. "My entire life has been nothing but hope and chances. A chance to escape my circumstances and the hell I lived in. A chance with coaches and teams. A chance with the woman of my dreams, and I was damn lucky to get more than one with her." I meet my mother's dark, bloodshot eyes. "I believe in chances, but there will never be one if you don't help yourself."

I take a step back, needing distance. "But don't do it for me. Do it for Bree. She deserves to have what neither of us ever did."

Her hand goes over her mouth as tears spill over the black circles surrounding her sunken eyes. "Sign those papers . . . Mom."

Chapter 47

LEX

I sit tipped back in Grandpa's squeaky, worn-through office chair, which I'm not sure I'll ever be able to get out of. A mass of pink and blue balloons surrounds me. So many they'd likely elevate a tank if tied together.

I slide my finger underneath another piece of tape to open one of the few remaining gifts. Krissy steps forward to snap another picture while all the guys sip beer from their lawn chairs and keep their ears tuned into the baseball game blaring on the old radio.

I peek over at Mark and Bree, who are in deep debate about which Taylor Swift song is the best. Mark, taking every opportunity to show her his deplorable vocal skills. They're two peas in a pod, and over these past few weeks, I've only seen further proof of what an amazing father he'll be.

He catches me staring and winks before that sexy smirk takes over his mouth like he just got away with something. But today, that sly smile doesn't quite hold its normal level of self-assured cockiness.

After visiting Linda, he's been in his head. His normal, playful self has been absent. Everything in me wants to get him out of here and haul him away from the pain that dwells in this place for him. I want my Mark back. The one who beams and lives high on life.

"What the ff . . . hell is that?" Carson says, his beer can halfway to his lips.

I hold up the box containing the wearable breast pump I picked out.

I watch Trig's eyes go wide. "Do those attach—"

"They'll fit right inside her bra so she can pump while she works," Krissy explains casually, and all the guys groan.

"You mean they're like two little portable milking machines," Wind asks, one side of his face scrunched. "Does that shit hurt?"

"I don't know. We should hook you up and find out." Slade sits slumped down in a chair, a beer bottle hanging between two fingers.

"You aren't keeping that in the fridge here," Wind throws out an arm, declaring it's prohibited. "What if it gets mixed up with—"

"Stop." Slade cuts him off with a growl, and I can only laugh.

"Damn, boys," Grandpa gripes from a chair in the back where he's been relaxing and surveying. "It's no wonder your sorry asses don't have a lady."

Wind rests his head in his hand. "If you have any other grotesque gifts, can you just hold off and save those for home? I think I've heard enough about nipple cream, feminine products, and placentas to last me a lifetime."

"Seriously, jackass. Did you need to use that word again?" Carson shivers.

Krissy lays her hand on Trig's shoulder, and I promise I hear Slade snarl. "Did you know some women choose to save the placenta? They store it—"

"Oh, for ffff . . . shit's sake," Wind holds out his hand to stop Krissy. "What the hell is wrong with you?"

Through their pansy complaints, I see Mark pull his phone from his pocket and step down the hallway that leads back to Grandpa's office.

"Ok," my mom says, taking the box from me. "Who's ready for some cake?" Bree jumps up and joins her as I wonder where Mark went. "You want to help me cut it?" my mom asks her.

She nods, and Bob steps up to help move the cake to the workbench. I try to wiggle forward in my seat, and Carson gets up to offer me a hand. He yanks me to my Fred Flintstone feet, but his scowl is pointed at Trig and Krissy, who are busy flirting. *Interesting.*

I stand, letting my midsection adjust to gravity and space, which is followed by an immediate urge to pee. I waddle to the bathroom and then peek into Grandpa's office to find Mark leaning against the edge of the desk, staring at his phone.

I move to stand between his legs, sliding my arms around his neck as he sets his phone aside.

"Everything ok?"

His hands glide over my large stomach and clasp behind my lower back.

"Rob wants to ring my neck?"

"Why is that?"

He presses his lips to my forehead and leaves them there. "Denver wants to meet?"

I pull away. "Really? They weren't on your list."

"Rob said they're making some changes and have some extra money in their budget."

"They have a pretty solid team. Don't they?" I know they definitely made it to the playoffs last season.

His eyes drop to my belly, and he doesn't answer right away. "Yeah."

"When?"

"Next week."

I move my hands to his shoulders. Linda's court date is set for next week, and even though we hadn't decided whether we were going, I suspect his lack of enthusiasm has to do with that.

"You're going," I say with conviction, and his eyes pop up to mine. "You're not staying to hear the gavel drop on what we both know will be a sentence. You being here won't make her sign the papers relinquishing her rights."

"Lex . . . " His tone is soft, but there's a level of determination to it. "I'm not leaving."

"It's just a meeting. Go see what they have to say."

His arms tug me closer, my stomach pressing into him. "Come with me, then."

I let my head fall to the side. "I can't travel. These babies need to stay in here as long as possible." I grab the sides of his handsome face. "Call Rob back and tell him you're in."

"You're being really bossy." His lips curve upward slightly.

I release his face, and he pushes my hair over my shoulders. "Sometimes, I should get to be the bossy one."

He leans in, his lips brushing against mine. "I think maybe you should be the bossy one all the time. It works for you."

His mouth moves over mine, soft and slow, before traveling to my jaw and downward. If he's trying to make me forget, it's working.

"Oh, sorry," Bob says, peeking his head through the doorway, ready to escape before stopping. "Just checking to see if you two want cake. I'll set some aside and leave you to it. Your time for that will be *pret-ty* limited very soon." He grins and pulls the door closed.

I laugh, my head falling to Mark's shoulder.

"I like him," Mark says, finding my neck again. "The man clearly understands priorities."

I relish the feel of his lips coasting down my neck to my collarbone for just a second before I pull away.

"Call Rob." I kiss his lips and step away, opening the door, not letting him delay any longer or convince me to change my mind. Any more of what we were doing, he would.

"You're a tease, Lex. You'll pay for that later."

I turn to grin at him. "I hope so."

I hear his laugh as I waddle myself back out to the party so that he can make the call his mind, body, and spirit need him to make.

Chapter 48

MARK

Shane wasn't joking when he said I should give myself a night or two to acclimate to the altitude. Given that I wasn't leaving Lex for any longer than I had to, I flew in late last night so I could get here early and be home by tonight.

The sun is high in the bright blue sky, and the crisp mountain air is enticing, but it's the football in my hand that has my body humming.

I toss another ball to a trainer, getting my shoulder warmed up.

Rob and Shane stand on the sidelines, yacking it up. One's low coaching voice is direct and firm. The other is like a kid let loose with a hundred dollars in a candy store of opportunities.

A couple of receivers finish warming up and approach. "You gonna get the ball to us?" One of them grins at me, knowing I'll drop the ball right into his hands.

"Get your young ass down the field," I say as he laughs, taking off in a route.

I drop back and let the ball fly. *Bam!* There it is. The other receiver takes off. The ball spirals long and far, hitting my target, and he pulls into his chest before jogging back.

We work for the next thirty minutes, and in that time, I'm ready to be back in it. The rhythmic schedule, rigorous training, and the comfort of consistency.

I'm ready to leave the nightmares of my childhood behind and start new again. But there's a deep-seated fear I'm trying really hard to ignore that wherever that might be, I'll be doing it alone.

Visiting with my mom did nothing but remind me of everything I endured and what I never had. I'm reliving every slap, punch, burn, and the visions of my mom half-naked, strung out on her momentary drug of choice.

My skin turns cold and pricks with sweat as my stomach surges into my esophagus. I fall back, launching one last ball, as my chest tightens with the idea of never escaping all that's resurfaced. All the horrors I thought I'd buried deep enough they'd never touch me again.

I take some deep breaths and stretch my shoulder, then join the coaches on the sidelines.

We discuss my training schedule, which was only slightly delayed while I transitioned to Ohio. The coaches and GM relay at a high level their goals for the team next season, and then we shake hands while they take some time to evaluate.

"They've got a hell of a setup," Rob says, and I think he might be skipping his way to the parking lot. "You might have just scored yourself a deal here, kid." He slaps me on the back.

"I told you. I'm not signing any deals until I know Lex and Bree are coming with me."

Rob's forward motion halts, and Shane's large hands move to his hips.

"They won't wait around for you to button up your personal life," Rob states, but he's treading lightly. "You heard what they said. They have every intention of making it to the end this season. You're key in getting them there, but they'll want to get started yesterday."

I run a hand through my hair. My previous high tanking back to reality.

"Rob, I have two babies that could be born any day. My sister is now my responsibility, no matter what any papers say. She can't leave the state without Lex and I obtaining permanent guardianship."

Rob rubs his jaw, and Shane looms with his usual stoic stance. He can't say a word when he would do the same damn thing every day of the week if it were Maggie and the kids.

"What will it take to get things moving?"

I widen my stance, crossing my arms over my chest. "Time. I've talked to a lawyer. It will never move fast enough."

He nods, looking defeated. "Well, I'll be in touch, but I'm going to be honest. This feels like I'm spending a hell of a lot of time and energy chasing a deal for nothing."

I bristle, and Shane must see it because he finally breaks his silence.

"Mark, you need to get back and talk with the social worker to see what can be done."

I already know the answer to that, and so does he, but rehashing it won't help things right now.

"Boys, I've got a plane to catch, but Mark . . . " He pauses for a second, looking at me like he's unsure what to say. "I'll let you know if I hear something."

I nod as he climbs in his rental, and I'm left with Shane, who I know has something to say now that we're alone.

I toss my duffle in the back of his truck next to my suitcase, waiting for his words of wisdom.

"Come on. Let me hear it. Whatever you've been holding back."

He starts the truck, his head turning toward me, and I ignore his gaze. "You're too damn good to quit."

He lets it hang there, and I want to punch something.

"But I'd do the same thing, and I'd never look back." He puts the truck in drive. "I'm proud of you. I know you're facing a shit ton of pain and suffering that might feel like a beating all over again." He turns out of the parking lot. "I'm damn proud to call you my brother."

I stare out the window, willing the growing itch in my throat to settle the hell down.

Silence lingers as he navigates us toward the airport, but eventually, he cuts in. "I wouldn't mind having you as a neighbor. Then we just need to get Sean here so we can survive all these kids." I allow only a moment to think about what that would be like, but then tear it down. "Shit, man. You're going to have two."

A smile tugs at my lips, knowing no matter what happens, I'm the luckiest man there ever was.

Chapter 49

LEX

Mark pushes out the door, holding it for me. His hand slips into mine. It's hot and a bit sweaty. I'm certain it's from him clenching his fist for the last thirty minutes.

It's been a week, but Linda's court appearance was quick and to the point when her appointed lawyer had difficulty contesting the charges. Her years of sobriety couldn't erase her former convictions, and she was sentenced to ten years with a possibility of parole.

We walk to the truck in silence, and he opens my door, helping me in. I sit for a second, letting the Braxton Hicks contraction do its thing. They're coming more frequently anytime I have to do any amount of walking.

I'd take another contraction over the big, fat reminder that our request for permanent guardianship will be a long, drawn-out process. Mark's evaluation was approved, and we are now joint guardians, but it wasn't the celebratory news we hoped for.

"These things don't happen overnight," were the social worker's exact words. As Mark circles the truck and climbs in, I know he's trying to reel himself back from the past while watching his career come to an end.

He closes his door and pushes the start button.

"Hey." I stop his hand from putting the truck in reverse. "We'll figure something out. Don't—"

"Have these people lost their damn minds?!" His voice is in that range that tells me to just let him go. "How can she retain rights? She had dealers squatting in the room next to Bree. She was cutting and stashing . . . " He grips the steering, his knuckles turning white. "How the hell is this even in question?! The whole system needs some C-4 and a match taken to it. It's complete shit! Her rights should've been obliterated when she showed up baked out of her mind and handed Bree over to you."

His head tips back toward the ceiling, eyes closed, nostrils flaring. It's all finally boiling over. I knew it would, and I've been waiting.

"She doesn't have to sign over her rights. I'll fight. I don't care how long it takes. I won't ever let Bree go back to that. Lex, she could have been . . . "

He groans in frustration, his jaw clenched tight, but the ache in his tone hits me square in the chest. It's one thing to think about all that could have happened, but it's another to have lived that life, and he did.

I inhale and let it out slowly, knowing I'm going to have the battle of my life on my hands. Mark needs football, just like Bree needs safety, security, and stability. I won't let him walk away, not after everything, and not when he needs it.

I grab his hand and put it on top of my belly where a foot is wedged, threatening to bust my abdomen wide open.

"Please don't give up," I whisper. "I've never wanted you to have to stay here and . . . live in this." I can't bear what it does to his insides.

"To hell with football. I'm done. I'm not going anywhere."

I can feel the fear rolling off him, backing him into a corner. Every past horror on one side, current circumstances on the other. The future and everything it could be, sitting just beyond—within view but still out of reach.

"You're not doing it without me this time. I'm right here. Bree, the babies, and I will be here. I'll fly to games . . . "

"It's not enough. I've seen guys try that. It'll never be enough for me."

I won't win this battle in the next five minutes, but I won't quit fighting for him.

"I'm not giving up." I bring his hand to my cheek. "I might not be very good at reading, but it's taught me how to fight."

He lets out a defeated huff. "Lex . . . I love you."

"I know. I think somehow, I've always known." His eyes draw up to mine, studying me. "It's why I married you within an hour of seeing you again."

I smile. His beautiful dark eyes show me a hint of sadness. I love him so much, so much so that I'm not willing to let this be the end of what has allowed him to survive.

"Pal, are you certain you should be doing this?" Grandpa leans over and whispers in my ear. It's not often this man is uneasy, but I hear it in his voice.

I lower myself into the metal chair and let everything settle. "He's not quitting. This is all I've got to make sure that doesn't happen."

"He'll lose his shit if he knows you came here. Then he'll kick my old, wrinkled ass for bringing you." Grandpa stands to the side of me, shoving his hands in his pockets while he surveys the surrounding tables.

There's no sense in arguing because both are true. Mark might not actually kick Grandpa's ass, but there will definitely be a long, drawn-out outburst we'll have to sit through.

There's a loud buzz, and Linda is led in, her hands cuffed, and her white jumpsuit making her olive-toned skin look pale. The officer leads her to the chair across from me, and she uses her foot to slide it out.

This isn't the woman I used to have dinner with. Her eyes are set on the table between us, but there's a hardness to them that I've only ever experienced once. The cold, absent stare makes me even more determined to get through to her.

Grandpa steps away, giving us a little privacy, but he doesn't move far.

"How are you?" I ask the question I'm pretty sure I know the answer to.

"How's Bree?" Her voice is soft as her eyes drag up to mine. Shame replacing the fierce avoidance.

"She's . . . okay. She's doing well in school and dance. Only a few more weeks, and then she'll be out for the summer."

"I remember." She adjusts her hands in her lap, and I slide a picture across the table Bree drew that she'd be ok with me bringing.

Linda stares at it as moisture collects in her eyes. "Why are you here?"

I shift in the metal chair, trying to get comfortable when nothing is anymore. I get right to the point. There's no sugarcoating it. "You're likely in here for the next ten years. Bree will be an adult by then. You've given her years of happy memories to carry with her." I pause, letting that sink in. "You've never given Mark a single one. You can change that."

Her eyes morph back into that hardened, shutdown state. But I don't care. Mark came back for me despite leaving and letting him believe I never cared. He put his heart on the line. He gave me a chance, even though losing would have likely broken his heart worse than the first time.

"You need to turn over your rights. Any day, Mark is going to get a call from a team wanting to sign him. He's not going unless Bree and I go with him. This is your chance to put your son first. He needs to get out of here and away from everything that haunts him. Football saved him."

I match her cold, guarded stare. "This is your chance to put him first. For once, do what you've *never* done for him."

A tear runs down her sunken cheek. "And I'm just supposed to let you take off with Bree. She's not yours."

"Like it or not, she's with us and will have a life full of love." I pause. "*You* are her mom. She'll never forget that."

An officer strolls over. "Times about up."

Grandpa's hand rests on the back of my chair. "He's never asked you for a single thing, and he never will. I'm asking you. He's suffered enough."

Her hands raise together to swipe at a rogue tear, and then she stands. She grips Bree's drawing and follows the officer without another word.

I slump in defeat.

"Come on, Pal. Your time is up, too." He holds out his hand to help me up. "I went against all sound judgment today and brought you here. Now, you owe me a burger and milkshake without a side of lecture." I roll my eyes at him as I slowly waddle myself out. "And if I'm in deep shit with Mark over this, you'll be buying my milkshakes and burgers daily."

I swing my arm through his, holding on tight. "You're the best Grandpa."

"Are you telling me that because you know I'm about to get my ass chewed by your hyper-vigilant husband?"

"No. I'm telling you because it's the truth." I squeeze his arm. "But you might have to deal with Mark's overprotective, slightly obnoxious reprimand."

"Awe, shit. I can't handle that. I'll have to move into the shop.'

I laugh as he pushes the door open, and we make our way to his truck. "Do you think it made any difference?"

Grandpa's eyes drift around the parking lot, and he shakes his head. "I don't know, Pal, but you made one hell of a case. No mother could walk away and not think about it. Linda's got a good heart. Shame, regret, no self-worth . . . They're like gasoline in a Styrofoam cup. They'll rot you from the inside out. It's why she's here." He offers his hand to help me in. "But I have no doubt she'll be doing a lot of thinking about *both* of her kids."

Chapter 50

MARK

I pull into the shop parking lot next to Cal's dually and down the rest of my Gatorade. My phone buzzes in the cup holder. Rob. *Shit.*

I close my eyes, debating whether I want to know what he has to say. My fingers itch to grab it and find out if there's a deal waiting on the other end, but turning down an offer will be like walking into a pool without knowing how to swim. A slow and painful death to a dream I wasn't done living.

My hyperactive tendencies override my senses, and my hand reaches for my phone, hitting the speaker button.

"Damn, Mark. I don't get paid enough for this." He lets out a breath. "The one time I need you to answer your phone, and it takes a million years."

"It was five rings."

"You sitting down?"

"I'm not sure I'm ready for whatever has you all worked up."

He quiets. "Believe me. You want to hear this."

I'm pretty sure that's not true.

"Denver laid out a deal, and when I say deal, I mean it makes what the Liberties were offering look like the clearance section at Walmart. They want you, and they're bringing it."

I knew I didn't want to hear this. My heart pumps a little faster as if it has something to hope for.

"Mark, I heard you loud and clear, but you'd be a complete fool not to seriously consider this. I want to think we can figure out something that will work for your family."

My family. Dammit. I run a hand through my damp hair. "Rob—"

"Mark, hear me out."

My jaw clenches while Rob runs through the deal of a lifetime, and he's not wrong about it making the offer from the Liberties look like chump change.

I inhale long and slow, staring in my rearview at the shop behind me. Lex is inside, likely doing something she shouldn't be. How could I walk away again?

"Rob, my babies are coming. I won't miss that. Bree needs me, and she has to remain here. I can't—"

"Mark, just sleep on it." His voice is soft now, almost like he's begging.

I fist my hands, wanting to punch myself for answering this call. My insides wage war with wanting to sign on the dotted line and be with the ones I need.

Rob has fought for Shane, Sean, and me more than most would have. I have to at least give him this and suffer the horrendous torture of letting the offer dangle before me like water to a dehydrated, starving man.

"Ok," I say, my hands gripping the steering wheel so tight it'll leave indentations on my palms.

"They'd send a plane to get all the paperwork out of the way." He pauses, and I know whatever he says next will make me want to ram my head into the brick wall behind me. "Camp starts next week."

"Shit, Rob. What the hell?!"

"I know," he says, like it will somehow make being ripped down the middle better. "They've got plans, and they're being aggressive. Just . . . think about it and call me in the morning."

I rest my head on the seat. *Just think about it. Yeah, freaking right.*

"Mark, you're one of the best players I've ever seen. The way you read the field is unmatched. I want you to take this deal. You're nowhere near done yet, but . . . if this is the end, you can walk away with your head held high, and I'll respect the hell out of you for putting your family first."

I close my eyes as I end the call. My lungs squeeze tight, and I fumble for the button to crack the window to get some air.

I'm not ready for this to be the end.

The truth singes the edges of reality, burning a hole straight through me. I force some deep breaths.

There's a tap on the window, and I jump, smacking my head on the ceiling. Cal stands on the other side, laughing so hard I think he might keel over. His face is red, and his deep chuckle carries throughout the entire parking lot.

"You all right, son?" The old man grins.

"No, not now that you made me shit myself."

He laughs some more. "I thought maybe you were sleeping. You need to get in there and get my granddaughter off the floor. I'm pretty sure she's about to flip me off."

I collect myself, momentarily brought back to the present and out of my complete mental freak out. "And you think I'll get a better response?" I grab my phone and push the door open.

"Use your powers of persuasion, boy," he demands, climbing in his truck.

I step into the shop, and Lex is leaning over, inspecting something under a hood. She straightens and pauses, holding her belly. She's having one of those false contractions, but it's enough to cause her brow to furrow.

When she notices me, her mouth creeps upward into a full smile, and the chaos pulsing through me calms.

I raise my hand, using my pointer finger to call her to me. One light eyebrow hitches up slightly before she surrenders. Her arms slide around my middle, and her head rests against my chest.

"What are you doing?" I press my lips to the top of her head.

"Helping." She draws out the word.

"How about you help me?"

She peeks up at me, resting her chin on my chest. "Help you with what?"

I'm so tempted to kiss her lips, but I refrain. For now. "I have ideas."

Her cheeks redden, and I want to kiss her even more. "That's not happening."

"Oh, I have other ideas."

Her eyes flick between mine as her hands slide up my back, holding me tighter. "What's wrong?" Her mouth softens into concern, and I have no idea what she's seeing that I'm really good at hiding.

"Nothing." I lie, not even wanting to discuss this. I know what she'll say, and I can't hear it.

She releases me, grabs my hand, and leads me to the back, where it's quieter. She pulls me into Cal's office and pushes me into the desk until I sit.

"What's going on?" Her brow scrunches.

"Why do you think there's something wrong?"

Her head falls to the side. "Mark Lucas Sandburg. Look at me right here." She points to her pale blue eyes. "Tell me there's nothing wrong."

Shit. I should've known she'd know. "Rob called." She doesn't move like she's been expecting this. "Denver made an offer."

"And?"

I rub my forehead, the heat of frustration building all over again. I want to peel my skin off. Maybe that will help.

"Lex, it doesn't matter. I'm not taking it."

"Did you tell him that?"

Her and her damn questions. "He told me to call him in the morning."

She stares at me, searching my face, and I look away, not wanting her to see the truth.

"It's an amazing deal, isn't it?" Like a defiant little boy, I don't answer. "You're taking it."

My eyes snap back to hers as she calls me on my shit. "Lex . . . " I stand.

She holds up her hand. "Tell me you don't want it."

"Lex, I'm not—"

She holds up her hand again, her eyes closing this time. "Tell me." Then, one finger pops into the air as her eyes flip open. "But before you say anything, let me remind you that we promised never to lie to each other."

Damn her and her memory.

I slump against the desk. I can't do it, and she knows it. She steps into me, resting her arms on my shoulders.

"Take the deal, Mark." Her fingers press into my jaw as she draws my gaze up to hers. "You have no idea how much I want this for you. I'll be there as much as I can be. You have to do this."

"I don't think I can," I whisper. *Either way.*

"Yes, you can. You'll get on a plane and sign those papers. Eli, Peyton, Bree, and I will be watching and cheering for you. You have to do this." She brings her forehead to mine. "You're not done yet, and this time, we're doing it together."

Her voice is so soft. If it cracks, I'm a goner. I want her confidence.

"How am I supposed to leave you?"

She pulls away, her warm hands holding my face. "Because you know this time, there isn't a thing that will keep me from you. I'm always right here." She places her hand directly over my heart. "You wrote your name on mine so long ago. Permanent ink. There's no changing it. Distance. Time. Nothing."

I hold her tight, wanting to take to Denver all the plans we left in Phoenix, only with the addition of Bree. The thought of it causes an ache somewhere deep in my middle that I don't allow access to often.

That deep-rooted fear is like muscle memory rearing its ugly head. Its taunting voice wants me to believe that if I leave, I'll lose her just like I did the last time I accepted an offer and told her goodbye.

I bury my head in her neck, breathing her in. "Eli and Peyton, huh?" My question comes out muffled.

"I don't know. I guess it's kind of stuck. They're already roughhousing in there."

I pull away, placing my hands on the sides of her face, needing to see her eyes. "I won't miss this."

That bottom lip gets tucked between her teeth. "You won't because I won't let you."

"So, you'll sign the contract and then go to camp?"

Bree sits on the edge of the bed, reciting what I told her while I'm sprawled across the bottom in the middle of a tragic downward spiral.

Why does it all sound so innocent and simple coming out of her mouth?

"Can I come to a game sometime?" Her eyes brighten at the idea.

"I'm not sure. Maybe one of the games that's closer."

I thought talking to her about this would involve sadness and her begging me to stay, which would give me an out. I'd tell Rob no because Bree needs me and to know she can trust me.

But no. Both my girls seem to be perfectly fine with me hitting the road for roughly the next six months.

"What about the babies?" Of course, she asks the question that takes my uneasy stomach and rolls into a giant ball of turmoil. I'm going to need a pallet of Rolaids to get me through all of this. I should tell Denver to add that to the contract.

I swallow down the bile that's taken up permanent residence in my throat. "Well, the doctor recommends we schedule their birth, so I'll be back for that once camp is over. I'll have a few weeks off before preseason training starts, but I should be able to come back on the weekends for a while."

Please tell me it sucks. Tell me you hate me for leaving and throw your clay pencil holder at me.

She pats my leg. "I'll help take care of the babies when you're gone."

Why in the hell is this child so agreeable and helpful? Where's the drama, the crying, and the neediness?

"So, you think you'll be fine if I take the offer?" *Say no.*

She laughs. "Yeah. I can't wait to tell all my friends you're playing for the Big Horns. Can you get me a jersey? I'll wear it on game days." She bounces toward me.

It's my turn to laugh. "Yeah, I think I can manage that."

"The babies need little jerseys. We can all wear them while we watch."

It's a punch in the gut. They'll be wearing my jersey, but I won't be able to see them.

"You know, I'm really glad to have a big brother. I never thought I'd have one, but it's even better that my friends think you're so cool."

I bump her shoulder as I roll up and stand. "Just remember that when you're sixteen." She frowns. "Time for bed, Obi-Wan."

She climbs under her purple quilt and sheets covered in flowers she and Lex picked out. "Who's Obi-Wan?"

"Oooohhh, we're going to have to fix that. Everyone should know who Obi-Wan is, but that requires a movie night."

"With popcorn and candy?"

"Popcorn and lots of candy. You can't watch *Star Wars* without a sugar high. You'll miss stuff."

She grins. "It's a date," she giggles, and I can't help but smile.

"It's the only kind of date you'll ever be having."

She rolls, laughing, and I tickle her side. "Goodnight, Breezy."

I pull her door closed and step across the hall to find my pregnant wife sitting up in bed eating.

"What is that?" I smell dill, and I know pickles are involved.

"The leftover pasta with pickles on top."

"That's just gross." I flop onto the bed beside her.

She presses a hand to the underside of her belly that's sagging a little lower each day. "Ugh. I don't know how much longer they can stay in here. They're out of room."

I wrap my hand around her thigh. "Only two more weeks, then they'll inject you with drugs, and you'll pop them out of there." She groans. "I can't wait to watch the whole thing." I wiggle my eyebrows, forcing a grin rather than spilling into the pool of fear that's growing around me.

"How'd Bree take it?" she asks around a mouthful, snatching me off the ledge.

I roll to stare up at the ceiling. "She's ready to step in and be a full-time parent in my absence." Lex laughs, her belly jiggling. "She's all mature and well-adjusted, and I'm like a spastic nutjob. Peyton and Eli will probably be better off."

She runs her fingers through my hair. I need her to do this every night, but if I sign with Denver, her fingers will be here, and I'll be there. Alone. Again.

"These babies are the luckiest to have you as their dad."

"I'm going to miss so much of the first months." My ribs suddenly shrink, and I have to sit up a bit, or else I might suffocate. "Lex, seriously. I'm terrified to say yes, and I'm terrified to say no."

She sets her mostly empty bowl aside and slides her hand into mine, linking our fingers. "Remember when I came to Phoenix to tell you I was pregnant?"

"Baby, I won't ever forget that."

Her thumb runs over my knuckles. "You asked me if I trusted you." She lets that hang a moment, and I wonder where she's going with this.

She moves closer, resting her head on my shoulder. I breathe her in.

My eyes burn, and my throat is so tight I hold my breath. I can't help the constant voice of my sucky past that tells me leaving is a mistake. To stay so I won't lose her again. That ugly voice jabs, '*What if it's for good this time?*'

"Hey." Her soft whisper pulls me from my dark thoughts, and I have to blink away the fear that's crept from my gut into my eyes.

"Yeah." I manage to choke it out, but only barely.

"Do you trust me?"

Shit. She shanks me in the chest and punches me in my already spasming throat.

She lifts her head to look at me, but I can't bear to meet her eyes. "I know last time, I broke something precious. Something that's not easily repaired, but I really hope you know this is different."

When I don't move, she grabs my face, forcing me to look at her.

"When you call me tomorrow night, I'm answering. When you call me the next night, I'll answer again. And again. And again. When you get through with camp, you're coming back here, and we're having our babies."

She releases my face, and my lungs are paralyzed. "When the season starts, your little Tasmanian Devils and I will be standing on the sidelines before the game and waiting for you after so we can go home. It doesn't even matter where that is." She pauses, sniffing and swiping at her cheek. "Wherever you are . . . that's where our home will be."

I slide my arms around her and haul her onto my lap, which takes effort, but needing to hold her. Her tears run down my neck.

"I need you to trust me. I promise you can." Her words are shaky but honest and true.

The ugly voice is drowned out with love. The overwhelming love I feel for her and the total and complete love she's only ever given me in return. She put me first over everything we had.

The desperation I felt only seconds ago evaporates into belief. Belief in her. In us. In what was always meant to be.

A swift thump-thump from her belly hits mine.

I hold her face, pressing my forehead to hers. "I love you."

Her hands slide to my neck. "I love you, too. I'm so proud of you." Her lips press against mine so, so gently. "It's only a couple of weeks."

Just a few weeks. "You have to stay off the shop floor."

She bites her bottom lip, hiding a wry smile.

I glare at her. "Don't make me stay here."

She kisses me hard but quick. "Never."

Chapter 51

LEX

I roll to a stop in the school drop-off lane. "I'm picking you up today, so I'll see you this afternoon."

Rather than hopping out, Bree sits for a second. "Do you think Mark will be able to call tonight?" She sets her backpack in her lap. "He said . . . he'd help me figure out the rest of my comic strip that's due tomorrow."

The worry in her voice reminds me that she's still learning to trust us, and our ever-changing world isn't helping.

The vision of him dropping to his knees this morning as he left for the airport and her hugging him tight bolts through my mind. The two of them have become thick as thieves, which will only make his absence harder.

"Yep. He said he'll FaceTime, and you can show him what you get done today. Ok?" *Thank goodness, because my ability to help with homework efficiently is seriously lacking.*

She nods, a hint of a smile breaking the corner of her mouth. "He said he has a good idea for Captain Gooey."

"Oh, I bet he does," I laugh as my phone vibrates in the cup holder.

She giggles, popping open the door. "I'll see you after school."

The door slams as the social worker's name appears. I press the answer button, waiting for the car in front of me to move forward. I listen as she relays the news I was certain we'd never get.

"Ok. Yes. Thank you." I end the call, watching the brake lights in front of me blink off and then back on again. My eyes dart to the clock on the dash.

I glance back at the cars in the drop-off lane, needing them to move IMMEDIATELY. I have the urge to lay on the horn, but it won't help.

My stomach has ached since kissing Mark goodbye this morning. Over these past months, my dreams have morphed into something brand-new. Something that resembles a house where Mark comes home every night, and I spend the weekend watching him like I've always wanted. A much smaller garage where I get to work on the rusty truck he bought me. I might've even allowed myself to think about a restoration business.

My skin prickles with heat and the need to get to the private airport. I crack the window to the let the fresh air in.

Mark didn't sleep at all last night as he tossed, turned, huffed, and groaned. The worry in his eyes this morning told me exactly what was going through his mind, and I hate that my past choices put it there.

I want to erase his fears, putting a nail straight through any lingering doubt, and I want to swing the hammer face-to-face.

The cars inch forward, and I glance at the clock on the fancy display. If these freaking cars move, I might just make it.

With only a tad bit of speeding and carefully rolling through a few stop signs, it takes me ten minutes to dive into a parking spot at the tiny airport. *Please still be here.*

I push the door open and swing my legs out, using the 'oh, shit' bar to help slide my increasingly immobile self to the ground. I don't care what anyone says. Those overhead handles were made for pregnant ladies.

I slam the door and hurry as much as a pregnant penguin can, swinging my arms, hoping it will propel me forward faster. As I near the entrance, I have to lose the arms and help support my belly.

If Mark is already gone, I'm going to hit my knees in tears and likely pee myself in the process.

Please be here. Please be here.

The doors slide open, and I can see the jet through the glass wall. I glance around the small space and there in the corner of the limited seating area is my husband. His elbows rest on his knees, his head in one hand, phone in the other.

I'm so out of breath that I need a second before I can speak. "Mark."

His head pops up, and then he's charging toward me. "What are you doing here? I was getting ready to have the car come back and get me."

I hold both my hands to my stomach as a damn contraction squeezes.

"Lex . . . are you ok? What's wrong?"

I give it a second to ease. "I was wondering . . . if you might have time this week to do a little house hunting." I wince as another takes hold. "Something near Shane and Maggie would be nice."

He frowns, stepping closer. "What?"

"One that has an extra-large garage or space to build one."

His large hands move to his hips. "Baby, I need you to be a little clearer on what's going on here, or I'm taking you to the hospital for questioning or whatever the hell it is they do when pregnant women start talking crazy."

I smile. There's my man. "I got a call when I was dropping Bree off." I step closer, sliding my arms through his and around his back, holding on. "Linda signed the papers."

"What?" he exhales. "Giving up her rights?"

I nod, pulling him even closer, although it's difficult with the twins between us.

"Seriously? I was sure she'd never do it."

I raise and lower one shoulder. "Maybe she understood it was time to do the right thing again."

He stares at me, and tears glisten as he finally wraps his arms around me and holds me tight. "I couldn't do this without you again. I need us . . . every day."

I hug him so tight. "Me, too. So, go join that team, play your ass off in camp, and find us a house in the mountains. After these babies are born and Bree is done with school and her recital, we're moving."

He chokes out a laugh. "Are you sure? What about help when I'm gone? What about Bree? Do you think she'll be ok?"

I relax against him, my heart finally settling into a normal rhythm. "It'll be another big change, but we'll talk to her. She's already missing you and worried you won't have time for her."

He stares at me like he's trying to make sure this is real.

I push up as much as I can, pressing my lips to his. "What I can't do is be without you."

When I pull back, he still looks in shock. "Besides, if Slade buys Grandpa out, I bet the old man can be talked into fancy plane rides, games, and late-night feedings. And if we're close to Shane, he's got a gang of kids for Bree to hang out with. That's something she's never had."

He hugs me hard, and I can't breathe. "I love you so much."

"I love you, too. Now, go get us that house while I try not to evict Peyton and Eli from their cozy little den."

He cups my face, kissing me again as a pilot swings open a door.

"Flight check is complete. We're ready when you are."

Mark doesn't look at him but stares into my eyes. "I'm about ready." His mouth spreads into a wide, boyish grin like he just won at the game of life. "How big of a garage?"

Chapter 52

LEX

"Ok. Again!" Slade yells from the rear passenger side fender.

I press the brake pedal to the floorboard and hold it. Bleeding brakes is the one thing I'm still capable of doing.

"Let it up!" he yells over the impact gun Trigger is using to tighten lug nuts as if he's training for a pit crew.

I release the pedal.

"Again!"

It's been a week since Mark left, and he's been blowing up my phone with the most ridiculous houses. Homes that cost millions of dollars but don't look like they belong to a family. He's a kid in a toy store, but it's not about the house. It's about us becoming a family.

When he gets back from camp, we'll talk to Bree. Moving will be a big deal for her. The two of them have spent the evenings laughing on the phone together, and I think Mark is exactly what she needs. We hope to get her into the same school Shane's family attends. She'll have the summer to spend with them and get to know her giant family.

She's asked about her mom, and I know her heart breaks a little more each time trying to make sense of what happened. She writes letters, and it takes weeks to get one in return. The social worker agrees that visiting Linda in this state would only do more harm than good.

Bree doesn't understand, and she needs to be with Mark. He's the only one who knows exactly what she's feeling and can help her through it. Years separate them, but they relate to each other in a way no one else will.

"Ok! Let up!" Slade yells. "Let me move to the other side."

"Who will you get to do this when you own the shop?" I ask as he attaches the hose on my side.

"Anyone I want. They'll do it if I say so," he grumbles while I wait for him to fit the hose onto the bleeder screw.

"Ha. We aren't going to listen to you any more than we listen to Cal," Carson tosses out.

"And we like him," Wind adds from the bench, filling out an invoice.

I laugh, and Slade lays out a string of curses under his breath. When he's ready, I press the pedal down and hold.

This shop has been my dream for so long. It hurts to think about it being handed over to anyone other than me, but I see now that Grandpa was right. I wasn't supposed to stay here forever.

I bring the phone to my mouth to dictate a message to Mark. "Stop sending mansions, but we need a room for Grandpa." I see three dots.

SEXY BABIES' DADDY: *Voice message* *So, two double wides and a warehouse in the back?*

Slade hollers, and I press and release the pedal a few more times while Carson and Wind bicker over who's patching a tire.

When Slade finishes, I hoist my legs out of the car first and then reach for the handle, but he sticks his hand out to help me. He pulls me to a stand and then—

Uh, oh. Oh, no. No, no, no, no, no, no, no. A trickle of warm liquid fills my underwear and proceeds down my legs. I would wonder if it's pee, but this is way too much when I just went.

When I don't move or let go of Slade's hand, his brow creases. Then he peers down at the pool, collecting on the floor between my feet.

"Um . . . is that?" He starts to back away like it might be corrosive or contagious.

The shop is quiet, and I realize my guys have gathered around the growing pool of bodily fluid.

"Shit. What do we do?" Carson asks as if any of them have the answer. I don't either because I wouldn't let Mark *read* this part of the book to me.

"Grab an oil pan and some shop rags," Slade barks, risking it and taking my arm again.

Trig and Wind dart around like they're lost in a maze while I try to think. All that comes to mind is that I need Mark.

Wind is back with a roll of rags in hand and starts ripping them off and tossing them to the ground like I might leak an ocean.

There's a stench that creeps up my nostrils that has me horrified.

"Shit! Alex, what the hell?" Slade shoves his wrist to his nose, about to gag, and if I could focus, I'd likely join him.

The smell! I begin to panic, trying to look around my belly, BUT I CAN'T SEE ANYTHING!!

Then, it hits me. "Wind!!!"

His cheeks turn pink as he continues to spread shop rags around me.

"Good . . . shit, man." Carson waves his hands in the air to try to get it moving as Slade steps away to breathe.

"Sorry. I can't help it when I get nervous."

"What the hell are you nervous about? Are you birthing babies? They're probably suffocating in there with your ass air."

I take two steps, and all four guys take two steps, following me with their arms outstretched like these babies might literally drop right out on the shop floor. I pull my phone from my pocket and dial Mark.

It takes two rings.

"Hey, baby. I'm heading into—"

"Mark, I need you to come back . . . right now."

There's nothing but distant voices on the other end, and if one more man, the most important one, freaks the hell out, I'm going to lose my shit.

Finally, he speaks, and for once, he's the calm one. "Like right now, right now?"

What the hell is happening? "Yes."

"Peyton and Eli?"

I think it's a question. "I'm pretty sure my water broke."

"Ok." He's still way too calm. "Ok. I'm . . . I'll be there. Just don't let anything happen until I get there. Ok? I'm coming. Right now."

"Uh . . . " Here I am, standing in the middle of the shop. My shorts are soaked, and I'm staring at three grown men and one sweet almost man, who looks two seconds away from putting on nitrile gloves and rolling over a creeper just in case.

I hear Mark's muffled voice and a commotion on the other end. Then, some skidding like he might be running.

"Uh . . . Mark?"

"Baby, I'm coming."

"Ok. Please hurry. You're the one who read about this part."

"Shit yeah! I read this chapter! I'll be the best damn birthing coach that hospital has ever seen. Just hang on. You tell Peyton and Eli it's not game time yet."

I take some deep breaths, trying not to panic or cry when my hero walks through the door.

"What in Sam Hill is going . . . "

I see the moment it registers, and he calmly walks to me.

He takes my arm from Slade. "Come on, Pal. It's time to go." And we're on the move. "Wind, get the rags. Slade, her keys." I look at him, his gray eyes meeting mine. "I love you, but you aren't leaking that shit onto my seats."

I laugh, and tears fill my eyes. I have Grandpa, but I need Mark, and he needs to get here . . . soon.

Chapter 53

MARK

Next time they run sprints for time, I'm in to get clocked. I've never run so fast in my life. My lungs burn, and I'm pretty sure my legs are about to fly off. I'm not even sure if I said anything to my Uber driver before I flung myself out of the car.

When Lex called, I was heading into a team meeting, and fortunately, when I told the group what was happening, one of the team jets was waiting on the tarmac.

Now, with the hospital in view, I'm racing up the sidewalk in the fading evening light rather than counting down until my last nerve jumps ship in backed-up traffic. Five blocks weren't going to keep me from getting to Lex.

I hit the sliding doors, running until I get to security. It's the same guy, and he grins as I stand, trying to catch my breath. Sweat drips down my forehead as his fingers tap keys, searching for Lex's room number. He pushes the button, and the doors buzz open.

"Good luck, man! Go, Big Horns!" he yells as I take off in a jog to Room 16. When I see the number and closed door, I don't even bother to wonder what's happening on the other side. I bust through like a defensive end aiming for a sack.

The door clangs open, and my sudden burst and appearance stuns the room into silent stillness. Three pairs of wide eyes stare at me, and the only ones I care about belong to the woman lying in bed.

I glance around the room. *No babies.* My chest heaves in and out. *I made it. I fucking made it!!!*

I've had a lot of important moments in my life, but this was the only one I'd never be able to get over missing. Not ever.

I move to Lex, leaning over to grab her face and press a hard kiss to her lips, not bothering to wipe the sweat off first.

"You made it." Her eyes fill with tears, and I kiss her forehead.

"Damn straight, I did. No way was I missing this." I find her eyes again. "Baby, this is my time to shine."

She laughs, as does her mom and the nurse standing nearby.

"The doctor wants to do a C-section. One of them is breech, so . . . " She doesn't say anymore, and I see the cold, hard fear in her eyes.

I sit on the edge of the bed, taking in her hand and pressing it to my damp chest. "We're doing this together. All of it."

She swallows hard as she nods.

Her mom stands, leaning over to hug Lex. "My work here is finished for now." She smiles. "I think you two have this handled. I'll keep the guys in line and from driving the nurses insane. I've got Bree tonight."

She smiles at me. "I'm so glad you made it. Take good care of her." She offers a hug, and it feels strange, but I hug her back. "I'll be back to meet my grandbabies."

As she leaves, Lex's eyes flick to the nurse, who's busy typing away on the computer, and then back to me. "I had to sign a bunch of stuff." Her voice is soft, and her eyes are filled with worry about what she agreed to.

I lean close, pushing a strand of hair behind her ear. "We'll make sure we understand everything, ok?"

She nods as tears fill her eyes again, and she tries to blink them away. "I don't know if I'm ready for this."

I swipe a tear away. "Ready or not, here Peyton and Eli come."

"Peyton and Eli, huh?" The nurse joins our conversation as she hands me a surgical suit. "You've got some busy boys in there, then."

"They have power and attitude, just like their mom."

Lex rolls her teary eyes. I love her so much I don't even know how to hold it all in.

"Dr. Marshall is on her way, so we need to get you prepped." The nurse moves around the room, grabbing things and unhooking others.

I zip up the paper suit, unable to believe that within minutes, I'm going to meet our babies. I ask a million questions, helping reassure Lex and wanting to know exactly what's happening.

The minutes go by slowly but also quickly. It's as if I've only blinked, watching every detail of the most miraculous thing I'll likely ever witness. All I can think is that I do not deserve this. I've done nothing to warrant Lex's unending love, trust, and devotion, nor the gift of these two lives it created.

Lex grips my hand so tight a pool of sweat forms between our palms as I stand and peek over the curtain as the doctor pulls one slime-covered baby free. When I hear the sound of its cry, I lean down and kiss Lex, my tears mixing with hers. A minute later, it happens all over again, and my blurry eyes stay glued to the two tiny babies who are pissed about being ripped from their safe, warm home.

I don't blame them for screaming their tiny lungs out, and the amazement of it paralyzes my own. The only thing I know as I kiss my wife is that I will spend the rest of my life doing everything I possibly can to keep their world safe and warm. I'll love them so hard, and they'll never go a day without it because these two have had my heart since the moment I saw Lex's small, rounded stomach.

Lex's tug on my hand tears me away from my silent commitment and wonder. I lean over again, pushing her tears away with my thumbs as the stapler clicks away.

She sniffs. "You ready for this hot shot?"

I grin, letting every ounce of joy I feel seep from me. "I've never been more ready for anything in my life. Besides, I knew exactly what I was doing that night you married me."

Her eyebrows raise. "You did?"

"Yep. Look at them over there." I tip my head in their direction. "I did a hell of a job, if I do say so myself."

Her fingers wrap around my jaw, pulling me an inch closer and pressing her salty lips to mine. "You really did."

This . . . this is the rest of my life.

Chapter 54

LEX

I guzzle ten ounces of water, trying to hydrate and hoping it will help me keep my eyes open a little longer.

I carefully shift onto my side, still getting used to not having the weight of two babies wedged inside. Mark sits next to me, resting against the headboard. Both girls are on his bare chest, with a soft, fuzzy pink blanket draped across them.

I'm pretty sure the man hasn't worn a shirt for the past week. I'm not complaining. His glorious tan skin and that tattoo can be on full display 24/7 for the rest of my life.

The books taught him all about the benefits of skin-to-skin, and since he's leaving tomorrow to head back to Denver, he's held these babies in nothing but their diapers against his chest NON-STOP.

I watch him stare at their tiny faces smashed against his pecs. "What are you thinking?"

He presses his lips to each of their bald heads. "That I don't want to leave tomorrow morning. I don't want to miss this."

I snuggle closer. "It won't be so long," I say, trying to convince myself. "You'll be back for Bree's recital, and not long after that, we'll close on the house and be there with you."

We talked to Bree about moving, and she had a lot of questions and was worried about what would happen when her mom was released. We reassured her we'd stay in contact and when Linda is released, she'll be there. When we got to the part about living close to Shane's family and all the kids, she was sold, excited they'd all be at the same school.

"Yeah. In the meantime, those jokers will rotate through here, stealing snuggle time with *my* girls. Just the thought of it makes me want to punch each one of them."

Mark detests the idea of the guys volunteering to take Bree to school and help with the babies in the evenings. I know these guys. The minute I get close to handing one of them over, they'll panic and ditch me with some lame excuse. I could tell Mark to relieve his clear and obvious misery, but his rare display of jealousy makes me giddy inside.

"You might want to enjoy your time. It's going to be you and a houseful of girls."

His face turns toward mine, a sly smile sliding across his mouth. "I'm exceptional with the ladies."

I raise an eyebrow. "Oh really?"

"I branded your young, ripe heart, didn't I?"

I laugh, unable to argue with him. "Does it ever get tiring being so full of yourself?"

"Nah. I'm confident in what's mine and always will be." The intense heat in his eyes as he stakes his claim stirs a herd of wild horses in my belly.

"Just wait until they're all teenagers," I whisper, leaning into him to peek at their soft, sweet faces.

His head falls back toward the ceiling, hitting the headboard like I just sucked all the joy out of life. "Don't. Don't even. Bree, Ellie, and Peyton aren't going anywhere with any guy unless I have a full background check, personal protection, and a very long conversation about what will *not* be happening."

I laugh. "What are you, the president?"

"I will be Mr. President to anyone taking out my girls."

I smile at him and all his protectiveness. The sight takes my breath away. It's hard for me to believe that this is real. That this is actually my life. Just a few weeks, and this will be every day and every night.

I lean over and kiss his shoulder. "I can't wait to see you play. I used to watch every game and wonder what you did when it was over. Who was waiting for you and wishing it was me."

His lips press against my forehead. "I never allowed anyone in the family and friends space except Shane and Sean. I couldn't stand to have anyone there that wasn't you."

I raise my chin to look at him, searching his eyes. "Really?"

One side of his mouth tugs up. "Yes. Really. Now, it'll be all of my girls, and I'm going to be skipping into that room no matter how the game turns out."

He slides his arms under the girls and stands to place them in their portable crib that's wedged in between the wall and our bed. He leans over, keeping them tucked into his chest as he lowers them. He wraps each tightly like two little burritos in the sleep sacks that I've learned really are as fantastic as they're described.

Once he kisses and lingers over them a few moments longer, he stretches his shoulder and climbs in bed, not taking a second before eliminating any space between us. His face is so close to mine that our noses touch.

"I don't want to sleep alone tomorrow night. I don't like it when I can't feel you near."

I slide my arms around him, holding him close, already missing him. He pushes the hair out of my face, letting it fall between his fingers and keeping my face close. His lips brush against mine.

If my incision were healed, I'd throw one leg over him, but I can't yet.

"You know that night I came back here and found you in the garage?" His voice is so soft it's almost a whisper.

"You mean after Grandpa called you?"

He pulls away just a little. "He told you?"

"Uh, yeah. After the car accident. I didn't know you'd been calling."

"I didn't want you to know. I just needed to know you were . . . ok . . . happy."

"I came home that night, pulled on your shirt, and cried, missing you so much." The admission is freeing, like it's releasing those years of suffering and sadness to make room for all the joy and happiness since and yet to come.

"Shit, Lex," he breathes out, his forehead pressing against mine. "I drove around, then sat outside the shop until you left and followed you home."

I pull away. "You did?"

"I had to know if you came home or . . . " He brings my hand to his chest. "I slept in my car until the morning when I had to catch my flight.

If I'd known, I would have climbed in this window and stolen you away from here. I would've done that over and over and over again."

I sniff because, apparently, birthing babies doesn't rid you of all the hormones. You just become more of a mushball.

"I wouldn't have gone with you." A tear rolls down my cheek, absorbed by my pillow. "I couldn't believe that you'd come back and that you really meant everything you said. I couldn't believe you still loved me after . . . "

His warm hand slides into the back of my T-shirt and up my spine. "I needed you. I wanted to know that you'd be mine forever."

I stare at his perfect face. It's my turn to push the strands of hair off his forehead. "I was," I whisper. "Even then. I've always been yours. There was just a sliver of time where we couldn't be together."

"It was like trying to live without my lungs. I hated every single tortuous second of it."

I smile. "We don't have to do that anymore. Me in your old T-shirt and hating each day. It's over. It's us now."

"Damn straight it is. It's always been. And we made Ellie and Peyton." His devilish smirk presses into my cheek. "Baby, we did that."

"We?" My grin finds his. "How about we finally find out what it's like to actually *be* together?"

He's careful as he slides his leg between mine. "I think it's about damn time."

Epilogue

LEX

Three Months Later

I stand just behind the white rope, rolling the stroller back and forth and searching the field for number four. The tall, dark-haired one that can make my heart race with that sly, sexy smirk.

"Hey, I see him," Bree points as she jumps, spotting Mark.

We watch him warm up, tossing a ball to a trainer. Flashes of him in the middle of a much smaller stadium with thousands of fewer fans zip through my mind. Same guy, but the man on this field and I share a life. We're more than best friends and lovers. He's my partner. The father of our girls. The one I'll spend the rest of my life loving up close. I'll never take it for granted, knowing exactly what it's like to not be with the one who owns my heart.

He jogs toward us, removing his helmet and holding it at his side.

He grabs my face, kissing me as if we're the only two in the stadium, not caring in the slightest that there are people and cameras surrounding us.

"For getting lucky," he says, grinning like he has a secret.

"You've never needed luck."

His lips move close to my ear. "Baby, I'm not talking about the game." I shove him, and his grin creeps even higher. He bends down and scoops Bree into a big bear hug. "All right, Breezy. I expect to hear you all the way down here, and when we get home tonight, we're finishing those next two slides."

Bree high-fives him. They've been working on a comic strip about a brother-sister duo who save kids from the monsters in their closets. I hear them laughing and carrying on through the house, and it's helped Bree adjust to all the changes.

She's fallen right in with Maggie and Shane's crew like they've known each other forever. We help her write letters to Linda and make sure that she gets the ones her mom sends back. The stability of having a permanent place to call home and her own room and space has helped her settle in.

"Give me my girls." Mark lifts Peyton out of the stroller, and I hand over Ellie as he beams like the proudest man on the planet.

He turns toward every camera, snapping away, kissing both of their chubby cheeks as they smile and coo. The man has always known how to play it up, but this is just Mark in dad mode. It's as if this is truly what he was born to do. It's obnoxious, and I love every second of it.

He kisses one and then the other as he hands them back to me, pressing his lips to mine. "See you in a couple of hours."

I smile. "I'll be there." Being here when the game is over might not seem like a big deal to some, but to Mark and me, it's everything.

He jogs away, and I put the babies in the stroller. Bree and I make our way through the stadium and up to the box to join Shane, Maggie, and the kids. When we get there, Bree joins the boys in the seats outside, screaming and yelling as the Big Horns take the field.

Shane scoops up Ellie with one arm, holding his guy in his other, and takes off as I release Peyton from her seat.

"Have you ever seen men more thrilled to have babies in their arms than these dudes?" Maggie says, watching him juggle the two.

I laugh. "I'm pretty sure Mark works the girls into every interview just to make sure everyone knows he's a dad."

Maggie rubs her stomach as she sips a Sprite. "Shane's practicing the double hold. He's been counting down the days until he could punch them in the face with us having number two."

"You're pregnant? Congratulations!" I slide my free arm around her shoulders and squeeze. "Thanks a lot. Now, Mark will be all over me about number three," I tease.

"We need Andie here. We've got to set these men straight that we will not literally be birthing a football team. If Shane had it his way, I'd never not be pregnant."

"I'm down for whatever kind of intervention we need to have." I laugh. "Mark is convinced he makes nothing but multiples."

"Well, I know Andie will join. She's barely sleeping with their two, and with this being Sean's last season, she said he's pre-planning for a celebratory number three. I'm calling the group home to find out what kind of cocktail they were feeding these nutballs."

"I think Mark got a double dose," I say, following her to join Shane and the kids.

The coin is tossed, the ball is punted, and Mark jogs out on the field to take charge and call plays.

I spend the next two hours swapping and feeding fussy babies while keeping my eyes glued to the field and Mark. Our group is loud and often on their feet, but I watch calmly and quietly, savoring every moment of the whole experience and getting to be a part of it.

With one minute and twenty-three seconds on the clock, Mark kneels and sets up to kneel a second time, ending the game. He pulls off his helmet and searches for our box, and when he spots us, his fist moves to his chest just like he did after every high school game. My hand finds my heart in return.

Like a mob, we move through the stadium. At an exit, I part ways with Maggie, Shane, and the kids. Bree was happy to join them and get a head start on the after-party, which will involve streaming Sean and Cole's games. I continue to weave through the crowd with the stroller, eventually showing my badge to get into the family waiting area.

With both girls sleeping, I roll the stroller back and forth, hoping their much-needed nap isn't disturbed. It's not long before players filter in. Mark strolls through the doors with a grin plastered to his face wearing a pink T-shirt that says 'Girl Dad.' This man is so into fatherhood I can't help but think about doing it again with him . . . someday.

His shirt is tight across his chest, his jeans are just the right amount of fitted, and his hair is a little messy, but it's the look in his eyes that has me biting my lip and holding my breath.

What Maggie said rolls through my mind, and I can't help but laugh as he bends to pick me up, lifting me off the ground. I wrap my legs around him, pressing my forehead to his.

"You know, I've been waiting for this moment for nine years."

I link my arms around his neck. "Oh, yeah? I think I've thought about it a time or two. You did good out there."

One eyebrow arches up. "That so?" I nod, holding his gaze. "It's never meant more to me than it did today." His eyes move to the stroller, checking on the girls, and then back to me. "You being here. Our family. Our life. Everything you've given me." He pauses, staring so deeply into my eyes I have to swallow. "It matters so much more than this, but thank you for allowing me to do both."

"I love you," I whisper, suddenly overwhelmed with so much joy it creeps up my throat and into my eyes. I nuzzle into his neck as tears drip from my eyes.

His hands grip my thighs. "Baby, I know. I feel it every day." His lips find mine, soft and sweet, but when I pull away, his smirk promises more to come.

He sets me down, and I link my hand with his as he grabs the stroller. "Nice shirt."

He smiles, lifting my hand and pressing his lips to the back of it. "The reporters dug it."

I laugh, stepping closer and wrapping my free hand around his forearm as we make our way out of the stadium. "Of course they did. I bet the ladies loved it, too."

Ugh. That grin. It kills me every time.

MARK

I set Ellie in her crib gently, hoping she'll stay asleep this time. These girls are spoiled being rocked every night, but I don't care. I'm rocking them until they fall asleep, and maybe even longer.

Lex might kill me as the season picks up, and she has trouble getting them down, but I'll suffer her wrath for this time with my girls. Making them feel safe and loved as they go to sleep is something I never had. I will do this for as long as I can.

I let the white noise machine work its magic as I close the door. Down the hall, I peek in on Bree. She's sound asleep after a long night of dance classes that are quickly filling up our evening schedule. Dance is giving her what football has always given me. Freedom. An escape. A space to let all the pain and hurt go.

I turn off her lamp and brush her hair out of her face, hoping she knows how much Lex and I love having her here. She's had to grow up quickly these past months, and she's way more mature and adjusted than any ten year old should ever have to be.

I pull her door closed and march straight to the garage.

I open the door to Lex's four-stall haven, where the Bronco sits jacked up off the floor. Country music plays low in the background, and Lex is on her back under the rear wheel well.

Metal clinks to the floor, and she groans. She scoots out from underneath and stands. Her hair is held back with a bandana, and she's wearing a white tank and old jeans filled with holes. *Damn.* The sight reminds me exactly why I'm here.

"How'd it go?" She wipes her hands on a blue rag.

"Ellie needed extra Daddy time."

She squats back down, peering underneath the truck again. "You're getting nothing but silence when I'm up all night trying to get them to sleep." She knows her silence is my Kryptonite, but I don't care.

"I heard. I'm choosing to suffer the consequences. Your idle threats kind of turn me on." I can hear her roll her eyes.

"Don't forget Slade is coming out next weekend to help me."

"Great," I grumble. I like that guy, sort of, but I don't have to like him working with Lex in this environment.

Her head swivels to peek at me over her shoulder. Her smile is blinding. "You're gonna have to get over it. This little jealous streak you have about Slade. He's like my brother."

"Why isn't he dating someone?"

She walks to me, her arms sliding through mine, propped on my hips. "Uh . . . maybe because he's a jaded, old crab who had his big, crusty heart broken."

"You make him sound like Mr. Krabs."

She laughs and presses her lips to mine. "He kind of is, but I need his help pulling the engine. I can't wait to get this baby up and running." She untangles herself and moves to the workbench to grab another tool. "Besides, McGowen's Aston Martin is being delivered this week. He can help me get a head start on that."

"When will there be space for my Mustang?"

Her back is to me, and she stills. The smile that creeps across my face that she can't see says, 'Gotcha!'

She slowly turns to face me, pulling her long blonde hair over one shoulder as her fingers find one earring. Twist. Stop. Twist. Stop.

Her bottom lip tucks between her teeth to hide a smile. "What do you know about Mustangs?"

I take a step toward her. "Hmmm. I know they're fast and . . . wild." I take another step closer, planning my attack. She crosses her arms over her chest as if it will deter me. "I know they can be flashy, but the insides are built to last." One more step, and I slide my hands around to her lower back and grab her butt. "I know once tamed, they are loyal to a fault."

Her head falls to the side. "Really? You know all that?"

"Yep." My mouth moves to her neck, my teeth gently grazing her skin. "I did research. I also know that if you had to pick a car, that's exactly what you'd choose."

Her arms are still crossed, but she lets her head fall further to the side, giving me access, and I make my way to her collarbone. "You sound pretty confident. Are you sure about that?"

"I know you'd take adventure over boring any day."

She shoves me back. "How do you know?"

"How do I know what?" I play innocent, which I suck at.

She glares. "You know exactly what I mean." My ass-eating grin deepens as her eyes narrow further. "You know what this means." She turns to grab a tool from the workbench.

"What?"

She spins back, pointing a long rachet at me. "I think it might be time for another tattoo."

"Done. Now, get over here."

She shakes her head, but that playful look in her eyes has my temperature spiking to a thousand degrees. "I need to see if I can get the midpipe off."

"Say that again?" I lift my chin, waiting.

She frowns. "What?"

"What you just said. Say. It. Again." I dare her.

Her grease-covered hands move to her hips. "I need to get the midpipe off, or we won't be able to pull the engine."

I close the space. "I've warned you that watching you work is the hottest damn thing I've ever seen. The girls are all in bed and asleep. The clock is ticking until one of those little Daddy's girls wakes up and needs me. So, we can do this the easy way, and you come with me willingly, or the hard way, and I will happily throw you over my shoulder and haul you straight to our bed. Your choice."

She steps back, her arms moving to her chest again, looking defiant, and that was the wrong damn move.

I bend, folding her over my shoulder.

She laughs. "I didn't even get a chance to vote."

"Nope." I stop at the workbench, letting her drop off her tool and rag. "You just had to go and look like you were going to challenge me. My last bit of patience wore off."

I step into the house and pull off one of her work boots and the other, leaving them by the door. I storm down the hall to our room.

"I wasn't aware you ever had patience."

I finally reach the edge of the bed and let her down slowly, her body making full contact with mine. "Definitely not when it comes to this and what we are about to do."

"Um . . . do I get to take a shower first?"

"Nope. After."

Her baggy jeans hang low on her waist, and my fingers find the soft, bare skin. She sucks in a breath. I know exactly where she's ticklish, and she fights not to laugh, her knee jetting up to put a little space between us. I snatch her back, not giving her a second to retaliate. I find the hem of her tank and pull it up and over her head.

Her hands slide underneath my shirt and slowly around to my back, pulling me close. Even a thin layer of cotton between us won't do, so I swipe it off.

Her nose presses into my cheek as her lips move along my jaw, taking her sweet time. The tips of her fingers brush the small black script lettering over my ribs.

I pull back, forcing her to meet my eyes. "Your love . . . it makes me forget." I rest my forehead against hers. "Nothing can ever erase it and . . . I don't want it to. It brought me here . . . with you."

Her eyes stare into mine as if she's making sure it's true. She blinks so quickly. "I loved you then . . . so much. But now . . . "

"I know," I whisper. And I do. I know because every day I see Bree, I know what she did for me. I feel it every time I watch her with our girls. When she's waiting for me after a game, the pride in her eyes almost knocks me over. Because I know she'd do it all over again just the same, to give me a chance.

Her arms link around my neck, her body pressing against mine.

"I love you, and it won't ever be enough," I whisper.

Her hands move to the sides of my face, her thumb tracing the scar above my eyebrow. Remnants of the last blow, not even close to the worst of them, but symbolizing the end of one kind of darkness only to enter an entirely different kind. Until she came along.

"It was enough to last me eight years apart from you." Her breath whooshes across my lips. "This . . . what we have, our family . . . it's more than enough to last me a lifetime and beyond."

I kiss her, no time for soft and slow. The heat in my belly roars as I toss her onto the bed and find the button on her jeans. Her hands glide over my skin, keeping me close.

Our mouths and tongues move in sync with practiced precision. I grip her waist, needing her.

She laughs, and I lean down to kiss her smiling mouth.

"You know, I was thinking." My fingers push at her bra.

"Uh, oh." Her hands move to the sides of my face, angling her mouth over mine, kissing me achingly slow. A distraction technique, maybe.

Not going to work. I brace myself above her. "Nice try."

She smiles, biting her bottom lip. *Damn her.* I hold her wrists, making sure she knows I mean business.

"Don't even say it, Mark," she warns, but I've never been good with caution.

She pulls up, gently biting my lower lip. It's another nice attempt to deter me.

"I was thinking . . . " She closes her eyes, lying perfectly still. I kiss her just below her ear. "That." Her cheek. "You." My lips move over her skin. "Need that Mustang tattoo."

Her eyes flick open.

I place kisses over her body with every shred of patience I can muster. My turn for torture. "Right . . . here." My lips run along her ribs right underneath her heart. "Just a tiny one."

She exhales slowly and smiles, one that pulls all the way to her eyes. "Maybe I should."

"What'd you think I was going to say?" I know exactly what she thought, and it's not that I'm not thinking it.

Her arms link around my neck, smashing my body to hers. "Don't even pretend you're not ready to give Sean and Shane a run for their money."

I grin. "Oh, I am. But baby, I'm saving up for round two. I plan on practicing. A lot." I brush my lips to hers. "Next time, I'm shooting for three."

LEX

One Year Later

"Would you shut up?"

"Man, one more comment like that, and I'm burning yours to a crisp." Mark points the metal spatula at Shane, turning back to the grill. He picks up right where he left off, singing Journey's "Don't Stop Believin'," directed at Hank, the oldest of Maggie's siblings that she and Shane have cared for.

I glance at him, and he looks like he's one second away from ditching us and booking an early flight to London.

"Come on, man." Mark is disturbed. "You're Hank Matthews. The young David Beckham. Shit. You'd probably be a better quarterback."

"I told him," Maggie says, standing. "But I think she's dating that blockhead, who doesn't know his right hand from his left, just to torture him since he WAS BLIND."

"Seriously." Hank's face turns red.

"Steal the girl, man," Mark interjects. "Find your play and make it."

Shane points a baby spoon at Mark. "He doesn't need your input."

"I think he does. Look," Mark points at me. "I slid in at sixteen, and I got the girl . . . forever. You can't give up. This is your last chance. She's going to be here, and you have to man up and do something about all this . . . " Mark waves his wand around. "Pent up sexual tension."

"I'm leaving." Hank stands, shoving his chair away.

"You can't leave." Maggie steps in front of him, bouncing the newest member of our giant family. Little Quinn already has Shane wrapped around her pinky, and the rest of us aren't any different. "This is *your* going away party."

"Like hell, I can't. I didn't want a party, and you all are—"

There's a loud commotion, and a parade of kids spews out onto the deck with Teddy in the lead, running toward the pool. I clutch the stack of plates just in time to keep them from crashing to the ground.

"Cannonball!!!!!" Teddy yells, taking a running leap.

Shane swings an arm out, snatching Aiden, and throws him over his shoulder like a wooden barrel. Sean and Andie bring up the rear with Ax and their little beauty, Lydia. Bree and Liv each have a hand on the girls waddling to the pool with their little diaper butts.

Sean retired after last season and is now the offensive coordinator for the Colorado Moose. He and Shane coach together, and we are all practically neighbors, which means there's no privacy in this family.

Shane points at Hank. "Sit down. You will suffer through this one final time. Mark, not another word. He doesn't need your input."

"I'm just saying, it's the eleventh hour. You're leaving in a few days. You'll miss your chance. Take it from me. Living without the one you love is like living with your chest gutted and everything inside spilling out."

Mark swings his arm around me as I set another plate on the table and presses a kiss to my lips before returning to Master Griller.

Hank huffs. "Dude, she *has* a boyfriend, and no one is suffering. We're friends. I'm leaving."

"That guy is an asshole," Sean pipes in, putting Ax on his shoulders.

"Is he coming?" Andie asks. "I need to know. I might punch him."

"Ugh, *is* he coming?" Maggie groans. "I'm texting Simone and asking. We didn't invite his incapable, chauvinistic ass."

"Firefly, if you want Hank to remain at his own party, let it be," Shane says, stopping her.

Maggie glares at him but shoves her phone in her back pocket.

"Why isn't anyone all up in Cole's business?" Hank throws his hands in the air.

"Because he's not here." Half the group responds in unison and Hank drops back down into the chair, surrendering.

Maggie turns toward him. "Don't worry. If he weren't required to be at the Stingray's camp, we'd be all up in his face about what's actually happening in Miami."

Hank groans. "You all seriously need to get a life. I can't wait to get out of here."

"But you are our life," Andie sings sweetly.

"Hey," Mark jumps back in. "You're going to miss us when you're on the other side of the world, realizing there's no one that loves you like we do."

This is my family. All of them, and I never want to be anywhere else.

When we aren't cheering for Mark, we're watching Shane and Sean coach the Moose, Hank's soccer games, or Bree and Liv's dance shows. Cole's games are streamed at one house or another, which just so happen to be within five miles of each other. It's football and sports and activities All. The. Time.

And when I have a little quiet time, I sneak away to the garage and work on whatever my current rusted-out project happens to be. I finish one, and Mark's friends have another delivered. Restoring these old cars and trucks is everything I've dreamed of.

"Maybe you should spend your time worrying about that," Hank points to the pool where Bree sits on the edge, laughing with one of Garrett's friends.

All three men turn in that direction, and I watch Mark's posture change from carefree to Captain America.

"Damn, man," Sean whispers. "Here it goes. You're gonna have fun with that."

Shane laughs, and Mark backhands him in the chest. "Laugh all you want, shithead. Liv's right behind her, and she's a lover of all lost things. You just wait and see who she brings home."

Shane growls, "Mark, I'm one second from drowning you in the pool."

Sean makes some kind of snorting noise and Shane's head whips in his direction.

"Hold on, asshole. Lydia will be there before you know it."

Maggie and Andie join me as we watch our men freak out about all of our girls' future dating lives.

"People would pay to see this," Maggie whispers.

Andie bumps our elbows. "We should video them and put it on YouTube."

"What about the boys?" I ask, just wanting to see their reaction.

Three big heads swivel toward us.

"We're not worried. They have the three of you," Sean says like it's a ridiculous question.

"Anyone who doesn't run within the first three minutes of your unrelenting interrogation will get our vote of approval," Shane adds.

"Besides, with the way Cole and Hank are going about things, there's no need to worry," Mark tosses in, eyeing Hank.

Hank stands, pulling a soccer ball off the side of the deck, and then joins the men's little observation party. He rolls the ball between his hands. "If I knock that little shit in the pool, you all will get off my back about Sadie . . . for good. We're friends, and that's all we'll ever be."

"Deal." All three guys approve.

"I'm not agreeing," Maggie protests.

"Firefly," Shane warns.

"Fine. I like Sadie enough to let it go. She's smart and beautiful, and she's the best babysitter we'll ever find. But Hank, for the record, you're a dumbass."

Andie and I laugh as Hank drops the ball. With a swift kick, it smacks the kid in the back, and he tips forward just enough to fall into the pool.

All four men stand with their arms crossed over their chest in complete satisfaction, watching Bree's eyes grow wide, laughter tumbling out of her.

"Nice aim, man," Mark bumps him on the shoulder.

"I'll have Teddy ready with the paintball gun while I'm gone." Hank joins their protective stance.

They fall into conversation about all the ways in which they will torture future boys who start sniffing around.

"Oh, this is just the beginning, ladies," Andie says. "I'm not sure who will drive us to the nut house first. All these kids or these men."

"The men," Maggie and I say.

"We already know these guys will take out any jackasses, but can you even imagine when one of these nutballs brings a girl home?" Maggie says as if the idea is unfathomable. "I mean, let's be real. We got crazy lucky that *we* actually like each other, but what if we don't like her?"

Andie and I look at each other. This is a revelation.

"That won't happen, will it?" I ask, fully aware my list of female friends goes no further than what I can count on one hand, and two of them are beside me.

"What if one of them brings home a whiner?" Maggie cringes.

"Or someone who cries all the time?" Andie adds.

"Or isn't capable of pumping her own gas?" They both look at me.

We survey the young males spread throughout the backyard that belong to us.

"Can we shoot them with paintballs if we don't like them?" I ask.

"Well, I say since that one in there is a boy, it's fair game for all of us." Maggie points to my growing stomach.

"What's fair game?" Mark asks, all three pairs of manly eyes on us.

"Just making sure there's equal opportunity for the boys."

Three sets of shoulders slump, and there's a majority groan.

"You all need to behave yourselves and play nice." Sean points at us.

"Don't worry," Maggie says, stepping toward Shane and sliding her arms around him.

"Yeah, right. I already know how you are with these boys." Shane wraps his arm around her.

Sean slides behind Andie. "You have to be nice."

Andie's head tips back to look at him. "Why? If I were nice, you wouldn't love me."

He grins and kisses her forehead.

Mark eyes me, a sly smile awakening.

I join him next to the grill, and he swings his arm around my neck, pulling me against him.

"I'm one hell of a lucky man to get to see you get all protective over this little guy." His hand runs over my stomach.

"Yeah, well, live it up. I think this is it, Casanova."

His lips press against my ear. "I am. Every second."

Me, too. I smile, watching our giant family. "Who knew you three abandoned boys would create this."

There's silence as we take in the absolute chaos happening before us.

"We did," Mark says, with complete confidence as he fist-bumps each of his brothers. "And hell, we aren't done yet."

Maggie, Andie, and I groan while the beautiful men surrounding us laugh like this is what they'd planned all along.

Acknowledgments

Writing this series has brought me so much joy and a whole lot of healing. These characters and these stories would not be what they are without all of the people I'm somehow fortunate enough to get to call my family and friends. You all have given me the courage to live out this dream.

Brian, you show me daily this kind of love exists. Because of you, I can write stories, knowing with my whole heart that happily ever afters are not just for fairytales but for real life. Thanks for choosing me and loving me regardless. Always.

To my kids, you guys are more patient with me than I deserve. You're proof that love stretches beyond limits. Spending my days with you will forever be my greatest gift and the most rewarding job I'll ever have. I love you guys to the moon and back over and over again.

To Mom and Roger, thanks for standing in my corner and loving me enough to tell me when it's time to go back to the keyboard and work it out.

To all of my beta readers, Lauren, Natalie, Abby, Jordan, Lizzie, Courtney, Marae, KJ: thank you for reading and for the endless text/voice messages. You helped me get this story just right. You guys make this process more fun than it ever should be. Your love, support, and total honesty helped me bring this story to life. Thanks for hanging with me on this journey. I'm a lucky girl to get to call each of you my friend. I love you guys.

To Taylor, thank you for your expertise and tolerating my series of one-off questions without any warning. I hope you're prepared for what's next.

To all of you who have read these stories, thank you for taking a chance on me and these characters. I couldn't do this without you. You make every long night, moments of doubt, and struggle for the right words worth it. Whether this story hits home with you or not, time is precious. I promise I'll never take the time you've spent on me for granted. I'm forever grateful and can't wait to share what's coming next, so stay tuned.

Last but not least, to those who want to give up. Those of you who think hope is for fools. I understand why you might feel that way. I wrote this story for you. For the ones who have yet to feel the kind of love that sticks around. The kind that shows up and really does last. Let that hope float up even when you're tired. Let it take flight and soar even when you think it won't. Be patient even when your patience is stretched so thin it's filled with holes and flapping in the breeze. Sometimes, love takes time. You are worth it, and so are they. It all starts with hope in what you can't yet see.

About the Author

Stacy Williams lives with her husband and children in Illinois. She writes in five-minute increments between homeschooling and extracurricular activities. She's spent years dreaming about writing love stories that, in a worn and broken world, remind us of what we're truly made for.

authorstacywilliams.com

 @stacywilliams.writes

 stacywilliams.writes

www.ingramcontent.com/pod-product-compliance
Lightning Source LLC
LaVergne TN
LVHW100507110826
845146LV00002B/543

* 9 7 9 8 9 8 9 0 4 4 9 6 2 *